Red Nexus

For Giuliano,
Enjoy the Nexus!

Benedict Leautier

Sep 1st 2017

Red Nexus

Benoit Chartier

ISBN: 1505870941
ISBN 13: 9781505870947
Library of Congress Control Number: 2014923010
CreateSpace Independent Publishing Platform
North Charleston, South Carolina

Thank you to my family, friends, and fans. You've been fiercely loyal and encouraging, and for that I thank you.

Table of Contents

CHAPTER 1

If you don't take it, someone else will.

—Nabeen Singh

WEN HARKWELL STARED, half-awake and eyes watering, at the emergency cut-off switch floating in front of him. For a moment his eyes rolled back, and he slipped into the half-daydream of memory: a wet quay at midnight and searchlights, mother holding him close, and panic gripping him. Dogs with bared fangs and glistening fur, getting closer. Their strained leashes barely held by uniformed men with guns, and then, running, running for his life under the light of a three-quarter moon. His head snapped back as his stool dipped backward and he almost went with it, the vision so vivid it might have been a moment ago.

How long has it been since I've seen it? he thought, the image of a gibbous moon seared in his mind. *Nine years, at least.*

With dirty, trembling fingers he pulled out a stained white tissue from his back pocket and dabbed at his eyes and nose. His face always lost cohesion toward the end of a twelve-hour shift on the factory floor, something in the air causing histamine overloads. He sniffled and slipped his worn gray leather gloves back on. It was only through a vague biological ticking that he could tell his shift was pulling into the last stretch, in the perpetual casino time of the factory. The green wake-ups he'd popped during break had long evaporated from his system.

The machine he was meant to watch disgorged saw-cut pieces at a dizzying rate. A protracted yawn caught his jaw, and he shook his head; at least he was in the middle of things today. Being stuck in the corner with the packing robots or wracking his shoulders on hydraulic screwdriver duty would've been a pain, especially on this, his

Memorial Day. Sitting near the center of the immense factory meant that he could see all the activity flowing around him as the rock in the middle of a maelstrom. The downside, of course, was mind-numbing boredom, inducing lethargy and the occasional visual hallucination. *Better this,* he reminded himself, *than the coming nights' work,* and pushed those thoughts out of his mind like unwanted guests. The sole advantage to this mindlessness was the freedom of thought that came with it. Even in his tired state, long wooden bridges over opulent lotus-filled waters danced in his mind's eye, surfacing from the past. Pretty memories he'd gathered like shiny pebbles before the storm, unaware that those dark clouds signified the end of life as he knew it, like the night he lost his father, the night on the pier. Things one could only know in hindsight. He shook his head.

Before him squatted the enormous blue sheet-metal press from which the endless reams of cut-outs flowed before his red, watering eyes, spewing a fine mist of metal dust out of its sides. It reminded him more of a postmodern sculpture than a machine, all bulges and soft angles. The rolls of raw material sank effortlessly into its maw, ejecting perfect shapes with that sharp metallic tang onto a thick black conveyor belt with a hiss. His hand sometimes hovered over the big red panic button in case the process went awry, which it never did, never would. Robotic meticulousness prevented it, yet there were laws in place so that a fallible human could counteract whatever nonexistent threats might arise. His head nodded a little, his hand wavering. A crick, and he stretched his neck first right, a crack, left, and then he massaged his temples, leaving gray smudges on his sweaty face. The incessant spewing brought on double vision. He wiped his face with the back of his glove and looked around again to regain some form of concentration.

The bare high ceilings revealed boring white-painted cross-beams and supports covered in spray-on particulate insulation. Thick trunks of multicolored electrical wiring ran from one end of the factory to the other, snaking through them and running down to the various stations where machines worked and people observed. He tilted his head back and followed a single wire with an imaginary finger to see where it began and ended. Somehow, the neutrally charged holiday garlands blurred with them and he ended up following those to glance one more time at the New Year's countdown clock, whose digital numbers told him 2327 was a mere forty-five days away. He shook his head and frowned.

T-minus five, he knew instinctively.

The whizzing of pneumatic screwdrivers keened at regular intervals, accompanying the whoosh of the presses, dulling his senses. The behemoth-like blue industrial equipment refined and cut, shaped and molded polished spools of metal, serviced by long, red, robotic arms rushing at dizzying speeds. These floated like ghosts on magnetic tracks throughout the hangar-sized space, on the floor as well as the ceiling. Slumped on his stool, Wen was content to watch them in a half-daze as they fluttered about, handing off pieces to each other with graceful torsions of their limbs. Servos singing, they would revolve, sending their pincers in a twist. There was a deep beauty in the precision of their movements. Their programming made them perfection, as they spun and twirled, pliéd and arabesqued. They bowed and curved and shared with their partners the fruits of their labor, mindless and awe inspiring. They lived without souls, danced without music, and smiled without faces, he felt. The drooling sacks of meat looked on with curved backs and slack expressions as the only seemingly volitional beings drove their usefulness further into obsolescence with a pirouette and a voltige.

I'm paid to watch robots dance, he thought, his lip curling in a sour expression, not for the first time.

The only other area in the factory he enjoyed working in was the stress-test section, where random pieces were pulled off the lines and put through rigorous pressure-point exercises inside sealed translucent plastic boxes. There was something inherently satisfying at seeing a brand-new equipment part explode with a bang and fly into a million pieces. He would then open the box, clean up the mess, and send the chunks in a small gray metal case to be analyzed in a department he had never been to. It constituted the bit of excitement he could afford in an otherwise incredibly dull job.

The sound of the buzzer reverberated throughout the immense factory, announcing the closing of the workday, and he looked up in relief. Red lights flashed from the ceiling. The black-haired young man looked up at the clock as an automatism. After having lowered his white paper facemask, he took a deep breath. Eight o'clock, and another shift over. Stepping off the stool, he shook his sleeping legs back to life. Already the other workers filed toward the punch clock, their faces expressionless; their gray coveralls coated in a thin layer of metal dust. He patted his own dirty, gloved hands down the front of his suit, a smattering of metal crumbs falling to the ground without a sound. He left his station and walked over to where the other men and women removed their gloves and touched the grounding rod. He stopped and let one of the enormous robotic arms slide by, silently, on its magnetic track. The thing was heading to its berthing station at the far end of the factory, its show now over; in a sense, he envied it.

He shared little of the general history of the other workers, apart from the fact that they were all descendants of refugees from other Asian countries, in their midtwenties

3

to early thirties. The others, though, were mostly fifteenth-generation islanders who had not seen their great-grandparents' homes sink below the waves. A few South Americans and Australians peppered the mostly Asiatic population. As a general rule, he didn't see that many whites doing manual labor in the depths of the city. He peered over the plodding throng, his height an anomaly among them.

The line advanced at a snail's pace, booted feet shuffling on a floor he would guess alabaster if not for the thin coat of metal filings covering it. The walls and ceiling shone with a blinding plastic whiteness. Wen took off his left glove and placed his hand on the grounding rod, ensuring he would not be shocked to death at the next metal object he inadvertently touched outside the factory. He swiped his forearm over a sensor, the green light signaling that he'd been registered as punched out. Eight o'clock—two hours to spare before the next job. There was much to do before then. The line split as the women headed for their own locker rooms, and he went into the men's. He sat down in front of his own locker with a sigh. A small yellow-rimmed mirror inside the door reflected his almond-shaped eyes, which burned with a quiet intensity, even after such a long day's work. Life had become a set of routines without end, there to make sure he could do the same thing he had done today, tomorrow. His shock of black hair was spiked, and his mouth a horizontal line. A picture of him and a boy half his age hung below the mirror. The boy was almost the same age Wen had when he arrived in Japan. Sammy looked like him in many respects, save that this younger version had not forgotten how to smile yet, and his eyes were blue, not green. He removed his coveralls, took his toiletries from the locker, and then headed for the shower stalls. The frigid waters woke his weary body with a start, leaving him feeling refreshed, if not stunned awake. He nodded in the direction of some of the other men, who barely acknowledged him. Dressed, he looked one last time at the picture of him and his kid brother, took his bag, and closed the locker, which beeped shut. Heading out the front entrance, he put in his translator earbuds, slipped on his clear, plastic, full-face rebreather mask, and went out into the darkness of the fiftieth level. The earbuds he wore out of long habit more than necessity, since he spoke perfect Japanese, English, and Cantonese. The Fujii-Hashimoto Heavy Industries Consortium neon sign flickered behind him, giant and red, switching from Japanese Kanji to English, above the entrance to the factory. The air was thick with soot and rank smoke. Massive fans about the base of the factory moved the eddies of filth away from its workers so they could find their way to the nearby elevators.

A group of six people of Filipino and Indonesian descent, chatting in a circle, hailed him down.

"Wen, you coming to the Izakaya tonight?" asked a small bleached-blond woman in her thirties.

"Can't go drinking, Yuka, sorry. I have to go home. Some other time," he answered as manner of apology. He always refused the offer, but it was professed anyhow. Tokyo's bars would once again count one less reveler. The woman smiled and shrugged, and he bowed to them and then walked away toward a large group of workers who were waiting at the industrial elevator heading back to the higher levels, the metal grating underfoot pinging musically with every step. Looking down, he could see the shear drop that went all the way into the black smoke rising from the ground unseen.

"You sleeping already?" came a voice beside him, startling him out of his reverie.

"Taz, hey. Long hours, you know?"

The other man grinned, his brown eyes twinkling. Scott 'Taz' Till extended his palm sideways, and they made their elaborate handshake.

"I really need to get some sort of tan. I think I'll turn green soon, or transparent. This vitamin deficiency'll kill me," he said, pretending to look at his pale arms through his protective brown suit.

"Not much in the way of beaches around here," Wen answered.

"Bah, my days of surfing are long gone. Besides, all I need is a booth; got to go live like the upper crust for that though. The shitty ones in *Sinjuku* will give you cancer!" He pronounced the last word with elongated vowels, and it sounded like *caain-sah*. Taz had long ago escaped the tedium of the doomed Australian resettlement, leaving his family behind for a chance at a better life and to try his hand at something, anything, that didn't involve soil desalinization on the hardscrabble coast.

"Work hard and you can do anything," Wen said without thinking. It was one of those phrases like: "Fly All Nippon Aerospace!" or "Drink Kirin beer!" that came out unbidden, an unconscious brain-bubble-like advertisement for a purer nationalism.

"Whoa! When did you turn into a propaganda commercial, mate?" Taz said, with an expression of mock surprise. "No amount of hard work will get me there; you know that." Taz was of the opinion that to rise like the cream meant that much scheming had to be done, that labor alone was good for suckers content to dream, stuck forever in their dead-end jobs.

"I do, I do. At least it's another shift done," he said, changing the subject.

"Day's not done yet though, is it? We'll be picking you up at ten o'clock sharp," Taz said, turning serious, staring his friend in the eye.

"Where is it this time?" asked Wen, looking away from him at the overhang of the monolithic building under which they stood.

"Wish I knew. Oscar never tells me anything; you know that."

"Regular guys?" inquired Wen, looking back at Taz with a raised eyebrow.

"Yup. It's you, me, Oscar, Andrei, and Sayeed, as per."

Wen's expression softened. "You mean New Guy. Anything specific we need tonight?"

Taz snapped his fingers. "Oh yeah, I almost forgot: bring your shovel."

Wen's expression soured, like someone who had just found the catch in a contract that sounded too good to be true. He hated digging with a passion, almost as much as he hated changes in personnel.

Taz chuckled. "Maybe we won't need to use them, but bring it anyway. That's orders from the top." Taz smiled, looking at his best friend's expression. "I have to go talk to some people, so I'll catch you later. Don't be sleeping when we get there, man, or Oscar will go nuclear on you," Taz said with a wink, and left, heading to another group of workers who greeted him with a whoop. Wen saw him raise his hands, and the others all did the same, clapping him on the back. Wen once again stared through the tarnished brown metal grating at his feet and observed the gray swirling mist that suppurated from the depths. He shook his head, suppressing a shiver, and walked to the main elevator shaft.

He got into the packed elevator with thirty or forty other people, and it began its rapid ascent to the 150th level. Though the darkness remained, the air began to thin, as a plane might surface above storm clouds into a starless night.

Once he got out, he took off his mask and put it in his ratty backpack. He crossed the pedestrian walkway that arched over the abyss, straddling high-speed motorways, heading to another immense structural pillar. Concrete, multishaped plateaus, interconnected by bridges and crosswalks, elevators and motorways, clinging to and surrounding supports: that was the city in a nutshell. Wen pictured petri dishes hung by mad gods, infected with humanity and left to thrive. Cars sped along below him; dirty little two passenger electric Daihatsu Ovae, Toyota Requiems, Mitsubishi Microns as well as long Fuso trailers ferrying goods from one end of the city to a hypothetical beyond. The rail tracks overhead vibrated with the passing Metro cars. He entered the station under its bright fluorescents and swiped his wrist over the scanner, flipping his rail pass as he did. It was an automatic gesture, one he had done a billion times before. Without even looking at the white-on-black signs hung above, he headed for the platform of the Yamanote Line at Yurakucho Station. He hurried up the stairs and got in line behind rows of manual laborers, mostly fresh releases from factory shifts in the Chuo Ward. A few were fitted with prosthetic limbs: rough-looking arm enhances, complete functionality minus the aesthetics, as well as some visual augments for the depths; ground workers all. Wen looked at them with curiosity. All he had in the way of implants was the Virtual ID chip in his forearm, like everyone else. Otherwise, he was a complete natural. He didn't have anything against augmentations, per se, he just wondered what it would feel like to have them. Not like his crew boss, the one Taz and he worked for; he hated anything that had to do with Augments and The Heights. Wen looked above the rail tracks at the behemoth buildings that towered like closed sentinels, their helmeted peaks invisible at this depth. Tarnished defenders made of concrete, bulwarks against time, saving the rubbish of humanity. "Work hard and you can achieve anything": official propaganda masquerading as the common narrative of hope. It was a tired message, and he was tired of hearing it. He felt bad for having spewed it to his friend. The upper levels eclipsed the true breadth and height of the city, giving the 150th the feeling of a gargantuan concrete cave. The crackle of the intercom boomed with a polite ladies' voice announcing the arrivals and departures, bringing him back to the hustle and bustle of the platform where he stood. He felt so tired; he wondered how he'd survive the night.

The old refurbished Metro train pulled into the station with a clunk and a sputter soon after, and he pushed his way into the packed car. The air was thick with the stench of sweat and machine oil, cigarettes and strong deodorants, as well as the foulness they were meant to suppress. He stood for lack of seats, ignoring the quiet coughs and sniffles around him, pulled out his Netware from his backpack, thumbing the on button. The purple light inside the black, semitransparent ovoid shone briefly, and he whispered into it that he was coming back before pressing the send button. He slipped on his VR glasses and turned them on.

The mail attachment in the right-hand corner of his sight came from Okumoto Fumiki san, Sammy's principal. He sighed as he read the reprimand, his frustration the fruit of a long string of complaints from the school's administrators and teachers. Switching schools again was out of the question. Sammy's reputation made it hard enough to get him into this last one. He transferred the letter to the already bursting Sammy Complaints folder and switched apps to a movie viewer.

He chose an old one and then tuned out the rest of the cramped ride home, images flashing for him alone. *What am I going to tell him this time?* he thought. *What bullshit excuse will I get?* His gaze was in the middle distance beyond the images and before the packed train car, hovering at an invisible point; zenless oblivion.

A pause on the viewer told him that he had reached Shinjuku1 Station. He put everything into his backpack. As he stepped out of the Metro car and headed down the stairs he was surrounded by the crush of the throngs. A giddy sensation overtook him when he stopped a moment to appreciate the shear amount of people, like ants in a hill, going in all directions.

Shinjuku1 never slept. Workers like Wen plodded home, partiers went out to be seen, and "businesspeople" stayed right where they were, hawking an array of goods arranged in quick-close suitcases under splayed hands. Artificial whores, almost human despite their staccato movements, offered their services twenty-four hours a day in front of love hotels, frilly uncovered asses harboring the establishment brand to which they belonged. Engineer pimps stood within tasing distance, eyes on the merchandise. Loud, revolving neons promised the full gamut of human sensory experiences, in most major languages. Red lanterns covered in gold Kanji symbols hung along the street, tonight packed with mainland Chinese expats celebrating a displaced holiday. In the deeper shadows waited and watched the grifters and fixers, hands holding the levers of the city. Little wonder the area had been branded the facile moniker of *Sinjuku*.

Night was the eternal bonding glue that held all together. In the bowels of the city, the 150th level in Shinjuku1 was the midnight beach where everything washed up to flourish or decay. Fierce ecosystem and human desire wed, feeding the carnivores and remoras alike. Wen walked in the general direction of the residential elevators, past pachinko parlors disgorging cigarette smoke and crouched-over players, praying mantises in dingy jackets, riveted to glaring screens. The din of the machines assured the passersby that "You WIN!" in the same repeating overjoyous mechanical tone, while Jamaican street performers set up their gear and prepared to play full rock concerts nearby. French bakeries let out the wafting scents of fresh croissants at every slide of their doors, the white-uniformed bakers bowing to each new customer. Laughter split the night as salarymen lifted their beer mugs in a toast under the awning of a half-patioed bar, spilling out onto the street. Shinjuku1 gave a human scale to the vertical city. The impossibility of the construction forgotten when faced with everyday life.

He stopped to say hi to the ramen cart owner posted between an anime toy store redolent with large-breasted plastic figurines and a miniature bar consisting of a single counter with five occupied seats.

"Zenji, old man. One ramen with pork, please," Wen said, slapping a New Yen bill down on the stainless-steel counter.

"You still feeding the old bum?" he asked, inspecting the money under the lights. He then scooped out a ladle-full of fragrant soup into a Styrofoam container, which he placed in a bag.

"I do what I can," Wen said, shrugging, taking the plastic bag. He walked back into the flow of the crowd. At a nearby Wi-Fi hotspot sat a hunched figure begging for cigarettes and coin. He waited until three toughs in navy-blue army uniforms had passed before approaching.

"Hey, Joe," he said to the disheveled old man. He looked about sixty or seventy, but he must have been much younger. He knew the streets sucked the life out of you over time when you were unable to escape them, which made him glad he had. Joe's beard was long and dirty yellow from too much smoking, his fingernails cracked and blackened. He wore many layers to fend off the chill and moisture of the November air.

"Hey there, buddy!" exclaimed the old man with a hint of Japanese accent, his eyes lighting up. "Spare some change?" Wen crouched down on his knees and handed the man his takeout bag with the Styrofoam bowl of ramen inside.

"That's all I can do for you today, Joe," Wen said.

"Can you stay awhile?" he asked, his eyes pleading.

"Not long. I have to get home." Wen put his hands in his pockets to fend off the chill.

"Just for a minute. I have something I want you to look at for me. Maybe you could help me out."

"Tell me what it is, and I'll see what I can do. You still using, Joe?" Wen asked.

"Nah, nah, it's nothing like that. Come on, just help me out, for old time's sake."

Wen hated to be reminded of his debts, but he demurred.

The old man lifted his dirty, matted white hair from the back of his neck, revealing two extended metal diodes, side by side.

"I can't seem to get them to work anymore. Can you have a look at them, please?" Wen looked at them with a raised eyebrow. *You've been keeping secrets, Joe*, he thought.

It was odd to meet someone with Netrodes with most of his mind intact living on the 150th. Those who underwent the permanent Net Connection only visited this area for entertainment, and even then, not often. The "disconnected," those sent down in exile from the Heights, were usually lobotomized; the removal of their 'trodes causing irreparable damage. This came as a complete surprise from a man he thought he knew well. The question was, if he was a Disconnected, why were his 'trodes still in place?

"How long have you had these?" he asked. The ends were worn, and they still had connectors on them, meaning they weren't wireless, but meant to be plugged in directly. They looked fairly old.

"I don't rightly remember now." Joe scratched behind one ear with one of his skinny fingers. Wen looked into his backpack and took out his Netware. The small, ovoid black box lit up with its purple inner light as he pulled a long, thin transparent cord out of its side. He slid on his glasses and touched the end of the cord to one of the protruding metal spikes on his friends' neck for a moment. He then touched the other one.

"Sorry man, it's not telling me anything. They're inactive, like you said. Let me get their model number and I'll try to fix them for you, all right?" he offered. There probably wouldn't be much good in his offer, since these were so old that nothing could be done about fixing them, save replacing both for new ones. He was no tech doc, and he had no idea where he'd get the parts, but there was no harm in trying.

"Thanks, my friend. I really appreciate it." Joe looked Wen straight in the eyes. He couldn't hold that gaze for long and averted his eyes to the sidewalk, his cheeks reddening. They were DaiSin Corp. implants, model 1805. *Those really must be ancient*, he thought. *DaiSin. Why am I not surprised?*

"I really do have to go, Joe. My brother is waiting for me," Wen said, putting his Netware back into his pack.

"Thanks for the soup!" the old man said, raising his chopsticks and the bowl as the young man got up to walk away.

"Don't mention it." Wen raised a hand without turning back.

Wen stared at the road, walking toward the local elevators once again. His thoughts drowned out the bustle of people. He was surprised at the revelation that old Joe was 'net connected. *Or rather, disconnected, or something,* he corrected himself. He himself could have been, but the opportunity had been stolen from him. Why did he feel he had to help the old beggar, anyhow? Hadn't he repaid his debt to him many times over? Yet still he felt he had to do more. He wondered if he would ever explain that mystery to himself. More troubling still was the DaiSin connection.

I'm looking too deep into this, he thought. *Everybody and their dog has DaiSin Netrodes.*

Even though Shinjuku1 was an immense, sprawling level, spanning many floors, he did not have far to go from the station. He had lucked out when the apartment had become free; only ten minutes' walking distance to the elevators from his train. There were only two dozen people waiting for the elevator when he arrived. He slipped out his Netware once again and whispered into it that he would be coming through the door in a few minutes. The rapid descent made him dizzy for just a moment, but he was feeling all right by the time he exited the elevator on the 132nd level. The chaos of the 150th was barely audible at all, but he could see the effervescence of light and constant animation on its streets up above. He walked along a quiet road. It was too late in the season now, but cicadas would sing their high-pitched song next summer, hidden amongst the glowing pink branches of the genetically engineered trees. They lit the way home for him, silent now. In the temporary quiet, he lost himself in thought, a state he tried to avoid but that haunted him whenever silence made it impossible to ignore. It was always about survival, never about living; the factory, its workers, the denizens of Shinjuku1, even Joe. Up above, in a different world, was the flip side of the medal, a better life; actual living. He shoved the thoughts out of mind, feeling himself slipping into uncomfortable thought patterns.

The apartment towers reminded him of impossibly tall industrial-looking stacked sunflowers, seen horizontally; all within touching distance, lit by thousands of identical porch lights. He came to an intersection and turned right, walking to the front door of apartment block 735, also known as the Cherry Bowl Arms. All had been bestowed horrendous, nonrepresentative names. Taz lived in one a few blocks down called the D'Artagnan's Cat. Wen was of the opinion that whoever had thought up these designations did so by pressing random on his encyclopedia application's entries, picking the most asinine with the aid of copious amounts of liquor and/or drugs. How else could he reason buildings that suffered the designations of Deify Plums, Market Pudding, or his personal favorite: Flannel Giraffe?

He lived with his brother in one of these outlandish-shaped sunflower buildings. Hexapods, as they were officially designated, were inspired by bee-hive design. At first, they had excited the minimalist crowd. Each block organized around the idea of space-saving through interlocking six-sided apartments. An integral part of the pillars, the drawback being a lack of outward-facing windows for tenants situated inside the first perimeter of the overlying design. This gave the whole construction a claustrophobic feel.

Wen had cared more about having a roof than windows, so the place had become theirs. His first reaction had been amusement when the concierge had mentioned the scheme, giving him the fast-talking sales-pitch like it was a barely used car, and would he be taking it, *now*?

Cheap and convenient, he had had to overlook the dark rust-colored stain, barely visible, on the bedroom's greenish carpet: a strong indication that the price was tied to superstition over foul play. Wen had no fear of spirits, brutally murdered or otherwise, but would refrain from mentioning the possible origin of 'the stain' to his then four year-old younger brother until he was mature enough to understand. His more pressing duties had been to explicate the various awful smells in the hallways, most of them urine-related. A common game they played now was Name That Disgusting Stench.

A movement over the door caught his attention. A fat spider rolled its latest victim in a cocoon of silk, pausing only to look at the interloper. Its web stretched between the porch light and the wall, the perfect place to catch juicy, unwary prey.

Wen shivered a bit and then opened the code box on the wall. He punched in his number and swiped his wrist on the scanner after the buzzer sounded, pulled open the door, and walked in. The house was lit by the holovid screen in the corner. A 3D cartoon played silently, enormous armed robots firing missiles at each other, the youths piloting them yelling orders, their mouths hyperextended like yawning fish, while flashing lights dazzled their faces. His younger brother slept on the couch amid the muted mayhem.

It was nest and home, cozy and messy, the fruit of many years of familiar accretion. Clothes lay bunched almost everywhere. Old-school games and consoles piled near the holovid screen in the living room, controllers like a mound of colorful, mismatched plastic puzzles in a red basket in their vicinity. Takeout and take-home boxes crunched as he squeezed past them with the open door. On the left, a miniature open kitchen cowered, a single table and two chairs taking up most of the space, themselves inundated with scrap paper, schoolbooks, tools, and odds and ends that hadn't quite made the transition from useful to trash yet, hanging in object limbo. The bathroom was past the kitchen, and the one bedroom, which he had given to his brother, was situated behind the puke-green convertible couch he called his bed.

He walked into the kitchen and flipped on the lights. Delicious-looking food waited for him in the wok on the range. He turned it on at low temperature and put the lid back on the wok, trapping the moisture underneath. There was a bit of rice left in the cooker that he put in the microwave.

"You're home." A half-woken voice came from the couch.

"I'm home. I guess you didn't get my messages. I got a complaint from school, Samuel. You didn't show up yesterday. Want to tell me what you think you're doing?" Wen said, exasperated.

"Sure, *mom*. I meant to tell you about that. Didn't feel like it," he said without conviction.

"You...didn't feel like it." Wen felt the familiar pressure rising in his temples, and he instinctively lifted his hand to massage them. "Tell you what. You skip out on school, get kicked out, and get a laborer job, and maybe you can help me pay the bills that are already behind. Maybe then we won't get kicked out of the house next month? How does that sound for a plan?" Wen said, his voice rising.

"Geez, it was only one day! I'm not going to do it again, all right?" his brother said, his arms crossed, pouting.

"You said that last time, and the time before that. Don't blow it, Samuel Harkwell. We're not doing so hot right now, as if you didn't know." He turned around and could feel his brother opening and closing his hand in a yadda-yadda-yadda gesture behind his back, bringing on the urge to slap him across the face.

"Did you get what I asked you to?" he snapped. His brother's head popped up from the sofa. He turned off the holovid with a swipe of his hand.

"Duh, yeah! It's on the counter next to the plate," he said, rolling his eyes. Wen turned around and saw the fat brown paper envelope next to the clean plate meant for his supper. He picked it up and threw it inside his backpack.

Sammy came and sat at the kitchen table, looking on as his older brother combined the rice with the mixed vegetables and tofu from the wok into his plate. He rested his chin on his hands and stared at his brother. Wen didn't want to complain, but ever since Sammy had started cooking, the meals had been a crapshoot of mild success versus resounding failures bordering on heresy, with the scales weighed down heavily by the latter. Sammy cooked when he felt the need to be forgiven, essentially. Wen sat down in front of his younger sibling and grabbed his chopsticks, praying for edibility. His brother smiled behind his hands as the food approached his mouth. His lips parted, and some of the vegetables fell in. His face convulsed for a moment but then regained its composure.

"It's takeout. I didn't have time to cook tonight. I had a project to complete *at school* today," Sammy said.

"You could have warned me," Wen scolded.

"And miss the show? Are you kidding me?" His brother laughed.

"We don't have time for this," Wen said, slamming his chopsticks on the table. "It's already late, and I want to be ready when they come."

"Don't worry; you'll be on time," Sammy said, his smile losing cohesion. Wen gobbled down the rest of his meal and put his dishes in the sink on top of the ever-growing dirty pile. Then the brothers grabbed their coats and Wen, his backpack, and they turned out the lights in the apartment and left.

They boarded the elevator to the 150th level, the graffiti-covered metal box almost empty. Wen felt the old urge to hold his brother's hand as they exited, something he hadn't done in years. Sammy seemed to read his mind and looked up at him. They walked along the road, through the crowd, passing the busy stores and restaurants, bars, and entertainment parlors. They came to a slim alley, which to the casual observer seemed to lead to nowhere. For those who knew, it was a sacred place. It was ensconced between two enormous square gray pillars, grappling the heavens. Pictures, drawings, hand-written notes, scraps of paper, plastic flowers, trinkets and mementos plastered the walls, all the way to a small red shrine, several meters away, at the end of the alley. The street sounds muted as they entered, as if shushed by solemnity. A well-dressed man carefully stuck someone's picture to the wall from the top of an aluminum ladder placed against it, while a woman held it. A leather-jacketed teen with a purple mohawk, on her knees, head bent and palms together, prayed in front of a burning candle against the concrete wall-face. Wen and Sammy walked on past her to the newly painted shrine, where an orange-robed, middle-aged man greeted them. Wen reached into his bag and took out the envelope. He opened it and removed a handful of incense sticks, a few white candles, and a photograph of a smiling lady.

The balding monk looked at the picture and asked:

"What is her name?"

Always in the present tense, Wen realized in surprise.

"Min Chen," Wen replied.

The monk spoke words in a low, guttural Japanese over the picture and incense while both boys bowed their heads. When the monk was done, they headed to the shrine and tossed some coins into a red wooden box. Eyes closed, they joined their hands and offered a short prayer. They then returned to an enormous copper bowl adorned in sacred Japanese Kanji near the shrine, in which burned several sticks of incense, the inside like a scale model of a forest-fires' aftermath: stumps, cinders and smolder. Lighting theirs, they inserted them vertically in the bowl and then bowed their heads and let the smoke envelop them. The enticing smell had a slight dizzying effect, like a mental piety pheromone. A free spot on the wall became the new home for the photo they had brought, as they lovingly pasted it to the cold concrete. They knelt before it and prayed in silence, lighting their candles and letting them burn a third of the way, wax pooling at their bases. Wen felt tightness in his chest as he looked at his mother's picture in the dark over the tiny orange flame. Her soft smile, her long brown hair, the tender hands that would caress his face and soothe him; all these things called out to him from the beyond to which she had been stolen.

When they got up, Wen looked at his watch. It was already quarter to ten! They would have to hurry back home, or he would be late.

"Do you think we'll ever see Mom again?" asked Sammy as they walked out of the alley, somber and serious now. Wen knew the question was coming, as it did every year on the same date. This year, Sammy did not cry. It was odd, under those circumstances, that he should feel like it.

"I don't know, Sammy. I hope so." His brother stopped walking. He looked up from the ground at Wen with clenched fists and set jaw. Wen opened his arms and Sammy went to him, wrapping his arms around his brother. Wen felt his lip quiver, but still he couldn't let the tears fall. The brothers were an island in the current of people. Time stopped for just an instant. Sammy released his brother from his grip and began walking again.

"Thanks," Sammy said over his shoulder.

Wen could think of nothing to say. He walked up to Sammy and put his hand on his shoulder. Their mother would never be returned to them, not after so many years of disappearance, they knew. She, like the thousands of others whose memories plastered the walls of the alley, was gone forever. Their bodies were never to be seen again, souls in limbo, leaving a legacy of uncertainty. "Disappeared" yet not forgotten; never forgotten. Eight long years had passed since their mother had dissipated into the ether. Eight years for the brothers to survive on their own, practically without help. The Administrative Police had claimed to search for her, but with so many cases to deal with, another missing person was the last thing they cared about, Wen knew. But he couldn't repress his bitterness over their seeming lack of effort.

He had contacted a detective agency and paid a cold-eyed man to investigate. Their mother had accumulated a bit of money during her days at DaiSin, the tech company that had hired her at their arrival. This he had used to find her. Soon, the money was gone, and the only thing they knew for certain was that it was no one on the street who had made her go away. The detective suspected a kidnapping of some sort, but without a ransom demand, he couldn't comprehend the motive.

With no one to help, they sold the furniture until that too was gone. On the last day, in the bare apartment that dominated the Heights, Wen looked out from the balcony at the uncaring sunshine and resigned himself to their fate. He took his four-year-old brother by the hand, each of them holding a bag of clothes and Wen, his father's old Netware deck, and took the plunge into the murky waters of Shinjuku 1.

Life was harsh in the Districts, but they survived. They even had a place to live, and Wen held a stable job. One day, Sammy would be able to work as well, if he could just focus for a moment, and things would get better. That was as far as dreaming went; one wobbly step at a time, up a dark staircase, with no end in sight.

They got home, and Wen told his reluctant brother to go to bed. Sammy went to school in the early morning, and he wanted him to have full attention when he did.

"Don't go," Sammy said, biting his lower lip.

"What do you mean, *don't go*? I have to go," Wen replied, his brow furrowed.

"You know, just for tonight, stay in, get some sleep. You need it too, you know. Besides, you guys never bring back that much valuable stuff anyway. Come on, bro, get some rest for once." Wen couldn't understand what had gotten into him.

15

"I have to go, Sam; it's my job," he said, his neck tensing.

"It's not a *real* job though! Why couldn't you get a real job?" He laughed forcefully. *What the hell is he talking about?* Wen fumed. "I'm going tonight. I have no choice. These guys are counting on me, OK? Not a real job. How is it a fake job?" he barked.

Face flushed, Sammy cried, "This *job* of yours is gonna kill you; that's why! What am I going to do if I lose you, huh? You might die for a couple of credits, how is that even worth it, huh? Why couldn't you go for a coders' pay instead of wasting your time?" Sammy ran out of the living room, in tears, into the bedroom and slammed the door shut. That hurt. Wen wanted to go to his brother and reassure him, to tell him he was doing the best he could. He also knew this would be a completely useless gesture. It was better to let Sammy cry it out. He would talk to him when he had calmed down. Besides, he had no time to waste on a whiny child. The others would be arriving soon to pick him up for his "fake job." Whatever Sammy thought of it, this is what he had to do for them to survive. This is what he had to do to put food (no matter how mangled) on his plate, to put him through school so he wouldn't have to do the same things he had had to endure when he was raising him. *Ingrate.* Wen's brain boiled slowly, his ears becoming warmer. He could hear his brother crying from the room. He should have expected this on the anniversary, but there was no way to mitigate it.

He went to the closet and pulled out his mesh-covered brown rubber protective suit and slipped it on, whipping up the zipper to his chin. He grabbed his backpack and threw it on. He took the grimy shovel from behind the door and tacked it into its holster on his back. He opened the secret panel behind the sofa and took out his H&K P3000 semiautomatic pistol and the spare clip, slipping them into his bag as well. He went to the front door and shoved on his thick-soled, metal-capped rubber boots, slamming the door shut behind him. After he walked out of the malodorant meanders, he stood over the rusted guardrail, tapping an electric cigarette with shaking fingers out of its chipped plastic box, popped out the used nicotine cartridge and slipped a new one in. He flicked the switch that would heat up the nicotine and give him an infinitesimal drop by turning it into smoke and took a long drag of it. He chucked the used cartridge as hard as he could into the night and watched it fall. Far above, the lights of the 150th shone, psychedelic festival decorations, glimmering in the relative darkness. The demented carnival for the adult crowd drew in those who yearned for a stroking of the amygdala, on a shoestring budget. The view to the bottom was a Mandelbrot set, illuminated at regular intervals until nothing more could be seen. He took another satisfying drag, and the plastic cherry burned brightly. He turned around to see how his neighbor was doing. The spider had finished wrapping its victim in a cocoon and was resting in the middle of its web.

"Cheers, buddy," Wen said, waving his smoke in its general direction.

He saw the crew coming toward him in the distance, down the walkway.

A muscular older man of around fifty led the way. His name was Oscar; leader of the group, bald, vaguely Mediterranean. He always wore high-collared sweaters that made his head look like a dick plastered with a serious face; a coiled fist ready to spring at the slightest provocation.

The second was Taz. He and Wen had been recruited at the same time for their present illegal activity when they were caught up in other felonious dealings gone south. The third was a darker-skinned, almost anorexic, much taller boy with a thin nose named Sayeed. He replaced Shawna, who had been arrested in a bar brawl a few weeks previous. Wen knew nothing about him save his name. He was a new guy, and Wen despised having to deal with newbies. More trouble than they were worth and not worth a damn in a tight situation.

The fourth was a short, squat man in his midforties. He harbored a trim, well-manicured beard and mustache, a style that was unpopular at best. Andrei was the point man. He carried the biggest gun, an ancient AK-47 automatic. Large shoulders rolled with every stride, making Wen wonder how he could have gotten so bulky, like some powerful animal storing fat for winter hibernation.

All were wearing protective gear against the toxic elements they were about to face, rebreathers slung under their arms. A few augmented their safety with military surplus bullet-proof vests, olive drab and worn-looking. They all had their own guns and ammo, proscribed as they were, the lack of which was a surefire way of turning up very deceased. Wen sighed and flicked the switch on his cigarette, slipping it back into its case.

Oscar walked by him without a word.

"Yup, let's go," Wen said, mocking the leader's silence, trying not to think about his sulking brother inside. They kept walking in the direction the group was originally headed. Wen shook Taz's hand.

"How goes it?" asked Taz.

"Alright, I guess. Sammy is throwing a tantrum." He shook his head.

"What's the matter this time?" Taz wondered.

"Today is his mother's Memorial Day. He still takes it pretty hard," he said.

"You mean *your* mother's Memorial Day as well, don't you? How are you taking it?" Taz inquired.

"It's not so bad." He lied. There was rarely a day when he didn't think about his mother, of course; this one always the worst of all.

"Uh-huh. One day at a time, bud," Taz said, looking at his friend and patting him on the back.

"Where are we headed today?" Wen changed the subject. He regretted having mentioned Sammy, but he felt better for getting it off his chest.

"I heard Oscar say some section out near the Bay, I think." said Taz. Tokyo Bay was replete with garbage of all kinds. Centuries of it accumulated in thick strata. It wasn't so much trash from the city as it was from *everywhere*, not just Japan, carried by the currents and hoarded up beneath the pylons. Oscar's team searched for the most valuable *gomi*, trash they could sell to various fronts in the upper city. Many other groups operated as well, but Oscar and Andrei had the best intelligence on where to look. Some of their rivals hunted for scrap metals instead of treasure. Remnants of twisted, broken ships also jutted sidewise here and there, frozen in the perpetual act of drowning, perfect pickings for the well-prepared. The laws of the jungle prevailed: it was dangerous to leave a discovery out in the open for too long. The fittest of the bunch would come and haul it away; hyenas taking the lions' prey.

This illicit industry began only ten years back, when the waters finally started to recede from underneath the towering megalopolis. Illegitimate and dangerous as well: trapped gas pockets, dug-out caverns, precipices, a rabid wildlife, other poachers, all of the ground level was a slow, roiling deathtrap for those foolish enough to explore it.

Wen had joined the crew two years ago. It paid little-to-middling, but enough to supplement their income and keep trying. Besides, surprises sometimes came to him in the form of rare artifacts. Those moments made the trek into sometimes pitch-black infernal dangers worth it. The past few months brought nothing of interest, only long nights of searching and wasted sleep. He felt tired in his being. He longed for a single night's rest but feared losing out on a discovery that would change his luck. Loot was only shared among those who participated in the haul.

"Touch metal then," he said, for good luck. They both knuckled the metal railing along the walkway they traipsed. Wen dropped back, ignoring Sayeed. He greeted Andrei with a firm handshake.

"Ready for another great night?" joked the Russian.

"Yeah, I guess," replied Wen, not daring to hope for too much, too fast. Andrei always picked the spots they would be excavating and searching. He sometimes went straight to a source that turned out to be pure gold; like the time they had found a cargo container full of ancient, intact bicycles. They had worked their asses off for a week on that one, but the payoff had been more than worth it. Booze flowed like a river for weeks on end after that haul; it was the reason Wen and his brother had a nice new holovid in the living room.

Andrei was the only guy crazy enough to live on ground level. No one had been to his hideout, but everyone speculated about it. Was it a self-built chalet in the middle of the dump, or a discarded concrete military tent? There were bets going on from all members. Andrei knew about them, but didn't care; an eccentric, undoubtedly, but highly intelligent.

"Cheer up, man. We'll have a good night for sure, OK?" Andrei smiled like a crevice that threatened to split his face. His infectious laughter always made Wen pull himself out of whatever abyss he was drowning in.

"Andrei, what do you know about DaiSin model 1805 Netrodes?" Wen had just remembered about his promise to Joe.

"Wow! Those are some *very* old tech! How do you know about those?" his eyes growing wide.

"Just a guy I know, he's got them implanted," Wen said, looking at the ground.

"Seriously? Those things haven't been used in a hundred years! No doubt they're illegal implants. Your acquaintance could get into a heap of trouble for owning them."

"Yeah, well, they don't work. I scanned them with my Netware and they don't report anything; no transfer, nothing."

"What are you using?"

"I have a Bergman-Strauss Zipper. It's old, but it still works well."

"Israeli Netware, da? Yeah, not as old as the 1805's, though, right?" Andrei chuckled.

"I guess not. What do you think?"

"Well, first of all, you're trying to scan for signal with a completely incompatible system. Your Zipper works on advanced fiber optics. The 1805's are pure metal connectors, so your gear wouldn't even register them. It would be like trying to play a vinyl record with a DVD player."

"Play a what with a what?" Wen said, confused.

"Nerdspeak, young padawan, never mind," Andrei said, chuckling.

"So they might still work, you think?" Wen asked, uncomprehending.

"Well, when they did the switch over to Wi-Fi only, a lot of people used the 1805's. Since they would have lost a lot of customers, DaiSin Corp. made these new inserts that could be slipped onto the existing 'trodes, making them wireless. Then everybody went directly to wireless, so they dumped all of them. I think I have a few somewhere. Don't tell anyone though." Andrei winked.

"Thanks, Andrei. I appreciate it." Wen felt good about himself. He thought he would be able to fulfill his promise to his...friend? Is that what Joe was? He couldn't classify him, really. Did he need to?

They came to a service elevator, and Taz opened the control panel. He bypassed the security protocols so that they could ride all the way down to the 50th level. The elevators were meant to stop before reaching the dangerous sectors, namely, anything after the 100th level. There, the air quality was bad enough that nothing human could survive for long without oxygen rebreather masks. It also made the danger pay at Fujii-Hashimoto Heavy worth it. They got in, and all put on their masks. The elevator slid without a sound into the depths. They got out at the 50th level and turned on their headlamps. The air, thick with dust and soot, made visibility a hard thing to come by. They walked along the metal catwalk until they reached a cart system like a miniature train meant for the maintenance workers. Once again, Taz worked his magic and by-passed the magnetic locks that held it in place. They boarded, and Oscar took the con-trols. The only sound was that of the whirring electric engine and whistling onrush of wind. It was like being on a roller-coaster with twists and turns but few ups or downs. They travelled on the edge of nothingness, Wen's heart squirming at every tight turn. Several times, Oscar stopped the cart and Andrei would tell him which direction to take. The onboard GPS was meant for localized areas only, and did not allow to pull back far enough to see a larger slice of the city. Andrei was cognizant of huge swathes of the ground level, and was better mentally equipped than most mapping softwares.

After an hour of zipping around in the silent darkness, they came to a stop near the edge of the bay, near a place called Odaiba Island. Wen wondered how long ago there had been an island here, and why they kept the name.

"Stay near the side of the pillars. The metal's almost completely salt-corroded down here." Andrei warned. Oscar took a safety line out of his pack and clipped it to his belt before handing it to Taz, who did the same, and then all the way down to Wen, who fastened it to his. They walked single file on tip-toes to the closest support structure and sidled along it, holding any protrusion in case the catwalk should fall away beneath their feet.

They came to a metal cage, a maintenance platform that descended all the way to ground level. The destroyed power box next to it looked as if it had been hacked to pieces.

"We aren't going down this way," mused Oscar.

"Hold on," Andrei said. He reached into his gear pack and took out a thermos-sized, red-and-white-striped cylinder. He grabbed two wires with alligator clips on one end, and inserted the plugs into the cylinder on the other.

"Always bring spare batteries, no?" Andrei smiled. He went behind the control console and unscrewed its rear panel and then spliced the power box cables and attached the alligator clips. When he turned on the battery, the console lit up.

Andrei took a bow and said, "Gentlemen, your ride." The crew erupted in muted applause and then entered the metal box. Andrei pushed the green button that closed the gates, and they began their descent. The air was almost opaque. Fires burned day and night, vomiting black smoke thicker than fog.

For this part of their journey, Oscar led the way. The five men walked in single file, the new leader scanning the ground for what he only knew would lead them to discovery. Wen took the gun out of his backpack and holstered it to his waist.

The ground was a sponged mass of garbage, felt more than seen. Wen found walking difficult and sinking exasperating, like taking a hike through marshmallow soup. He constantly lifted his boots to chest height to take another step. His headlamp's stream bounced in front of him, illuminating his steps, pointing at the next man ahead. Flying debris stuck to his visor, forcing him to wipe, lest his lowered vision be reduced to nothing. The ambient air was toxic enough for even the flies to avoid it that day. Wen trudged on, able to see less than a meter in front of him.

The rope pulled taut, and he jerked forward, falling on his face. He began to slip toward the others ahead, unable to stop. He saw Sayeed slide as well, flailing about. Wen grasped at objects on the ground but kept on skidding. He fell vertically, his heart leaping out of his throat, and his hands reached out to grasp anything that could stop him, without success. The wind got knocked out of him when the cord holding him by the midriff snapped back and held him before he could go any further. He hung, Sayeed above him, his headlamp dancing on the ceiling of a garbage cavern. Sweat dripped from his forehead, stinging his eyes. His head spun and stomach churned, his hands white-knuckling the rope.

"Are you OK?" He heard a shrill voice from above him as he dangled. His headlight swung with him, and he could see that the cavern into which they had fallen was enormous. He would have to drop another hundred meters before hitting the ground.

"I'm all right! Pull me up, will you?" He looked up and saw Sayeed holding onto his end of the cord, reaching up out of the hole and grasping someone's hands. The walls of the cavern were compressed garbage, the cavity dug by water currents. The bottom still looked wet. Corroded street lamps lay like giant burned matchsticks in the mud. There were a few vertical rectangles, way at the bottom. They must have been twenty stories tall, but seemed small from this distance.

He felt himself being dragged up. As soon as he could, he grabbed the crumbling edge of the garbage pile to pull out of the hole. The others lay in the detritus, panting.

"I recommend we get away from the edge, my friends." suggested Andrei, breathing heavily, his hands on his knees.

"I second that emotion," said Taz, as he lay on his back, his chest heaving, lifting his right hand.

"That's 'motion.'" said Sayeed.

"I know what I said." the other man replied.

They crawled away from the opening on their hands and knees, careful not to disturb more garbage. Once at a safe distance, Oscar came up to Wen and lifted him by the front of his suit.

"You almost got us all killed, you little shit! What do you have to say for yourself?" he hollered from behind his mask.

"What? How is this my fault? I'm the one who fell in! Back off!" he retorted, shoving the belligerent leader away. Oscar fell a step back and brought his arm back to hit Wen, who got ready for the imminent attack. Andrei grabbed Oscar's arm and yelled at him over the wind. Smaller debris was rolling along the mucky floor, some of them alighting, announcing a heavy garbage storm.

"Now isn't really the time, don't you think? We'll have to leave soon. The wind is picking up," he said. Oscar lowered his fist and shoved past Andrei, pushing Wen's shoulder.

"Did you guys see the bottom?" Wen asked, shaking. Oscar was pacing, mumbling to himself about incompetence and stupidity.

"No, why?" Oscar asked, stopping mid-rant, his head whipping up, teeth bared.

"There are buildings down there," Sayeed said, pointing at the hole.

"Yeah, a bunch of them," Wen chimed in. Oscar looked at Andrei.

"Do you think that's what you were looking for?" Andrei asked.

"There's a definite possibility. Didn't think it would be this easy though," Oscar mused. "Or this hard." The incredible height made it impossible to lower themselves without better climbing gear. Above the hole, visibility was getting worse. "Trade places with me," he told Andrei. They switched positions on the security rope, and Oscar ordered everyone to hold onto the rope as he approached it, crawling on his stomach. The swirling garbage made it difficult for Wen to see Oscar plunge his head into the aperture. The wind was picking up, as Andrei had warned. Wen felt a perverse urge to sever Oscar's rope and kick him into the hole, but he backed away from the hole and got to his feet before Wen could enact his fantasy.

"I think this is the place," Oscar said to Andrei, beaming, his anger forgotten.

"Good, now will you tell me what it is you're looking for?" Andrei replied.

"Sorry, comrade, can't do that." Oscar shook his head. He took a peg out of his satchel and stuck it in the ground. Then he pressed the top. "That'll tell us where we need to come back tomorrow." He turned to the others.

"All right, ladies, we're calling it quits for today. Drinks are on me tonight." The wind howled and garbage flew about, making it hard to see the way back. Andrei led the way, with sure footing and his unerring sense of direction. The orange metal cage came into view and they clambered aboard. It rattled like an old jalopy all the way up, getting stuck for an interminable ten seconds once.

Andrei disconnected his battery and slipped it back into his pack. They walked in procession along the side of the support pillar, careful of their footing. From the maintenance cart that brought them back to civilization, they could see the foul storm that rained hell below, billowing garbage-devils and gas explosions sparked by colliding metal objects. The tiny cart zipped back into the city at breakneck speed, the rising tide of wind and flying debris making their position a dangerous one.

Once they were back in Shinjuku1, the group began to disperse. Oscar, Taz, and Sayeed planned to have a drink to celebrate for reasons only Oscar seemed to be aware of. Of course, neither of the other two would turn down a free cold one. They removed their reinforced rubber coveralls, placing them inside their bags. Only Andrei and Wen stayed dressed in their protective suits.

"You girls not coming?" Oscar joked.

"Things to do, unfortunately," replied Andrei.

"Ha! Imagine that! A Russian turning down a free drink," Oscar said, laughing. Andrei smiled and said nothing. Wen stared at the floor, waiting for his level so he could go home. When the doors opened on the 132nd level, Andrei exited the elevator with Wen. They nodded to the rest of the crew as the doors closed and the elevator began to rise once more. They both removed their facemasks.

"What are we looking for, Andrei?" asked Wen, turning to him.

"Walk with me, my friend. It is not good to stay here too long," said Andrei. They headed further down the hallway, in the direction of Wen's apartment. "In answer to your question, I don't know. I haven't been picking out the targets for the past little while," he said, shrugging his shoulders.

"Is that why we haven't been finding squat for two months?" Wen asked, whirling to look at him, anger rising in his voice.

"Hey, hey! Relax, my friend. He is the boss, you know. He's been looking for something specific, but he won't even tell me what it is. So tonight, maybe we found it—who knows? He's a weird guy but usually doesn't steer us wrong." Andrei's shoulders rose and fell as he spoke.

He doesn't sound convinced, thought Wen. *Or he's trying to convince himself and not just me.*

"I'm tired of taking orders from that gohmert. You should be our leader, not him." Wen told Andrei.

"I am honored by your faith in me, but that is not my job. The problem is what you feel about Oscar. You should know him like I do: Under his gruff exterior, his holier–than-thou attitude, and condescending superiority complex, there is a worse bastard than you could ever imagine," said Andrei, smiling.

"That's really not what I thought you'd say. How does that even help me?" Wen said, knitting his brow.

"There are people you have to deal with in life, unless you can find ways *not* to have to deal with them. Oscar brings out the worst in you; in everybody, really. His anger is his own, don't make it yours," Andrei advised.

"Sometimes I think you're brilliant, Andrei."

"Thank you."

"There are times like these, though, when I wonder if I'm right to think so," Wen said, shaking his head. Andrei started laughing so hard that tears ran down his cheeks.

"That, my friend, is not the worst that has been said of me. Have confidence. Tomorrow, we should be fixed on the situation. What time you going to sleep?"

"That's a weird question. As soon as my head hits the pillow, Andrei." Wen raised an eyebrow.

"OK, OK, I see what I can do," he said, explaining nothing. "Good night, Wen." They had reached his apartment door, and Andrei was walking away. *What the hell am I doing with my life?* Wen wondered, his head shaking. He punched in the code to the door and walked into the darkened room. The oppressive silence made him wonder if there was anyone else there. He removed his boots and suit, taking the suit into the bathroom to rinse off the reek in the shower. He then hung it on a pole in the bathtub. He went to the bedroom and peeked inside. The table lamp beside his brother's bed was on, but his brother was sprawled on his stomach, face into his pillow, wearing his blue pajamas. His arms clenched his drenched pillow, looking like he wanted to tear chunks out of it. Wen approached without making a sound and took a different pillow from beside his head, tugging at the one his brother held in a death grip.

"Mommy!" Sammy whispered in his sleep. Wen's heart thumped at the word, a hard ball rising in his throat. He let go of the pillow he was trying to remove, placed the dry one close by, turned out the table lamp, and walked out of the room. He closed the door as slowly as possible, muting the creaking hinges. He headed for the shower and cleaned himself in the frigid water, wiping away the cancerous grime with rapid, sharp movements. His headache was coming back, and he had trouble staying awake when he lay down on the couch.

During the night, he woke up, hearing a faint tapping on the wall, coming from his brother's room. The knocks came at regular intervals. Groggily, he rose from the couch and went into the room. Sammy was standing by the wall, his nightlight on.

"I'm sorry," he said.

"I forgive you," Wen replied, rubbing his eyes. He would never tell Sammy about his plunge into a hole that could have ended with his splattering on the ground below. Sammy's concerns were genuine, but it seemed impossible to back away now. Maybe Oscar knew of a haul so fantastic that it would buy their way out of this place. Maybe he would be getting his share after tomorrow. Maybe he would never have to go digging through wet *gomi* for the rest of his life. Maybe.

"How do you like my Morse Code skills?" asked Sammy, lying back down in bed.

"What's that?" asked Wen.

"Well, it's a series of dashes and dots. People used to use them to communicate before computers and the Net. Every letter is represented by a bunch of them. I learnt it in coding class today."

"So what were you Morse Coding on the wall, just now?" he said, sitting on the bed by his brother.

"I'm sorry," Sammy said, looking into Wen's eyes.

"That makes sense."

"Did you guys find 'the big haul' tonight?" Sammy asked, imitating Oscar's gruff voice.

"Nope. Soon, though. Maybe very soon." Maybe, always maybe.

"I hope so. I can't stand it knowing you're out there," Sammy said, frowning.

"I know, Sammy. I don't like it either. Go to sleep; you've got school in a few hours."

"OK. Good night, Wen. I love you."

"I love you too, Sammy." He walked out the room. It took him several minutes to find sleep again. His mind was racing with the thoughts of Sammy having to fend for himself on the streets of Shinjuku1. He could never let that happen. As his mind blurred between reality and his unconscious, his mother kissed him goodnight, and was gone.

CHAPTER 2

B Y THE TIME he woke at six, Sammy had left already. School began early, and many Metro transfers away. Wen's mind buzzed from lack of sleep. He stepped into the frigid waters of the shower again to shoot the cobwebs out of his brain. Walking into the kitchen, he saw a clear plastic bag with a note taped to it, and beneath it, a letter written by Sammy that said: *I found this in the mail slot this morning. Have a good day at work, and I'll see you tonight.*

Wen put his brother's letter down and picked up the bag. Inside lay two purplish capsules, both smaller than pen caps. He opened the note and read: *You were wondering about this yesterday. I found you some that still work. Just slip them over the existing plugs and they should activate. —Andrei.*

The Wi-Fi 'trodes! Andrei had gone *somewhere* and found the upgrades for the DaiSin 1805's. Wen wondered if the man ever slept. He removed the note and put the bag in his backpack. Sammy had made a full pot of coffee, and he poured himself a tall cup. Then he drained the rest into his thermos. He cooked up some grilled tofu and miso soup, grabbed a large spoonful of rice from the cooker, and turned on the holovid in the living room. The black-haired Japanese woman told him that crime was up, employment was down, and that it was going to be a sunny day, somewhere far, far above his level. Breakfast finished, he rolled the rest of the rice into fist-sized flattened patties and wrapped them in seaweed. These he put into a plastic wrap and inserted into his pack.

He eyed his surroundings: disaster zone. Shame overcame him when he thought too hard about how they *should* live versus how they did. Mom wouldn't have let things slide like this. She would have told them to pick up their crap. She wasn't there; this is what it was. It had been so since Sammy had turned four, a few months after their mother had vanished. It was nigh impossible to go back to the life they'd had before, but Wen was willing to give up *his* dreams so that his brother could have a better future. He'd vacuum the pigsty tomorrow, maybe do some laundry if time permitted. Always a million things to do and no compunction to accomplish any of them unless the situation became dire.

The door closed behind him at a few minutes before seven, and he was headed out into the usual dark dawn. The streets of Shinjuku1 watched him saunter by. The drained prostitutes sat hunched up in groups against the walls, their depleted batteries recharging. Stores were shuttered for a few hours more, until traffic picked up again. Entertainment parlors had lost their eagerness to declare winners. A city-wide hangover until the night returned. Wen walked among the hordes of salarymen heading to the elevators of the upper levels, an army of white-shirted and black-panted men, most of them wearing glasses. As in a sea of milk, he followed the flow under the streetlamps. He spotted Joe near his designated Wi-Fi post. Time was lacking before work, but he thought it would be better than being forced to hunt him down if he failed to be in his usual spot later on that night. It was the first time he saw him up this early in the morning. On any given day, he was in some alley overcoming the night's abuses, Wen believed.

Joe's attention was focused on a single point on the ground before him. Wen stopped and observed, curious as to what could command his contemplation like a man hypnotized. As if sensing his presence, Joe looked up and saw Wen staring at him. He smiled, displaying his rotting and missing teeth.

"Hi. Good morning, kiddo," he whispered.

"Morning, Joe. What are you looking at?" Wen asked.

"Come closer. I'll show you. You gotta be quick though; it'll be gone real soon," he declared cryptically. Wen approached and saw a light beam, square in shape, smaller than the palm of his hand, touching the dirty concrete in front of Joe. Wen sat on his haunches, head cocked, transfixed. He reached out a tentative finger and slipped it into the light stream. It was warm and made his finger tingle. He looked up to see its source, but it was painful to try to pinpoint. The walkways, roads, buildings, and overpasses blocked most of the light, save this one rare and tiny beam. Then it was gone. Wen felt his heart beating faster, and his body ached for a return to the surface. He missed the sun almost as much as he missed his mother.

"Beautiful, isn't it?" said Joe. A great sadness was gripping Wen, and he couldn't find the words to describe how he felt. Joe could see the troubled look in his friends' eyes. "Hey, it's just light, you know. You can come back here every day to see it. It shows up around the same time, more or less. It'll be our secret." Wen made a sound somewhere between a giggle and a sob.

Secret.

The 'trodes! He remembered the gift he had come to bestow on his friend. He reached into his backpack and removed the plastic bag with the two tiny purple bulbs.

"Turn around, Joe. I have something for you. Can you lift your hair for me, please?" Wen asked, popping off the protective cap from the bottom of the upgrades. Joe complied, lifting his matted hair from the back of his neck. Wen slipped on the first 'trode, and it clicked into place. With more confidence, he placed the other one and took a step back.

"I don't feel any...oh, wait," Joe said, his expression going blank. "I'm there. My connection is back," he said, beaming. "Thank you, man, thank you!" He rose to his feet, quavering a bit, and grasped Wen by the shoulders. "I'm in!" he yelled, looking into an imaginary sky. The salarymen paid no attention and kept on walking without looking back. Wen realized he would be late if he stayed much longer. He gently took Joe's hands and placed them back by his side.

"I have to go now. You take care, all right?" Joe had begun to wring his hands and did not notice Wen anymore. He walked away gibbering to himself, his fingers dancing in the air, his stare a million miles away. Wen lifted his shoulders with an intake of breath and dropped them again, exhaling, watching the man stumble away. He resumed his walk to the Metro station, a ray of sunlight dancing in his mind's eye.

He thought of it for the whole day and felt as if there had been an exchange. Joe had given him something grand, and he wanted to hold onto it for as long as he humanly could. He repeated the gesture in his mind, over and over, feeling the heat and watching the light play on his skin, ending the loop with the extinction of the light. He observed his hand, his physical hand, as if it changed during the interaction and wondered what true difference existed between the memory and the experience. He closed his eyes again and again and saw the light, embraced the heat. He wanted the moment to be eternal, etched in his memory as the passage of a moment of greatness. In this state, he did not see the hours drain away. They swirled through the hourglass at breakneck speeds, taking him from beginning to end faster than he could believe. His head jerked up in surprise as the closing bell rang, and he returned to the exit of the factory, which he had entered just a few seconds ago. He remembered now how he took the light for granted when it was all around him. How nothing mattered when he was a kid.

"You ready for tonight?" Taz asked, scaring the pants off him.

"Holy hell, dude; you have to quit sneaking up on me like that!" he exclaimed, having been oblivious to his surroundings.

"Geez, sorry! Didn't you get enough sleep last night? You look half-awake again. I went out, and I feel great!" he said.

Except you have great big black circles under your eyes, thought Wen. "How was the beer?" he asked, uncaring.

"He paid us a beer all right. One beer, in a bar where it was 400 yen per glass. It was beer-flavored piss-water. Scratch that; water might have been more intoxicating. Sayeed and I went on to some better places after having sent Grandpa Cheapo home," he said, shaking his head.

"That comes as a complete shocker. Do I need my shovel tonight?" he asked with apprehension.

"I don't think so, but bring it anyway; better safe than sorry." The memory of the light beam faded a bit as the night's work prospects loomed larger in his mind.

"Makes sense, I guess."

"Tell you what; we'll go for a drink, you and me, after this is done. From what Oscar's been saying, this could be a huge haul: *the* haul. He could be telling the truth, for once," Taz said, putting his hands in his pockets.

"I sure as hell hope so. I'm getting sick and tired of dredging the garbage heap for the ghosts of promises." Wen glared into his friend's eyes.

"You and I both, man. Buck up, buttercup; this'll be a wild one," Taz said, serious for a moment.

"Yeah, that's what it'll say on my grave marker," Wen replied.

"Cheerful today, aren't you? I'll see you tonight," Taz said, clapping his friend on the shoulder.

"See you." His bitter words hid a desire to return to his memory.

Wen left his friend and returned home. The Metro ride seemed shorter than usual. The clanking of the rail ties was softer than he was accustomed to. The hustle and bustle of Shinjuku1 was a pleasant scene, which he felt and smelled. Gazing higher than usual, he saw the upper floors of those businesses he walked by every day. Lancatlgue Coffee Shop, Cocue Massage Parlor, Freak's Store, The Lonely Ronin Whisky Bar; each name a story in itself. Shinjuku1 was built vertically as well, stores like barnacles hugging the sides of the pier but stopping just below the water line, unable to survive the rarefied air of the Heights.

This place is plausible only if you don't try to think about it, he mused.

His steps lightened as the road home grew shorter. He wished he was Netted, so that he could share his memory with his brother. He'd heard rumors that that was one of the advantages to the implants.

"I'm home!" he said, stepping through the door.

"Great, I made supper tonight," replied Sammy, nodding his head in the kitchen's direction while keeping his eyes on the holovid screen. He stood before the 'vid set, chopping the air with his hands, his avatar slicing through purple humanoid enemies in 3D before him. The background was displayed on the wall, and other enemies were approaching in the distance.

"What have you done *this* time?" Wen said.

"Nothing! Why do you always think I did something wrong?" Sammy said, indignant.

"That's the only time you cook!" Wen answered pointedly.

"Well, not this time, OK?" Sammy answered with exasperation.

After removing his shoes, Wen went to inspect the simmering stewpot on the range. The odor wafting from underneath the lid was enough to make his mouth water. Sweet green curry and chicken was one of his favorite Thai dishes. He turned to his left to wipe a few bowls for the evening meal but was startled to see that not only was the sink empty, it was clean as well. The dishes, sparkling, lay piled neatly beside it.

"Thanks for the dishes!" he yelled over the sound of the massacre in the living room.

"No problem. I cleaned my room too."

A demon has taken possession of my brother. Do I want him back that badly? thought Wen.

"Anything else I should know about before I die of shock?" he said.

"Mm, nope. That's it," Sammy answered, kicking and felling a large, axe-wielding anthropomorphic tree approaching him. He paused the game and came to the kitchen.

"Help me, will you?" he asked Wen, looking at the pile of papers, school supplies and junk littering the table.

"Where do you want to put this stuff?" said Wen.

"My room for now. I'll sort it out later," Sammy said, picking up an armload and heading to his bedroom. Wen took his share of the mountain and followed his younger brother in disbelief. His back stiffened as he walked into the room. A *floor* lay before him. Heaped in a corner rose a tottering pile of dirty clothes, overflowing from the hamper like a geyser. The bed was made. Sammy's toys had disappeared. Only the hypermasculine superhero posters on the walls belied the fact that a teen boy lived there.

"What happened?" whispered Wen rhetorically.

"Nothing. It was time to clean up," Sammy said, putting the stack of paper on his neat bed.

Wen kept looking around the room, expecting it to revert to its original capharnaum if he blinked hard enough.

Sammy wiped the dining table and placed coasters on it. He brought the pot of green curry, the rice, and chopsticks to the table.

"Get the water, will you?" he told his older brother. He filled their respective bowls with rice and topped them off with the curry. Wen brought the water glasses and sat down. Sammy sat as well and invited his brother to try the food. Too shocked to think of preparing for an onslaught of horrible flavor, Wen took a big bite of his curry. It was delicious.

"What do you think?" asked Sammy, leaning in.

"Mmm-mmm!" replied Wen, giving the thumbs up sign with one hand while covering his mouth with the other.

"Spicy enough?" asked Sammy.

Wen wobbled his hands in a so-so gesture, his mouth still full.

"Good," he replied. They both ate in silence, stopping only to take sips of water. Wen had to admit, reluctantly, that his brother's cooking was on the upswing. He hoped this was no fluke but a sign of better things to come.

When ten o'clock came, he was ready, by the door, dressed in his gear. Sammy stood near him. A look of determination had replaced that of despair he wore when his brother was about to leave.

"Be safe, bro," he told him, as Wen crossed the threshold.

"I'll be careful," Wen told him, hoping that that would be enough to reassure him. Sammy nodded, his jaw set and his expression serious. He then turned around and went to the kitchen to clean up. Wen slipped the door shut and walked down the wet corridor to the overlook. He stared at the identical apartments on the other side of the chasm. A young couple walked home on the level below his, the girl's head nestled in the man's neck. She wore large, golden hoops in her ears that shimmered under the lamps. They held hands and softly stroked each other's fingers in a way that made Wen ache.

A disheveled drunk man in a stained suit stumbled down the walkway a few levels higher. He tottered near the guardrails, oblivious to the danger of falling over. *He wouldn't be the first to fall into the darkness*, thought Wen. He observed the inebriated man's progress until he saw his crew approaching from afar. Oscar looked joyful, for once. The others talked and joked behind him, carrying their masks under their arms.

"Ready to fly?" Oscar said as he came up to Wen.

"Let's go," he said, surprised to be spoken to. "What's the good news, man?" he asked Taz, who had been chatting with Sayeed. They kept walking toward the service elevators.

"Well, Oscar is 90 percent sure we've found a great place, according to his archives. We've hit pay dirt, and now we're gonna get rich. How's that for news?"

"Spiffy. You still up for that drink later on?"

Taz grinned: "Guaranteed. Tonight we celebrate, for real. You're looking cheery for once; what's going on? Did you get laid after your shift?" Taz mock-punched Wen in the shoulder, and he couldn't repress a smile.

"I wish. I'll tell you about it later. Could be good, could be bad. I don't know, honestly."

"Alright, Mr. Mystery, better not forget though."

"Where you guys going?" Sayeed asked from behind them, butting in.

"Sorry, man; it's just me and Wen tonight. Got some catching up to do. Nothing against you. I made a promise," Taz said to him, sincerely.

"That's all right. I'll see if the old men want to go for a pint." He smiled, pointing his chin at Oscar and looking back at Andrei.

"Who are you calling old, tadpole?" Andrei called out in feigned anger.

Taz laughed. "Wow, you have good ears, for an ancient."

"*Ay ay ay*, the things you have to hear," Andrei said, putting the back of his hand to his forehead and throwing it back in an exaggerated movement.

"Alright, my little drama queens, simmer down. We have a long, hard night ahead of us. Save your energy for the job," Oscar growled, turning around to scold them.

They made their way back to the site of the previous night, lowering themselves to the garbage heap along the length of the immense concrete pillars. The fog was less thick than the night before, and those massive stanchions could be spied by mask-light at regular intervals, plunging deep into the morass. Flies and wasps the size of thumbs rose in clouds from the filth to greet them, aggressive and hungry. They clung to the men in buzzing fury, biting at their suits until the crew turned on the repellers, ultrasound waves that drove them away.

"I'm having trouble finding the signal," Oscar said, tapping his device with his index finger.

"It was that way," Andrei said, pointing toward the distance. They slogged through the muck, sweat dripping into their eyes. Oscar stopped. Before them, a great depression fell away, an immense crater of garbage. The walls dropped as sheer verticals, with what Wen guessed would turn out to be crumbling handholds to help them down. They had trouble seeing all the way to the bottom, but the outlines of structures could faintly be guessed at.

"The cavern collapsed overnight," Andrei said, hands on his knees, peering into the pit.

"That explains my vanished beacon," Oscar said. He walked back a few meters and searched for a solid anchor point. A thick metal railing protruded vertically from the garbage about three meters away. He looked it up and down, testing its rigidity with both arms, nodding in satisfaction as it didn't budge a centimeter.

"This'll do it, I think," he said, taking a long rope out of his pack. He looped it several times around the railing, trailing the loose end toward the chasm. He clipped himself in and began the descent while the others looked on. They pointed their helmet lights toward his position to help him out. Several minutes later, they heard a yell come from the bottom of the pit:

"All right, next!" Taz attached the rope to his waist and descended, grabbing handfuls of loose garbage as he did.

Wen saw an orangeish-red light in the distance. It was across from the crater, approaching from the northwest. He peered at it with knotted brow. He tapped Andrei on the arm and pointed toward the glow. It was getting larger, like a dim sun rising. Andrei told Sayeed to hurry down the rope and tell Oscar a sentry bot was coming. Sayeed said he had never seen one before but had heard of them.

Administration's attempt at policing the Heap, they resembled squat, black nuclear submarines, hovering about the carpet of garbage, scanning in infrared from a flexible periscope above their rotund, tubular bodies. It was the light emitted from the end of the periscope that gave them away. Lethal, they were equipped with stun guns that would pump you full of current until your heart stopped or your body exploded. They would bring back your fried corpse to Police Central for processing.

Wen kept an eye on the approaching bot as Sayeed shimmied down the crumbling embankment of dreck. Andrei grabbed Wen by the arm and told him to dig into the pile to bury himself. He then got on his hands and knees and dug a hole to hide in. Wen followed suit, ripping out piles of scrap to hide before they were spotted. The top layer of rotting garbage let off heat as it disintegrated, making it a perfect hiding spot. As he covered his head with the refuse, the sentry bot began to follow the rim of the large bowl it had just stumbled upon. It gave off a high-pitched metallic squeal of curiosity, its periscope swaying to and fro, looking for clues as to the reason for this new declivity on its territory. Wen peered from under his trash pile, lying on his back and trying to be as still as possible. He had done this before, but every time was as nerve-wracking as the first. He wondered if the others were also under heaps of trash a hundred meters below. He felt the vibration of the sentry as it came closer and closer. Wrappers and tin cans, bottles and diapers shimmered and rattled over his face, clanking and sloshing. His pulse quickened, his hands sweating. The sentry was five meters in length, and maybe half that in height. It hovered nearer, and the ground shook beneath it. Wen could hear its vents exhaling air as it moved. He closed his eyes, hoping it would go away.

Don't see me, don't see me, don't see me, he repeated inwardly like a mantra. A fat rat made the unfortunate mistake of popping its head out of the ground a mere meter away from Wen. The sentry bot's turret spun toward it, the periscope's eye becoming small and bright. A porthole opened on its side and a long rod extended from it. White lightning crackled and flashed, and the rat exploded where it stood. Wen twitched at the kill, thinking the sentry was aiming at him. A questioning sound emanated from the bot, as it inspected the remains of the animal it had just destroyed, leaving a tiny smoking heap. It turned around to investigate the slight movement. Two holes opened beneath its belly, and long pincered arms extended, beginning to rummage the spot where Wen was buried. Just as one of its extended arms scraped by his ankle, Andrei jumped out of his hiding hole. He flipped his automatic weapon from his shoulder to the firing position, flicked the safety and let loose upon the sentry bot's red eye. The shots went wide as the bot anticipated the trajectory of his bullets. Andrei rolled away from it as it shot a bolt of lightning in his direction. He ran toward the sentry, zig-zagging to avoid getting zapped. The thing sent bolt after bolt at him but kept missing by centimeters as he managed to duck and dodge in time. Wen popped out of his hole, behind the now distracted sentry. He unholstered his gun, aimed at it, and fired off a few rounds, which ricocheted. He attracted its attention though, and was now in mortal danger. Wen jumped out of the way as the bot opened another porthole on his side and began shooting bolts in his direction as well. Its periscope swung from one man to the other, aiming for both Wen and Andrei. The air crackled with bursts of lightning shooting from its sides. As Wen avoided being shot, he took a wrong step and fell over the edge of the precipice. He caught the dangling rope in time and climbed back up as fast as he could. At the lip of the hole, he saw Andrei straddling the bot, attempting to open the cargo hold at its rear. Wen climbed over, propping his gun on the ground while the bot spun about, trying to get rid of its unwanted passenger. Andrei held on with both legs like a cowboy riding an enraged bull. Wen shot twice into its eye while it was distracted and shattered it on the second shot. He ducked again as the thing sent off a volley of lightning at Wen's last known position. He peered from his cover again and saw Andrei slamming his shovel as hard as he could into its cargo hold door. It had stopped firing, now blind, and wobbled side to side, making Andrei slip and almost fall. His shovel fell out of his hand as the periscope whipped back and hit him. Andrei now held onto it with a death grip so as not to be ejected. Wen climbed out of the hole and took his own shovel off his back. He jumped onto the machine as well, making it sag a bit lower to the ground. This new weight on it revived its desperation to flip off its assailants, and it rolled deeper and spun faster. Andrei caught Wen by the waist as he was close to being thrown off, clasping his legs around the periscope. Wen bashed at the door with all his might and broke it open with a clang.

"Now what?" he yelled at Andrei over the fury. Andrei reached into his bag and pulled out a hand-grenade, gripping it as hard as he could. Wen took it from him, popped the pin, and threw it into the hold. Both men rolled off and ran to the hole, where they slid down the near vertical slope at breakneck speeds. They tumbled head over heels in the trash when they heard more than felt the explosion that rang out over them. They both came to a rest in a thick, plush pile of refuse at the bottom of the hole and remained prostrate for only a few minutes before lifting their aching bodies from the mess and limping to safer grounds. The trash that had been the cavern's ceiling the night before had cushioned their fall. Chunks of fiery debris landed around them, extinguished by the ambient humidity. Oscar and the others appeared from the other side of one of the buildings that stood in the distance, staring up at the wreckage the sentry bot had left in the wake of its extermination.

"Oy, Andrei, what are you going to do about the other sentries that are going to rain down on this place in a few minutes?" Oscar yelled.

"I make it my problem, just like the last time. You go on ahead; I'll catch up to you later," he said, turning around and beginning to climb up the rope, his movements slow yet steady. Wen joined the others near the cluster of ancient concrete apartment blocks with shuddered windows and doors. He was amazed that they had stood the test of time in such harsh conditions.

"What happened last time?" asked Sayeed.

"We found the sentry bot's beacon and brought it somewhere else in a hurry. He doesn't have much time though. Neither do we. Let's go." Oscar raised his hand, commanding the others to follow. Oscar led them between the mud-caked buildings, looking at each for the detail as to the exact location he was hunting. Most of them were between ten and twenty stories high, some having crumbled under pressure. The fog was thinner at this depth, their light beams stretching further. At the sixth edifice, Oscar took out his GPS device and looked at it long and hard before pointing at the fifteen story complex. The front door was a massive piece of intricately carved copper, green rust running all the way down the stairs. A small metal panel rested on its left, at chest height.

"Check it out," Oscar ordered Taz, who ran up the short flight of steps and inspected the panel. The other men pointed their headlamps toward him and approached. He tried opening it with his gloved hand without success. He rooted around in his canvas duffel bag for a moment before taking out a crow bar and prying at the panel. Underneath it was a keypad with stainless-steel buttons surrounded by waterproof sealant. The buttons lit up at his touch, and Taz recoiled in surprise.

"Holy crap, this thing has current!" he said.

"You wouldn't happen to have the code, would you?" he asked Oscar, who slapped him on the back of the head.

"No harm in asking," Taz said, rubbing his bruised scalp.

Jerk-off, thought Wen.

Taz removed a device the size of a credit card from a pocket in his belt, placing it overtop the keypad. The side of the card facing him illuminated to show him an x-ray of the keys, as well as the cables running from them to the computer off to its right. He ran the card along the length of the cables, pinpointing the processor through the wall. He then tapped his card, sending a charge to it. The keypad lit up red on numbers 1, 3, 6 and 7. He removed his card from the wall and changed programs, selecting his hardware cracking application. It asked him for the numbers and symbols he wished to use, and he duly typed in the numbers that had appeared on the keypad. He then placed the card over the keypad again and ran the program using all combinations of those numbers up to nine digits, the maximum amount of numbers that could be entered onto the keypad screen. There was a resonating click, and wheels that hadn't been oiled in centuries began to turn. The sound was deafening, and must have been heard all the way to the 120th. The massive door began to roll sideways, across the front of the building. They covered their ears to block out the painful screech that threatened to leave them writhing on the stoop. The blessed silence returned once more after the door came to its final resting place with a thud.

"I don't know how far Andrei's gotten, but that racket must have alerted *something*. Hurry up, hurry up!" Oscar said. On the other side of the immense metal door were two smaller, yet thick, glass ones. Oscar told Sayeed to go in first. Sayeed gave him a curious glance and walked toward the inner doors. They slid apart and he was thrown to the ground by a rush of wind.

"Did you know that was going to happen?" he asked Oscar, angered, picking himself up off his back and rubbing his thigh.

"Yeah, I did. What are you going to do about it?" Oscar answered, taking two steps closer to Sayeed. He didn't answer, but his red face spoke volumes about what he would have wanted to do.

"Let's go, chicken-shit, time's a-wasting," Oscar said, leading the way again, without even looking back at the rest of his team.

The interior was decorated in a style that was even more ancient than the building itself; wooden paneling, plush rugs covering marble floors, copper accents; this was a gem of a lobby. There was even a security desk ten steps in, beside the gold-barred elevators to its right. Their booted feet broke the silence of the tomb. They had closed the outer doors, to drag in as little of the fog as possible. The black-tiled floors had a thick coat of debris, and what must have been red wallpaper was now pinkish white. On the left were rows of small wooden doors with etched-gold numbered plaques.

"Mailboxes," Oscar said, explaining nothing. He walked up to the elevators and pressed the call button, but nothing happened. Whatever current fed the outer doors was not connected to this part of the building.

They walked past them to the wooden staircase that spiraled all the way up to the fifteenth floor. The pink carpet sent plumes fluttering into the air with every step they took, like ripe dandelion seeds blown into the wind. There was no way they could charge up this elevator's current with what little power they had; therefore, they opted for the long way up.

By the fourth floor, Wen started praying they'd find something worth the pain. By the tenth, he just wanted to quit and go home. It was on the thirteenth floor that they finally stopped in front of the sealed door. Its construction was identical to that of all the others. This one was, however, closed and untouched. Taz went to work on it and got it open in a little under five minutes. He said that the coding was extremely intricate for something that age, much harder than the front door.

"Open it," Oscar ordered Wen.

"No. I don't think so," Wen said, shaking his head.

"Don't look at me. I don't want to be blown off the landing again!" Sayeed said.

"Damn pussies," Oscar said, gritting his teeth. He grabbed the door handle, and with his back to the adjacent wall, turned it and pulled the door open. A slight pop resounded, but otherwise the pressure was equal on both sides.

"Get in there," he roared. Sayeed peered inside the room, looked left and right, and then took a tentative step inside. Wen looked on in amusement, thinking he looked like a terrible cartoon parody of a cat burglar. Wen entered next. He stood flabbergasted at the entrance, and Taz tapped him on the shoulder for him to move. Oscar came in afterward, looking around in amazement as well. It was impeccable and opulent, from the deep, dark wooden floors to the fine tapestries on two walls. The rugs covering the floors had not lost all of their many hued and intricate beauty, each one different in design yet similar in style. Wen imagined the dusty bazaar in Tunisia or Iran where the globe-trotting owner of these treasures might have hand-picked his prizes under a scorching sun to adorn his home; places that were more earth than steel and glass.

The living room was immense, the adjacent apartments having had their walls knocked down to increase the size of the dwelling.

"Wow," Sayeed exclaimed.

"Wow is right," Taz said.

Wen looked on in silence, taking in the beauty that surrounded him. This mysterious person's tastes were influenced by European and Middle-Eastern flavors. Because the apartment had been air-locked, nothing had aged during the time of its entombment. Three gorgeous, thick brown leather couches were arranged in a semicircle on the right side of the living room, desiccated as mummies' skin. They faced an enormous black marble fireplace coated in dust. On top of it stood two slender gold candelabra, adorned with climbing leaf and vine patterns. Glass-topped, circular end tables supported delicate gold lamps with stained-glass shades adorned with powdery spider webs. Wen thought of how the person who had dwelled here might have spent his evenings with a snifter of some fine and expensive liqueur in one hand, holding one of his books with the other, the only light by which to read being the orange fire's crackling glow. The chandelier that hung in the center projected long, slender, black branches reaching down from the ceiling, with tear-drop shaped crystal shards in their grasp. Dark oak libraries overflowed with thick old tomes on almost every wall of the room. Fascinating. Wen had never seen books that ancient, let alone an entire room full.

"Don't touch those," snapped Oscar, following his gaze, before going back to the task at hand.

The others began to gather the precious heirlooms and bibelots that decorated the room and giddily stuffed them into sacks. They too were awed by the book stacks, but treated them like cursed objects. Wen perused the shelves while the others searched the other rooms for treasure. He noticed, while flashing his headlamp about, that a book was missing from a top shelf. It left a small gaping hole like a missing tooth in an otherwise perfect mouth. He looked about for the missing book, its absence a puzzle to be solved. He then noticed it under one of the glass tables near the fireplace. As he walked to it, Oscar's voice rang through the apartment.

"Wen, get in the bedroom." He took a step forward and hesitated. He glanced behind him to see if anyone was looking and hurried over to the table, reaching out his hand to take it. They were here to take all that they could, but these books were most definitely proscribed. They had been squirreled away before the Selection Committees had even been a twinkle in Administrations' eyes. There couldn't be any harm in taking just this one, could there? No one would ever see it but him. He would keep it safe in his home. Even under the couch cushions, not a soul would dare disturb it.

"Hurry it up!" yelled Oscar.

A short, sharp shiver zipped up his spine as he walked away from the scene of the would-be crime empty-handed. What could be the problem of taking this one book? It was worth less than a lot of the treasures they were plundering as he thought about it. It was fine. Everything they were doing that night was illegal, so why worry?

He headed in the direction of Oscar's voice. A corridor opened up on the opposite side of the couches. It was narrow, with small, square paintings of tiny birds along the left wall. On the right stood three carved wooden doors in Arabic style, the first of which was open, and one at the far end of the hallway. He looked inside the first room to find the others stuffing their satchels and backpacks with all manner of memorabilia, trinkets, and ornaments. The dresser, end tables, and headboard were loaded with such valuables, reinforcing Wen's admiration for the previous owner's eclectic taste and a knack for collecting beautiful, exotic, if not expensive things. They harkened back to a day when it meant something to bring back a souvenir from some distant land, the living fabric of its culture. Made there by skilled craftsmen, the memory of the place embalmed in it forever, the new owner never needing to doubt its origins. Taz handed him a small jade dragon with a wooden base, his bag overflowing to the brim with treasure. Wen placed it carefully in his bag. Out of curiosity, he opened the drawers in the dresser and found them empty. He peaked into the closet, but apart from several more works of art and paintings resting against the wall, no clothes hung from the pole. He removed the artwork and placed the smaller pieces next to the jade dragon in his bag. Wen looked around and saw that there was still a cover on the bed. He lifted one of the corners of the duvet, but there were no bedsheets, only the duvet over a naked mattress covered in plastic wrap. He knew what he would find, but he went to the window and pulled aside the long purple velvet curtains, tufts falling off where his fingers touched. The windows were sealed, of course, since the apartment remained spotless and without water damage. The more Wen looked around, though, the more he thought everything was arranged like in a museum. It didn't seem as if someone had left in a hurry and abandoned all his earthly possessions, neither had the owner moved out, since everything was arranged just so. Wen couldn't put his finger on it. Apart from the expected thick layer of dust, it was spotless. He would have thought to see at least a shirt thrown nonchalantly over the divan, perhaps a pair of shoes left askance at the entrance, but no such careless gesture came to mar perfection. He left the bedroom and visited the second room down the hallway. It was bare, and so was the third. The last one down the hall was a bathroom, with an enormous claw-footed porcelain bath resting on blue glass tiles of varying hues. The taps and pipes that fed it were golden and carved with elaborate designs, staying with the vine and leaf motif. Nothing had been left that could be lifted, so he returned to the living room. The men were busy turning the kitchen over, trying to find any baubles they might have missed.

"Alright, I think we got everything," said Oscar. "It's getting pretty late. Time to go." He took one last look around the living room, scrutinizing every corner. He nodded in approval and raised his hand to say "Let's go." As they left the threshold though, Wen obsessed about the lone book he had left under the coffee table. It gnawed at his mind the further he walked.

"I forgot something inside. I'll be right back," he said, turning around and running up the stairs before anyone could protest.

"Dumbass. Hurry it up, will you? We're not waiting for you," Oscar hollered after him as he went back into the apartment. He stepped up to the coffee table and only skimmed his second thoughts before leaning under it and picking up the tiny volume, slipping it into his satchel with the rest of his treasures. He rushed out as fast as he had entered, catching up to the others making their way down the stairs a few floors below. They walked out of the building and scanned the area for more sentries. Andrei had done his job well; if pursuers there were, they were busy tailing the Russian far away from their present location.

The rope tensed to its load capacity as they clambered out of the pit. Wen watched from below as Oscar peered over the lip of the crater, looking out for the telltale red glow of the sentries. They clambered out of the hole, muscles tense, sweating heavily after the effort. They once again fastened the rope to their midsections after having hauled up their line, Oscar leading, followed by Taz, Sayeed and Wen trailing behind. Wen felt the last of his energy drain from him. Volutes of smoke petered out from under a nearby trash heap, where Andrei had covered the smoldering remains of their foe. Wen was surprised that none of its kindred had been attracted to the area by its demise. He surmised that they were more interested in knowing the location of its black box beacon, now in Andrei's care, and why it was still moving. He pictured a phalanx of the killer sentries, buzzards on the trail of elusive quarry. He wondered how far afield he had had to go to lure away the killer bots. It felt as if *something* was out there in the wastes, peering at them, hidden and waiting.

They stepped through the trash with great care, eager to avoid another cave-in, more so now that they were weighted down with so much. Wen peered over his shoulder constantly, the eerie feeling of being spied on not leaving him until they were back on the 50th level.

The little maintenance cart creaked under the combined weight of the men and their bags, groaning often and loudly when they took a turn faster than it would have preferred. Oscar was forced to slow down or risk their plummeting over the side of the level. Instead of going back to Shinjuku1, they headed toward the Shinagawa Ward, a disaffected industrial district that bordered the bay to the west. That section of the oceanfront was mostly abandoned on the 50th, new factories having opened either on the Asian mainland or in the Chuo Ward, where Wen's workplace was situated. The salt waters gnawed tirelessly at the gridiron, making the place just as much of a death-trap as a safe haven. They had set up shop in a disused parts supplier's building: three floors high, little street frontage, and a whole lot of privacy. Rusted corrugated metal curtains covered the few windows in the front from nosy neighbors. The addition was superficial at best, since no neighbors of a reputable disposition had elected domicile in the area for at least twenty-five years. Even those of less trustworthy standing tended to adopt hideouts with a better and fresher supply of breathable air than the 50th.

Andrei had finagled an air system that pumped out the raw sewage and turned it into palatable oxygen, via found tech and a bit of splicing on the grid. They entered through the back door after having squeezed down the slim alley with their over-burdened sacks. Andrei was there already, waiting at a terminal in the main room, the screen reflecting the streaming colors on his face in the semidarkness. He turned around and his frown turned into his usual wide smile. He slid his computer chair over a bumpy carpet near the terminal.

"You have returned alive!" he said, raising his arms in greeting.

"Glad to see you too," Taz said, clapping one of his outstretched hands.

"How did you get rid of the other sentries?" Wen inquired.

"I ran as quickly as my legs could carry me to the higher levels, stole a mainte- nance cart, and drove around for a few hours until I thought you would be done. I then left the black box on the 50th, somewhere out in the East Bay area. It'll take them forever to find it. How about you; how went the hunt?" he asked, crossing his arms. Oscar flicked the switch and turned on the minimal lights they permitted themselves to have inside the building. It was one thing to have a fully functioning air system, but burning up wattage with flood lights would have tipped the scale against them in their theft of electricity. It was in their best interest, of course, to remain as inconspicu- ous as possible with the local Electric Power Corporation. Sooner or later, they would send an able-bodied and overzealous employee to travel all the way from the cushy seats of headquarters to the crusty outer rim of hell and would realize that there was in fact no baby-bottle manufacturing plant at this address.

Andrei had hooked up the system, but it was Wen who had falsified the records and given them temporary peace of mind.

"Bathroom break," declared Wen, walking past Andrei and mirroring Taz's high- five. He headed to the second floor and hid his secret treasure in a metal work desk covered in dust. Once done, he went to the toilet and flushed, returning to the ground floor where the others were opening their bags and emptying everything onto a sol- id wooden table near the station Andrei had been using. Sayeed hosed down the suits and protective gear hanging in the corner, the nauseating smell catching in their throats and noses.

Dragon and candelabra, trinkets and antiques lay in a jumble on the table. Oscar separated the loot in piles, according to which street dealer or front would give him the best prices for the various items. The man's saving grace was his knowledge and working of the Tokyo criminal underworld. It kept them in the clear with the local mafia, a small tax notwithstanding, and gave them a wide variety of contacts to deal with. Bargaining was a cinch when the crook you dealt with knew you could bring your spoils to the competitor's place.

Large blue plastic boxes marked "organs" were loaded up according to Oscar's di- rections, each cushioned with packing pellets. The boxes were brought to the garage, where they loaded them onto a tiny delivery truck. Oscar and Andrei would take their haul to the dealer in the morning, but for now, they promised booze, and lots of it. Wen made sure to sneak back upstairs and grab the book before they left.

The gang headed back to Shinjuku1. Genbe's, a tiny, back-alley Izakaya greeted them with diminutive open arms and big glass mugs of flowing beer. It was the kind of place where half the bottles of whisky behind the bar had their owner's names labeled on them, cozy and personal. There was only one private booth, but at this hour the place was mostly deserted. They sat on the floor with their feet under the table, a black curtain muffling outside noises. Food covered the tan wooden table under the single lamp that hovered above it. Steaming skewers of fried chicken, chicken skins and pork, bowls of vinegar-dipped cucumbers, tuna salad, mayo shrimp, and a host of other succulent finger-foods accompanied the highballs of Yebisu beer they toasted with. It was a hair past two in the morning, and Wen was starting to feel it. Oscar was louder than he had ever heard him before. He tried to force joviality but was too weary and ended up simply satisfied that the day was over. Andrei kept lifting his glass and yelling "Za vashe zdorovie!" a Russian toast, which everyone else echoed with a Japanese "Kampai!" and the glass bottoms would surge to the ceiling and another beer was ordered.

Taz told of how he was shot down by his latest attempt at a conquest who had heard of his reputation as a player. Despite its size, the factory was still an incestuous place to attempt relationships, no one being an unknown entity. Wen told himself that this was the reason why he never did. They all laughed as Taz exhorted in exaggerated gestures about it. Wen smiled without saying a word, his eyes closing on their own.

Taz raised his glass to Shawna, the only woman in the group, now incarcerated at Administration Central. Shawna: five foot nothing, long auburn hair, and a carnivorous smile. Idiots learned not to mess with her, but she was in the slammer for just that kind of payback. *Shame that*, thought Wen. He'd wait for her release. Like all the others. No use visiting and being tacked as a known accomplice, acquaintance, friend, or what-have-you. Short fuse and long memory—that was Shawna. But she was fun to be with and had an eternal question lingering on her lips, ready to replace the last. There was no way of knowing if she was all right, but due to the nature of her crime, the odds were that she was treated well. You don't walk far after crushing a beer mug into a man's face, but they don't hold it personal at the Shinjuku1 PD, either. The douchebag lived, concussion and scratches notwithstanding. Another month and she'd be breathing the stale outside air again.

The food began to dwindle and the beautiful Malaysian server Taz had been shamelessly hitting on came around less and less.

Around this time, Oscar declared, "You're the best crew I've worked with in a long time," which coming from him sounded like an admission of undying love. "I mean it. You boys worked hard. Except you, Sayeed." And they all laughed. "Seriously, we won't be getting together for our night runs for at least a few months. I'll be cashing this shipment in and delivering your pays in the next two days. Tomorrow is Sunday, so take it easy. Might as well take Monday off too, if you can. You might not even need to work for a long time. I know I won't!" he said, lifting his glass. They echoed his sentiment, calling out, "Cheers!"

"Since we're the best crew, why don't you show us how much you appreciate us?" Wen said, arms crossed, slightly tipsy, looking crookedly at Oscar from across the table. A chill ran up and down the entire room, the silence ominous and dry. Oscar stared right back at Wen.

"You know what; you're right," he said, his fangs melting into a vicious smile.

He called for the bill and paid for it, to everyone's shock.

They ended up on the pavement in front of the establishment in the ungodly hours of the morning. Each was heading toward home. Taz promised Wen that they would have their night out the next night, since it was already so late, or early, depending on your point of view. Wen minded not one bit, he being already comatose. The group split up into the very early dawn like atoms in a supercollider, twirling away drunkenly.

Wen barely remembered how he got home, or how he ended up in his boxers on the couch, but that is where he woke up the next day, his brain a mass of jingling broken glass and staunch regret. He found his wet pants in the bathtub, his shirt in the kitchen sink.

The bag. His heart leaped and seized at the same moment, giving him the urge to vomit through his nose. He imagined the acid putridity cascading through his nostrils and ran to the toilet to be sick.

Damn hangover, he thought. In general, this type of awful feeling put a brake on his drinking. He would spend the day hating himself, downing strong coffee and liters of water. First he had to find the bag, and by extension the book. Looking around, he was glad Sammy had kept his word and cleaned the living room. Neatness, a concept peculiar and unsettling in their tiny home, had temporary roost. Because of it, he could plainly see that his bag was nowhere to be found. Neither was his brother.

Sunday cram school, his mind reminded him creakily, vapors drifting through it. His stomach churned as he bent over to peek under the sofa. Cushions went flying in his feverish search, and he found the bag tucked beneath them, under the exact spot where he had slept the night before. Breathing a sigh of relief, he sat on the hard sofa, with the bag in his hands. He grumbled and got up, retrieving one of the cushions from near the front door, placing it once again where it belonged. He then sat and opened the bag. Inside was the small tome. He placed it on his upturned palms and gave it a bit of a heave, testing its weight. It was light. He inspected its cover, spine, and the outside of its pages to define its age. It seemed old. A date of publication below the title told him it was published in 1910. Ancient then. Thin, yellowed cardboard cover holding fragile browned pages. The title began with four Chinese characters, under which was Sun Tzu, and then, one line below, *on The Art of War.*

Curious, he opened to the cover page. Apart from the obvious gags, he couldn't think what such a novel might entail. A strip of *something* made the paper bulge beneath the cover. It went from the outside edge to the inside and seemed to continue to the back cover. He opened the last page, and the bulge made its way to the outside edge as well. It was almost imperceptible. He had noticed it more because he had run his fingers across the page. Returning to the first page, he began to read but felt too sick after a few lines to continue. Certainly, whatever he found inside would be fascinating, but his present condition precluded any heavy mental lifting without a massive dose of ibuprofen. His gun went into its hiding spot, the fake panel fastened in place, a poster of Gozen Samurai, his brother's favorite rock band, rolled back onto it for good measure. The stereograph tilted left and right, giving the impression of a three-dimensional landscape in trompe-l'oeuil. Lifted from their old album *Rock Child Demagogues*, the three band members stood in action poses with their instruments on a stage made of giant vertical razor blades, surrounded by wolves, blood dripping from their lip-curled maws. Wen always felt dizzy after staring at it too long, doubly so after a night of drinking.

After showering and dressing, he went out for a walk in the district. His stomach cried famine, rumbling and complaining. A bit of food would do him some good, he thought. It was 12:30 when he hit the streets of Shinjuku1. Business had picked up, the morning hump overcome. Labyrinthine city of lights, it flashed and flowed. This version was a reproduction of the original, now piled high with *gomi* at the bottom of the towers, like the apartments they had encountered on their previous night's plunder. The confusion of dead-end streets, alleys, and byways forced a filter over the observer's eyes, telling you that this place was much bigger than it seemed. Straight lines were a rarity, therefore getting from point A to point B meant a disconcerting walk out of reality. Wen wondered how much had been planned and how much was simply organic human substructural growth, the superstructures remaining immutable as fossil bone. An entire city grew like coral in and around the chimneys that touched the sky.

The inhabitants were scatterings of dress and origins, reflected by business facades catering to all imaginable tastes. His ran toward the ordinary and breakfast-like at the moment, and he walked up the main thoroughfare, keeping his eye open for a restaurant window with the plastic food item that would attract him to the real thing. Japanese methods of customer enticement had spread to the other cultures that shared the need to do business. Panoply of food simulacrum adorned every serious restaurant window, true to the point of mouth-watering realism. Wen searched with eager anticipation for one that might have mountains of pancakes or stacks of waffles covered in whipped cream, syrup, and strawberry coulee. He remembered one, not too far away, that had been recommended to him by Taz. A ridiculous name attached to the recollection of a delicious description. *Something about books and birds*, he thought.

Turning the corner at a used electronics shop spilling old motherboards out of milk crates, he walked down the covered arcade, one of the only areas of Shinjuku1 with a straight line of sight. Sunday was almost a festival, judging by the crush of people attempting to make their way one way or the other. Sharp-dressed, thin men with broken teeth stood in packs, eyeing the potentialities through slitted eyes with affected *désinvolture*: seeming too cool to care until you noticed the snake's tongues. Vicious and lithe, their markings were the scarification where their ID tags used to be; tribal tattoos of those who had rebelled against tech. Wen knew how to fly under the vulture's radars and had taught Sammy the same early on.

He turned again a few blocks further, a quiet side street with wrought-iron street lamps, matte-black and faded to match the bumped cobblestones underfoot. Five businesses sprouted from the walls in cream pastel colors. Beside the mint-liqueur green flower shop on his left was the oddly named Turn the Pages of Your Life Electronic Book Café and Breakfast Nook. He swore he remembered something about birds. The storefront was a pale blue with hand-painted, slim green trees surrounding its name on a wood-simulacrum plaque. The street was reminiscent of old Parisian alleys, perhaps, having undergone disneyfication to augment the nostalgia quotient. A few metal tables with broken-pottery mosaic as their eating surfaces, complemented by wrought-iron chairs adorned each side of the front door. Already, three customers lined up in front of the CLOSED sign dangling in the front window, awaiting its revolution. He stepped into the waiting line and looked around for the remaining few minutes.

The roofs of the stores looked like overlapping flat wooden shingles, stained to a gleaming coat but otherwise left unaltered. Artificial chimneys let out volutes of white smoke for effect. A man wearing a vertical-striped apron arranged flowers, plopping handfuls into green buckets on the floor inside a shop. Each building stood three stories tall, with dormers on the last floor. The windows harbored elaborate reconstruction of handmade glass, some thicker in the middle, like bulging bull's eyes that distorted the view inside. He spied three women dressed in traditional-garb replicas cleaning the interior of his intended destination with unrestrained zeal, their forms warping behind the deforming windows.

An enormous display recessed within the wall, showing all manner of crepes, waffles, ice cream desserts, and a plethora of amazing sugar-filled foodstuffs that made his already aching belly cry. He removed his Netware from his backpack and slipped on his glasses. He searched for the store's Wi-Fi signature, and tabbed it for when he would have paid for his breakfast, the access becoming free for him to use. He checked his account to see if he would be able to pay for this extravagance and decided that it was within the realm of affordability, if barely. Besides, he would be swimming in it in two days, so why worry about the now? His brother had left him a message.

"Going to spend the day with Mustapha from class. Enjoy your day off. See you tonight? Be home around 7:30 at most." Maybe not. He texted him back, telling him he would try to be back around then. The reply came a few minutes later. "Roger."

It seemed a bit dry, but Wen needed his day. He would spend the next with him, perhaps tell him to take the day off as he intended to do.

I'm forgetting something, he thought. The rotting corpses in his mind were lazy in their departure. Illness tap-danced on his body still, the wrong effluviums reigniting his earlier nausea.

The wooden front door opened with a tinkling of bells, and Wen realized that the line had grown exponentially behind him. He stepped up the concrete steps and onto the long wooden floorboards inside. A carved pine-imitation table stood in the middle of the space, offering such goods as sourdough bagels, croissants, apple strudels, and other light pastries. He sidestepped the crudities and went straight to the counter for the main course. He stared up at the chalk-written menu behind it and realized why he had been confused. The walls were covered in tear-drop shaped cartoon birds, circa mid-twentieth-century American animation studios. That must have been what Taz had spoken about.

He ordered a mountain of waffles with a spire of whipped cream, drenched in blueberries, strawberries, and raspberries, and then went upstairs to grab a window seat. He observed the more interesting denizens with intensity. He never lost his enthusiasm in watching the machinations and purposes of people doing what they did, not since he was a child. He recalled quite clearly when he did the same with his mother at the big department stores.

He sipped from a steaming mug of coffee and observed the line downstairs, as well as the passersby entering and leaving the street. He invented stories for them and futures such as they could never have believed, while peering over the top of his coffee cup, poised on his lower lip. Whenever he looked up too high, he averted his gaze and came back to Shinjuku1. No use inventing stories about the Heights, ever. No one tried to go back to live in Atlantis, so why should he? The end of the street was a wide downward staircase, flanked by concrete lions or some other dull material, facing away from him and toward those brave enough to scale its steps. Meanders began once again beyond it, the eye getting lost as soon as it wandered.

The mountainous breakfast arrived, a new coffee ordered along with orange juice. *Might as well go balls out.* He smiled. He drenched the tower of whipped hydrogenated oil with a river of high-fructose corn syrup and then took a mouthful of that sweet, sweet mound. Heaven: no other way to describe it. The last time he had tasted something even remotely similar was years ago at one the swankier bakery/cafés of Roppongi Hills. The crimson of the strawberries had stood out like a crime scene over the virginal white of the walls and ceiling. He closed his eyes and he was there, with his mother and brother. He felt a surge of guilt at not having taken his brother with him but pushed it away knowing that they would be back; no use ruining his recovery.

His feast devoured, he slipped on his glasses and pressed his Zipper's on button. The heads-up display told him the day and time, as well as the weather; nothing to type home about. He pulled down the app he had hidden in the corner of the screen, a black market Shadow Net ware that connected him to the Outer Net. A host of the nation's hackers had pulled old servers out of the trash and jerry-rigged a World Wide Web of sorts. Nothing fancy, just a skeleton that connected the knowing user to anonymizer proxies and black market cracking tools constantly under development. Wen didn't often go trolling down the avenues of the backend Web, especially not near home. Curiosity kept calling him back when he had a spare moment though, and he felt like he relived the good old bad days of playing cat and mouse with the Administrative Watchers, server-hopping and giving them a disconnect signal at the last millisecond. The only person he knew that could best him at the game was Taz, and they hadn't played in a long time. Not since they'd been caught. He flowed through the distant and archaic computing machines, flicker of lists appearing in the air in the middle distance. His hand poised on the Zipper, manipulating the cursor with deft fingers on the surface of the console. A consortium in Nairobi offered discounted malware and Trojan horses; not really his stuff. Server jump to Albania where an enclave of gray-hat hackers operated east of Tirana in a smaller sector of the capital named Kombinat, same as the hacker's group. Backdoor specialists and ghostless entry made their wares especially alluring. He would have to come back with currency.

If the Net was like an egg, seamless and encompassing Tokyo, the Outer Net was the spider's web that it rested upon, invisible unless one knew where to look. It was possible to exit using stealth-dodging defenses but very difficult to get in. The players who dealt on the Shadow Net didn't find any allure in the available products of the official Net; people who dealt in the electronic equivalent of atomic bombs found little use in booby-trapped, rubber-bladed knives. He wished he could access the second tier of the Net, where even better apps hid, but getting through the barrier of the upper levels was like a salmon trying to swim up the current of a fighter jet's afterburners; it couldn't be done.

Wen felt a pressure behind his right eye and knew it was time to backtrack, flaming his steps as he did. Whoever was lurking came nowhere near his address, didn't even know he was located in the Metropolis. "The Waver" is what he called it, that feeling he got when he knew he was being watched, and his inner radar pinged before he even knew it was there. It was, to him, like standing on a high-wire in the dark, and feeling the oscillation of an interloper falling upon it. It served him well, most of the time. He felt it coming on strong this time. Taz, despite his expertise and technical proficiencies, admired Wen for that innate sense that he himself wished he could cultivate. Wen had logged in longer hours than he had, having helped his father in his crusade.

He disconnected and put away his gear, satisfied at having indulged his guilty pleasures. He looked out the window at the deformed street and the fun-house mirror people strolling down it, ready to become one of them once again.

I'm free, he thought, a lightening of his heart creeping in against his will. He strolled down the street, aware that he could go almost anywhere he wanted. He looked into a shop chock-full of brick-a-brack—antique chairs and sofas, mirrors and mannequins, racks and lamps, as well as an unending assortment of baubles and doo-dads—and they fascinated him. They were the treasures that hunters like him subtracted from the refuse, infusing them with new value. The apartment full of exoticism came back to him, museum-perfect. *That* is how he would like to have lived: traveling the world in previous centuries, back when it was still in one piece, bringing back the proof of his adventures and impressing those around him with them. He wanted to be distinguished and admired, not to mention rich. A few more hours and he would be. Not beyond his wildest dreams, of course, but perhaps within his more modest ones.

A music demo shop attracted him into its colorful interior. Various stands with earphones allowed customers to try a vast selection of new and old music, available for purchase and download on the spot. Posters and video-clips played in silence on the walls, announcing show dates and album releases. Gozen Samurai had released a compendium of their greatest hits, which were many, considering the group was no more than ten years old. Wen double-checked his account, weighed the pluses and minuses, and bought it for Sammy without thinking any longer on it. He would it give to him when he got home instead of uploading it straightaway to his brother's Netware. The row of shops and restaurants were on one side of a drop. He walked along the guardrail, cars speeding by several meters below. With his hands in his pockets, he followed the curve of the street, turning without thinking about his next direction, either trying to get lost or trying to find himself. For a few hours, he emptied his mind, living in the now. He saw neither people nor places for what they meant, only as tactile surfaces, disconnected from meaning. Skin-deep reality devoid of purpose, he engrossed himself in the rebellious act of existing without other purpose than to be. Was that the truth as well, if he could imagine it? Did he always have to pose gestures to justify his continued existence?

The pressure in his head made him snap to attention. The alley he had stumbled into was devoid of people. But no, there was a gray-suited razor youth leaning against a wall, fondling his pocket-blade and smirking at his newfound prey. He didn't need to turn his head to feel the others closing in on him from behind.

So stupid, he thought. He bolted toward the lone boy, a rictus of pure hatred distorting his face. The nuisance's smirk melted into concern and then fear, as Wen ran at full bore, jumping as the other lifted his arms to stop the train bearing down on him. The click of hard, flat shoes behind him rang down the wet concrete as his own foot slammed into the slight chest obstructing his escape. He saw the look of surprise beneath him the instant before the boy's head cracked open on the hard wet ground, and he kept on running. Pain shot through his left leg as he landed.

"Stop, motherfucker!" he heard yelled from behind him.

Not bloody likely, he thought, grabbing a street lamp in passing, changing direction like a boomerang, avoiding surprised bowling-pin passersby. Three lupine bodies reflected on dirty store windows he spied at crazy speeds, arms-lengths away. Three red-faced, greyhound-lithe youths, huffing after what they had mistaken for a dazed rabbit, revealed racing hare. Now on a main avenue, the crowds slowing him down, he aimed at two burly navy-blue army suits, backs turned to him. Centering between them, he lightly tapped their spines, ducking the gap as he did. Both bodies turned, batons drawn, angered and startled, flung back a short distance like tackling dummies by his pursuers. The beating that ensued left more than a few gawkers gasping in shock. Three wannabe gangsters, bloodied to a pulp by real men, limped away as Wen watched from around a corner, breath rasping hot and metallic in his throat. The crowd dispersed in amusement as the beef returned to their perambulations, wiping crimson off their nightsticks.

He leaned against a garbage can, energy burned out of his system, his hands trembling. His jeans stuck to one of his legs, and he noticed the blood seeping through it for the first time. He swore when he lifted his pant-leg and saw the smooth gash left by the idiot's blade as he had leapt on him. It wasn't deep, but it still needed attention. He hobbled to a nearby pharmacy, getting some gauze and disinfectant. He bandaged himself as best he could after pouring the burning liquid over his calf, cringing as it bubbled and solidified. In a few days, the only proof of his encounter would be a smooth patch of skin devoid of hair. He couldn't believe how dumb he had been, or how lucky. If those men hadn't been patrolling...they weren't cops. They wore no insignias, come to think about it. Had he seen them before?

His Netware rang, and he realized it was past five.

"Where do you want to meet?" Taz asked.

"Old hangout, Bingo's Arcade," he said.

"Alright, six o'clock; I'll be there," Taz said. Click.

He had spoken without thinking, but nostalgia ran deep today. He limped all the way to the arcade, his leg under anesthetic. He wouldn't run for a few days, but otherwise he was fine. He got there at a quarter past the prescribed time. Taz sat on one of the dilapidated couches at the rear, sipping a peach juice from the can. The din from the front was muffled by two graffiti-scrawled walls, some of them belonging to a younger version of himself. He walked by rows of tall boxes, high as people, with screens covered in ancient moving pixels on flat screens that could be manipulated with bright plastic buttons and joysticks like oversized lollipops. Kanji fighting games and Cyrillic tank games, American shooting games, as well as some of the earliest Net simulation games like Neurotrancer. The place was awash in tweets, bleeps, and boops that brought fond memories back to Wen every time he set foot on the gum-encrusted carpet. A balding man of indeterminate age stood behind the black Formica counter at the far end, a worn token dispenser clipped around his bulging midriff. He bowed slightly as Wen entered, and Wen returned the bow.

Taz shook his hand and extended his arm, inviting him to take the couch opposite his. Taz's flat deck-card lay on his right leg. Wen thought he saw a dot like a radar in the center of the screen. Taz glanced at it one last time and then flipped it to sleep mode.

"What the hell happened to you?" he said, noticing the blood-encrusted pants.

"Lo-Fis tried to jack me down in Old Town," he said, running a finger down the vertical slash in his jeans bordered with what now looked like brown rustproofer.

"One guess as to who won," Taz said, grinning.

"Only just. Have you noticed some new patrols around town? Guys in blue, no markings? For sure not cops," Wen said, leaning forward.

"I have, actually. Nobody knows. They swagger like ex-military; foreign, a lot of them, I think," Taz said, palms up.

"I owe them a beer then." Wen relaxed back into the deflated couch.

"How's the hangover?" Taz grinned.

"Better. How's yours?" he said, looking into his friend's bloodshot eyes.

"Dying down. I can't do it like I used to. Whatever happened to waking up in the morning and feeling fine, and then doing it all over again the next day?" he asked, serious.

"I don't drink anymore, that's all. Apart from the odd time with you guys, of course. I haven't invited that much pain into my body in a long time," Wen admitted, staring at the dingy carpet.

"We're old, man," Taz said, laughing.

"We're twenty-six; how did we turn into fossils so quick?" Wen smirked, looking up.

"I don't know, but I don't think it'll get any better anytime soon. Better start investing in adult diapers. You were going to tell me about Sammy the other night." He touched his temple with a finger.

"He's gotten weird," Wen said, matter-of-factly.

"You mean *weirder*. He dressed up in your grandma's underwear, did he?" Taz said, leaning forward.

"No, dumbass. He...he just...he cleaned the entire apartment yesterday," Wen said, staring at the table, knowing how foolish that sounded.

"Oh fuckenell, call the cops! Your baby brother's a psycho on the loose, mate!" Taz laughed.

"Shut up; I'm serious. It's not that, really. He went from being a messed up kid to... not. You get what I'm saying?" Wen said, looking him straight in the eye.

"Bah, he's growing up, is all. You worry too much." Taz took a slow sip of his drink.

"He's only thirteen, man. He's not us and doesn't need to be," Wen said, gimping over to the vending machine and plunking in coins.

"How old do you figure he'll have to be before you come to your senses and see he's his own person?" Taz said, head lolling to the side.

"You think I don't know that? What, am I supposed to push him out the door? Is that what you mean? He's a flake sometimes, but he's blood." Wen took his cola from the out tray and popped the top.

"No, of course not! You're twisting my words. What that boy needs—"

"What, a mother? A father? You're damn right he does, but he doesn't have that. All he has is *me*. That's his family; I'm all he has." Wen's voice went up an octave.

"Relax, mate. All I'm saying is, he's not doing *so* bad under the circumstances. Yeah, he did need a mother and father, but that's not what I was going to say. He needs better opportunities than the ones he was handed, but so did you. He might still get 'em if you could straighten him out somehow," he said, tossing the empty can into the bin a few meters away. "As it were, we're both going to profit from our last little endeavor, so maybe you'll get to spend the time with him that he so desperately needs. Steer him in a proper direction. Talk to him; find out what he wants. It's no wonder he gets into so much trouble. Idle hands live in glass houses, or some shite."

"You have a way of shooting metaphors in the gut, you know that?" Wen said with a smile. The tension he had felt the moment before was leaving him in spasms. Taz was right, he knew. Sammy was his own person, as much as he was loath to admit it. What did he want his brother to have, as a life? Not what he did, that was certain. Where did that leave *him*, though? He wasn't ready to face the eventualities of a life on his own.

"What are your ambitions that you have something to look forward to?" Taz asked, lying down on the couch.

"I just take it day by day. That's all the ambition I need," Wen said, taking a sip of his drink.

"That's not enough to live! Don't you ever wish you could go back up there?" Taz exclaimed, pointing at the ceiling and glaring at his friend.

"It's not a place for me. It's complicated, Taz," Wen said, mentally kicking himself for having told Taz so much about the Heights.

"I'm going. Maybe I'll buy my way in. Maybe I found a way to get up there. You want, I can get that door cracked open for all three of us. Are you with me?" Taz said, his eyes gleaming.

"I won't go back, Taz. Even if I could, I wouldn't," he said, frowning and shaking his head.

"I'm really sad to hear you say that. I thought we were friends." Taz looked hurt as he sat up.

"Are you planning on leaving me behind, Taz?" Wen said, half-joking. A long pause like a shroud dropped on the conversation.

"I'm going no matter what, mate," Taz said, stern determination clenching his face. "I'm going, and if you knew what was good for you and your brother, you'd at least try to go back too. With me."

"Good luck then," Wen said, his voice dry ice, feeling as if something had broken, just a little, and he didn't think it would ever mend back to new. The conversation turned to trivialities, and they avoided more meaningful dialogue from then on.

Wen left the arcade around eight and got home half an hour later.

"Hey, Sammy, I got you something!" he called out into the silent apartment. He flicked the light switch and went to knock on the bedroom door. No answer. He was out then. He went to the couch and moved the poster out of the way to retrieve the book. He had been curious about this *Art of War*, and now that his body was back in working order, he felt like perusing its brittle pages. It wasn't there. He hadn't put it in the hiding place, he realized. He displaced the couch cushions. It wasn't there either. The morning was a blur he couldn't quite put into focus. He had left the book on the floor, he seemed to recall. Sammy said he'd be here.

The book was gone.

Sammy was gone.

Panic jumped at his throat in a rising tide as he fell down the dark stairs he had so painfully climbed for so many years.

CHAPTER 3

Fear is the pin; anger the bomb.
—Yusuke Daiko

SAMMY'S NETWARE RANG and rang, but he didn't pick up. Wen left a message in case he couldn't hear it. His hands shook when he called Taz.

"I have a problem," he said, hoping the trembling in his voice was under control.

"What's the matter?" Taz asked.

"I did something I'm regretting right now. I took one of the books from the site the other night." Wen closed his eyes, his lips taut. There was a pause on the line.

"And?" Taz replied flatly.

"It's gone. So is Sammy. I have to find him. Right the fuck now!" Anxiety rose in his voice.

"Should I just tell you good luck with that?" Taz said, acid bitterness seething through the handset.

"Come on, Taz! If he gets caught, we all go down," he said. *And you can forget the Heights*, he thought.

"That's a solid bar of shit you are dropping on me, Wen, especially now. Hold on."

Hold on to what? he thought. *What could possibly be more important than this?* Wen fidgeted, waiting for Taz to come back on the line. The doorbell rang, and he dropped his Netware, running to the side of the door.

"Who is it?" he asked, his pulse racing.

"Oscar; open up."

Right, payday. Wen took a deep breath and shook his arms out.

"Just a sec," he said, and opened the door, smiling as broadly as he could. His face met the soft cover of a book with a hard, stinging slap, followed by a kick in the gut, and he flew to the ground, the breath knocked clean out of him. He sat a moment wheezing and clutching his midsection, and points of white light danced before his eyes before he recognized the missing book in Oscar's hands. How had he gotten ahold of it?

"Did I tell you you could take this?" Oscar bellowed at him, kicking the door closed behind him with one deft move as he stomped in. He waved the tome about like a street preacher clutching his bible, invoking damnation as he yelled.

"I thought it would be all right, just the one..." Wen cowered on the floor, trying to get up using the couch's armrest. His nose felt smashed and his fingers came back bloody when he touched it.

"No, I did not tell you you could take this. I told you *not* to touch it. Now you almost went and fucked everything up. Too bad you don't listen too well. Do I need to tell you that you no longer work for me? How's this? Keep a low profile, your name is poison from now on," he said. He looked as if he was done berating him, and he turned around, but then he came back and backhanded Wen in the face. "That's what bitches get. You don't even deserve a punch," he said, standing over Wen, wagging his finger in his face. Wen's throat constricted, and he spat blood into the other man's face. Fear forgotten, slow, simmering anger was taking its place.

"Where's my brother?" he said, bracing for impact. Oscar looked at him with surprise.

"You do have a pair, don't you? I wouldn't know, shitbird."

"Where did you get the book from, in that case?" Wen said, his right eye beginning to swell shut.

"A concerned citizen had a punk kid show up earlier, trying to sell him some truly jail-worthy material," he said, smiling broadly. *Arnquist's Used Books*, thought Wen. *That twitchy, fat bastard Remi must have called Oscar. That's the only place Sammy would have known about.*

"Good-bye, Wen. Let's see how long you survive out there." He patted the battered man on the head. Wen tried to lift his leg to hit the big man in the groin, but he moved aside without effort and then cracked Wen in the jaw with a right hook.

"Wen? Wen? Man, are you still there?" he heard Taz shouting from the Netware's speakerphone. He groaned and tried to hold himself up on his elbows. His head weighed three tons and felt like a piano had fallen on it.

"Urrrgh," he said, and then threw up what felt like a bucket of blood on the carpet. *So much for the damage deposit*, he thought. "I'm here. How long was I out for?" He touched his swollen eye and winced.

"I've been yelling at you for five minutes now. What happened?" Taz said.

"Oscar. He found the book. I don't know where my brother is. He says he doesn't either, but I know that's bull. I'm certain my brother went to Arnquist's to pawn the book, but I have no proof. I feel like curb-stomped shit right now." Wen got up in unsteady increments, holding on to the wall until he reached the bathroom. He turned on the light and flinched at the sight of his face in the mirror. His right eye was purple, turning black, and the right side of his face was swollen and red. His lower lip was split, which explained the copper taste in his mouth. His nose wiggled as if the cartilage had fallen out, dripping hemoglobin like a leaky faucet.

"We have to follow him, find out where he's going. Your brother might be there," Taz said from the living room. Wen poured cold water over his face and then went into the freezer to retrieve ice to put on his eye and face. He held a moist towel over his nose and the ice on the side of his head.

"I look like a Picasso," he said, returning to the living room.

"Must have been quite a beating. I always said you were a piece of work."

"Yeah, his hand is probably aching as we speak, poor guy." Wen sat down on the couch for a moment. He tapped his pocket for his cigarette case, without luck.

"Listen, I'll try to catch up with Oscar. I'm on my way to your place. You go check out Arnquist's and maybe, you know, beat the crap out of Remi. If he did sell out your brother, you should at least make sure he regrets it. Actually, beat the shit out of that wanker anyhow; he's got it coming to him," Taz said, hanging up.

Yeah, just let me stop bleeding all over the place, and I'll get right on it, thought Wen. His head felt as if it had been replaced with a cement balloon animal; comical, if it hadn't hurt so much. He pushed himself off the couch and grabbed his backpack, throwing his Netware in it.

What a bloody mess, he thought. *So much for Sammy's cleanup*. He grabbed his aluminum baseball bat and stuck it in the bag and then headed back to Shinjuku1. The evening crowd was making its appearance and the going was slow. They avoided the man with the mashed up face like they would a virulent contagion. Wen averted his gaze from reflective surfaces, striding toward Remi's store. His head throbbed, but he felt electric. Somewhere, Sammy was in trouble.

The electronic door chime sounded once, and the fat man behind the counter had time to say "How can I help—" before turning around and bumping the side of his head against cold metal.

"Maybe you *could* help me, Remi. I'm looking for my brother. You remember him, right? One head shorter than me, thirteen, face *not* mashed to burger because some rat turned him in?" Wen said, holding the bat level to the large man's face. His eyes kept darting from the tip of the bat to Wen's face. He licked his lips and said:

"Hey, Wen, is that you? You look like shit, man! I don't know your brother! Never seen him in my life!" Remi blubbered, trembling on his seat. A bead of sweat was forming on his lined brow.

"I think you're lying Remi. Scratch that: you lie like you breathe." Wen raised his bat and smashed it into the glass case in front of him. Shards sprayed everywhere as Remi's hands flew up to protect his face.

"I swear I don't know, man!" Remi said, shaking from behind his upheld arms. Wen dragged the bat down the length of the shattered case's metal frame, making an awful squeal. He slipped the tip of the bat against Remi's protruding gut through the broken glass case.

"Where is he, Remi?" Wen said, slitting his one good eye. Remi grabbed for the bat and held it.

"Go fuck yourself, asshole. I wouldn't tell you, even if I knew," he said, from behind porcine eyes. Wen yanked the bat away from him, the large man still grasping onto it, and he jabbed it into his flab. The fat man doubled over in pain, his head bashing into the cases' rim, forehead cut on pieces of glass.

"One last chance, Remi, or it's your watermelon *head,*" Wen said, raising the bat and rounding the corner of the case. Remi groaned, clutching his belly, his face green.

"Oscar. Oscar took him. I delayed your brother, and he came for him. I'm not going to prison for some stupid asshole's pleasure. You have no idea who you're messing with," he said, drool dripping down from the corner of his lower lip.

"You're a turd, Remi. I should kill you," Wen said, walking out of the store, whacking a stack of ancient newspapers by the window to vent his frustration. He called Taz.

"Remi says Oscar has him. He must have stashed him somewhere," he announced, walking down the main strip.

"Impossible. I've got baldy in my sights and he's alone. He's headed to the elevators. I think I know where he's going," Taz said.

"Don't lose him," Wen said, walking faster.

"Have no fear."

Wen walked past the ramen cart and saw Joe looking around. Joe spotted him in the crowd and called him over. Wen gritted his teeth and went over to him.

"Listen, I don't have time right now..." he started.

"Oh, I know. Your brother is in trouble!" he declared, wide-eyed and frantic.

"How do you know that?" Wen asked, grabbing him by the front of his jacket.

"What happened to your face?" the old man said, as if he saw him for the first time.

"What do you know about my brother?" Wen yelled, clutching Joe's clothes even tighter. His eyes seemed to fade into the distance and snap back to reality, like an appliance that was turned on.

"Big guys, they were taking him somewhere. I followed, but I didn't see where they went. I'm tracking them, but they're erasing their tracks," he said in a conspiratorial voice.

Poor guy is crazy, Wen thought.

"Can you let go, please? I think you're ripping my jacket. That's my only jacket," Joe said, looking down where Wen was gripping him. Wen released him, the homeless man getting off the tips of his toes.

"What did the guys look like, Joe?" Wen asked, looking him straight in the eyes.

"Dark blue uniforms, army, looked like, but they didn't have any markings," Joe said, tapping his shoulder.

Those guys again? thought Wen.

"Do you want me to find out who they are?" asked Joe, his gaze once again floating away.

"Sure, Joe, you do that," Wen said, walking away and dialing up Taz as he did. "I just talked to somebody who says those weird military guys are involved somehow. Where are you?"

"I'm going toward the bay. You better get your suit and meet me at the site. If we get the jump on him, maybe he'll tell us what the hell is going on. Hurry it up," Taz said, and hung up.

His heart racing, Wen hurried back to the apartment, getting his hazmat suit and gun and then getting on the fastest Metro to the bay area. He hacked a maintenance elevator and dressed inside it as it descended to the nether regions. Once back in the smog of the 50th, he called Taz again. "I'm on the maintenance levels, where are you?" he asked, walking along the girders.

"I'm in the Heap already. I'm close behind him. Do you think you can find your way to that old apartment?" he said. Wen felt a sinking feeling at the thought of getting lost alone in the swirling mists of the trash pile. He walked at a brisk pace, avoiding the crumbling outer walkways as much as he could.

"Yeah, I think so. Give me...ten minutes." He hung up and found the metal cage that led to the ground floor. Once there, he sloshed his way to the crater, sweat dripping from every pore in his body, his injured leg screaming. His face still pounded, more so under physical activity. He felt like lying down right then and there and giving up but kept lifting his leg, moving it forward, lifting the other, and repeating the laborious exercise with his brother's face well in mind. He climbed down the rope and almost ran to the apartment complex. He stopped at the door to regain his breath for a moment, rivulets of sweat drenching his forehead, and swore off smoking for the rest of his life. Gun drawn, he climbed to the thirteenth floor. He threw a glance around the corner and saw Taz standing over some inert form on the ground.

"I'm coming in!" he yelled to the side of the doorframe.

"You got nothing to fear; get in here," Taz said from inside. Wen looked in, and Taz looked back at him.

"He's dead," Taz said. "Damn, you look like crap, man!" he added after seeing his friend's face for the first time. "I barely recognized you!"

Wen walked in and saw that the shape that his friend had been standing over was Oscar. A pool of blood framed his head, and he was lying face down near the libraries in the living room. The bullet hole was a bit off to the right of his head, straight through his unprotected headgear. It was presently rolled down, the bald head with a single shot through it exposed.

"Why did you kill him? Now we might never find out where my brother is!" Wen said, looking over the big man's corpse.

"I didn't. I got here and found him this way. Check this out," Taz said, rolling down the dead man's sweater. Underneath it, in the middle of his neck were two small, off-white, circular patches. "Next-generation Wi-Fi 'trodes. No protrusion, nothing."

"What? Oscar was Netted? That's impossible! This dirtbag was always railing about how he hated the scum of the Heights!" Wen exclaimed. Confusion swirled inside him. Who was Oscar, in that case, and who were those men who had taken his brother? He got up and looked around him, trying to find an anchor of some sort to tie him back to the real world. Things might be crap there, but at least they were understandable. He noticed a book sticking out from the library. It was only pushed in halfway. The spine read: *The Art of War.* And his nose began to throb again. He slammed it all the way in and a short tone sounded. Taz yelped, and Wen turned around to see Oscar's body thumping up and down by the chest. It was a sickly pantomime that he stopped by pushing the corpse over sideways with his foot. Wen avoided looking into the hole of the dead man's face, concentrating instead on the rod that was rising from the floor where he had lain the moment before. It came up to his chest and stopped. It was metallic and square, the tip cut at a forty-five degree angle. The top recessed and a whirring sound was heard, a smaller platform rising within. A set of pincers came up holding a tiny diamond, clear as glass. Taz and Wen just stared at it and then looked at each other.

"You take it," Taz said, getting on his hands and knees to inspect the lump of dead flesh on the ground. He found Oscar's wallet in an inside pocket and stuck it in his own.

Wen stared at the jewel with intensity. He plucked it from the pincers with his thumb and index, holding it in front of his eyes and shining his headlamp on it. He slipped it into one of his breast pockets and resealed it, patting it to make sure it was safe.

Their heads swung up at a sound. Steps were creaking outside, faint but audible. They turned off their headlamps and stepped as lightly as they could out the door, walking up the stairs by hugging the wall. They climbed two floors, and Taz laid down his Netware near the banister, turning on the infrared camera. They hid inside one of the abandoned apartments, looking at their heads-up displays inside the facemasks of their suits. A few moments later, they spied the outlines of ten human figures, faint and irregular.

"Optical camouflage," whispered Taz. Two of the figures stayed on either side of the doorframe at the apartment they had just left, the other eight rushing in. They came back out a few seconds later carrying the cooling outline of Oscar's body down the stairs. One of the figures by the door bowed slightly and then took a small oval shape from his hip, tossing it into the apartment. Wen and Taz turned off their visors as the incendiary grenade flared up, blinding them for a second. The fire spread in waves, catching on everything, licking its way out the door, and devouring the rotted carpeting on the landing. It snapped up the dry particles in the air and set them ablaze. Taz grabbed his Netware and they bolted for the nearest emergency exit. The door resisted any attempts at being opened. They pushed and jumped at it without success.

The wooden staircase began to catch. Their escape was almost blocked. They had no choice but to climb to the roof. They ran up the stairs as the air was being heated by the blaze. Wen felt his arms getting toasty and his rebreather was having trouble with his hyperventilation. At the escape hatch on the last floor, Wen climbed the ladder first, but it was locked solid. There was a code box by the ladder, and Taz jumped on it, hooking it up to an emergency battery he had brought. The fire was catching up to them and the smoke was making it difficult to see. Taz had his face pressed against the code box, his cracking gear inserted between number blocks. The fire darkened the ceiling in the stairwell as it licked it. Finally, the code box went green and they heard the click of release from the trap door above.

Whoever thought of putting a lock on an emergency exit should be shot, Wen thought, as he scrambled up the ladder. He was glad it hadn't been anywhere as hard as the front door, or they'd have fried for sure. He pushed the hatch, and nothing happened. It was stuck. He pressed on it with all his might, and it barely budged. Taz came up beside him, and they pushed, getting in each other's way, pressing and hitting with all the strength they could muster. The fire was climbing up the walls around them when they got the hatch busted open with a clang. The roof was flat with broken antennas, vent shafts, and shattered glass strewn around. They looked around for a way down. Overhead, the bulk of one of the towers loomed in the smog. They found a fire escape ladder on the backside and released it straight down. No matter how loud it would be hitting the ground, the fire was making a bigger racket, bouncing out metal curtains left and right like popcorn kernels.

They scrambled down the ladder to the ground, windows exploding out around them in fiery shards, and stood still against the wall after spying around the corner. Two hovertanks rested in front of the building, their angular shapes absorbing much of the light from the blaze. Oscar floated away, carried by invisible men that shimmered as they walked. The fire glistened through their camouflage as if seen underwater. One of the tanks swallowed the corpse of his ex-boss and nemesis. Wen and Taz had to leave the underside of the crumbling building; bricks and rubble rained down all around them.

"What do we do now?" Wen yelled over the noise. Taz went to grab one of the metal curtains but dropped it immediately, flailing his hand in pain.

"Go straight to the next building. If those guys see us, we're toast," Taz said, pointing to a nearby apartment block with the hand he was not blowing on. The blaze enveloped the whole building now, blinding flames lapping out the windows, and they held their hands over their heads, running behind cover to the other block. A falling brick clipped Taz on the shoulder, and he fell down. Wen helped him up, and they continued running headlong until they reached safety.

"Gah, I think it's broken," Taz said, holding his arm. A small gash was open near his trapezius, but no blood was coming out.

"We have to get back before that gets infected," Wen said, looking around for other sources of trouble. They made their way back to the climbing rope in a round-about way, avoiding open spaces. Taz went up first, Wen pushing him from below. A high-pitched whine came from the pit, and they ran as fast as the muck and their sore legs would allow them to go. They reached one of the pillars as the hovertanks rose into the air, disappearing as they did. They waited for the sound to dissipate until they left their hiding spot and returned to the service elevator.

"Where do we go from here? I don't think returning to the surface is such a hot idea," Taz said, wincing, clutching his shoulder.

"Let's go back to Shinagawa. We can lie low for a while and decide what to do."

Taz seemed to waffle, but agreed. They took one of the rattling carts back to the hideout, Wen driving as fast as he could. They snuck in through the back door, certain they had evaded pursuit. Their headlamps danced around the silent building, the halogens left off for precaution. Wen ran to the bathroom to get the emergency medical kit, spilling the interior of the pharmacy into the sink. Taz stayed downstairs and attempted to remove his suit.

"I can't get it off," he said, sitting in one of the utility chairs as Wen came back down the stairs. Wen put the kit on the table and helped his friend out of the top part of his constraining suit. After taking it off, Wen washed the gouge and then sprayed disinfectant over it, Taz gritting his teeth as he did. He wrapped the wound in a gauze bandage and gave his friend a minor analgesic.

Wen sat down next to his friend and let out a deep sigh.

"What the hell was that all about?" he mused out loud, tilting his sweating forehead back. "Where is Sammy in all this? Can someone explain to me just what the heck is going on?"

Taz just shook his feverish head, at just as much loss as his friend. "I don't have a clue, mate. I'm tired and I need some sleep, that's all I know." Taz rolled his head back over the top of the chair.

"Sh...did you hear that?" Wen said, raising his finger. They both fell silent. There was a ping, like a ball-peen hammer knocking on metal. It came from the barricaded front. Wen helped Taz slip his hazmat suit back on, and they both reached for their guns. They turned off their headlamps and slid behind the worktable, hearts pounding. A bang reverberated at the front, the door slammed back, and shadows slithered through the offices toward them. Kneeling behind the table, it was hard to see who might be coming after them. Taz put down his gun and took out his deck, handing it to Wen. With the infrared turned on, the intruders' hazy outlines could be seen sneaking into the building.

"Out the back, quick!" Wen whispered to Taz, putting the deck into his friend's pocket. They crouched to the back, stopping when they saw the door fly open and more blurred shapes duck in. Wen pointed to the computer terminal, pushing the computer chair slowly and lifting the carpet underneath. They lifted the hidden grate it covered and slipped into the sewer system, closing the grate again as they did.

Wen pointed the way, and Taz followed. As far as he knew, only he and Andrei knew about the hidden passage, having explored the edifice to discover its underground electrical systems. Cables ran the length of the putrid sewers they now plodded through. Blood pounded in Wen's ears, the splashing of the water much too loud with every step they took. Taz looked like he was going to pass out, and Wen half-carried him through the slime. His respiration came in ragged breaths, the tell-tale sign he might have picked up some nasty bug earlier in their escape. Despite fogged masks, trembling hands, and the morbid fear of death, the two ran on.

A gray metal door appeared on their left, and Wen dragged Taz through it. Discarded tools and rusted metal tubes lay in a jumble around a spiral staircase that wound upward. Before making their escape, Wen wedged a few of the rods against the door. Taz held onto the staircase for support, his expression slack.

"More climbing, huh?" Taz said, his voice raspy.

"What do you have against climbing all of a sudden?" Wen replied, smiling tiredly at Taz. He took him by the shoulder and began the ascent, the splashing of water and excited voices coming from the other side of the door. They froze a fraction of an eternity, until they were sure those voices had gone by. They dragged themselves up a whole level before exiting, staying away from the edges of the rotten floor plates. From one of the missing ones, they saw hovertanks lingering in the void, their floodlights sticking to the walls like knives.

"Take out my deck," Taz said, and Wen reached into his pocket to retrieve the Netware. "Click the zoom app in camera mode."

Wen did so and recorded the hovertanks, as well as the men no longer in optical camouflage. They were soldiers, that much was obvious. Dressed in black from helmet to boot, faces protected by reflective visors, they carried some heavy firepower. There were at least six men out front, and who knew how many inside searching for them. It was time to go. Wen clicked off and put the deck back into Taz's pocket. Taz limped back to the pillar they had come out of and slid down to the ground. Wen extended his index and cocked his thumb. He fired off an invisible bullet into the flank of the closest tank, making it rock sideways and discharge a blast of ion pulse canon into the façade of the building, killing all of the intruders instantaneously. So much for fantasy.

"Where to now?" Taz said, feeling déjà-vu.

"The only logical thing to do would be to call Andrei. He's our wildcard. If Oscar didn't know how to find him, maybe his buddies won't either," Wen said, wondering where he could plug in so he could make an anonymous call.

"You mean, our wildcard before we found out about Oscar, don't you?" Taz said, smiling, and then coughed.

"Yeah, something like that. Listen, are you going to be able to walk? We have a ways to go, I think," Wen said, staring into the distance. The level they were on was devoid of buildings; only catwalks and grating as far as the eye could see; deep-sea drilling platform architecture on a monumental scale.

"Are you going to leave me behind, Wen?" Taz said, smiling.

"Tempting, but no. You're coming with me," Wen reassured him. He gave Taz a hand to get back up, and they started the long trudge to Shinjuku1.

Questions, like an avalanche, threatened to submerge Wen, and none with any readily available answers. His head swam as he shouldered the weight of his ailing friend. The faint ping of their boots brought a strange kind of comfort, something concrete to anchor the intangibles, if not enough to make them disperse. He thought of how his idea of going back to base had almost gotten them killed. He had to start thinking more clearly instead of pulling dumbass moves that would endanger them both again, assume that everything equaled danger until he figured things out. An old construction worker test access port allowed him to tap in with his ware. He rarely went wireless, easier to mask his ID at the port than give off a funny wavelength that begged to be triangulated. He thought back to the afternoon at the café and thought: *moment of weakness. Won't happen again. We're hunted now; time to double down on security.* He sent off a quick burst to Andrei on his usual channel and waited for a reply.

Taz sat slumped on the wall, head between his knees and panting.

Wen received an answer back. He checked for authenticity, and it cleared. Andrei would meet them at the base of the Fletcher Consortium Megastructure. He checked his map software, and they took the long way around, doing the length of the 50th. It was maybe five or six clicks away, and Taz was losing energy fast. No available worker carts meant they had no choice but to hoof it. There was nobody around, but rows of construction exoskeletons bolted to the girders for the night in front of a maintenance hangar. No matter how much "smartcrete" they had used to construct the city, living in a place that suffered 1500 earthquakes a year still demanded extensive repair work. He felt small walking under those lifeless giants. Every once in a while, an enormous support pillar would loom in front of them from out of the mist, and they would be under a different structure. The clicking of their boots on the metal crosswalks and platforms barely broke the silence. The girders looked fresher and better maintained as they went along, alleviating Wen's fears that they would fall through to a lower level. The sound of the wind and their breathing were the loudest, apart from Wen's thoughts, which were threatening to blow his mind up.

"You want to play cliché?" he asked Taz.

His friend smiled faintly and said, "No, you should just leave me behind." Taz furrowed his brow, a hint of a smile stretching his lip.

"Point! You know I couldn't do that; you have to carry on!" Wen said with an exaggerated look of determination.

"Point," Taz huffed. "I'll only be a burden to you. You must leave me here!"

"Nice one! Point. There's no way I'd leave my best friend! Besides, what will my sister say when I tell her I abandoned her husband?" Wen said, lifting his fist to the sky.

"Now you're just making shit up. I'll give you half a point for that one," Taz said, limping forward.

"Just play along, dammit," Wen said, as sternly as he could without laughing, his back starting to hurt.

"Man. Um...she'll understand...she's made of sterner stuff?"

"You don't even deserve half a point for that one," Wen said. They had played this game forever, mimicking the horrible dialogue from TV and movies.

"Are we there yet?" Taz said, slumping a bit.

"Almost, not quite. You still want to go to the Heights?" Wen said, lifting his friend upright.

"I'm still going to the Heights," Taz said, steadying himself on his friend. "Damn, that Oscar did a number on your face. I'm almost ashamed to complain."

"You should be. You ain't got nothing on me." They laughed quietly, making their way to the meeting point. *How did we get this far without dying?* thought Wen. *We've been living on a high-wire for so long we forgot it could be cut, no net underneath to catch us.*

They came around the corner of a gantry system used to repair the support structure of a building. In the distance, three enormous construction trucks were parked. They walked toward them in a roundabout way, sticking to the walls. Andrei appeared from behind one of their massive wheels, gun at the ready. He was dressed in dark camo gear from head to toe and was practically invisible.

"Took you guys so long?" he asked, glancing about.

"Sightseeing," Wen said.

"Pfff...let's go," he sighed. He was not pleased to see them, and Wen could understand why. He would have hated to see them too, if he had been in his shoes. More trouble for Andrei, really. They walked over to a panel and Andrei slid a knife into its side. It opened and revealed a tiny metal cabin, barely big enough for the three of them. He flicked the red lever and they shot down fifty levels. Wen felt nauseated the whole way down. They exited, and it began its ascent back to the 50th. The garbage they walked over was comprised of electronics and circuit boards, the mother lode of Tokyo's electronic archeology. Like broken green shale, the strata would reveal the transitions from earlier ages. Andrei was surefooted as he walked, while the other two slid on circuit boards and tangled rainbow-colored cables.

Andrei pulled a small box from his pocket and pushed a button. There was a rumble from below, and a trash-covered door opened before them. The electronics were artfully attached to the portal, no way to tell it was there otherwise. Wen nodded in approval. Andrei pressed the button again when they were halfway in, and the door rumbled close. The overhead halogens flickered a bit before staying on. It looked like a midsized garage but could have been an underground car park. There was a huge vehicle with an oily tarp over it in one corner. Bits of welded metals and gears, wires, and motors were arranged in dusty gray piles of various heights on the floor. Andrei led them into another room, much smaller, but with walls covered in thick army blankets. He took off his mask.

"It's all right. I got an air filter rigged up down here," he said. "Take a seat." It sounded as much as an invitation as an order, but being so beat stopped Wen from caring. He sat on a huge, ugly brown couch, and Taz found a dirty fluorescent orange armchair to pass out in. Andrei had left the room through a wooden-beaded curtain. He returned shortly with a medikit.

"What the hell happened to you?" he said, noticing Wen's face for the first time.

"Oscar happened. Everything happened," Wen said, shaking his head.

"What kind of trouble are you in that you have to bring it over here?" Andrei asked, his mouth a straight horizontal line as he dabbed an alcohol swab on Taz's sweating arm.

"Too much. I don't know where to start."

Andrei jabbed a needle into Taz's arm and then sprayed disinfectant foam over the affected area. "Well, you better start somewhere. Nano-antibodies—they'll do a body good. The injection should start taking effect within an hour," he said to Taz. "Wen, help me drag him into the room."

Wen took one elbow and Andrei the other, and they lifted Taz to his feet. They marshalled him down a hallway to a room with thin, particle board walls covered in more thick blankets. They tucked him into a double mattress covered in olive green covers, and Andrei put a sensor on his forehead. Another mattress lay nearby, arranged in the same manner.

"That'll warn us if there are any complications," Andrei said under his breath. "Come," he said, going back to the kitchen. "I have to admit, I was reticent to let you boys in. When I say I never have any visitors, I mean I *never* have *any* visitors, and it's not because I'm antisocial. Do you understand?"

"I think so," Wen said.

"Good. Since I'm not a complete bastard though, I realize you wouldn't have called me unless the situation was fubar." He reached up into a cupboard and removed a large clear glass bottle, half filled with a translucent liquid.

"Fubar?" Wen said.

"Fucked up beyond all recognition. Fubar."

"It's that all right," Wen said, leaning on the melamine counter.

"That's what I thought. Grab two glasses from that shelf. Are you treating that?" he said, peering at Wen's face.

"Yeah, I put some ice on it earlier," Wen said as Andrei headed through the beaded string room separator that led into the living room. He grabbed the glasses and followed the older man. Andrei was indicating a square piece of plywood that covered an industrial-sized wooden spool used to unwind commercial grade electric cable in its previous life, which now served him as a coffee table. Wen put the glasses down next to the bottle and sat back on the shit-brown sofa, crossing his arms.

"Start from the beginning, or whatever you think might be potentially relevant to the situation," Andrei said, pouring a few drops of the liquid into each glass. He then tossed Wen a tube of antiseptic cream.

"Well, my brother is gone, Oscar is dead, and there is an army after us. The three are related, but I have no idea how," Wen said, palms extended, catching the tube. Andrei handed him a pocket mirror that Wen placed on the wooden board before him.

"I think I might prefer the long version then, if you don't mind," Andrei said.

Wen explained everything that had happened, leaving out no details as he dabbed the cream on the worse-looking areas of his face. Andrei listened intently, never once interrupting. "That is some fairly heavy drama, my friend. I'm glad to hear Oscar is dead."

"You are?" Wen said.

"Of course! I told you, that man is...was...a piece of shit. He'd been blackmailing me for years!" Andrei said, smiling for the first time.

"Over what?" Wen asked.

"What, and give you something on me?" Andrei said, raising his eyebrows. Wen woke up to the fact that he knew little about the people around him. Was it willful stupidity on his part? He liked to believe that it was plain omission, but these lacks were beginning to pile up and made his life difficult, to say the least.

"What am I supposed to do about my brother?" he said, changing the subject.

"We have to find out who Oscar was working with or for. It obviously wasn't a one-man show. You said something about having his wallet?" Oscar said. Wen went to the bedroom and got the wallet out of Taz's pocket. He thought he wouldn't mind if it meant saving their lives. He tossed it at Andrei, who rifled through it and took out all relevant pieces of info. He had a driver's license, three credit cards, a work passcard and Metro card on top of the usual receipts and junk people amass in their effects. They were all small rectangles the exact same size.

"One of these things is not like the other, can you guess which one?" Andrei said in sing-song, a kid's nursery rhyme. Wen perused them close up, trying to see the detail that differentiated one of them.

There it was.

"His Metro card is thicker than it should be," he said.

"Therefore?" Andrei asked.

"It's not just a Metro card." Wen guessed.

"Give the man a prize; we have a winner!" Andrei said, clapping his hands and nodding solemnly.

"One point," Wen said. Andrei looked at him with curiosity. "Sorry, never mind," he added, not feeling the urge to explain the game.

"You also mentioned video footage of these men," Andrei said. Wen went back to the bedroom and returned with Taz's deck. He tried to turn it on, but it was password protected. No use trying to hack his friend's deck when he could turn it on in the morning. "That'll have to wait then," Andrei said, handing a glass to Wen.

"What are we drinking to?" Wen said, eyeing the liquid with distrust.

"To freedom and anarchy. It's not because we're in trouble that we can't enjoy the finer things in life." He lifted his glass and threw the booze down his throat. Wen did the same and immediately regretted it. The firewater burned all the way down to his stomach, sending him into a coughing fit.

"More?" Andrei asked after pouring himself another drop or two.

Wen retched. "I'll pass. What do we do about the fake Metro card?" He sat there red-faced as Andrei dunked the other glass, his features screwing up.

"Damn that's nasty. Now we go to the workshop." He picked up the Metro card and the rest of Oscar's belongings, led Wen into the kitchen, and pressed a hidden button beside the refrigerator. A door slid open where a blank wall had been a moment before. Wen followed him and glanced back as it slid closed. A short concrete hallway led them into a warm room with low ceilings, filled with mountains of electronic equipment in various states of undress. The walls and ceilings were covered in padded reflective foil and an assortment of robots and rocket-riding pin-up girls. Wooden work benches lined the walls, topped with soldering tools, spectroscopes, computers and other gizmos and tools Wen failed to identify. The air hummed with electric current and he could only think of the uncanny resemblance the lair had to a mad scientist's in the serials.

Throw a bucket of water in here and we're both crispy critters, he thought.

Andrei lifted his leg over a chipped-chrome swivel chair and plopped himself into the seat. He noticed Wen's gaze, lost in the overwhelming junk pile of the workshop.

"The place is insulated against pirate signals. Nothing can get out unless we want it too, and nothing can come in without our say-so; perfect protection from a completely 'wired' world," he said with a hint of pride.

"You're pretty paranoid, aren't you?" Wen said without thinking.

Andrei grunted: "Who's running for his life at the moment, hm?" he asked, turning on a flat plastic box the size of a microwave oven with a screen above it. He opened a slot along its bottom and slipped in the Metro card and then tapped a green button along the side. An x-ray image of the card appeared on the screen. Where only one chip should have been, there were two.

"That one," Andrei said, pointing to the top right, "is a Metro chip. This one," moving his finger to the bottom left, "is bigger by far and is meant for something a bit more complex. I would guess a flash drive, or a personal ID badge of some sort." He added. He twirled his finger in the air a few times and pointed to the far end of the room. He got up and followed his extended finger into a junk pile that lay heaped against the far wall. He picked up item after dusty item, muttering under his breath, placing them atop other discards until he came up with what looked like a handheld laser radar device. Wen watched him with amusement as his friend beamed with a "Eureka!" smile. He walked back to his chair, blowing sawdust off it, and then plugged it into an outlet and calibrated it using the rotary dial on top.

"You going to take my speed?" Wen joked.

"No, but I will clock you over the head eventually, wiseass," Andrei said, waving the plastic machine in his direction. He pushed a button on the side of the scanner he had been using previously, and pointed the new device at the card. He clicked the trigger, and a readout appeared on the screen:

Balance: 637 yen.

"Wrong chip," Andrei said, frustrated. He pointed the laser at the opposite corner and pulled the trigger again.

Oscar Logias,
#1250, 243rd level, Shinseki Arms,
Shibuya ku, Tokyo.
124 6771
Social Security Number: 423 555 0982

"So he lives in the Heights. That much we had figured out on our own. That still doesn't tell me where my brother was taken, or who he was working for," Wen said, disappointed.

"You make a piss-poor hacker with that kind of attitude, son. Now you have his Virtual Identification Data. There are many things one can do with a valid VID. The fact that his wasn't implanted makes our job a whole lot easier." Andrei held up the card. "Our 'friend' is a ghost. Whose ghost; that is the question that interests us. We can do many things if we do not officially exist, if we wanted to use this VID."

"Such as?" Wen asked, knowing full well the uses of this particular information.

"Such as breaking and entering, for one. Such as impersonation, for two. Such as…" Andrei's voice trailed off when he noticed a blue light flashing on the wall. He got up and ran to a screen around the corner, tapping it with the tip of his index. "Company. Lots of it. Get over here, you," he ordered Wen, who complied and ran to the screen, swearing as he did. "These your friends?" Andrei asked. A contingent of loose obscurity swayed on the screen, blurred and diffuse. Andrei slammed his hand on a big red button on the wall.

"Probably; they're wearing optical camouflage," Wen said. Andrei pushed a switch that flipped the view to infrared. The shapes lit up and became more humanoid, seen from above. A dozen at least, in groups of three, fifty meters apart.

"One of you two is bugged. You led them right to me," Andrei berated him.

"What do they want with you?" Wen asked.

"Shall we go out there and ask?" Andrei said, pointing at the screen, his eyes bulging.

"How far are they?" Wen asked. The view was bouncing from camera to camera, keeping the invaders in sight.

"Three hundred meters and closing," Andrei said, his gaze darting to the camera numbers at the corner of the screen.

"Well, is there anything we can do?" Wen asked, worry creeping into his voice.

"I think we've done enough for tonight. It's time I made a confession," Andrei said, smiling. "I lied to you yesterday." Wen dug at his memories of the previous day like a dog trying to find a lost bone. The blurred figures approached the hump he recognized as the front entrance to the hideout.

"Can you just skip the suspense, please? Just tell me we aren't about to get killed because I led a platoon of assassins to your door!" Wen said, pacing in small circles behind his friend's chair, his eyes riveted to the screen.

"You remember when I told you that I hid the beacons out of reach after we destroyed that sentry bot? I actually deactivated the thing and brought it back with me. I've been doing that for years. I didn't tell Oscar because he was an anal retentive bastard with a hair trigger. I have them set up around the perimeter, hooked up to sonic amplifiers." He sat down on a chair before the screen and placed his hands behind his head. "Watch." He smiled. A different camera view appeared, with a big red dot surrounded by a dirigible-shaped body coming closer. Other camera sensors were tripped and more of the blimps made their way closer to the hideout. They soon encountered the heat signatures of the soldiers, and arcs of lightning began to shoot from all compass points, followed by gunfire. The vicinity of the hideout was now a battlefield, explosions going off, rocking the ceiling of their bunker. Wen and Andrei stared at the screen, transfixed by the sight of a platoon of floating death-machines raining hell onto equally well-prepared, but hopelessly outnumbered, soldiers. The camera screens lit up with silver light, flaring from all directions, but the humans were doomed. They called for a retreat, and the surviving diffuse blobs tried to run as far and fast as their legs would carry them. The robot sentries caught up to them and made them burst one after the other in arcs of pure electric fire, their every death a brilliant flash across the screens, a climax of blood fireworks. Andrei turned off the beacons with another whack at the button on the wall, and the sentries were left to pick up the charred corpses of the soldiers before floating away, their rallying cry extinguished.

"What do we know?" Andrei asked Wen after everything was over.

"I don't know; what, professor?" Wen said, shaken after the carnage but irritated that Andrei would have let him believe they were about to become more compost for the Heap.

"You're not all that interested in staying alive, are you? First, we know that one of you is tagged. Fortunately, they could only guess at our general vicinity, thanks to these thick walls and my tinkering. That explains why they were in a searching pattern, not in one big clump. We'll have to check both of you for homing devices. Second, those guys weren't Administration, or they would have turned off the sentries in the first place. In that sense, we were very lucky. Third, we'll have to get the hell out of here soon, before they send more people after us. Have I missed anything?" Andrei asked rhetorically.

"I think that about covers it," Wen said, watching the last of the sentries pick up the remaining charred corpses. "I'll take you up on that shot now," he said, rubbing his forehead with a trembling hand.

They sat back down on the dingy furniture in the living room, Wen still vibrating from what he thought were too many near-death experiences for one day. Andrei served them a bigger glass of firewater, and they both toasted to life, love, and the pursuit of a way out of their predicament.

"I'm sorry for everything," Wen said. "I feel like such a novice."

"Bah, relax, you did what you could with what you knew," Andrei said, his accent and deep, rolling Rs coming on thicker after a few shots. "You can only do so much with limited information. Knowing too little is what gets people in trouble in the first place. Besides, how were you supposed to be ready for such a full-on tactical mission against you? There's a reason they let you live back there. They knew you were on the run. The question now is, what do they want with me?" Andrei said.

"Maybe it's not you; not entirely, anyway," Wen said, reaching into his pocket and taking out the diamond.

"Ah, I see! Maybe you're right. I forgot about that. I have to inspect this little guy. I bet it's the reason Oscar was killed in the first place. Why else would he have had such an interest in a mere book? Enough for one night, though. I'm falling asleep. You can take the cot next to Taz's. Let's go check on him, shall we?" he said, pushing off the couch and stumbling a bit.

Taz's vital signs were normal, and the fever had died down. Andrei showed him where to find a washroom and staggered off to bed. Wen washed himself and slipped into bed; he pulled the warm, scratchy covers up to his ears. Taz's snoring was reassuring, a sign that his friend would survive the night. Wen fell into a dreamless coma a few moments later.

The smell of bacon woke him up. The hangover had passed him over this time, but he still felt groggy from lack of sleep and extenuation. He rubbed his aching eyes and scratched his head, noticed Taz's empty bed, pulled on his crusted pants and walked the cold, concrete floors barefoot to the kitchen.

Taz was at the controls, manning the stove when he walked in. Sizzling bacon and eggs made Wen's senses tingle. His stomach howled in basso profundo, wanting to partake in the feast.

"Morning. How are you feeling?" Wen said, still rubbing his black eye as gently as he could.

"Hey, you're up! Good as secondhand, thanks to you guys. Andrei got me up to speed. He's a wily bastard, that guy," Taz said, all traces of illness gone.

"Where is the wily bastard?" Wen asked, yawning.

"In the workshop, checking out our diamond," he said, shaking the skillet and pointing behind him with his spatula. A scream resounded through the halls then, and they both dropped what they were doing and ran to find its source. Andrei was hopping up and down in front of one of his screens, smiling as if he'd seen heaven.

"The hell is wrong with you?" Taz said, spatula raised in self-defense.

"The diamond—it's not a diamond!" Andrei said, taking him by the shoulders. Streams of information flowed down the screen behind him.

"That's hardly a cause for alarm then, is it?" Taz said. He remembered the food in the skillet and ran back to the kitchen to get them off the burner.

"Well, what is it then?" Wen asked.

"A memory chip, of sorts. It is one of the first crystalline memory chips ever made, that I'm sure of. It's crude, but when you point a laser at it, the data is transferred through it!" Andrei said.

"That's...pretty neat, I guess. What is the data about?" Wen asked, nonplussed.

"I don't know. That part eludes me. It's all encrypted. I don't have the key, so I can't unlock it," Andrei said, a bit less enthusiastic than before.

"Then, Oscar was after this. And now they're coming for us because we have it. Sammy got in the way and they took him. That sounds plausible," Wen said, pensive.

"We only need to find out who 'they' are, and then we can retrieve your brother. We have a very powerful bargaining chip, pardon the pun. I don't think they would harm Sammy just yet; not before they get this back," Andrei said. The data stored on the diamond kept downloading onto his computer, and they went for breakfast.

Taz served them on the coffee table. The bacon was a bit crispy and black, the eggs a tad hard, but no one dared complain, lest they feel the cook's wrath.

"Thanks again for saving my life," Taz said to both of them after taking a bite of his eggs.

"You would have done the same," Andrei said, pushing his knife with all his might against a piece of bacon, folding it like aluminum, without breaking it.

"That's a gorgeous setup, by the way. How the hell do you get your signals out without getting traced?" Taz asked, looking around.

"Easy. I have a decoy transmitter out in the middle of nowhere, and set up my receiver aboveground. It's all wireless, and I bounce my signal from server to server," Andrei said.

"Where did you get all this *stuff*?" Wen asked, thinking about the mounds of junk in the workshop and the hardware in the garage.

"Bartered, bought, found. I know a few guys. I don't need much in the way of luxuries, so I get interesting gear instead. We are standing in the biggest pile of garbage in the world after all." Andrei's usual good humor seemed to have returned, and he was no longer shy of having his privacy intruded.

"What's our next move?" Wen said.

"Well, I went over both your suits and found no bugs. Now we scan the both of you to see what comes up," Andrei said, holding up a flat, plastic paddle. He passed it over Wen's and Taz's front and back. The green diode on its side never wavered.

"That's odd. Something should be transmitting. There has to be a way they tracked you down," Andrei said, puzzled.

"Maybe it's been turned off," Taz suggested.

"Maybe," Andrei said, putting away the paddle. "Here is the tricky part: we have to get someone into Oscar's apartment. There's no way we can access his info from the outside; the Heights' firewalls are too strong to let anyone in. Even with my best military cracker, all we would do is attract attention back to us again. Besides, since the man was wearing his VID in a fake chipped card, something tells me he wouldn't show up on any official databank anyhow."

"How do you propose we get into the Heights?" asked Taz, leaning forward.

"Oscar's VID, for all intents and purposes, is still usable. Perhaps not for long, though, so we have to hurry. One of us has to pass as him and break into his place," Andrei said, holding up the card.

"Didn't you say you always wanted to go to the Heights?" Wen asked Taz.

"How, though? It's not like any of us look like Oscar!" Taz replied.

"Never fear; I can get someone in there. It will require a little alteration though," Andrei said cryptically. "Those men you showed me are definitely not Administration, obviously. Like you boys said: no markings, insignias, nothing. Whoever hired them has money. Those tanks are top-of-the-line Republic of Texas make. The weapons are from Free Pakistan. We're not dealing with amateurs," Andrei posited as a tone sounded from somewhere beyond.

Back in the workshop, the data signal had stopped. A blinking line of code stuck to the bottom of the screen.

"We need insurance," Taz said. "Let's make a few copies and keep them in a safe place in case anything happens to us."

"Sounds good. Gentlemen, your devices," Andrei said, holding out both hands. Taz gave him his card-sized deck, and Wen handed over his Zipper.

They were plugged into the computer one after the other, downloading the data at terabytes per second.

"Can I use your secure line?" Wen asked, after his Zipper had been filled with the crystal's code.

"Sure, what for?" Andrei asked.

"Insurance of my own," he said.

Andrei opened a drawer in the workbench, pulled out a wireless sensor, and stuck a cord into some rough-looking, pock-marked military hardware. The sensor pad, a convex lens, glowed a soft blue. Wen got his Netware and turned it on, applying its sensor to the lens. Contact was immediate, and they magnetized. He got his glasses out of a pocket and slipped them on. He pulled up an ancient wooden swivel chair, and Wen had a seat. He slipped forward from his toolkit screen over to the military machines' options.

The view Wen was used to was slick and round-edged, with soft colors. This thing was hard-core. The only descriptions he could give it were grim and functional. The specs were solid. He could get into just about anything with it. He wished Andrei had told him about it before. He kick-started the thing, and it created a maze of false addresses to slow down potential pursuit. He hunted down the drop box he had made for himself out a still functional but unknown server bank out of Cape Canaveral. He'd have to find a more reliable one before all the lights blinked out of existence. The information transferred smoothly from his deck, after which he deleted it. No trace would be left if ever the Zipper fell into the wrong hands. He logged off and disconnected the Zipper from the military unit. Andrei stared with evident concern at the screen next to the diamond.

"The file or files are gone. The laser burned them out. Guard your copies well, gentlemen."

CHAPTER 4

THEY LEFT THE underground soon afterward and walked across the barren Heap, encountering the occasional charred and smoking Sentry carcass. Back on the 150th level, they headed toward Nogata and its fish vats and gray markets. Three-story tall, clear, plastic, barrel-like aquariums, million-gallon tanks full of murky green seawater and packed with mackerel and bonito swimming clockwise loomed just beyond barbed-wire fences. Smells of fish, brine, and spices filled the air. Men in black rubber aprons carted frozen quarters of tuna, oblivious to the trio. Clear plastic lats hung from open garage doors where chilled breaths hung in the air, plumes of frosty, serpentine fog writhing along the ground from within. Yellow forklift's orange flashing lights warned them to step aside, Kanji-riddled white boxes of goods stacked high on wooden pallets. The sound of delivery trucks backing up melted into that of the workers' whistles telling them to stop. The Piscean odors retreated, replaced by the hospital smells of disinfectant and rubbing alcohol. Enhancement clinics flourished in the work district, cheap and mostly clean.

They came to endless rows of five-story, dirty white blocks like player-piano keys, drab and windowless; human chicken coops for the working class. Ankle-height fog wisped across the dark, deserted streets in snaking rivulets. After a left at a nondescript intersection dominated by the blank-faced, identical staff apartments, they followed Andrei into the first one on the corner and took the elevator to the fifth floor. The music from the speakers was a slow-sax rendition of popular rock songs. Wen was taken aback when he stepped out into the hallway; the quiet luxury within belying the anonymity and baseness without. The hallway was brown carpeted and impeccable; the only sound was that of their hushed footsteps. White, frosted-glass, half-shell lampshades adorned silver stems at regular intervals along the hall. Andrei knocked on a door with no number and it opened immediately, the peephole going dark for a millisecond. Wen realized that none of the other doors had any numbers either.

"Come in!" came a mellifluous voice from within.

"I brought you customers, Zegni," Andrei said, walking in with the others.

The door closed of its own accord, and Wen saw a camera attachment on the peephole, under which a set of guns were held by robotic arms, pointing toward the hall. A shiver went dancing along his shoulders like a wave.

"It's Zella now," a tall, Asian, black-haired woman said, coming around the corner, white teeth flashing behind blood-red lips.

"You went back! I thought you were happy as a man?" Andrei said.

"I was, but the muses always *drag* me somewhere else," she said, making *drag* sound like it was carrying something heavy. "My neighbor is a wonderful genetic surgeon who happened to have kept some of his younger daughter's DNA: voila! Besides, who said I got rid of all the manly bits?"

"Zeg...Zella Marchenko, this is Wen Harkwell and Scott Till," Andrei said.

"Call me Taz," he said, bowing.

"It's a pleasure," Wen said.

"Andrei tells me you need access. I think I have what you need," she said. She led them inside the apartment to the dining room, where they sat down around a large oak table.

She took out a static-proof bag from a plastic drawer and placed it in front of them.

"This is a doppelganger chip. It'll take anyone's VID and make it *you*. I have to remove yours, of course, but you can always switch back to your own ID by squeezing it," she said, gripping her forearm and pressing, "like this. This isn't for anything illegal, is it?" She looked at them sternly down her pert nose. The three looked at each other, uncomfortable and at a loss for words.

"Ha ha—just kidding! I can never bug my customers like that; I wouldn't get repeats. I just had to," she said, covering her mouth in amusement. "Who is it going to be?" She looked from one to the other.

"I can't. I have my reasons for that," Andrei said, shaking his head.

"Of course. I wasn't asking you, dear," Zella said, eyeballing the youths.

"My friend Wen here will volunteer," Taz said, clapping Wen on the shoulder.

"I will?" Wen exclaimed, surprised.

"I'm still feeling ill. Besides, you have a greater stake in this. You also know the Heights, whereas we are but poor country folk who would get lost in that terrifying urban jungle. You do want to get your brother back, don't you?" Taz said. Wen looked defeated, yet too proud to refuse the charge that had been placed on him.

"Yeah, OK, let's do this. Why can't I just use the card; that should work, no?" he said, as a last-ditch effort.

"What do you do if they ask to scan your arm?" Andrei asked. Wen resigned himself to his fate.

"You don't have any other implants, do you? Net trodes or other?" Zella asked him.

"Just my VID, why?" he asked.

"This thing's electrical signal would interfere with them. It's recent, and for obvious reasons, they can't publicly market test them. Congrats, honey, you're a guinea pig," she said. "Don't worry; I'm a certified tech surgeon." That didn't make Wen feel any better. "Dolly! Molly!" she called, and two female sex-bots dressed in nurse's uniforms came out from a room behind them. "My assistants," she explained. "I've reprogrammed them to perform simple tasks."

"Sure you have," Andrei said with a wide grin. The two androids with their anime eyes and short pink and purple hair led Wen into the surgery room without a word. He sat in a dental chair, and they strapped his wrists down, putting a gas mask over his face. *I'm doing it for my brother,* he thought. *I'm doing the right thing.* His eyes grew heavy, the room blurred. The Asian with the toothy grin stood over him. She was saying something, but the words were coming from the other side of a wall.

"*This old herd a bit, love,*" she said, and Wen blanked out.

⋏ ⋏ ⋏

His face was in the grass. The grass was wet. He lifted his face and the wetness was blood. The blood came from his face. He lowered his outstretched hand to touch his forehead. It hurt! He looked at his fingers. They had blood on them. Time was slow. Slow time. There was a booming sound all around him. A swing swung back and forth a little ways away, and further still, some knotted, twining ginkgo trees stood silent watch. There were boys near him. They were booming. *No,* his mind said, *they are laughing.* Wen Harkwell lifted his tiny frame up on his bruised elbow. Asian faces, all around him, mean black eyes, forced laughs. *They hate you,* his mind said. *You are a stranger.* The laughter stopped, and the boys ran away, like crows taking off in a volley, angry at having lost their prey. His father picked him up. His *English* father, picking him up. *You are a stranger. You will always be a stranger,* his mind said. And he believed it.

⅄ ⅄ ⅄

Wen woke up an hour later from sedation, the shards in his head throbbing, bobbing in the sea of memories. His face no longer felt swollen, but his forearm did. He rolled his heavy head to the side and stared at the area that felt swollen. There was only a red welt, no other indication that there had been flesh manipulation at all. What he wanted more than anything was to be free of his restraints so he could scratch the swollen place, and to go to the bathroom.

"He's awake," he heard, coming from someone near him. It was a woman's voice. "How do you feel?" she said.

"Dizzy. Itchy. I have to go to the can," he said, and the doctor unclasped his restraints.

"Dolly and Molly will take you to do your business," she said, and Wen felt a vague sense of inappropriateness, as if someone had said, *This blind man will drive you home.* The sex-bots took him by his shoulders and helped him walk to the washroom, sitting him on the toilet after removing his pants.

"I'll be fine," he told them, and they left, closing the door. He slumped over on the side of the cabinet and had to call them in when he was done so that they could pull his pants back up. He had to resist the feverish urge to scratch the itch that emanated from his arm, like a thousand bed bugs biting at his tender flesh. The "nurses" sat him down on a leather sofa in the living room next to Taz. He and Andrei were having a cup of tea served from a tall, slender pot with a curly handle. Zella put the bone-china teapot back onto a placemat on the dark, wooden coffee table. A silver clock's pendulum swayed to and fro on the wall behind the couch where Taz sat. Outside the large picture window, a beautiful, sunny day shone on a perfect lawn. A delicate wind tilted the grass at smooth intervals. White lace curtains undulated before the window, pushed by a fan in the ceiling. Wen took a deep breath, and the thought of his grandparents came to him, unbidden. Zella tapped a button on a remote control, and the scene from the window became an aerial view of Mount Everest on a cloudless day, white craggy peaks dusting a powder of snow in volutes. The moving panorama made Wen slightly ill, forcing his attention to stationary objects.

"How you feeling, mate?" Taz said, tapping him jovially on the back, making Wen rock forward a bit dangerously.

"Crusty. I could sleep three more days."

"We don't have that much time," Andrei said, raising his eyebrows.

"I'll have a pot of that tea, if you don't mind," Wen said, turning to Zella.

"Cup?" Zella said.

"Did I stutter? When will I feel less like beaten horsemeat?" Wen said.

"Give it another hour or so, Mr. Grumpy Pants. Oh, I fixed up your face a tad. Nothing major, just something to accelerate the healing; you're welcome," she said. Wen grunted, and Taz helped him put the cup to his lips. His desert throat yelped as the hot liquid poured down it.

"Shall we give it a try?" Andrei suggested, taking the Metro card and pressing it against Wen's sore forearm. It felt like the fire of a thousand suns had suddenly ignited on his skin, making Wen scream in pain, throwing his arms up and sending the teacup flying.

"Doctor recommends waiting a bit," Zella said from behind her teacup. "You always were the impulsive one, *moya lubov*. It should work anyhow, but give it some time. Try this," she said, handing Andrei a fist-sized, matte-black module bearing a lighter plastic strip at one end. "Scan; don't touch," she suggested. Andrei did as told and the readout on the thing's face told them that the owner of the arm was Oscar Logias, inhabitant of Shibuya District, Tokyo. One of Zella's assistants picked up the spilled teacup from the white, Asian-patterned rug while the other fetched a new one.

"Works just fine," Andrei said with approval. He leaned over to squeeze the VID out of the system, and Wen cradled his arm protectively.

"No way. I'll do that myself. No need to rush things, Mr. Impulsive," he said, and Zella smiled as Andrei rested again on the sofa, Taz giggling behind his fist. Zella tossed him a small plastic container filled with a transparent, shimmering cream.

"Put some of this on whenever you feel an itch," she said, pointing to the bottle. They finished their tea, Wen making frequent use of the unguent.

"The check is in the mail, Zella," Andrei said.

"Forget it; I'll just rip it up. Consider it payback for Sevastopol," she said.

Zella waved them off at the door, her two assistants bowing deeply to them as the left.

The door slammed shut as they walked down the corridor.

"You two uh..." Taz intimated to Andrei, pointing his thumb the way they had come.

"In several other lives. I don't know about this one. I'm not sure I'm that adventurous anymore," Andrei said, looking Taz straight in the eye. "Answer your question?"

"One hundred of the percent, my liege," Taz said, curtsying. Wen was too itchy to join in the fun and had to restrain himself from rubbing his arm every other second. He applied the cream in great dollops, torn between excess and lack.

The plan was simple, or rather, simple enough: they would choose a point of entry to the Heights where it was improbable Oscar would have. This saved the trouble of any recognition by the elevator guards, if they happened to double-check. Since he had his VID implanted, there was no need for picture ID; his face would do the trick. He would need cash to go from one end of town to the other, and using a credit card was out of the question. Who paid for their train ride with a credit card anyhow? The Metro pass was one ride short of being depleted. Taz and Andrei transferred as much credit as they could onto his Zipper, giving it enough of a balance to get there and back. Wen had one chance of doing it right, so he made sure he had all the right hacking tools he needed in case he had to break into the man's apartment.

"You don't look right, mate," Taz said, sizing him up.

"What, my face again?" Wen said, distraught, touching his swollen visage.

"No, no, idiot! You don't look like you would fit in the Heights. You look street, just not Ginza street, know what I mean?" Taz said, annoyed. He was right. Wen looked at himself in the nearest store window and thought he did look pretty ratty. His clothes might fall apart at the next wash because the glue that held them together was his own sweat.

"No two ways about it; we're off to Shinjuku1," Andrei said. "We need to get you some new clothes."

"Hold on, there, Andrei. I think I can lend our friend here some dapper dos. I was saving them for myself, but seeing as he needs them more than I do…You will repay me the favor someday, won't you, Wen?" Taz said.

"What, you mean like save your life?" Wen said distractedly, trying still not to scratch.

"Ah, well yes, there is that," Taz said. "Anyhow, why don't you two park your asses somewhere, and I'll come get you in a bit," he said, leaving them standing there.

They found a coffee dive called The Drunkard in one of the less crummy side streets of the Chuo Ward. Recycled vinyl car seats lined the walls under peeling paint, on the 150th level. Photocopies of last centuries' celebrities' autographed pictures lined the back wall behind the knife-etched counter. It was a hand-me-down café with the rows of shelves meant for liquor decorated with cheap claw-machine plushies, dust-covered and grimy. The constant white noise on the holovid blurred the stolen Net signal. The rest of the place was filled with burly workers with tech prosthetic enhancements designed for heavy labor on the ground. This was the other side of the procurement coin. Whereas Oscar's ex-crew searched for treasure, the hard-working people in this fine establishment toiled in the recycling business, dredging up any and all garbage that could be smelted and put back into circulation. Wen wondered what they used for Sentry repellent as he sipped a thin coffee from a stained mug. They kept their heads low and avoided looking in anybody's direction, occasionally peering out the window onto the wet street. A fine mist suppurated at waist height, the chill emanating wet dog stench. November frost drew postcard corners on the dirty plate-glass window, organic crystalline growth framing a picture no one would want to send.

I'm really doing this, Wen thought, trying to come up with excuses not to go. Even when he hacked as a child, there was nothing *personal* about it. He was an operator at the end of a wire, disconnected from the real, absorbed in a persona that could be cut off at any time. His body was not included in the deal. It was as safe to think *I'm going to break into the Telecom's intranet* as *What will I have for breakfast?* Now there was no running away; no floating out of the puppet like a spirit. He clenched his fists under the table, staring hard at the bruised reflection in the window.

"Calm down," Andrei said, putting his hand on one of Wen's knees.

He noticed that he had been tapping his heel unconsciously, and concentrated now on not letting it resume.

Taz paged them a little under two hours later and met them in the mists of Taito Industrial Park. Above them was Ueno Park and Zoo. Andrei was certain this was the safest point of entry—anonymity at the egress and a little-guarded elevator mostly used by the zoo workers. Wen took the brown paper bag of clothes and shoved it into his backpack. He walked out alone from the security of the shadows near the automotive shops and into the circular plaza where the support pillar harbored two smaller elevators. Two guards in gray uniforms stood at attention by them, their faces impassive. Black batons hung from their hips, luring Wen's gaze as he walked toward them under the circular orange light of the street lamps. Somewhere behind him, Andrei and Taz would be hidden in the blanketing gloom, following his progress. Would they help him if anything went wrong? His legs and spine felt stiff and jerky; his head swam. He walked between the guards, placing his wrist over the scanner. It pinged and turned green, a turnstile opening before him.

"Stop," a guard ordered as Wen took a step toward the elevator. He froze, his organs seizing. He tried to breathe from a constricted throat and was afraid it was coming out in wheezes.

"What...what is it?" he asked, swallowing drily.

"May I ask where you are coming from, Mr....um...Logias?" said the guard, glancing at the readout on the turnstile.

No, no you may not, thought Wen. He was so close. He was going to get arrested and thrown in prison. He would never see his brother again. His adrenaline surged at the thought, and he felt his palms growing warmer. They prickled with heat, as soon did his ears. Pins danced on the back of his neck.

"I am on business," he said, glaring at the guard who had had the temerity of trying to question one of the Elite. He was *Oscar Logias,* dammit, and no one fucked with him. The guard seemed to have second thoughts about his questioning. There was no dropping the mask, not even for a second. Forget the fact that he was dirty and dressed like a bum. What if they checked for proof of residence or called in to Central for confirmation? Wen's clenched hands sweated profusely, but his stare into the questioning man's eyes never wavered.

"You may go through, sir," he said, looking uncomfortable and returning to his post.

"You're damn right I can," Wen said, glaring in his direction. He strutted to the elevator and haughtily plinked the sensor with the second joint of his index finger. The doors whooshed open and he stepped in, turning around to press the next level's button angrily. It was only after the doors had closed that he leaned against the wall to steady himself. With trembling fingers, he unzipped his backpack and attempted to open the sealed paper bag. He got annoyed and ripped it open. He then remembered the cameras in the elevators and closed his bag again. Through the porthole of the rising elevator, he spied the shrinking plaza, followed by motorways obscuring his view, Metro lines and busy streets lined with stores, and then pure concrete as he broke through the womb-like threshold of the lower levels. A piercing white light shone into the elevator as he achieved the park, forcing him to avert his gaze. The doors opened with a tone, a voice announcing Ueno Park and Zoo, and he exited, his eyes adjusting to unfiltered sunshine for the first time in years.

CHAPTER 5

T HE AIR WAS brisk and chill, pushing along elephantine cumulus clouds, but the intermittent rays warmed his skin. He breathed in the purity and strolled through the park, trying not to get distracted from his quest. Cherry tree–lined dirt avenues remained deserted save a few strollers and their attendant nannies. The bare cherries held promises of bloom and swirling petal, but not yet. He felt as if he was meeting an old friend under sad circumstances. There was no time to waste.

Wen headed to the nearest public restrooms, inhaling the heady scent of dirt and moss that surrounded him, spying the silent high-speed trains further up and outside the park. From here, he could see the tips of the behemoth towers, Glasteel panels gleaming, looming high above. Green terraces adorned many of them, endowing them with warmth and nature. A crow's raucous cry echoed in the distance, and a sparrow couple chased each other through the branches in the tree above him. He felt dissipation, fear turning to calm and serenity.

The worst is over; I just have to get in and out, he thought.

In the toilet stall, he put on the clothing he had been given; a cream-white shirt with hand stitching on the edges of the collar, gray cherry floral patterns around the breast pocket and straight-legged black pants, smooth and shiny with red dots connected by straight lines around the back pockets. The gray suede shoes with black soles complimented the whole, three straight black lines crossing at a perpendicular angle across the tips. He looked once again into the bottom of the bag to see if anything was missing and found a glass bottle slipped in a small black paper box and a clear plastic bag. On the cover of the box were wavy lines in a lacquered black. He pushed out the glass bottle from its slipcover and looked at the amber liquid within. It released a pleasant cinnamon and musk aroma when he sniffed it. He dabbed his finger on the front of the glass bottle and the cologne suffused through it. He tapped each side of his neck once and put away the bottle, placing it in his backpack. There were two little white round stickers in the plastic bag, and he looked at them curiously. What were they supposed to be? He practically slapped himself in the forehead when he realized they were imitation Netrode links. He was in the Heights, after all. Nothing would stick out more than a man with no 'trodes. He peered out of the stall and went to the mirror, placing each sticker as fast as he could on the back of his neck. He inspected them, turning this way and that before being satisfied that he could pass off as one of Them. It suddenly dawned on him that he had gotten on the elevator without the guards noticing he was an Unconnected, and a cold wave washed over his body. He threw the packaging into the garbage incinerator in the restrooms and departed.

How long have you been saving your paychecks to afford this, Taz? Wen wondered with a touch of guilt.

He left the park and found the nearest Metro station, a mere hundred meters away. The pedestrians he noticed walked and dressed like fashion models. Serious men in high collars displayed platinum cuff-links and showy analog timepieces, with price tags that were no laughing matter. Electric Lamborghinis and Porsches drove by, gliding over the tarmac and taking off into the air at the end of the street. Children like perfect dolls demurely held their nannies' hands, busy as they were being careful not to get a single smudge on their spotless garments. A parade of private school girls glided by, giggling behind cupped hands, dressed in identical navy-blue sailor suits. Their scent was spring, in all its forms, wafting from delicate skin. He ached for the season he would never see, the perfume a too-strong reminder. The stores he passed held no more than three of the same item, which had no price tags, the thought being that if you had to ask, you couldn't afford it. Wen could feel the change in himself as well: his slouch turned into a strut, his attitude self-important and carefree. The art to *being* was returning in a hurry. If the clothes made the man, the man had to buck up to the situation; and he did so admirably, he thought.

He replenished his stolen Metro card at one of the station wall consoles. It had been refurbished since last he had come. The walls had been replaced with holovid screens; 3D patterns flowing in smooth succession. Wen was mesmerized by a medley of living Dali paintings, succeeding each other in animated chase, running along the curving walls. The Tokyo Art Museum logo pursued the artwork from left to right in Dali-esque font. The ceilings were concave egg shapes, held up by slim, cream-colored pillars. A shifting rainbow of soft, liquid pastels soothed the eyes. A sultry woman's voice announced that the next train was arriving in the next minute, bringing Wen back to his present endeavors. He walked with a sure step to the platform, the other passengers business men and women in black and gray attire. A few young men joshed around, feeling the camera of their life turned squarely on them and wanting to make the best of it, living to be noticed—the exact opposite of Wen.

The low-pitched whine of the mag-lev train entered the station before it, the smooth bullet-shape coming next. Wen rode in the front seat of the driverless train, a pull from his heartstrings making protest moot. The accelerating train augmented the beat in his breast. He was fourteen again, going to the department stores with his mother and baby Sammy. The towers whooshed by as he stared at the open sky, so blue, so vast. It was like flying. Silent electronic tags flashed on the windscreen, announcing the names of the myriad buildings and a brief history of their existence.

He was no longer fourteen years old, though. He had a job to do. Sammy had to be found before it was too late. He sat down on one of the plush seats and considered his plan. All he had to do was get in the man's apartment and break into his computer, finding out who he was working for: simple. Why was he so scared then?

There is no plan beyond this, he thought. *What the hell am I going to do when I find out who did it? Go knocking on their door and ask for Sammy back, please?* He felt ridiculous for even trying, but he could not give up. Not so easily. Not again. He leaned forward from his seat and closed his eyes, turning his face up to the sun, feeling the tingling heat on his skin. *One step at a time*, he thought.

He got off at Shibuya station, a monster of glass and steel. A high-pitched voice announced and repeated the station name twice over the loud-speakers as he left his compartment, the sound echoing in the immense hall. A glass half-dome hung above the multiple train tracks, tapering at the station itself, ten floors higher. A city alight spread out beyond the dome.

An animated cartoon tiger danced in midair over the parallel tracks, grinning from an anthropomorphic mouth, its tongue lolling out. The work crowd thickened now, the click-clack of heels thunderous on tiled floors. An enormous Victorian-style antique black clock hung from the far glass wall announcing four o'clock. Orange skies contrasted purple clouds, the lights of the city taking over.

Shibuya was the worker's Heights, affordable luxury for those who still needed to work for their pay. Wen walked out of the sprawling station, trying to get his bearings. He was tempted to visit his old home but knew it was a foolish waste of time. He turned left along the station, avoiding suits hailing yellow taxis lined up for what seemed like kilometers. In the sky he guessed the brightest stars as he walked along the polished sidewalks, shoulders relaxed and concentration returned. The towers bore wide, clam-shaped balconies like tree mushrooms, their gardens lichen.

He closed his eyes and was back on the edge of a balcony, staring into Tokyo nights, the smells of the kitchen wafting out the sliding doors as he avoided home-work. He opened his eyes again and turned right, crossing the street, following a wide avenue lined with stores and fine dining restaurants on the first floors, apartments overtop. The Shinseki Arms was a short rectangular stack, twenty iron balconies high, red brick, clean, and no visible sense of humor.

He swiped his arm on the scanner in front of the building and walked into the lobby, the glass doors sliding closed behind him. He pushed the button for the twelfth floor and fidgeted, tapping his foot until the door opened. He walked right, saw the numbers were ascending, turned around, and walked down the hall until he found the wooden door marked 1250. His arm was trembling as he put it over the scanner. *Please, oh please work!* he prayed. His hair stood up on the back of his neck. The door unlocked with a satisfying click, and he pushed the golden lever down and crept inside.

Austere was the first word that came to mind when he entered. The dark cubic libraries were barren, save a few pictures of Oscar and some other man. There was also a group picture of men in army fatigues, half of them crouching before the others, nineteen in all. He did not recognize the man he was impersonating until he saw his surly face, with a full head of hair, arms crossed, off to the side. A weight bench squatted near the porch window, just a bar with some circular iron weights strapped to the ends. A naked kneeling stone statue flexed by a full-length mirror. On his immediate left stood an open kitchen with a giant slab of gray marble countertop like a horizontal tombstone, spotless, aseptic as a mortician's embalming room, depressing and impersonal.

How fitting that Oscar's ghost should come back to haunt his home, he thought.

Wen headed down the corridor to the left, finding the master bedroom. A round-ed glass display case like an erect phallus paraded medals and ribbons. He opened the closet out of curiosity and found three sets of navy-blue uniforms with no insignias sandwiched between clothes he had seen him wear before, and clothes that he would only wear here, in the Heights. A gray uniform caught his eye. It had an insignia he would recognize anywhere: DaiSin Corporation's guards. His heart beat faster until he noticed a black tag inscribed: M. Lewes. This wasn't his, in that case. Who was M. Lewes? Perhaps Oscar Logias wasn't even his real name after all.

He walked to the next room, the office, where a dead screen held sway over a neatly arranged workspace. He sat at the desk before it and swiped his hand in the air, the screen turning on and greeting him. The screen was password protected. Like most people who thought they were secure in their own homes though, the password was already entered, awaiting a mere click to go into the guts of the system. Wen approached his hands on the desk, and a laser keyboard was projected onto it. He pressed the enter key and the screen flipped away, going to the desktop icons.

There, in the left-hand corner was an icon titled "Oscar Work." The ubiquitous DaiSin logo, a mandala containing a tripartite yin-yang symbol, hung above it. He had it. He had what he had come for. His emotions seesawed between jubilation and unbridled anger.

DaiSin, he thought, *DaiSin is behind this after all*. His brain sang with ache and melancholy hatred. He wanted to rip out the screen and throw it through the window. He wished Oscar was still alive so he could stab him to death with an ice pick. Everything DaiSin touched left shit stains and misery. He would have loved to believe that Sammy's disappearance was related to his mother's, but he had no proof—yet. If they were gutless enough to kidnap a thirteen-year-old, wasn't it likely they had done the same to his mother? Why did they take his brother? Why? What the hell could they possibly want with him? He banged his fist on the desk. Wen wished he had one of those hovertanks so he could go pay them a visit and ask. He had to get back to the others with the news. They wouldn't be thrilled, but at least they would know where things stood.

DaiSin, he thought, his mind boiling over. *Motherfuckers*.

"Oscar, I'm home! You left the door open. Oscar?" he heard from the other room.

Shit! He felt punched in the gut. He looked around, but there was nowhere to hide. He flipped off the computer and got up, unsure how to proceed.

What do I do? he thought, his mind skidding at a thousand miles an hour but getting nowhere. He searched the room for possibilities and then realized: *This person doesn't know Oscar's dead!*

"I'll be right there," he replied loudly, twisting his abject fear into a little ball and walking out of the room. He marched up to the man setting two grocery bags on the slab in the kitchen. Fit and in his early thirties, he was dressed in a white shirt and black tie and pants; the salaryman's uniform.

"Who are you?" the man asked, astonished to find someone roaming his home.

"I'm with the DaiSin Corporation, sir. I'm sorry to inform you that Oscar Logias has passed away," he said, arms rigid and by his sides, palms sweating. This was the man from the pictures in the library.

"What? When?...What?" the man said.

"I am sorry, sir; this was all confidential. We could not tell you over the Nets, you understand," Wen said, his face as serious as stone.

"What did you say your name was?" the man said, starting to go around the corner of the counter. Wen lunged for the door, the man grabbing air behind him. He closed the door on the man's arm, and he howled in pain and whipped the door open. Wen sped on an adrenaline spike toward the elevators, changed his mind, and charged for the emergency stairwell, jumping down the stairs four by four, his Adam's apple bobbing in his throat. His hands slipped on the guardrail and his knees threatened to buckle, but he kept on running. Above him the man was running after him, feet pounding hard down the concrete stairs. The sounds reverberated, making the pursuer seem right behind him, ready to kick him in the back. Wen ran even faster, sweat dripping into his eyes, making his shirt cling to his soaked body. He threw himself against the door on the first floor, running outside into the night. A police car was landing in front of the apartment block, lights flashing but with the sirens off, two officers stepping out.

This can't be happening! he thought, in complete panic.

The man chasing him screamed, "Him! It's him! Stop him!" and Wen kept running toward the train station, at a loss for a plan. He grabbed his forearm and pressed, hoping to erase any trace of the identity he had stolen. There was a sting in his shoulder. His muscles seized and he fell forward onto the sidewalk, hitting it hard and fast. He tried to turn around but another seizure cramped his muscles, shooting pain through his inert body, jerking him like a fish out of water.

"Don't move," he heard from above him, a knee jabbing into his back. His left arm was yanked behind him, followed by the right, clasped together in cold metal. The officer removed the Taser dart and patted him down, taking his backpack. One of them scanned his forearm. He was lifted by both officers and thrown into the back of the cruiser. One of them stepped into the front driver's seat, while the other followed the man back into the apartment block. *How did they get here so fast?* he wondered.

"Where will you take me?" he asked the officer.

"Downtown. It is my duty to advise you not to speak unless you have counsel." The officer looked at him in the rearview mirror. Wen stared outside at the apartment block. The other officer returned and sat down without a word. The two looked each other in the eyes and nodded, finishing a silent conversation. There was complete quiet inside the cruiser as they lifted off into the dark Tokyo sky. Red lights flashed intermittently at the topmost levels of the skyscrapers, the rest a wash of white glow. A three-quarter moon cast a baleful eye on the activities of man. The red flashers pushed other cars to the side, making their flight a quick one, and Wen saw with fresh eyes the

Tokyo he had dreamed of as a child. The endless sky caressed by the longing spires; the infinite possibilities. Gazing downward he saw the trails of red and white glowing ants that were wheeled traffic's call signs, speeding down avenues like cold, clean entrails. If he could have rolled down the window, he would have inhaled the chill November breeze of long ago. Yet he could not; this was no longer his city, and everything considered, it never had been.

They headed to the center of Tokyo, Central Administration. It was no small infraction that Wen had committed, but as the officer had said, it would be best for him to keep his mouth shut until he could be represented. He had no idea how much they knew beyond the visible facts.

The CA building dwarfed many of the larger ones in Tokyo. Sharp angles of concrete and vertical slashes of darkened windows over five hundred stories tall, it imposed by its presence and grim bearing. The police vehicle began its descent, a virtual grid forming on the windshield. They dropped vertically from the Heights to halfway down the tower, between both worlds; a great many floors eaten up by Tokyo Police Department. They slid into a wide open bay door and the cruiser came to rest on the tarmac next to identical police cars. The officers led Wen out of the car, past rows upon rows of TPD cruisers, trucks and vans, as well as a few hovertanks of their own. These were a sky blue and of a different make than the ones he had seen before. It smelled of oil and grease, and a tinge of floor polish. Cruisers alighted and landed periodically, the whine of their engines a whisper of wasps. The police garage was overlooked by office windows on the third and fourth floors, the open garage doors as tall as the ceiling, with a view of the next high-rise several hundred meters away.

He was led to processing, where they made him sign off on his backpack, taking it away from him to be held as evidence.

I hope I get my Netware back, he thought. They took his picture and led him to a windowless closet of a room, a single camera on the corner of the ceiling. The officers unclasped his handcuffs and told him to go sit down at the metal chair behind a table. He rubbed his sore wrists and pressed vigorously on his right forearm again, knowing full well it was too late if it hadn't worked the first time. He traipsed about, attempting to dissipate the ants in his legs. The room was five worried paces by four annoyed steps; this, of course, varied by degree of both emotions.

Around a thousand steps later, a woman marched in. She had serious, short black hair to compliment her furrowed brow. Tight lips and a haughty nose crowned the rest of her face. She wore a severe black suit with a conservative knee-length skirt and carried a small brown attaché case.

"Mr. Harkwell, sit down," she ordered quietly.

He took a seat, his expression falling even lower, but inwardly thankful he had been able to erase Oscar's VID copy.

"May I?" pointing at the chair.

"Y-yes, of course," he answered.

"Thank you." She sat primly, crossing her long, stockinged legs with quick, precise movements and putting down the attaché case.

"I am Special Investigator Mariko Ishikawa," she said, taking a card out from a metal case and holding it out to Wen from the top corners with the tips of her index fingers. He hesitated and then took it from her with the tips of his fingers. He was looking at it as if it were a new species of beetle, the kind that bit.

"You are in trouble, Mr. Harkwell. You know that, and we know that. Fortunately we can help each other. This may sound trite, but the City of Tokyo needs you." She said this with set jaw and her scrutinizing gaze piercing into his face.

He could not react for a moment because it felt as if someone had just smacked him upside the head out of the blue with a very large, wet noodle.

"Needs me for what?" he said.

"Glad you asked," she said, taking it as a signal to pick up her attaché case from the floor. She rifled through it briefly and removed a folder marked "Eyes Only" in big red stamp.

She opened it, and as she rifled through some papers, Wen asked, "Why don't you have some sort of protection?"

"Because you're not a threat to me," she said matter-of-factly, placing a tablet computer on the table.

"How do you know?" Wen asked, feeling the urge to prove he might be dangerous.

"What am I thinking?" she said, her gaze sharpening as she stared into his eyes. *What is she thinking? What the hell?* Wen thought.

"Strawberry cream cheese on a plain bagel, toasted," he said, throwing his palms in the air.

"Sounds tasty. No, you are no threat to me. Nice try, though," she said, pointing to the picture that was displayed on the screen. "This man, Oscar Logias. You know him." This was not a question. *So it wasn't a fake name*, he thought.

"Yeah, obviously, I was in his apartment," he said. "Hey, wasn't I supposed to get a lawyer or something?"

"In certain cases, your right to an attorney is waived. This is such a case. Why *were* you in his apartment?" she asked.

They don't know everything, do they? he pondered. "Paying a house call," he said defiantly.

"Careful, Mr. Harkwell. This is no joking matter. The man disappeared off the radar yesterday. Why did you tell his husband he was dead?" she asked.

He blinked. *His husband? Really?* he thought. "To see his reaction," he said, trying to keep his composure.

"Mr. Harkwell," she said, closing the file. "We can arrange for a nice cell in the same dimensions as the one in which you are presently located, or," she said, punctuating each word with a tap of her finger on the screen, "you can try to be more cooperative. DaiSin is up to something. We know some of the players, but we want to know the endgame. You are caught up in this, somehow. It would be in your best interest to have someone watching your back, don't you think?"

Wen pinched the bridge of his nose. "You want to help me?" he said.

"Only if you help us," she replied.

"Where was your 'help' thirteen years ago when my mother vanished?" he said, becoming angry at the woman's earlier threats. He wanted to get his brother back, but to get in league the people who had snubbed him so easily when he needed their assistance? That was a kick in the crotch that would take a lifetime to heal.

"I assure you, Mr. Harkwell, everything that could have been done, was," she said, never losing her composure. "You know who Oscar Logias is, you know his employer. You might want to listen to people who are trying to look out for you. DaiSin is no friend of yours, Wen, not by a long shot. If you are involved in his disappearance, you can bet they'll try to find you in the worst possible way. Work for us, and take our protection," she said, trying for a smile, tight lips extending like a rubber band.

"I know what DaiSin is. I won't help you. Go find some other idiot to manipulate," he said, crossing his arms. Her expression went blank, unfocused. She mouthed some words without making a sound.

"Very well," she said, the attempt at a smile gone, her attention back on Wen, "have it your way. You are free to go. There is a formality first, but that won't take long."

"Free to go? Whatever happened to the tiny cell with my name on it?" he said, incredulous.

"I have no time to waste on a...person like you, Harkwell," she spat, standing up and knocking on the door.

Is this the weirdest day of my life? he thought.

"Aren't you even going to torture me to find out what I know?" he said, pretending to flog himself.

She stopped midstride and turned back like a viper lashing out. "I'm sure you'd enjoy that; the Tokyo PD is above such crude and ineffective methods. Good luck with your troubles," she said, getting the last word in and slamming the door.

Another lost opportunity, he thought, shaking his head. *Would I have been better off?*

He was taken to an infirmary soon after, and a police doctor asked him to lower his shirt.

"What are you going to do?" he asked.

"Vaccine. It's not going to kill you; don't worry. As much as I'd like to spay and/or neuter you, it's just a simple precaution to keep you healthy," the man said, holding up a short needle. "We do this to all the strays we pick up."

Wen grudgingly lowered his shirt sleeve and the doctor swabbed his shoulder, inserted the needle, and pushed the plunger.

"There; all done! You can thank me later when this saves your life," he said as Wen rubbed the sore spot.

"I'm sure I'll be thinking of you," Wen said, and was led away. An officer escorted him to the personal articles desk, and the attendant handed his backpack to him. They then took him through meandering corridors full of suspects being led one way or the other by uniformed police. He was taken to the nearest elevator and let down, all the way back to the dreary darkness of the lower levels. He stepped out of the elevator and the first thing that hit him was the smell: the foul stench of despair and poverty, sewer runoff mixed in for good measure. This was his home. He took a few tentative steps, walked off in the direction of the nearest Metro station, and occasionally checked to see if he was being followed, but nothing police-like was to be found on his trail. *Good luck with your troubles*, he thought, wondering what his next move might be. The pungent smell of mold and rotted food caressed his nostrils in putrid ecstasy from a Dumpster along the way. *DaiSin is no friend of mine? No kidding. I have to find out what kind of enemy it is.*

He paged Andrei and Taz, meeting them at the same dingy coffee shop he and Andrei had waited in earlier. The Drunkard was almost empty, the ambiance crepuscular. The cheap coffee hadn't budged all day, black sludge bubbling in the pot, smelling like burnt tires. He half-expected to see a mammoth slowly sinking in it. Retired prostitutes married to their pimps chatted in hushed, somber tones under the dingy lights of their own booths.

"So, what happened?" Taz said, eager to hear about his "adventures." Wen stared into his glass of water, watching the fine particles swirl in a hypnotic counter-clockwise spiral.

"It's DaiSin," he said, morose.

"I should have known," Andrei said, becoming gloomy as well.

"Ah, shit," Taz said, putting his head against his hands on the table.

"Those guys in blue fatigues are DaiSin as well. I found several suits in Oscar's closet. The cops got there way too fast," he added.

"The police? Why were they there?" Andrei asked, leaning forward.

"They just showed up! One minute I'm trying to get away from Oscar's husband, the next thing you know I'm getting Tased and booked," he explained.

"Oscar's *husband*?" Andrei asked.

"Yes, his husband. Anyway, as soon as I hit the door, there were the cops. Nothing I could do about it," he said, shaking his head.

"Them ap hammen?" Taz asked from his prone position, his face on his hands.

"Excuse me?" Wen said, and Taz sat up.

"Then what happened?" he asked.

"They took me downtown. This is the weird part: Some lady detective," and he reached into his pocket to take out her card, "came to talk to me after they made me wait for a hell of a long time." Andrei reached for the card and turned it over, looking at it through the fluorescent hanging over the table.

"It's clean," he said, relief in his voice.

"What did she want, this..." Taz said, looking over at her card, "Mariko Ishikawa?"

"She wanted to offer me some sort of deal. She wanted me to help the cops out or something, or else they would throw me in jail," he said.

"What did you say? You aren't in jail, so you took the deal then?" Taz inquired.

"No, I told her off. I told her I would never help the bastards who left me high and dry when I needed their help the most."

"You what?" Taz said, an eyebrow lifting.

"I told her to fuck off, Taz. Jeez, chill man," Wen said, offended.

Taz bit his lower lip and said, "You moron! What if she could have helped us take care of our problem? Did you think about that?" Taz said, his voice rising slightly.

"Do you think it would have made a difference if Wen had helped the cops out? They're not the most reliable bunch in town you know," Andrei said, looking at Taz.

"Taz, I did what I thought was right; whose side are you on, anyway?" Wen said.

"I am on *my* side, Wen. I am on the side that needs to find a solution to every single one of *your* fuckups, Wen. I am on the side that had to deal with the fact that you can't handle the simplest of tasks, *Wen*. I need to think," Taz said, cupping his face in both his hands, drawing out a long sigh.

"What is the matter with…"

"*Shut. Up*," Taz bellowed, getting up, revealing a red face from behind his hands, slamming them on the table. He massaged his forehead with the tips of his fingers, gritting his teeth. Wen stared outside the dirty window without a word. Andrei looked at Taz with a curious stare, but he too stayed quiet. The whole café was silent, the old ladies glancing surreptitiously at Taz from the safety of their booths.

Taz turned back and said, "Mind your own business," and white heads slipped back into their alcoves. He sat back down, clasping his hands together.

"All right. Here's what we're going to do," Taz said, tapping his index fingers on the edge of the table. "Wen goes into DaiSin Corporation. He tells them we have what they want. They have to call off the hounds or we release whatever info was on that diamond in a very public manner."

"Wait, why the hell do I have to go in?" Wen said, recovering from his initial shock.

"Because you've *been* there. You *know* the place. *Your brother* is the one they have. Why must you question everything? Don't you *want* to help your brother, Wen? Isn't he *worth* something to you? Frankly, I'm getting sick of your shit. Will you do it or will we have to run for our lives for the rest of our days? Make up your mind, Wen," Taz said, looking at his friend squarely in the face.

"I'll…I'll do it," Wen said, ashamed to have doubted his own resolve for even a second.

"Good. That's my boy," Taz said, grinning. "Remember, you have all the power. As long as we hold on to those files, they have to let him go. You will tell them they have twenty-four hours. If in that time you and your brother aren't released, and the chase for us isn't over and done with, the files become public domain. When you get out with Sammy, we'll tell them where to find them."

"I don't know if…" Andrei said, doubtful.

"Andrei, please, trust me! What other choice do we have, really? Everything will be fine, you'll see," Taz said, giving him a wink.

Good luck with your troubles, Wen thought.

He rented a capsule hotel room under a fake name, cash payment. The orange, coffin-sized room felt like a suitable facsimile of a final resting place, and he thought he should look forward to his imminent funeral. He'd look great, he thought, in a nice suit or perhaps Taz's purloined clothes. They would slide his body into the incinerator, same size as the tiny space he lay in now, and turn on the flames of hell. He felt a shiver zigzag up and down his spine. He wasn't dead yet. Going in unarmed to blackmail one of the biggest and most heavily guarded corporations in the world did not *guarantee* a one-way ticket to a small funerary urn, but the odds were not in his favor, clearly.

I really ought to have more confidence, he thought. At least now there was a clear target: an enormous, immovable rock of a target. He took a deep breath and let it out in spurts, lying on his back on the egg-container shaped temperfoam mattress. He slid the single thin sheet over his shoulder. There was so much riding on his success. His stomach was knotted, twisted, and sick. Alone to face down a giant. *I've been here before,* he thought. *It's been so long it feels like another life. I am in control of my own destiny now. I choose to do this. No one else can do it for me.* He felt better at the thoughts, and repeated them until he fell asleep.

⅄ ⅄ ⅄

The dream was always the same. He knew it was the dream because the scenes always cut and jumped. He experienced it both as himself and as an observer, but never to change anything, always watching. One moment he was in the Japanese Immigration Processing Center with his pregnant mother. A kind lady in a navy blue uniform behind a desk would speak to his mother in Japanese. He did not understand. The dream skipped to the next scene, and every one would flash by at incredible speeds, each a memory he could not express in his waking state.

He was in the Hospital Holding Compound, with his mother, in a one-bedroom suite. He read a book on the sunlit bed, back against the wall. A man in a suit came to visit his mother and spoke to her for a long time. When he left, his mother said that she had been offered a job. They had been "sponsored."

"What does that mean?" Wen asked.

"We're going up in the world," his mother said with a smile. He looked up at the light from the window and the scene tilted.

Sammy was in the bassinet in the living room, being looked after by the live-in nanny. Wen liked her. She had dark skin that complemented her smoky eyes. Her lips were always pink and sparkling. He liked this apartment, with his own bedroom, a closet, a bed, and toys.

He felt good, cocooned in undular architecture of seafoam-white; thick carpeting warming his feet, plush between his naked toes. On the balcony now, he peered down at the tiny people on the street. When they looked up, he would wave back from the top of the world. From here he could see the peaks of the city swimming among the clouds. As hard as he tried, he could never manage to see the bottom from whence he had been plucked. But it didn't matter. He would never have to go back there again.

He asked his mother about the bumps on the back of her neck and she would tell him all that she was permitted to. He pouted and wanted them implanted *now*.

"You have to wait until your body is ready, Wen," she said. "Don't be so impatient. You'll get yours soon enough," she said in her sweet voice.

The procedure had to wait until he turned eighteen, chemical and biological changes potentially disruptive to the process. This was the most anxiety-ridden time for him. He remembered how he would constantly pester and ask his mother what it felt like to be a permanent connector of the Web.

"Like a soft blanket," she would say, caressing his cheek with the palm of her hand, and he would envy her even more. Wen wished she would tell him more, but she always said it was a secret. She merged with the furniture, and everything shifted.

He was doing his homework on the balcony, at night. The dazzling, moving lights reminded him of the fireflies that had populated the woods behind his childhood home in Guangdong Province. He would turn off the small study lamp and look out across the city in awe on those sweltering summer nights and then turn it back on and return to his work. His mother came home, and he ran inside to give her a hug. He often made supper for the two of them, since his mother always worked late. Tonight, though, she called in advance and asked him to guess what kind of takeout she was bringing home, and they both ate on the balcony. It melted away.

They shopped at the fancier department stores in the Heights, Isetan or MaruiMarui, Saks Fifth Avenue or Harrod's, people-watching for hours on end while Sammy slept in his stroller. It was Sunday, and they picnicked among the cherry trees in Ueno Park, on the 200th level. Spring was that magical time when they would all bloom spontaneously into the most incredible display of pure white petals and yellow stamens, as far as could be seen. Not everything was candy and video games, as life seldom is, but it was *better*. Better was a long way from easy, except whatever wasn't easy was acceptable and survivable. Ueno and the cherry blossoms drifted.

It was *that* November day, Wen waiting for his mother, the chill air outside preventing his usual admiration of the city at night. It was already much later than his mother's usual arrival time. He called her several times, letting the Netware ring forever each time, only getting the android voice-message box for his trouble. Sammy slept in their shared room, no longer a baby but a four-year-old boy; no use in waking him. Homework done, he watched the holovid—crime stories and terrible news from around the world, game shows and talk shows, history and mystery—flick, flick,

flick, flicking from one channel to the next. He fidgeted on the plush sofa, jumping at every noise from the hallway, expecting her to pop in the door looking distraught and apologetic. She would say, "I'm so sorry, honey! I got caught up at work! Some big project I had to finish tonight on a deadline!"

Then he would say, "It's OK, Mom; I'm happy you're home!" as nonchalantly as any seventeen-year-old could.

He sat on the couch, flicking the channels with his hand, repeating to himself, "It's OK, Mom; I'm happy you're home!" He practiced it out loud until he thought he had removed all traces of worry from his voice.

He would wake up the next morning when his brother gently tapped him on the leg. He looked around and saw that he was still on the couch, the holovid gone into sleep mode, but turning back on as soon as Sammy had stepped in front of the sensors. The outside windows had darkened a bit to stop the full brunt of the morning sun from penetrating their home.

"Where's mommy?" Sammy asked, rubbing his eyes.

"She's at work, Sammy." He always lied, in his dream. His stomach knotted with worry now that he was awake and realized that their mother had still not returned.

"Why are you sleeping on the sofa?" he asked.

"I watched too much TV!" he answered, making a face.

"You're silly," Sammy said.

"Yes, I am." Wen would nod gravely, which made Sammy giggle. He got up and led his little brother back to their room and picked out his morning's clothes. Sammy was old enough to dress himself, but his taste in mismatched clothing, when left to his own devices, made Wen wonder if he was cross-eyed or just color-blind. While he was putting on his clothes, Wen prepared breakfast.

Sammy ate while making little animal sounds between every bite. Wen bit his tongue. He took his brother to the daycare center twenty floors below and several blocks away. As Wen kissed his red cheek in the chilly November air, Sammy said, looking at the ground, "I wanted to tell Mommy my dream this morning, but I forgot it now."

"It's OK; you can tell her later when you remember."

Kids in colorful jackets and mitts played in the yard beyond the gate, and a teacher waited for him at the door.

"I'll see you later, OK?" Wen said, roughing up his brother's hair as he twisted away from him to avoid the tousling.

"OK!" Sammy said, smiling, and he hopped on the terracotta tiles that led to the entrance of the daycare, avoiding stepping on the cracks. The daycare vanished.

He was headed straight for his mother's work. From afar, it looked like an impossibly long, slender blade slashing the sky. It was curious then, that it had been given the nickname of The Needle. He went through the revolving glass doors and headed to the wide, charcoal-colored security desk on the 200th level. Workers wearing suits in varying shades of grim streamed in, scanning their forearms before being let in through turnstiles.

"Wen Harkwell to see Min Chen," he declared without emotion. The guard behind the desk looked at him once and then to his computer monitor, pressed a button, and looked at him once again.

"She left already. Last night," the guard said evenly, peering over the desk.

"There...there must be some mistake. Are you sure? Can you check again?" Wen said, trying to look over the counter at the monitor before the guard. The guard lifted an eyebrow and tapped at his keyboard again.

"Yup, she left last night...around 9:30 p.m. What's this about, anyway?" the guard asked.

"She never came home last night. Can I please go check her office?" Wen said, gritting his teeth.

"Sure, why not," he said, shrugging. He called over a young man in uniform from the other side of the desk.

"Can you take Mr. Harkwell here up to the 313th, to office 56, name of Min Chen?" the guard said.

"Will do. Can you follow me, please, sir?" the younger man said, waving his hand at Wen.

The turnstile scanned his arm, and he accompanied the gray-uniformed officer toward the elevators. He stared up the vertical shaft of the hollow edifice designed to awe the senses. The elevators were situated in the center of the building, two face-to face rows of six, all rising and descending in clear Glasteel tubes. Wen's heart would lurch as the elevator sped up the tube, stopping after a rapid deceleration on the 313th floor. Walking with determination, he crossed over the long bridge, not looking down at the miniature people below. He turned right at the end and scanned the numbers on the closed office doors. He knocked on 56. No answer. He knocked again. The guard swiped his keycard on the scanner, and it opened with a click. Wen grabbed the door handle and entered.

There was only absence in the darkness: the stillness, the shuttered drapes, not even her smell. He poked around the office, examining the opposite side of her desk.

Nothing.

Nothing out of the ordinary. He looked on the desk for a clue, opened the cupboards. What had he expected? His mother alive and well? A corpse? Some sort of evidence of malfeasance? A crumb of a trail, perhaps, to tell him what had happened to her? Nothing.

His shoulders slumped, and the guard led him out of the room. He shrugged him off and took the elevator ride down with resignation. He was dizzy. His eyebrows were holding back the sweat that suffused from his forehead. Some of it slipped past by angling down his nose and aimed straight for his eyes, in the curve. He wiped it away with the back of his hand. His stomach churned, a fist having taken hold of his lower intestine and twisting ever so slowly. His head thumped, thumped, thumped, thumped, each hit increasing the pressure inside his brain until he thought his mind would scream before he could. A tone sounded inside his ears, long and drawn out, like a fuse. When the doors opened on the 200th with a ping, his legs were stiff and robotic. All he could hear was his breathing and his own brain pounding black blood through acid veins. His Adam's apple rose and fell spastically, his neck becoming tighter, his breathing more difficult. He could feel himself imploding, turning in on himself. He needed release somehow.

"Where is my mother! What have you done with my mother!" he yelled, taking the guard behind him by surprise. Wen no longer questioned: he accused at the top of his lungs, screaming over and over again, wanting only to find someone out of whom to beat a confession. He was electric tension and forces unchained, his voice reverberation on the thousand facets of a prison.

Guards poured from the front and rear, wrestling him to the floor as surprised employees walked by, shaking their heads. They subdued him and took him to a holding cell, straining to get ahold of this wild animal that had wandered into their midst and turned feral for no apparent reason. There, they let him rage and rant until all they could see on the camera was a broken youth rocking back and forth on the concrete floor.

Bloodshot eyes stared at the padded steel door. Wen's thoughts disjointed and incoherent, it took him a moment to realize that another person was in front of him—three, in fact. Pinched face and heavy suit, flanked by two eager-looking guards, the man harbored a mild worried look. Wen thought he might be bothered about how to cancel a Web subscription or if it was time to euthanize an old and unloved pet. The worry on his face was one micron deep and not at all sympathetic to his plight.

"Mr. Harkwell," he said to Wen, "I'm Director Douglas Deguchi. I hear you have a problem. Why don't you tell me about it? Calmly." His voice was almost a tenor's whisper. There was a hypnotic, soothing quality to it that was pharmaceutical. He was the kind of man Wen imagined had been the soft-spoken school bully from the very first day he had stepped into kindergarten, whispering monotone threats to children he held by the jugular.

He shivered and lifted his handcuffed arms to him. The man turned his head and nodded. One of the guards came forward and put his thumb on the small green box on the handcuffs. They chirped and clicked open. The guard took them and stepped back into position. The man named Deguchi leaned in, looming over Wen as if to say *Try. Go ahead. Try something. I'm waiting.* But Wen did nothing. He looked the man straight in the eye.

"My mother never came home last night. Where is she? What have you done with her?" he reiterated, all emotion and energy drained from his body.

"We have no idea what you're talking about, Wen. As we said, your mother left last night, end of story. We'll be glad to contact the authorities and get someone on the case. Your mother is a valuable employee. We want to have her back safe and sound, just as much as you do, maybe even more so."

I seriously doubt that, he thought.

Wen felt the tension leave his body at the man's words. He rose to his feet on shaky knees and the man named Deguchi let him out of the holding cell.

The police came and took their depositions. Wen resolved to tell Sammy about their mother. It was better for him to know the truth, but at the time, there was also the hope that she would be found. He cried for days; they both did, Wen in secret, Sammy openly. The investigation dragged on for months. Wen called the police department often and always received the same reply: no news.

"There's nothing we can do," the cold voice said at the end of the line. He got tired of hearing that voice at the end of all his dreams. It sounded too much like, "There's nothing *you* can do."

Good luck with your troubles.

⋏ ⋏ ⋏

A buzz sounded on the in-house telephone. He tapped the button and grunted.

"Your wake-up call, sir," a female voice said, coming from the wall at his side.

Seven o'clock, the dream was fading, leaving a feeling of unease in its wake. Wen dragged himself out of the capsule and dressed; grateful to still have Taz's clothes, at least. Only one other customer was up at this hour; a Japanese man in white briefs and undershirt pulling on a powder blue shirt further down the row.

Either worked too late to take the last train or had one too many and missed it, he thought. The life of a Japanese salaryman was a hard one, twelve hour days and practically no breaks. Wen had a deep respect for those who kept the machine of state in working order. He half bowed to Wen as he noticed him, while he pulled on his black dress pants. Wen walked out of the blank-faced wall of the capsule hotel fifteen minutes later. A black circle on the wall served as both entrance and calling card; perfection in minimalism.

A humid frost shrieked across his bones, making the already difficult trek a painful one. The streets were only beginning to wake, a smattering of workers headed for their daily commute. Shuttered shops displayed the territorial markings of rival gangs, scribbled graffiti the glyphs of an incomprehensible secret language. It felt like the death-row ghost walk, where the only certain point was death, but the tiny worm of hope in his mind was that light at the end of the tunnel, the one everyone said was there but no one had ever seen.

Andrei and Taz are in hiding right now, he thought. *Somewhere safe and warm.* He clapped his arms with his frozen fingers, his meager sweater no match for the weather. Breath plumed in the still morning, the tips of his ears and nose reddening.

In the distance, on the other side of a wide bridge, rose the DaiSin Building.

The Needle.

Employees streamed in one by one. Three guards stood outside, wearing the gray uniforms of the DaiSin Security Apparatus. Black epaulettes harbored the DaiSin logo, just like the uniforms in Oscar's closet. Wen's body warmed as he spotted them. He no longer felt the shred of the wind or the frost on his cheeks. He burned. The pavement was like a raging sea, uneven and swaying, but he walked on, determined and ready.

I do not fear. His heart raged in his breast, threatening to explode with hate.

I do not fear. His hands clenched reflexively, and he felt as if he was floating above his own head.

I do not fear. The guards saw him crossing the bridge, their eyes widening. One of them touched his ear and talked without making a sound. He neared the steps that led up to the row of glass doors. The beating of his own heart sang in all parts of his body like a choir. He walked up the steps deliberately, staring down the guards.

"I'm here. Take me in," he ordered them. They looked confused and searched around behind him and then guided him eagerly inside, Wen barely registering the soft click of the shutting door, like the padded whisper of a bank vault sealing shut.

They escorted him with the same respect and disdain they would have for a foreign dignitary from a despotic yet resource-rich neighboring country, to a room only slightly bigger than the interrogation room in which the police had held him the day before, glossy white-painted cinder block walls and no prying cameras he could tell of. It smelled of disinfectant and industrial-grade carpeting. He stood by a black board-room chair, clenching his hands behind his back and staring at the door with disciplined anticipation. He controlled his breathing as much as he could. Whenever his heart, like a rebelling dog on a leash, tried to get away from him, he would yank it back into line. The gray metal door before him was doing something grating at the moment: it was not budging. He wanted to pound on it for someone to come, but that would have shown weakness.

He was in control.

Had to be.

Was.

He was in control. Always. He had to remain in control until the parlay was at an end and he left with everything he came for. That was it, no compromises.

After a million years had passed, there was a knock at the door, and he heard a voice say, "Enter." It was deep and far away and did not sound like his own at all.

The large man walked in, and Wen tried to stifle a look of surprise.

"Mr. Wen Harkwell. What a surprise. We've been looking all over for you," said Mr. Douglas Deguchi in his inimitably deep timbre. The years had only managed to make the man look more powerful. His hair had turned salt and pepper, but otherwise, he retained the quiet intensity he had cultivated like a poisonous garden.

"What are you doing here?" Wen asked.

"I work here, Wen. They thought it might do you some good to see a friendly face. I'm close to retirement now, but I do a bit of training for the company." His soft voice still hid strong undercurrents, the outline of his massive hands visible through the fabric of his gray suit-pants pockets.

"What have you done with Sammy?" Wen asked.

"He's around," Deguchi said.

"What do you want with my brother?" he asked.

"Oh, I don't want anything, Wen. He's someone's safeguard, I believe," he said, un-sheathing the monstrous appendages and rubbing his palms slowly, like milling stones.

"You have to return him to me," Wen said.

"Or what?" Mr. Deguchi said, sounding bored.

"The files go public," he said.

"Now we're getting somewhere. Do you know what those files are?" Mr. Deguchi asked, smiling, something venomous staring at Wen in the slantwise edge of his gaze.

"We'll find out soon enough," Wen said, but his voice sounded hollow.

"Oh, sure you will. I bet you have the encryption key necessary to crack the code, don't you?" Mr. Deguchi said.

"Listen, do you want it back or not?" Wen asked, growing impatient.

"Of course we do, Wen, but that won't take long. You see, we know where your friends are," he said, the corner of his mouth lifting in a not-quite-smile.

"You're lying," Wen said, with slitted eyes.

"Am I?" Mr. Deguchi said, uncaring. "Why did you kill Oscar? He was up for vacation after this assignment."

"I didn't kill him. We don't know who did," Wen said. Deguchi observed Wen for a moment, nodded.

Wen pointed at Deguchi, smiling: "You have twenty-four hours to let my brother go and give up any attempts on our lives, or those files get sent out to the world," he said.

"You know, blackmail only works if you hold on to parts of the incriminating evidence, or else it's worthless. Let's say you do somehow get it out there. What will stop DaiSin from killing you afterward? Hadn't thought about that, had you? Don't worry; it won't go that far. In twenty-four hours, I will come back and you will tell us the things we want to hear. I'll even offer you a more comfy guest room until then. See, we're not monsters here," he said with a pinched smile and turned toward the door.

Wen's smile wavered. "You have twenty-four hours; don't waste them," he said feebly, his stomach constricting.

"All righty then," Mr. Deguchi said with an implied chuckle while exiting without looking back, leaving Wen with the agonizing feeling that all had gone awry once again.

A few moments later, a guard came to escort him to another room down the corridor. What surprised Wen most was the shear amount of guards they encountered in the short span of steps it took to transfer him. This room was larger, just as windowless, and had a black pleather sofa on the far wall. They had confiscated his backpack and Netware; he was cut off from the outside world. He sat on the stiff sofa, staring at the industrial carpeting between his legs.

Please be bluffing, he thought. *Please be the lying sack you so obviously are. Andrei and Taz are too smart to get caught. In twenty-four hours, we'll both be out of here and have the last laugh. They can't do shit to us, unless...*He killed his doubts as quickly as they bubbled to the surface. He stared a hole into the floor, the walls, the ceiling, wondering in what part of the immense monolith his brother was being sequestered. He took an unsteady breath and mentally screamed, gritting his teeth and clasping the sofa cushions. He released the cushions and lay his head back, eyes closed, letting out a shudder.

On a low coffee table in front of the sofa lay a slim remote control. He picked it up and pressed the red button in the upper corner. A sliding panel opened on the table to reveal a flat inlaid keyboard with metal keys. A retractable screen lowered from the ceiling on the other side of the room, while a projector lowered from above his head and turned on. He went to the wall and lowered the lights. His heart beat faster when he noticed DaiSin Corporation's homepage loaded on the screen.

Boom! I'm out, he thought. He typed in a search query, and it came up, pretty as you please. *This is too easy*, he thought, trying to access one of his fake public mail boxes, but his request was denied. *So much for that*, he thought. There was at least the possibility of searching for whatever he might need; but he was barred from sending anything. Caution was of the essence, of course. Nothing incriminating could be entered. Someone was watching his every keystroke, waiting for him to make a mistake. The hours were wasted away looking at old movies and gossip sites, slouched on the sofa.

A while later, a guard entered the room and put a tray of delicious food on the table. He jumped on it as soon as the man left, devouring every last morsel. He lay down on the hard sofa after his meal and attempted sleep.

The clock on the screen told him that he had sixteen hours to wait. Eight hours had slipped by in total. There was nothing to do but twiddle his thumbs, sleep, or cruise the Net. That was the most awful part, the wait. He would rather have been chased by bears than to have to stay confined another minute in this tiny cubicle, fixated on the grains of sand slipping through the hourglass like molasses. He could pace, but that would solve nothing and make him look weak; that, he was against. He played a game of chicken with the thought that he was royally screwed but kept swerving away just before ramming into it. *Be careful; thinking bad thoughts attracts bad things*, he considered and then laughed out loud for thinking such nonsense. He clamped a hand over his mouth. *It's not like anything worse could happen just because I think it.* He returned his attention to the screen, watching show after show, movie after movie, page after page, and never quite being able to alleviate his boredom but dulling his mind enough that it just didn't matter anymore.

The hours stretched on, and someone brought him another meal. He took his time and savored every bite this time, and he fell asleep on the sofa again.

He woke up in the dark feeling grungy in his wrinkled clothes. The clock on the computer said it was past nine o'clock in the morning, and he jumped on the Net.

There were several sites that would make a big fuss about such a file dump, encryption or no.

There was a knock on the door, and Mr. Deguchi entered. He flicked the lights on. "You've lost your bet, Wen. There's nothing out there. You can guess what that means, can't you? Don't be so surprised; it's not like I didn't tell you the outcome," he said. He was right. There was nothing on the site about a strange file being uploaded in the past hour. Wen's heart sank. He checked another and another until he knew for a fact that nothing was there. Now Taz and Andrei were in DaiSin's custody. He lost his bet with the dark thoughts, and they came careening into his conscious mind, crashing in fiery explosions with no way to stop the burn. No way out. Done for. *Fini.*

"Now, let us get down to business. We don't want to kill you, Wen; that would be a great waste of potential. We have a job waiting for you, if you'll take it," Mr. Deguchi said. Wen's eyebrow lifted.

"What if I refuse?" Wen said, crossing his arms.

"That's entirely your prerogative. You will, however, end up a small trash fire in the Heap, along with your brother and any of your associates who refuse this simple offer," Mr. Deguchi said offhandedly.

"You don't give me much choice." Wen blanched.

"Well, we certainly can't leave you running around being a nuisance, can we?" Deguchi said, winking at him.

"How long do I get to decide?" he said, his lips becoming taut.

"Sixty seconds. Do you feel suicidal or sociopathic?" Mr. Deguchi said.

"No, of course not!" Wen answered.

"Then that narrows it down considerably for you, doesn't it? You are lucky those files weren't released. The conversation we'd be having right now would be quite different. Thank your friend's incompetence for that. Sixty seconds are up. Who goes first?" Mr. Deguchi said.

"Ah, *dammit*, no one! I'll do it on one condition," he said, feeling as if he were taunting the firing squad.

"Which would be?" Mr. Deguchi said, taking a pad of paper out from behind him.

"I get to see my brother," Wen said. Mr. Deguchi paused, his focus a point beyond Wen's forehead and then came back. Wen could feel something along his spine stiffening, becoming taut.

"Granted," Mr. Deguchi said, putting on the kind of smile Wen would have loved to wipe off with a twelve-gauge shotgun.

CHAPTER 6

I know the way forward. I can take you there,
but only if you are strong enough to obey me,
every step of the way.

—Nabeen Singh

EGUCHI PUT A legal pad in front of Wen and handed him a pen.
"Just put your initials here, here, here, and here," Deguchi said, marking Xs on
four pages of the thick document. "And I need your signature...here," he said,
after turning to the last page.

"What's this?" Wen asked, as he read the document's legalese.

"Standard contract. You will not hold DaiSin liable for any mishap, whether inten-
tional or accidental, which might result in your amputation, lobotomization, or demise. There's a nondisclosure agreement as well; no discussing your past with anyone,
and, no discussing with anyone outside the company what it is you might do here.
There's much more, of course, but that's the gist of it."

"That's ridiculous!" Wen said, thumbing through the pages.

Deguchi leaned in close to Wen's face. "I guess you still don't understand that this
is your last and only chance." Wen took the pen, tight-lipped, and scribbled his initials
near the Xs, signing his name so hard at the end that the plastic pen snapped, spilling
red ink at the bottom of the page.

"That's OK; I've got others," Deguchi said, smiling.

"Did my mother have to sign this crap?" Wen said, slapping the contract with the back of his hand.

"Of course she did! Every employee has to. I did. I'm glad I did. You will be too. Welcome to your new home," Deguchi said.

No, never, not on your life, you solder-sucking ass-monkey, Wen thought. "Thanks," he said. "Now that that's been twisted out of me, where's my brother?"

"Not so fast, bucko," Deguchi said, putting the contract away. "We have a ton of things to do before that."

"I distinctly remember being promised to see my brother. Are you reneging on that promise already?" Wen said, his face turning red.

"We did promise that. We never said *when* you'd get to see him, though, did we? Always read the fine print," Deguchi said, his finger in the air.

I am going to kill you very, very slowly, Wen thought. "I see," he said, his stiff neck cramping up, a twitch developing in his hand. The stiffness along his spine was making his brain begin to hurt. It felt like he was being pulled like a bowstring to the breaking point.

"Lighten up; enjoy it. You're part of a big family now. Let's go meet the other members, shall we?" Deguchi said.

I'll start with the bottom and work my way up, and then I'll take off the head. I'll keep that for last, he thought, sizing up Deguchi.

"Yeah, *let's*; it'll be a *ball*," Wen said.

"There's still time to change your mind, you know. Give me the word and someone gets the Oscar treatment. Adjust your attitude a bit," Deguchi said with a soft, menacing voice, looking straight into Wen. He did not reply but clenched his teeth, hard.

They walked out into the corridor, no guards escorting them yet surrounded by them. Men and women in white lab coats carried small metal boxes and sometimes stopped to slip them into what appeared to be niches in the walls. Deguchi pinned a temporary "Initiate" pass on his lapel with an alligator clip. They went a few floors higher and came to the double doors of an auditorium, where fifty or sixty young men and women milled around a table at the large reception area in the hallway. All wore the initiate tag, some had a "Hello, my name is" sticker on the opposite side of their tag. A few seemed to know each other, but the majority acted sheepish and out of sorts.

Deguchi walked Wen to the table and got him a pamphlet and sticker, which Wen filled out and affixed to his sweater. Deguchi wandered off to speak to some of the other attendees. As Wen's gaze wandered around the throng, he saw him. Sayeed stood stiffly amongst the youths that seemed out of their depths. He peered about, shifting from one foot to the other, and then he caught sight of Wen and made a bee-line toward him.

"When did you get here?" Sayeed asked, wide-eyed.

"I walked in yesterday," he said.

"They broke into my house! Can you believe that shit! I'm not even supposed to talk about it either! They made me sign a *contract*! Screw 'em," Sayeed said in a harsh whisper, one fist clenched, punctuating his words.

"You probably shouldn't talk to me about it either," Wen said, peering around.

"What is this about, Wen? Why am I here?" Sayeed asked.

"I can't talk about it!" he whispered, leaning in close.

"Does this have anything to do with the scrounging? Where are the others?" Sayeed asked, searching the area for hypothetical crew members.

"I'll tell you later; not now, OK?" Wen said and began to walk away. Sayeed caught his arm and spun him around.

"You better not hide anything from me!" He gripped his arm tight; Wen twisted away. Others stared at them, whispering to each other, and Sayeed let Wen go without another word.

"Alright everybody, inside please!" Deguchi said, his arms raised. The auditorium was equipped to receive five hundred people, on four different rows, and the group looked small and scattered in that vast open space. Wen picked a spot toward the back, Sayeed going to the front. Deguchi sauntered down the stairs and to the stage, where he stood at a podium.

"Ahem. Can everybody hear me? Good. First off, I'd like to thank and congratulate all of you for volunteering for this program. It has produced some of the best and brightest lights the world has seen; I kid you not. My name is Douglas Deguchi. I am one of the senior program managers at DaiSin. If you are selected, some of you will be working under me."

Crap, thought Wen, *hope I fly under the radar*. He crossed his fingers and closed his eyes briefly.

"I'd like to introduce you to our head of security. This is Mauritius Lewes," he said, extending his arm as a tall man walked onto the stage. Wen leaned forward. It couldn't be. He looked like…no, he *was* Oscar's husband: M. Lewes.

Crap, crap! he thought, sliding down in his chair so he could disappear underneath.

Mauritius Lewes cleared his throat. "Thank you, Mr. Deguchi. I'd like to remind everyone of some simple procedural rules. Until you graduate, you *must* confine yourselves to your quarters after curfew for security reasons. We wouldn't want any of you to wander where you are not supposed to." He stared everyone in the eyes, making sure that all had understood. Some people were joking around and looked as if his words hadn't even been heard. He saw Wen, and his eyes narrowed.

His brow furrowed, and he said in a booming voice, "Some of you may be tempted to test this rule. I repeat: for *your* safety, do not wander out of your quarters after curfew. *Is that clear?*" The attendees ducked as if they had heard gunshots. This time, all eyes were on him, and heads nodded, slack-jawed.

"Good, I'm glad we understand each other. Also, do not attempt to use the elevators to go to restricted floors. Your present clearance is for floors 150 to 170; *that's it.* Apart from that, you can come to me during the day if you have any questions or problems. The Security Floor is located on the 150th. Thank you." He stepped down from the podium, and Deguchi took his place.

"Always nice to get the important things out of the way first, don't you think?" He smiled, giving Lewes mild applause. "A few things about DaiSin: it is one of the largest corporations in the world. It has 1.2 million employees in sixteen countries. We are the top supplier of Net technology. It is one of the only family-owned firms that can still trace back its ancestry to its founders. The present CEO is Nabeen Singh. We pride ourselves in using biodegradable and recyclable materials wherever we can in our products. Any questions?" Deguchi asked, and a hand went up on Wen's left.

"Yes, you, with the blond hair," said Deguchi, pointing.

"What happened to the Daiko half of DaiSin?" a young woman asked.

"You might have known if you had simply looked it up on the Net, miss. The Singh family bought out the Daiko stock 150 years ago, consolidating its assets. Any more questions? Yes, you, with the sweater."

"What is the rate of retention at DaiSin?" a man asked.

"We have between fifty and two hundred applicants worldwide every single day. We can only hire five to ten percent of those."

He avoided the question, Wen thought. *How many of your employees disappear without a trace?* He wanted to ask. Deguchi pointed to a person at the back.

"What kind of expertise are we expected to bring to the company?"

"Most of you are programmers. That's a good starting point. There are qualities we need from you that you didn't learn in school: aggression, intelligence, will power, but above all, loyalty. These will make or break your futures here. You." To someone sitting in front of Wen. He didn't hear what she said.

"Good question. You will be implanted tomorrow, if all goes well."

We'll what? Wen thought.

"All right, let's break for lunch. I'm sure you're all famished. I know I am. If you have any more questions, come and see me after lunch."

Sayeed waited for him behind the door of the cafeteria.

"Hey there, buddy," he said, teeth clenched.

"What do you want?" Wen said, ducking his head.

"You are going to help me escape, tonight. The way I see it, you got me into this mess; you and the other guys," Sayeed said, putting his arm around Wen's shoulder and gripping his arm.

"How the hell is this my fault?" Wen asked, staring into his eyes.

"I never signed up to be kidnapped and put into slavery! Weren't you listening? They're going to put *implants* in us! I'm getting out of here, and you're coming with me," Sayeed whispered as they walked toward the food line.

"Neither did I! Why should I go with you?" Wen said, trying to shake him off.

"Don't even try! Taz told me; you know this place better than anyone. You'll take me out of here, and that's final," Sayeed said, squeezing harder.

"There's no way! I can't go! I don't even…" Wen said, but Sayeed had let go and was walking away. Wen looked around for the nearest wall to bash his own skull in but resisted temptation. He slouched to the lunch counter and slammed a tray on the railing. He picked up a sandwich and plopped it on the tray, grabbed a juice box and threw it next to the sandwich. He clasped the railing for a moment and stared at the ceiling. Then he made his way to a table, where he dropped the tray and let himself fall into the chair. He ripped open the wrapper and stuffed the sandwich in his face and then guzzled the juice, crushing the empty box when he was done.

The babble of happy voices around him grated on his nerves. Didn't they know it was a trap? What could possibly make these unconscious idiots so joyful? He went back to the auditorium with his head buzzing. He only heard the rest of the afternoon's speech as background noise while he lay his head on the desk before him.

They were quartered in dorms with three bunk beds. Each dorm had an attached bathroom, and on the opposite side, the door to the hallway. Wen lay in his bunk, staring at the unlocked door. Sayeed was in the room next door; Wen had seen him go in before curfew. He had looked hard at Wen before going in. He sighed and stared at the bunk above him. It just got worse and worse, he thought.

Around nine o'clock, the door opened, spilling hallway light into the room. Sayeed tiptoed inside, followed by someone else. Wen pretended to sleep, but Sayeed found him and shook him.

"Let's go," he whispered.

"No, you idiot, they'll kill us!" Wen retorted.

"If you don't come right now, I'm sounding the alarm and telling them you were the instigator, asshole." He grabbed Wen's ear and pulled. Wen fell out of bed and got up, swearing under his breath.

"Who's this?" he said, looking at the other guy following them.

"Another malcontent. I promised to get him out of here as well."

"You're a *moron*," Wen whispered loudly.

"Lead the way," Sayeed said, pushing Wen to the fore. Wen looked left and then right, down the corridors. He took a step in one direction, changed his mind, and crept in the other. They snuck around corners, sticking to the walls, peering around edges, their senses on high alert. All corridors looked the same, every door identical.

"Stop right there or I'll shoot!" came a voice from behind them.

Ah!, thought Wen, ducking his head between his shoulders. They froze.

"Hands up where I can see them. Good. Faces against the wall. I said, faces against the wall, *now!*" A strong hand grabbed his arm and whipped him away from the wall. He heard steps running down the hallway, and they were surrounded by six guards. Wen was grabbed by two of them and dragged to the lower floors. They were all thrown into the same interrogation room. Wen slumped into one of the three metal chairs behind a table.

Mauritius Lewes walked into the room, glowering.

"Sit down," he barked. The other two scrambled for a seat. Wen rolled his eyes and then rubbed his face, frowning.

"It was his idea!" Sayeed said, pointing at Wen. Wen put his forehead against the cold table, letting out a weak grunt.

"I don't care who instigated. We're going to play a game," Lewes said, staring each of them down. Wen lifted his head from the table, cocking it to the side.

Lewes stared at them and said, "I am going to put my gun on the table. I will count to three. On three, the first person to pick it up and shoot me gets to go free. It's that simple." The trio glanced at each other in turn.

Mauritius Lewes unclipped his gun and placed it in the center of the table, pointing it toward himself. Sayeed licked his lips, and Wen crisscrossed his fingers before him on the table, his face impassive.

Lewes raised his hand, lifting a finger for each number: "One, two…"

Sayeed reached for it at the same time as the other escapee. Lewes' finger was already in the trigger guard. He spun the gun, pulling the trigger twice.

Wen jerked twice, wincing and closing his eyes, raising his arms in a feeble attempt to protect himself. He opened them when he realized he was still alive.

Wen stared in horror at the two men, chest wounds spurting blood onto their white pajamas. They both gurgled, clutching at their chests and looking horrified at the blood gushing out.

Lewes picked up the gun in slow motion, aimed it at each of their heads.

BAM! BAM! Sayeed and his accomplice jerked back in their chairs, heads rocking back.

Wen sat transfixed, gripping the table, wide-eyed. Lewes looked into the upper corner of the room, where a camera was affixed. He nodded his head, and the red light that had been blinking turned off.

"What happens to me?" Wen asked, rigid with fear.

"Do you plan on running away?" Lewes asked, emotionless, holstering his gun.

"No," Wen said.

"Then you will go back to your room," he said, putting his hands together.

"Why did you let me live?" he asked, looking straight at Lewes.

"You did me a favor. Don't take my act of kindness for weakness; it's not."

After you just shot two people in the face? I would never do that, thought Wen.

"Get up," Lewes ordered. Wen rose, holding the table to steady himself. He avoided looking at the dead men.

One of the other guards escorted Wen back to his room. He slipped into his covers and relived the experience over and over. Death had come knocking that night, and he had been ready to accept it; it seemed there was nothing else to do at the time. He had been wrong, of course. Could he chalk it up to sheer luck? Not entirely. A tug-of-war formed in his mind, two opposite thoughts competing for dominance:

I could have died!

I didn't!

One hopeful, the other dreadful, both tearing him apart for loyalty, keeping him awake, sleep always slipping away as one or the other resurfaced, until he passed out from exhaustion.

The next day, he had breakfast in the cafeteria. The handle of a coffee cup lay at the tips of his fingers. No one noticed Sayeed's or the other man's absence. The usual euphoria blanketed the room, young men and women chatting in smiles and laughter, expectant of their coming transformations but otherwise unconcerned.

It's like they're blind, he thought, grim-faced, dark circles under his eyes. *We're a herd of cows on the way to the slaughterhouse, and all they can think is, Oh what fun, a truck ride!* He grinned at the irony.

After breakfast, they were sent to the infirmary, where he stood in line with the other initiates. One by one they were scanned and x-rayed. A shrill alarm sounded as Wen went through.

"Have you ever worked in the Recyclers' Unit for Administration?" asked the technician, inspecting his screen.

"No, why?" he asked.

"You have the same model of GPS tag implanted in your shoulder. It's giving off strong signals," he said. "No matter, we'll remove it." He waved Wen away.

Vaccine, huh? That's why they didn't try any harder to convince me, he thought.

Everyone was brought into what looked like a classroom for medical students, complete with worn body charts on the walls, and a complete skeleton off in the corner. Orange plastic chairs were arranged in rows in front of a white screen.

"Good morning, everyone," a balding man in a white lab coat and thick black-rimmed glasses said from the front of the class. "My name is Dr. Howard Merkle. I'm here to explain the process to you." He waved his hand at the screen and a cross-section of a human head appeared. From a desk in front of him, he picked up a long needle with a circular, flat end and a chipped end.

"This is a Net 'trode," he said, holding up the object, and then he pointed a laser at the rear of the head on the screen. "It is inserted here, into the upper spinal cord, on either side. It connects to the brain stem. The operation is harmless and painless. It will take you roughly a day to recuperate. This," he said, holding up a tiny jewel, "is your crystal memory chip. It will record all experiences and memories you have. It is implanted along with the Netrode set. Any questions?"

"How often will we have to change the crystal thingy?" one woman asked.

"The crystal memory chip will record for over one hundred years and then will need to be replaced. You won't have to worry much about that," he said, and a few initiates chuckled.

"Can we access it directly?" a man asked.

"Yes. You may access all your memories instantaneously. It works better than your actual memory; more vivid, more precise."

"What are the downsides?" Wen asked.

The doctor paused.

"There are no downsides that we know of. It's a proven technology; all the kinks and bugs have been taken out of them as far as we know," he said. "Any more questions? No? All right, please step into the next room and change. We will begin shortly." Wen got up and shuffled glumly, following the excited group. Like them, he had anticipated this moment most of his youth. It hovered like a curse now. The 'trodes would be a new set of chains on his back, he thought; a method of control, not of liberation. There was nothing he could do about it. He was handed a white hospital robe and directed to a cubicle, where he put it on.

He was handed a folder and told to wait down the hall near operating room J. He sauntered down the corridor, voices chatting and laughing around him. The other initiates sat in groups of five along the corridor, called by name and brought into operating rooms by blue-clad nurses wearing masks and hairnets. Wen kept an eye on the letters above the doors until he got to his. He sat next to a cheerful youth, eighteen years old by the acne, who kept looking up every time the door opened.

"Pretty exciting, huh?" he said, turning to Wen.

"Oh...yeah," he answered, not looking at him.

"What's wrong? Chance of a lifetime, if you ask me!" he said.

I didn't ask you. Wen thought.

"Getting Netted today. Wow. Been waiting forever!" he said to no one in particular. Wen stared straight ahead at a bulletin board covered in notices and health warnings.

The hours progressed, and he bumped up to the first seat in the queue. There were few people left in the corridor.

"Wen Harkwell."

"Yup," he answered, getting up. He was led to a bed covered in a disposable paper sheet where he was made to lay on his stomach, his face through a hole, the sheet crinkling as he did. They pulled straps across his back, clicking them in place. The bed rose headfirst to a forty-five degree angle.

"Are you comfortable, Mr. Harkwell?" a man asked from behind his mask.

"I'll live," he answered.

I hope.

A nurse placed a mask over his mouth and asked him to count out loud to twenty. He made it to fifteen.

⋏ ⋏ ⋏

The hard June sun seared the vast, mostly empty parking lot in Shenzhen's Wholesale Mall. The humongous derelict building barely stood, like a man waiting to die, wracked by leprosy. A few foreigners walked in, their three children in tow. The vast majority of stores stood as empty as the cavities behind pulled teeth, the factories they represented gone out of business; China's economy was in freefall.

Eight-year-old Wen, sitting beside his dad in their eggplant-colored Geely Family Wagon, the air conditioning at full blast to repel the intense summer heat. They both wore Net glasses, plugged into their handheld Netware. They leeched the mall's Wi-Fi through a series of dummy fronts.

"Careful, that's a trigger," his father said, pointing to an unguarded ISP address. The Defense Ministries' barriers were rock solid, but Wen's father knew the ins and outs better than anyone.

"What are we doing, Papa?" asked Wen, looking over at this father.

"We're helping our friends," his father answered as they plunged into the Ministry archives.

"Is it OK to be here?" he asked, corrupting the defenses.

"It depends on who you ask," his father said, manipulating the databases.

"Won't the government people be angry?"

"Yes, very much so," his father said. "Cut and copy this list into your drive, Wen. I have to look for some other files. Sometimes you have to do things people don't like if they're not doing what they're supposed to."

"Are they evil?" Wen asked, thinking about his cartoon heroes and their nemeses.

"There is no such thing as good or evil, only people, Wen."

"Then why are we fighting them?" Wen asked, confused.

"Because you have to pick a side and then fight for it," his father said, erasing a series of files.

"And the government is bad?" Wen asked.

"The government is supposed to be there to make people's lives better, or else it has no purpose other than to enrich themselves at everyone's expense. That is, unless you remind them what they are there for. I fight for the majority."

"I don't understand," Wen said.

"Do you think that people should be punished if they rob you?"

"Yes!"

"Do you believe it's fair if someone goes unpunished if they do?"

"No, that's not fair."

"What if the rules said that this person goes to prison if they rob you, but this person will be rewarded for the same thing. Worse yet, you will be punished for complaining."

"That's not fair at all!"

"Those are the people I am fighting, the ones who get rewarded for robbing everyone. They make the rules, and I am the one who will be punished for stealing from the thieves. Do you understand?"

"Yes, I understand," Wen said. The files were titled Known Dissidents, Enemies of the People, Political Anarchists, Freethinkers, and contained thousands upon thousands of names. "What if we just go live somewhere else, Daddy?" he said.

"It is the same everywhere, Wen."

He felt a pressure on the side of his head. "We have to go, Papa. Someone is there!" he said, and they logged out.

A forest green army helicopter circled above the mall in the distance, its rotor the buzzing of a gnat.

Wen looked at his younger self from above, disembodied. He had not thought about his father since his death. He did not know about this memory at all until now. It was the very first one recorded to his crystal memory chip.

⋏ ⋏ ⋏

He woke with a start, rubbed the circles on the back of his sore neck, getting a feel for the implants. There were stickers with wires coming out of his forehead, connected to an oscilloscope by the bed.

A nurse came to his hospital bed.

"How are you feeling?" she said.

"It's a pain in the neck."

"Never heard that one before," she said, smiling. "We'll be monitoring you for a day. Until you get discharged, please try to remain as immobile as possible, and do not attempt to unlock the firewall."

"Firewall?" he said.

"Yes, you've been equipped with a DaiSin manticore firewall, for your safety. It's standard procedure; no need to worry." She handed him a plastic cup full of water, which he drank in one gulp.

I don't even know how to access this firewall, let alone bypass it, he thought. He closed his eyes, and the memory of his father began to play back. He wanted it to stop, and it paused, like a video. *This is seriously strange*, he thought. He was in the station wagon again, blinking at the other cars' reflections. This time, though, he saw the color of each car and could focus on any one he wanted to. He stared at the faded walls of the Shenzen Wholesale Mall, noticing the sparrows making a nest in a hole big enough to dump a refrigerator through on the fourth floor. *Go forward*, he thought, and the memory sped up, reaching the end before he knew it. He opened his eyes. He refused to remember anything more for now.

There was a Net set above his bed, and he looked for the remote. He waved his hand in front of the set, but it remained dead.

I wonder how you turn it on, he thought, and the set came to life. He stared at it, wide-eyed, holding the bars of his bed. *Turn off*, he thought. The screen went blank.

Holy shit! he thought.

"Oh, good. You figured it out on your own," a nurse said, walking up to his bed. "Just don't strain yourself too much for now. It's like a brand new engine; it needs time to adjust to the different speeds. You wouldn't want to burn it out in the first day, would you?" he said, smiling.

"This is just unreal!" Wen said. "It's magic!"

"Ha ha! It sure feels like it for the first little while. That's one of Clarke's laws: 'Any technology sufficiently advanced is indistinguishable from magic.' Don't worry; you'll get used to it. Besides, there are much funner things to do than turning on Net sets. Like I said, take it easy today, all right? What kind of subjects do you like?"

"Monocycle races and hover cars," Wen said.

"Sounds good. Be right back." The man walked away and came back a few minutes later with a stack of dog-eared magazines. "Whenever you're done, ring the buzzer," he said, pointing at the cord behind Wen. "I'll try to find you other stuff to keep your mind busy." For the rest of the day, Wen avoided thinking about Net sets and buried memories, concentrating on brand-new, turbo-charged Lexuses, Mercedes, Teslas, and BMW hovercars, and the Suzuki monocycle team's latest wins.

During the night, an alarm sounded, and he turned his head toward a flashing red light coming through the separators between the beds. A few cots over, a loud "whoooot" kept repeating, over and over. The ward lights turned on, and nurses rushed in.

"She's flatlining," he heard.

"Get me cortical stimulators and prep the emergency room, stat!" said another anxious voice. He got out of bed and pulled the curtain. His neighbor was doing the same. A team of nurses and doctors were unhooking monitors on the girl two beds down. The sound stopped and they wheeled her away in a flurry of animated voices.

"What just happened?" he asked the male nurse who had brought him the magazines.

"Don't worry; that happens sometimes. She'll be OK in a minute," he said, a strained grin on his lips.

"Are you serious?" Wen asked.

"Yeah, yeah, it's just minor shock. Some people just aren't mentally equipped for the 'trodes, that's all. We just need to adjust the sets; she'll be fine."

You're lying, a voice said inside Wen's mind.

"You can go back to sleep. Everything's OK."

Wen took a step back, looked in the direction where the girl had gone, and went back to bed thinking there wasn't much he could do.

The next day, he was discharged and given company-issued clothes: black pants, white shirt, and gray tie. He followed the throng of new recruits back into the auditorium and went to his now usual spot at the back. He scrutinized all the faces he could see, but none of them looked like the girl who had been evacuated the previous night.

"Good morning, ladies and gentlemen," Mr. Deguchi said from the front of the class. "Today is a new day in the story of your lives. Today you will learn to do things you never thought possible," he said. "First things first: close your eyes. Now, I want you to think about a very personal memory. Something only you would know. I want you to take that memory, and then put it at the back of your mind. That's it." He looked at a boy in the third row. "You're not concentrating hard enough. You have to focus all your attention on that one memory. OK, now, can you see the memory in your mind? You can play it perfectly, pause it, fast-forward it, rewind it, focus in and out of it, do anything you want with it. Give it a try." There were a few gasps of surprise.

Big deal, thought Wen, *I did that this morning without even trying.*

"Good, now I want you to think of this logo." A stylized manticore appeared on a screen behind Deguchi. "Don't enter anything yet, just think of the logo. This is very important. Close your eyes and picture it." Wen closed his eyes and stared at the bat-winged lion, its scorpion's stinger swaying. It approached him.

He could touch it, he thought, if he only reached out. A portal opened in the middle of the manticore's chest when he did. *Enter your password, please,* a female voice said in his mind.

"You will all be asked to enter a new password after I have given you the factory default. Think of a strong memory you won't soon forget. Remember, that'll be the memory you'll use to unlock the firewall every time, so try to make it a pleasant one." Deguchi said. "I want all eyes on me before you enter the default. I don't want anybody getting lost. All eyes on me, now. As soon as you are through the firewall, rotate 180 degrees and go back to the point directly behind you. Just relax. I will give you the password now." A thought appeared in the porthole in the middle of the manticore, and a voice inside Wen's head asked: *What is your new password?*

I don't know anything that's been pleasant in the past little while, he thought. *Wait. There is that...*Supper with his brother appeared before him like a thought-bubble, and even though the day had been stressful, he thought it might do. He opened his eyes a moment and saw Deguchi staring right at him. He turned his gaze elsewhere. *He knows,* thought Wen. *I can't use that one.* The shared memory of the beam of light he had with Joe came back to him, and the voice asked him to confirm his choice. *Yes,* he thought, and the hole in the manticore expanded, showing pinpoints of light beyond.

It was like falling through a trapdoor and into the vast universe. All around him shone points of light in an all-encompassing darkness, some of them within touching distance. When he looked closer, he saw that they were connected by thin strands of light, invisible from afar. It was like being underwater, swimming in a night pool, surrounded by glowing, spherical jellyfish. A stronger light incandesced before him. It sent tiny arcs of electricity along the filaments that connected all the orbs. He turned around and was blinded by a crimson sun, shining from far away and what *felt like* above; direction a meaningless concept. He averted his eyes to avoid being blinded.

I can't breathe! he thought, panicking. He was drowning, and he mentally turned around, kicking in space, seeing a ball of light the size of his head behind him. He swam to it and was asked for his password. His lungs felt like they would explode if he did not get any oxygen soon. He thought of the sunbeam and was back in the auditorium, panting on his seat.

"...job, now go back to your mind. That's it. No need to be afraid," Deguchi was saying, at the front of the class. "You'll experience weightlessness, that's normal. You don't need to hold your breath; you are still inside your body. You're only projecting. Breathe as you normally would."

He closed his eyes and went through again. This time, he did not feel like he was in an ocean but flying in the air. He floated a bit around his orb, never letting it out of his sight. He spied other tiny lights doing the same around their own globes. He floated back to the front of his sphere and noticed the string of light that went straight to the slightly bigger one in the distance. After staring at it with intense curiosity, he put out a tentative hand, lightly touching it. He sped to the bigger light at breakneck speed, making him dizzy and nauseated. He bonked against it, and Deguchi's voice said, *Back to your mind, Harkwell. Don't get ahead of yourself.* There was a push, and he was sent back to his orb. He went into the portal and opened his eyes.

"Nicely done, everyone. That's enough for this morning. Let's break for lunch and come back at one," Deguchi said. Wen walked out of the auditorium, feeling Deguchi's gaze on his back. There was a crack, a tiny little split, rending his resolve. Wen had gotten a taste of the Net, and it beckoned to him now, a silent ache at the back of his mind.

At the next session, Deguchi asked them, "What am I thinking?" Everyone frowned and looked around at the others.

"Come on, let's go; what am I thinking?" he said. Wen looked at him and pictured himself in Deguchi's head.

"The trick is, you have to concentrate on..." he continued, but Wen saw instantly. *Green horses, green horses, green horses,* the thought was huge, and Wen could see green horses running in a desert.

"Green horses," he yelled.

Deguchi stopped. "Correct." He smiled. The thought was cut off, and Wen was ejected from Deguchi's head.

"Concentrate on my mind, my thoughts. If someone's firewall is down, you can go rummaging through their thoughts, their memories, or do other things as well. This is why you should never leave your Gate open. If you leave your house in the morning, you don't leave the doors wide open, do you? Same for your mind; that should go without saying. Go ahead and try. Close your eyes, now."

Wen plunged back in, and this time saw a flight of people, gliding through the air over a summer prairie, their arms spread like wings. A warm breeze pushed him along. Wen realized that the others were the initiates in the room in a shared fantasy created by Deguchi's mind. He said nothing but enjoyed the feeling of flight, going higher or lower, brushing the tall grasses with his hands. The land cut off, and they passed over a cliff, a sea of green swaying below them. A jungle spread out in all directions. Wen turned around and saw the incredible height of the cliff. Deguchi led the group, gliding lower and lower until he landed in a clearing.

"These are just some of the possibilities available to you. With proper training, you will be capable of much more. Back to your minds now. Open your eyes." Wen felt a push, as if falling backward, and opened his eyes. The other initiates were beaming, laughing to each other.

"That's enough for today, I think," Deguchi said, glancing to his left. The initiates left in a burble of excited voices. Wen waited a bit at the exit. There was a young man slumped over a table. Wen hid behind the door. Deguchi turned the boys' head. Wen recognized him as the excited youth he had encountered before getting implanted. A pool of drool had formed on the table, and the boy's eyes stared, glassy and wide open. An attendant closed the doors, and Wen walked away. It left a sour taste in his mouth, this feeling of elation that wrapped him up while people were suffering around him. Was it fair for him to enjoy it? Was he now putting on his own blinders?

He caught up to the group. He counted about forty people in all.

I wonder how many of us will be left by the time we graduate? he thought. He sat in his corner of the cafeteria and observed the other initiates chatting together. A few seemed to be trying to read each other's minds.

What am I thinking? You're no threat to me. Am I a threat to you now? He thought. *That is some crazy superpower. Wonder what else I'll be able to do.*

A young blond woman in a gray uniform sat down in front of him.

"Mind if I join you?" she said.

"Little bit too late to refuse, don't you think?" he said, unamused.

"So it is. You've been picked, Wen."

"Really? I'm getting goose bumps. What do I win?" he said sarcastically.

"Seriously, finish your supper and come with me," she said. He popped the last bits of food in his mouth and got up. "There are thousands of posts in DaiSin, but not many as prestigious as the one you've been chosen for," she said as they exited the cafeteria.

"CEO, already? I thought I'd be here at least a week before they handed me the reins!" Wen said in exaggerated excitement as they walked along the empty corridor.

"Not that prestigious. No one will ever have that unless they're a Singh. No, you're going all the way to the bottom."

"Remind me again how this is *advancement*? Shouldn't I be going *up* the ladder?" he said, cocking his head.

"This is going up the ladder. You shouldn't be so literal. It's not because something is below that it isn't above, as well," she said, rolling her eyes.

"I have to ask; why me?" he said, as they stopped before an elevator.

"I have no idea, I'm just the messenger." She pushed the elevator button.

"So, how far down are we going?" he asked, their voices a hollow echo inside the tiny cabin.

"All the way." The doors opened, and they stepped inside. She put her hand on the level readout above the buttons, and a green light scanned her hand.

"Name your floor," a male voice said from a speaker above them. She looked at the screen, and Wen heard her voice in his head: *The Barrier Department.*

"What's the Barrier Department?" Wen asked, as the elevator started its descent.

"You heard me? I guess now I know why you were tapped. You're a second day initiate, aren't you?" she said, an eyebrow raised.

"Yeah, what difference does it make?" he asked.

"None, but it means you catch on quickly."

"Have any of the others been 'picked'?"

"Not that I know of. It's not often that we add new personnel to the group. The Barrier Department exists only to those who get chosen; although lately, the numbers have been increasing."

"So, I'm a chosen one?" he said. She laughed melodiously, throwing Wen off.

"Sorry, you are just as 'chosen' as the thousand or so other people in the department. No offense, but you're not special. Everybody has talents, even those who haven't been 'chosen' for this particular job. They might be really good office workers or on-site managers." She smirked.

"Way to make a guy feel special."

"Also not my job," she said.

The elevator doors opened, and the woman led the way into a dark corridor. The walls, carpet, and ceiling were black-purple auras illuminating from behind large, square, matte-black wallplates. Wen could "feel" the walls in his mind. They had an electric quality to them, like pleasant static.

"They're amplifiers," the woman said, turning around. "If you can feel that, they're designed to strengthen your signal at this depth. You can get around at much faster speeds with the kind of boost they give."

"Get around where?" he asked.

"Anywhere."

He paused and then hurried to catch up to her.

Wen imagined he was inside the base of the support structure for the DaiSin Building. Outside, the winds howled and dust devils churned. The fires raged on the surface of the Heap, several meters outside of the circular concrete walls.

His feet lit purple patterns on the carpeted ground, lighting the way in a whisper. The woman turned several corners and came to a door marked with the Kanji for "war." She knocked twice and entered. The room was arranged in three concentric circles, each one lower than the other. A holographic map was displayed at the center of the room, at its lowest point. What looked like black leather massage chairs were arranged facing the center, all around the different levels. Several people sat at the comfortable-looking seats, their eyes closed. Various characters moved on the holographic display in the center. A large figure rose from a console on a dais at the far left.

"Your new boss," the woman said.

It was Douglas Deguchi.

"Welcome, Wen," he said, coming down to greet him.

"What the hell is going on?" he asked.

"You've been given your first post, that's what," he said, crossing his arms.

"Aren't you supposed to train the new recruits?" Wen asked, irritated.

"That's a part-time occupation only. I'm also a recruiter for some of our more interesting positions at the company. I supervise operations at the Barrier Department. I wear many hats."

"I'm still waiting to see my brother," Wen said.

"So you are," Deguchi said evenly, letting silence hang in the air.

"What am I doing here?" Wen asked, exasperated.

"You'll be part of a team that protects the interests of the company, Wen. There's a war going on. It's an invisible war, and only units like ours get to see it. It's quiet at the moment," he said, looking over at the center console, "but we can get attacked at any time, without warning."

I'll be defending the thing I hate the most; great, thought Wen.

"Don't look so glum, Wen. There are many opportunities that can open to you if you do well. I expect you'll do well."

"What do I have to do?" Wen said, staring at the ceiling, his hands shoved in his pockets.

"Have a seat," Deguchi said. Wen found an empty chair and sat, crossing his arms. "Close your eyes and exit your firewall. I'll be there to guide you."

Wen did as he was told. He did not fall into space this time but went into a different room. The glowing white walls were covered in all types of weapons, armor, and shields from every era of history. There were guns, bazookas, grenades, and pulse weapons as well. Deguchi appeared beside him.

"Nice armory, huh? This is the default loading screen before stepping out onto the turrets. He pointed to a door at the other end of the room.

"Am I going to be a gladiator?" Wen asked, distractedly checking out a scythe.

"No, not quite. You'll be a hacker-soldier; a digital mercenary, if you will. These are your tools. They look like weapons, but of course, in the virtual world, they are code. They are a simulation of what the weapon represents. This room is the sum total of our research into new program-based weapons technology. Sure, we had to start basic," he said, looking at a serrated dagger, "but we got the hang of it eventually." He gestured toward a shoulder-mounted energy weapon.

"So this is a *game*? I grab a gun, go out there, and shoot the bad guys?" Wen said.

"Sure, you can see it that way. Thing is, in this game, you play for keeps. If you kill someone, they might become brain-dead at the other end of the line. If you get killed..."

"I can expect the same. Right," Wen said, scratching his chin.

"That is, of course, a worst-case scenario. Most of the time, people pull out before their defenses are breached. The goal isn't to massacre; it's to gain advantage."

"Over?" Wen asked.

"Other corporations. If someone breaks into our systems and steals our secrets, our market value goes down. Theirs go up."

"That sounds pretty silly to me."

"War has always been about domination. We just made it bloodless. Would you feel better if you could slaughter people in their homes instead?" Deguchi asked.

Wen felt sick. "No, but it just feels unreal."

"It'll feel real. You can count on that," Deguchi said, walking along the wall of weapons.

An alarm sounded, and men and women began to appear in the room. They wore custom armor and had their weapons at the ready. Copper cubes half their heights levitated behind them. The soldiers saluted Deguchi in passing and ran through the far door, followed by their cubes. Wen's pulse pounded.

"Do I have to...you know..." he said, looking in the direction the soldiers had gone.

"Not tonight. You need training before we even think of putting you out there."

"What were those floating things?" Wen asked.

"Your backup. Completely artificial constructs with independent AIs. Part of the High Yield Virtual Entity, or HYVE. They help you on the field, follow orders, attack, defend...they're your personal guards, and they're called Golems. We should go back; I have a defense to organize. Go through that door." Wen did so and was back in the chair. The woman who had brought him greeted him as he got up.

"We should leave the professionals to their job," she said, escorting Wen out the door. The chairs that had been empty only a few moments before were now occupied.

On the holographic grid, blue and red pins were coming together in the center. Deguchi stood at the front, watching every move. He had a helmet on and did not speak a word, but Wen knew that he was firing orders by thought. They left the war room without a word.

Wen looked back the way they had come as he walked. "How often does that happen?" he asked.

"Almost daily. We have many secrets at DaiSin. Our competitors would love to get their hands on them. We haven't stayed the best for so long without some fierce fighting," she said, her mouth screwing up. She stopped at a door. "Your quarters."

"One last thing," Wen said. "Who are you?"

"Oh, I'm Jenna. Jenna Wolinsky. Didn't I introduce myself?"

"I don't think so," he said.

"There. It's done. Good night," she said, walking away, leaving a trail of purple glowing steps behind her. Wen shook his head and looked at the door. There was a handprint beside the door, and he pressed it. His hand was scanned and the door slid open. In the middle of the room stood Sammy.

CHAPTER 7

If you know the enemy and know yourself,
you need not fear the result of a hundred battles.
If you know yourself but not the enemy,
for every victory gained you will also suffer a defeat.
If you know neither the enemy nor yourself,
you will succumb in every battle.

—SUN TZU, *THE ART OF WAR*

W EN'S KNEES GREW weak and he dropped to the floor. The door slid closed behind him, leaving only oppressive silence within. Sammy was frowning, staring down.

"A-are you OK?" Wen said, looking at his brother. His eyes felt moist. The corners of his mouth twitched violently.

A tear fell from Sammy's downturned face. "I didn't mean to…I'm…I'm…" he said, his fists clenched tight.

"Are you OK?" Wen said, vaguely noticing his knees getting wet. Sammy blurred before him. He got up on his unresponsive legs and walked toward his brother, his head throbbing.

"I really messed up, Wen. I really…messed…things up," Sammy said, sobbing.

"Hey, hey, it's OK, it's OK! I'm here now. It's OK…" Wen said as he extended his hand and put it through the image of his brother, Sammy repeating the same words over and over mechanically, his head tilting left and right.

A hologram. This was how they had decided to weasel their way out of their contractual agreement; they had given him a holographic projection of his brother, a mere *recording!* Wen looked at his hand and then at his brother's image, in disbelief. A shudder electrified its way from his groin to the top of his scalp, and the tightening sensation he had endured since the day he had arrived snapped like a too-taut rope. It felt as if his brain made a slow-motion roll toward the right, as a ship keeling starboard. He gulped, choking on the words he wanted to say. His teeth unclenched, and he let out a howl of pain that resonated like a bomb inside the dome of his skull as he struck the closest wall with all his fury. He punched it over and over and over again, trying to destroy the pain inside himself, to expunge the all-encompassing hurt that coursed like burning steam through his entire being. He fell to the floor, panting. He looked at his raw knuckles and turned around to look at Sammy. Then he looked at the walls and ceiling.

"What the fuck is this game? I want to see my brother! You promised! What is this fucking game? What the fuck do you want from us? You...you...you...Aaaaaaaaaah!" he screamed, clutching his head.

"It's really me, Wen. I asked them to see you in person, but they wouldn't let me."

His anger turned to surprise, and he was struck silent, staring. Sammy stood there, motionless, not daring to peer into his eyes, afraid of what he would find. Wen's anguish redirected like a laser sight. "Why did you take the book, Samuel? Why did you do that?" he said, with a demented look in his eyes.

"I wanted to help. That's all I wanted to do! I thought if I could do something good, you wouldn't have to worry about the money so much for a while, you know?" Sammy said.

"How did that help? Do you think we're in a better place now?" he said, waving his arms like a windmill.

"I just wanted to help! I'm tired, OK?" Sammy yelled.

"You're *tired*? Tired of what?" Wen said, incredulous.

"Tired of being the *baby*! I wanted to do something you'd be proud of me for, *for once!*" Sammy shot back angrily. Wen paused, rubbing the back of his neck.

"I was...am proud of you, Sammy," Wen said, gazing at a spot on the carpet near Sammy's virtual feet.

"Sure you are. Now that I've gotten us in this mess, *sure you are,*" Sammy said, his eyes glinting.

"I'll get us out of here; don't you worry. Do you know where you are?"

"I think I'm..." a long, shrill tone sounded, overpowering any words Sammy could have said. "They won't let you know where I am."

"Have you seen Andrei or Taz?" Wen asked, his anger abated.

"No, I haven't. There are plenty of others though. They got me going to class again. Not at my old school, mind you..." Sammy said, looking around.

"They put you in school?" Wen said.

"Yeah, I know. I thought I'd be in a prison cell or something. I'm in this..." and the same strident tone overtook Sammy's words again, forcing Wen to block his ears.

"I'll find you; don't worry."

"They're telling me I have to go." He turned his head. "Can I just have one more minute?" Wen reached out to touch his outstretched hand and grasped air. His brother was gone.

Sammy's alive. Sammy's alive! That's good, he thought, reorganizing his priorities around this solitary certainty. He had no idea how he would be able to break out of this jail. The Sayeed method was conclusive; escape was not an option. There had to be other ways of getting out. Even if they did, wouldn't DaiSin employ every dirty trick to reclaim them or eliminate them as nuisances? Where were Taz and Andrei then? Different part of the complex, probably. Kept separated for the simple reason that if they weren't, they could hatch a plan to topple the company. *Relax, imagination, come back to reality, please*, he thought. *What do I know?*

1. *Sammy's alive.*
2. *I now have Netrode implants.*
3. *I've been hired by the guerilla arm of the company. That could be useful.*
4. *My fingers hurt like hell.*

Wen felt drained. He found a sofa, dropped into it, and took a deep breath, looking at his sore, bloody knuckles. The surroundings were comfortable, if a bit Spartan. He at least had his own room. There was a screen on the opposite wall.

On, he thought, and it illuminated. He wandered to the kitchen and turned on the tap, showering his aching, bleeding knuckles in cold water, and then found some paper towels to wrap them. He was reminded of the fresh meats his mother would buy from the butcher's a block from their house, folded in Chinese newspapers. Wen got up and inspected his apartment, opening each door with the tips of his fingers, his hands in pain, imagining what Sammy's quarters might be like and how they treated him.

There were four rooms: living room and kitchen shared an open space, bedroom, bathroom, and chair room. He called it the chair room since it had one of those comfy massage-looking recliners in it, and that was all.

Place is classier than our old one; that's for sure, he thought.

The room was black, the walls covered in those same black plates suffusing a purplish light from behind them. Wen had no interest in sitting in the chair. Once for the day had been enough; besides, he was sure he would be using it soon enough anyhow. Another screen was situated on the wall in front of his double bed in the bedroom. There were two small navy-blue end tables near the head of the bed and one three-drawer dresser. It was empty save for two sets of gray pajamas and white underwear and socks. He took a peek inside the closet and found five gray uniforms of the same type Jenna Wolinsky wore. He lay on the bed and put his hands behind his head as gently as he could manage.

It could be worse, he thought. The voyage from China floated to his consciousness. *It could be much worse.* Eyes heavy, he slipped under the warm woolen blankets pulled tight over the bed frame. He took off his clothes like a man sloshing through a marsh, drained of energy, every move a great burden on his soul, and fell into a deep sleep.

He was standing alone in a large, stone cave, a bonfire crackling, dancing in the middle of the dirt floor, surrounded by a tiny wall of carefully placed stones. His head ached like never before. The flames shone on the cavern walls, archaic depictions of men hunting wild animals moving sluggishly after one another. He couldn't tell outright if the images were in fact shifting or if it was some kind of illusion created by the dancing flames upon their colorful painted outlines. Outside, the night sounds closed in on him. Jagged-toothed beasts prowled, shuffling and snuffling on coarse ground. Wen took a branch he found nearby and put it into the fire. The branch lit, throwing light into the night. Yellow eyes glowed in the darkness, always a step away from the light.

Hyenas laughed outside the circle of fire. Nervous titters of killers contemplating homicide. They waited for Wen to sleep so they could enter. A cacophony of yelps like voices ensued, sounding like *Let us in...*

"You can't come in!" Wen yelled into the cold night. The torch he held became a flame thrower, the tip exploding in a blaze, straight out of the cave. Yelps of pain resounded in the night, the beasts scattering. Wen sat again by the fire and looked at the wall paintings. Little red stick men with pencil-thin lances pursued blue deer and brown mammoths. *That could be me,* he thought, his headache fading.

A bell rang at 6:00 a.m., the flat-panel Net set flashing in front of the bed. He got up, his hands aching.

Did I break something? He thought, flexing his knuckles. The dried blood crusted on the paper towels he had wrapped around them. Dark brown smears stained the pillows behind his head. He went to the shower and the bell rang again, this time followed with a knock. He went to the door and opened it. Jenna was standing there smiling.

"Morning! You're not ready yet?" she said.

"No. Can you come back in a bit?" he said, hands behind his back.

"You better hurry or you'll miss morning training! You've got ten minutes," she said and then walked away.

Wen shuffled to the dark, gray-stone-floored bathroom and wiped the paper towel from his knuckles with the tap, picking at the crusted bits carefully so that they wouldn't start bleeding again. He walked into the glass shower and was startled by the steaming hot water that came out unbidden. He fiddled with the knobs a bit and got it to something approaching comfortable. It had been a long time since he had taken a hot shower, and he enjoyed the warmth coursing over his body, steam rising from the coarse, heated floors. He left the shower feeling rejuvenated, molted from an ill-fitting skin.

He rifled around the medicine cabinet and found flesh-colored bandages, which he duly applied to his sore, split knuckles on the tiny cuts he had inflicted on himself.

Dried, and choice not being part of the deal, he realized, he picked up the first of five identical gray suits in the closet.

The doorbell rang again and he answered the door, now fully dressed.

"Let's go," Jenna said, smiling.

"What's the program?" he asked, tugging at his suit jacket. It felt like a military dress uniform for cadets, dour and plain in its martial way. He saw Jenna's had a few in-signias his did not, slim two-toned slivers, like elongated diodes, above her left breast.

"You need to learn how to control your 'trodes, and quick. You're going back to school, Wen Harkwell." She looked back at him and nodded. "Uniform suits you." Wen felt his cheeks redden. The last time he had worn something this dressy had been in the heady days of Kokubo Private High School, where all students wore mandatory navy-blue uniforms, which, he now realized, had been paid for by DaiSin Corporation, in a roundabout sort of way.

They marched down several winding turns, acknowledging other similarly dressed employees, and came to a door. Jenna knocked and a voice sounded from within. "Enter!" The door slid open.

A chubby man with a kind, round face in his midthirties stood in the middle of a small classroom with a dozen of the same seats as the one in his room, arranged in a circle around him. Three students were ensconced within their seats.

"Wen Harkwell, this is Robert Gardner, your Outer Training Teacher," Jenna said.

"Nice to meet you, Wen. Come, take a sensornet chair," he said, indicating a spare seat.

"Gotta go; see you!" Jenna said, waving her hand and leaving. Wen sat at one of the comfortable chairs and lay his head back, clearing his mind.

"Now, as I was saying, most of what you will do consists of going out of your mind," Gardner said. Two of his students giggled. "No, not like that," he admonished in a mock-serious tone. "You exit your consciousness, projecting your minds to various locations. Let's try again. Exit your firewall and come to me. You too, Wen." Wen closed his eyes and opened the gate of the manticore, floating out into space. In front of him, a few meters away, a larger glowing orb. He found the filament that led to it and touched it and was there in an instant. Three other small lights surrounded the larger one—the other students.

Don't let go, he heard Gardner's soft voice say in his head. He mentally clung to his light and tilted toward another one, this one further in the distance. A sickening sense of intense acceleration washed over him, and he saw a host of other glints whoosh and warp, elongating past him as they rushed forward. They came to a stop near the one orb that had stayed static during the trip.

May we come in? It's for a class, he heard Gardner's voice say. A voidal port opened on the light-sphere, and they were sucked in. Darkness then, looking through someone's eyes, walking down a corridor. Other people walking by acknowledged them with a nod, the muffled carpet sound of footsteps coming through in stereo. Wen heard the excited chatter of the other students near him, invisible, and a grumble of complaint, as if from an echo chamber.

I'll have to ask you not to speak while we're inside other people's heads; it can be a bit unnerving for the host, Gardner said.

I have things to do, Gardner. Make it quick, he heard. It was Deguchi's tenor growl. They were inside Deguchi's head!

All right, time to go. Hold on to me, everybody, he heard Gardner say. Night surrounded them once more, pinpoints of light moving along their physical paths. The acceleration once more made Wen wince, and they returned to the classroom, holding on to Gardner's glowing orb. He nudged them back into their own orbs, and Wen opened his eyes, the thin hairs on his shoulders rising at the experience.

"There are many things you can do with that technique: read minds, use far-sight, like we just did, as well as body manipulation. Once you've gotten up to speed, you'll be able to travel wherever you want, as long as it's within a 'Netted device or person.'"

Wen snapped back to attention. "How can we know where we're going if we don't know what's at the end?" Wen asked.

"Easy. Put mental tags on the filaments. For instance, when you are near me, you can see my filament; just make a 'mental note' of who that string belongs to, and you won't be flying blind next time you go in. It's a bit annoying, I know, but believe me; it's a lot simpler than it used to be," Gardner said. Wen projected, and spotted Gardner's string. A tag appeared before it, labeled with his name.

"You should do that with as many people's Netminds as you can; that way you won't get lost. Don't tag yourself unless you want the world to know who you are. Netted devices usually have a code instead of a name. You'll need your updated software to decode the location. You don't really need to enter the device to activate it though. No use getting in the Net set to turn it on, right?" Gardner said, and the other students chuckled.

Wen thought about the Net set in the hospital ward. *I can get in the TV?* "How come your orb is bigger than ours?" he asked.

Gardner smiled. "Good question. Knowledge, power, and experience increase the size of your data set; therefore, your presence on the Net is augmented. As initiates, you barely have a presence at all, but in time, you will grow. Now, get to know your fellow employees."

Wen exchanged names with the other students, and they spent the rest of the class running up other people's filaments, tapping on their orbs and trading information, networking with all they would chance meet in the vicinity. Wen noticed certain filaments went straight up, but when he tried to follow them, he was rebuked by a glass ceiling. In fact, after inspecting his surroundings, he realized that he was confined to one level of the Barrier Department. It was like staring into infinity through a sealed glass disk or trapped inside the confines of a lens.

Jenna fetched him after class for breakfast. "How was it?" she asked over a bite of pasta.

"It was...instructive," he said. "Will you be leading me around for much longer?" he asked.

"Getting tired of me already, Wen? No, I won't. Only until you get the hang of the place. Here's a helpful hint: if you get lost, press one of the amplifiers on the walls. A screen will pop up, and you can ask it where you need to go," she said, smiling. The sound of the eating hall was muted, as if someone had sucked all the sound out and bottled it like a genie, most people communicating through thought. Gray-uniform clad men and women sat around tables of eight in a room that was centrally located on the level.

"It's so quiet in here; it's eerie!" he said.

"Then just tune up the ambient volume. I'm warning you though; you might want to practice doing it in a less crowded space," she said.

"Why is that?" he said as he concentrated on the noise level of the room. An explosive clamor of voices boomed inside his head. Wen double over in pain and turned down the sound as fast as he could, attempting to block out the point-blank mental canon blast he had just invited. His ears felt like bleeding and writhing off his head like dead leaves, simultaneously.

"That's why. Can't say I didn't warn you," Jenna said, peering over the side of the table at Wen's sprawled form. He picked himself up, his face red, as he unbuttoned the top of his collar. "You might want to take some meds for that. Even at low volume, mindspeak can be a strain." She handed him two small capsules. Wen gulped them down with water and felt better a short while later.

The next class was with a man named Ulrick Werber. He was introduced as the Defense and Attack Teacher, a thin, sharp man harboring a permanent sneer. They were back in the ovoid control room where Wen had first been brought the previous day and was left alone with him.

"Harkwell, sit down," he ordered, pointing to one of the seats from the end of his thin nose. "Go into the control room, now."

"How do I do that again?" Wen asked.

"Are you going to be a problem, Harkwell?" Werber said, raising his thick eyebrows. "Close your eyes and go through your portal."

Wen appeared in the white-walled arsenal, which he studied more closely than the first time. A hangar-sized space with no visible supports, it was a perfectly blank slate of a room adorned with weapons bristling on every square centimeter of its flat surfaces, every single one different from the next, the common thread among them a seeming progression of refinement and lethality, he noticed for the first time. When Deguchi had brought him here, he had merely stood in awe of so much firepower, but now he saw that there was order to the chaos. As if hung from the ceiling by invisible wires, armored and camouflage-painted vehicles levitated near its surface, upside down. Werber appeared beside him.

"Do you have your new interface, yet?" he asked.

"New interface?" Wen said.

Werber gripped his temples with one hand: "Yes, your new interface. The one you get after you are implanted. You don't expect to get far with the bare-bones package, do you?"

"I don't think so, no," Wen said.

"You'd think you knew if you did," Werber said, shaking his head. He lifted his arm, palm up, and a carrousel of two-dimensional screens floated above it. "These are your choices. You can customize as you go along, but there are eight 'skins' to choose from, all based on the same Operating System." The various screens circled around the axis of his palm. There were choices for most tastes, in a generic and broad sense: a seasonal theme that was presently stuck on fall, falling leaves cycling through a short sequence; pink and pretty, sickeningly sweet anime-style characters and not at all to his taste; dark and gothic, with some imposing fortress looming above a dark forest; military camouflage, a hovertank firing the same ion blast at five-second intervals; science fiction, with a space theme of flaring propulsion engines behind a scout-class dreadnaught in flight; jungle hunter, featuring a clearing surrounded by a lush tropical forest; artistic, juxtaposing various famous art pieces; and finally, standard gray, like a stark period, for the completely unimaginative.

"What difference does it make which one I choose?" Wen asked, observing each choice as they came round and round.

"None, or rather, it's purely psychological. These are basic themes. You can download many more. It's the program behind them that does the real work," Werber said.

"What does the program do?"

"Nobody told you this, really?" Werber said, irritated. "Attack and defense-based programming, with the purpose of making you a better defender of DaiSin. That's it. If you had gone up into management, it would be spreadsheets and organizational charts. Just pick one, all right?" he said, tapping his foot. Wen cupped his chin in his hand and looked at all the choices of skins.

It's psychological, is it? he thought, reaching out and picking the jungle hunter theme. He was transported into the hot, humid forest, in the middle of the clearing. The sweltering sun blistered overhead. A tiny bamboo hut stood further ahead, made of sea-washed driftwood, and in the center of the clearing was a black metal pot over a charred fire pit. A bamboo rack was located beside the hut.

"Interesting choice," Werber said, appearing ahead of him. He walked over to the cauldron in the sandy glade. "This is your..." he stopped and turned around, glaring.

"Get over here. Are you stupid? How often will I have to explain things to you? Could you have the courtesy of paying attention, at least? Give me strength!" he said, looking into the blue sky. Wen walked over, reflexively clutched his hands, imagining the irritating character before him within their clutches. Unpleasantness aside, the demeaning theatrics of this little man grated more than anything, the showpieces of one with no real power but that of annoying others.

"Good. Now pay attention, *please*. This is your crucible. With it you can create any program you want. Granted, the ones you *want* to make are attack and defense-related."

"How do I do that?" he asked.

Werber sighed. "You can take any of the weapons that are in the arsenal and improve on them, as well as think up new ones."

"I can *think* of weapons, and this *pot* will make them?" Wen asked.

"Yes! No one taught you anything, did they? What are Netrodes?" Werber asked.

"They're...a way to access the Net?" Wen replied.

"And?" Werber said.

"And turn on Net sets? Read people's minds, travel to other places..." Wen said, trying to recall all the different applications, real or imagined, he had heard about the 'trodes.

"Close, but not quite. Netrodes are a translation device, Harkwell. They turn thoughts into program, and vice-versa. You can manipulate code and machines with your mind; that's what you can do."

Wen was dumbstruck. "So how do I make weapons?" he asked, staring at the crucible, considering the possibilities.

"Activate it by pressing it," Werber said. Wen pushed the side of the pot, touching rough cast-iron, and a fire sprang up from underneath. "Your program is on now. What do you want to make?"

"A knife," Wen said, putting his hands on his hips.

"What kind of knife?" Werber said. Wen thought for a moment, and above the cauldron, a long, sharp, Bowie knife appeared.

"Whoa! Just like that?" he exclaimed.

"Just like that," Werber said. "Keep in mind, though, that the quality of the weapon is directly proportional to the experience of the craftsman."

"What's that mean?" Wen said, taking the floating knife and waving it around in the air.

"Stab me with it," Werber said, extending his arms by his side and grinning. This was a dare that not even the kindest of men could have resisted.

Gladly, thought Wen. "Are you sure?" he said, feigning concern.

"Come on, dumbass; show me what you got," Werber said. Wen lunged with the blade extended, thrusting it into the man's breast. The blade made a keening sound and broke, falling into the sand.

"That's what I mean. You need time and practice before you can make anything worthwhile," Werber said while Wen looked at the hilt of his broken knife, trying to hide his disappointment.

Werber walked up to the hut and opened the door. There was a simple cot, TV hung on the wall, and bamboo garbage can arranged around a hand-woven red carpet. Three large windowless openings on each wall let in the sunshine and a slight breeze.

"TV is to look up your memories, garbage is to toss out the stuff you don't like, or don't need; your inner space can get cluttered after a while," Werber said.

"And the cot?" Wen said.

"To relax. It helps you bring up memories more easily. You can get other stuff from the Nets, if you like to populate your mind with all sorts of garbage," Werber said.

Wen looked around the tiny house and then outside through the windows. He liked it here, he had to admit. Even the fake sun made him feel replenished. They walked out, and he asked about the rickety yellow bamboo rack.

"To hang up the stuff you made. By the way, if you make anything that's decent, it'll be shared in the arsenal automatically. Doesn't mean others will use it, just that it'll be available to the HYVE."

"What if I don't want to share?"

"You don't have a choice," Werber said. "You are connected to the HYVE, and everything you do or think is shared within it. Not with every individual, but with the computer stacks." Wen's heart sank. Everything he did? Everything he thought was stored somewhere, by some giant computer?

"Don't worry, it's not like anybody ever looks up your thoughts. What are you trying to hide, anyway?" he said, eyeing Wen suspiciously. "Everybody who works for DaiSin is hooked up to the mainframes."

"What about privacy?" Wen said, and Werber shrugged. They exited the jungle theme and returned to the Arsenal.

"Use the same password on your Operating System as your Manticore Firewall. Simplifies things a bit. Try to get used to the new system. Explore it when you have a chance. The clearing is just the beginning; it's your safe point. Don't go wandering around outside the glade without a weapon," Werber said, enumerating on his fingers.

"What's outside the glade?" Wen asked.

"The jungle," Werber said, smiling. "I knew you'd be causing me grief. Try to be more attentive tomorrow. I don't like dealing with morons." His smile dissipated, and he waved Wen out of the room.

"Pleasure working with you," Wen said, his shoulders hunched, avoiding looking at the man as he walked out the door.

Jenna was on the other side, hand raised as if to knock. She held a full grocery bag with the Fukudaya Groceries logo in the other. "Oh good, you're done!" she said, putting her hand down. She peered inside at Werber, who stood with his arms crossed, shaking his head slowly. Her smile deepened, and the door slid closed.

"How—" she started.

He cut her short. "Grating. Annoying. Infuriating. Is he always like that?" he said, his fists balled.

"No, sometimes he's in a bad mood. You caught him on a good day. Ulrick is kind of a character. He knows what he's doing, though, and that's what counts. You don't have to be his friend if you don't want to," she replied, smiling broadly.

Can I punch him? he thought and then remembered she might be able to read his mind. A sideways glance revealed no change of expression on her part, and he sighed a bit in relief.

"Where to next?" he said, resignedly.

"Your apartment. It's time to study mental defense," she said.

"Wasn't I just in a defense class?" he asked as they walked down the hallway, the purple steps dissipating behind them.

"That was prep for *outward* defense and attack. I'm talking about defending your mind. It's the last bastion of your sanity, if all else fails. It'd be useful to keep it intact," she said, stopping before his apartment door. He scanned his hand and they entered.

"Mind if I get some supper ready?" she said, walking over to the kitchen without waiting for an answer.

"Um..." he said, feeling like a betrayer.

"Great, it'll be ready in no time." She flashed him one of her smiles that could melt an iceberg. Wen sat on the sofa and felt the tips of his ears burning. Soon, the sweet yet tangy aroma of caramelized onions and *real* beef wafted throughout the apartment.

"You aren't a vegetarian, are you?" she asked, a look of apprehension on her face as she sautéed the onions.

"Not by choice." He tried to look nonchalant. Wen gave the mental order, and the Net set on the wall turned on. He found a news channel and pretended to watch the male announcer with serious mien.

"Hey, how come I can't leave this floor? When I mindtravel, I mean," he asked over the sound of sizzling from a griddle pan.

"You're an initiate. Give it time," she said, shaking the pan. The savory smell of peppers, fried onions, and thick, brown gravy tickled his nostrils. "Alright, time to eat," she announced, and Wen set the kitchen table with whatever utensils he could find in the drawers.

"Sorry, I don't really know the order of things," he said.

"That takes time too." She grinned. Jenna placed a piping hot steak covered in mushrooms, onions, and a peppercorn sauce accompanied by broccoli in front of him. He had not had steak in forever. It tasted like heaven, the beef melting in his mouth, cooked just right.

After the meal, he patted his stomach and said, "Wow! That was incredible. Do you always cook like that?"

She pinkened and said, "No, not really."

"My compliments to the chef. That was amazing."

"Glad you enjoyed it. On to business." Her demeanor shifted to a harder expression. She picked up the plates and put them in the sink. Then she sat back down in front of Wen. "What do you know about mental defense?" she asked.

"Only that I have a firewall to protect me. There's more to it?" he asked, leaning forward.

"Much more. The firewall is basic protection. You have to defend your mind from those who know how to get around it. Out there," she said, pointing to the wall, "that's just about everybody." Wen's shoulders stiffened. "You have to work on concentration and building your mental armor. Be especially careful of things that don't belong."

"Such as?" he said, raising an eyebrow.

"Well, if you find objects or memories that aren't your own, they are most probably implants, placed there to spy on you or to alter your thoughts."

"Like the HYVE?" he said, his lips curling.

"The HYVE normalizes and regulates everybody. It keeps us on the same page. We're stronger because of it. The HYVE is a good thing," she said.

"Did you come up with that one yourself, or did it tell you to say that?" He smirked.

She sighed. "Wen, you're just going to have to trust me on this, OK?" she said, cocking her head.

That's something I can't afford to do, Jenna, he thought.

"It's also important to keep an eye out during your dream state. Intruders might try to fool your mind into thinking they are welcome, or force their way in. They'll use the dream as a portal into your mind."

Wen shuddered. "Seriously? How do I tell if it's an intruder and not my bizarre dreams?"

"Something feels strange, or off. It's very hard to get rid of an invader that enters your mind once it's there, so do be careful. We'll be doing mental exercises in the coming weeks, so you don't have to worry too much about it now. Stay alert, though. You're now connected to the Net. Even though you might not be able to go very far at the moment, others can come to you. Even with our defenses, we're not invincible; no one is," she said. "It's getting late. I have to go. Nice having dinner with you. Next one's on you." She rose from the table, and Wen followed her to the door. She flashed him a last toothy smile before the door slid closed.

Wen felt out of breath. She was beautiful and alluring, but ultimately the feeling of double-cross that had hounded him won out. His heart did not beat for this woman, and never could. He sat on his sofa, replete with silence in the cocoon of his enemy, a thought he had to put aside until he knew what to do about it.

Another sentiment, though, had seized him. His mind bubbled and flittered with black butterfly wings, interstices shimmering in the hushed inky murk, breaking with the light of the world. For the first time in his life, he thought he was able to see outlines of the shape of life filtering through his very synapses; there a moment, elusive, sharpening, and then gone, leaving only an impression to yearn for. Everything he was partaking in made him stronger, increased his vision, broke apart that which he dared not consider, becoming the edge of revelation, and then, the darkness dropped, evaporated, leaving only those things he had hidden from himself. A horrible sight, perhaps, but unclouded by illusion, its power prickled his body with needles of ecstasy. Even in all its ugliness, an infusion of beauty surfaced from the concrete, factual, mathematical equation of the real. Access to the essence shredded the curtains of fantasy he had so painstakingly, erroneously erected to protect himself against the world.

Wen Harkwell *saw*.

A terrible, sweeping sadness surged in fibrous jolts for a moment at the loss of his old self, as one contemplating the soft tissue beneath a shed scab and then calmed to a murmuring tremor. There was no turning back from the molt. Electric joy swam in a peaceful pool of dopamine, his transformation now complete. He was resolve and unquenchable, cold retribution; he would be the chameleon and the panther. He would be no one's puppet.

He went to sleep that night without fear or anger, only molten will taking the shape of his new body.

▲ ▲ ▲

I am a stranger now more than ever, he realized, ducking out of the captain's cabin, peeking around corners. All familiar territory crumbled thousands of kilometers away, lost forever. China was destroying itself under the weight of its own paradoxes. He let his mother sleep as best she could while the ship fitfully rocked side to side. Hidden away on the reeling container vessel, he had snuck out when the ship's horn had announced their nearing the harbor. The hum of the electromagnetic coil drive vibrated through the hull, putting his teeth on edge. Against his mother's wishes, he had climbed on deck, risking discovery to catch his first glimpse of what would become their home. His heart filled with anticipation while teetering along the hallway as he held onto opposing walls, the floor slipping this way and that, adroitly navigating the vessel as any seasoned sailor would have. The first breath of outside air came filled with sea water, choking and soaking him. Choppy seas tossed him, wet, worn sneakers making him slide in all directions but those he willed, threatening to throw him overboard. Stacks upon stacks upon stacks of dour-colored containers lined the deck of the lumbering liner like the construction blocks of a dull child. Gray skies spat fine mist and cold misery over his shivering body. Still he struggled to open his eyes while salt-water waves sprayed and splashed at his legs. His soaked clothing hung heavy on his slight frame—three sizes too big, stolen from down below deck. The Swedish Liner SS *Ragnhild*, rocking on angry waves, lumbered its way to its nearing port of call. The robotic sailors ignored the drenched boy peering into the distance, busy as they were ensuring the stability of the cargo and reeling in the parasail. Out of the corner of his green eyes, he could see their hectic back and forth; their hydrophobic skin sloughing off water, making his own feel even more chilled.

Wen gripped the rust-red container, his eyes fixed above the waves. Each one crashed onto the high concrete ring the ship now approached and obliterated into fine particles that obscured the view beyond. The ring was comprised of enormous cement caltrop-like constructs named tetrapods; the same that lined the Japanese coast in previous centuries to lessen tidal displacement. The shadows against the roiling sea were like nothing he had ever seen before. He guessed more than saw where the city began; a darker gray against that of the sky, vertical stripes as thick as nuclear power plants and as tall as the universe plunged into the ocean's madness. His mind's eye saw an emergent infinity of alien obelisks petrifying him to his core. Nothing could have prepared him for the awe, the sheer momentum of depth that went on forever. It cleft his heart in two, squeezed the pieces to the bursting point, sending his blood gushing to his temples in a hideous symphony of fear. He felt his bladder emptying itself as he slid to the cold, wet metal deck of the ship, no longer able to withstand their judgmental gaze.

Immense harbor doors stuttered, opening with a metallic boom and whine, allowing the cargo ship entrance into its circular sanctuary. The bells rang clear across the deck and blank-faced cybernetic men regained their posts. The ship went in, doors grinding closed behind it, and he felt as if he had been eaten. He slunk back below deck, his hands trembling, tears streaming. Not even close to what he had hoped for.

"Where have you been?" his mother cried, rubbing her distended belly.

"I don't want to go anymore! Can we turn back, please?" he said between sobs while she searched for a dry towel. She enveloped him and gently held him on her knee.

"I'm sorry, Wen; we can't. Even if we could, we'd...get in trouble. Don't worry; everything will turn out fine," she said, her most reassuring smile wavering on her lips. There was no turning back, he already knew, and closed his eyes. Her soothing hands stroked his back, calming his shaking, but there was no calming his mind. Her hands were no longer there, and Wen opened his eyes. Mother was gone.

A sharp rap came from the cabin door, and Wen pushed himself back on the bunk, pressing his back against the wall.

"Who's there?" he cried.

"It's your mother. Open up, sweetie," a muffled voice came from the other side.

"What are you doing on the other side, Mom?" Wen asked, his brow furrowing as he got off the bed.

"I got locked out. Please let me in. You have to hurry," the voice said.

She's lying. It's not your mother, his mind told him. Wen's temples hurt.

"What's behind our house, Mom?" he asked, creeping to the door.

"That's a silly question, Wen; you know as well as I do. Come on, open up." Wen looked at the door. There was some sort of portal attached to it.

"Honey, I need the code. Can you just give me the code?" The voice sounded desperate.

"You're not my mother," said Wen, returned to his true age, the sham of the dream broken. "I don't know who you are, but you're not getting in."

There was a pause on the other side of the door, and a different voice said, "This is the captain speaking. You have ten seconds to open this door, young man, or you are in a heap of trouble. One, two, three…"

Wen looked around the room and imagined his H&K under the pillow. He walked over to the bed and lifted it, finding the gun where he thought it would be. It was loaded. He chambered a round. "I'm coming out now," he said, and the counting stopped. He saw the door opening before him, and the clean-shaven Swedish captain stood there, eyes hard beneath his white cap's visor.

"I'm glad you came to your senses. I need that code—"

Before he could continue, Wen took the gun out from behind his back and pulled the trigger once, level with the captain's heart. The frightened captain lifted his hands at lightning speed to protect himself and the bullet bounced off his hand. He compressed and imploded, turning to light and dashing away like a will-o'-the-wisp. Curious, Wen exited the room and turned to light. The "captain" was speeding down a filament. His light entered an orb and disappeared. Wen floated at its edge, locked out. Circling it, he probed for weaknesses until, on its lowest point, he found a flaw. Not enough to break in, but he could see inside it as through a window.

"I couldn't get in! He saw through the disguise!" said a frightened male voice. Deguchi paced before the man.

"You didn't get him to tell you where he hid the code?" he snarled.

"I told you, he saw through my disguise! He even forged a gun in his sleep and *shot at me!*" the man said, his hands dancing before his face.

"He *what*? Are you serious?" Deguchi said, his usual calm demeanor shaken, as he stood in stupor.

"I think he followed me, but I locked him out before he could get in," the panicked man said.

"You idiot! Let me in, now!" Deguchi howled. Wen turned away, returning to his mind. He woke up covered in sweat, wondering where the next attack would come from. At least now he knew they couldn't come in without his knowledge.

The code. They probably meant the program he and Taz had found and stashed. If they were trying to get it out of him that badly, then Andrei and Taz had to be alive.

CHAPTER 8

ENNA PRESENTED HERSELF at his apartment's door at 6:15, but Wen was ready and dressed when she showed up. He had gained the habit of getting up early while at Fujii-Hashimoto Heavy, and he had somewhat recovered from the turmoil of the past week, if not by choice, at least from necessity.

"What's on the menu today?" he asked, smiling, as they walked down the hall to the Command Center. There was an unusual commotion, the black hallways filled with eager men and women greeting each other as they headed toward their posts. Wen detected a kind of fever in the air, an infectious joy he felt within himself. He fought the urge to touch his grinning face.

"Today is Monday. We're going for the weekly address. It's kind of fun, actually. I think you'll enjoy it," Jenna said, giggling. The employees around them chatted joyfully, jostling about playfully, smiling. Wen thought how wonderful the day would be as they went through the door to the Command Center and they found free sensornet chairs. He sat and closed his eyes, opening them to a bowl-shaped arena, which he estimated could hold over fifty thousand people, each seat taken by a white-robe-clad man or woman. *How strange*, he thought, and looked down to see that he, too, was dressed in white, as if they were all senators in a Roman coliseum. All around him stood people he had never met, all of whom smiled beatifically, staring at the bright green field down below. He was near the very lip of the arena, way at the top, and he wondered how he would ever see anything from this far away. Laughter surrounded him on every side then, and strangers encouraged him to laugh as well. He suddenly felt nervous and alone, encompassed as he was, laughing against his will.

Down on the field, a lone figure strode with what Wen guessed was confidence, distance making it hard to discern details. As the man approached center field, though, he grew larger and larger, both in height and size, making the crowd erupt in a frenzy of cheers and acclamations. The man wore a stunning pale blue suit, fine as silk, with a mother of pearl handkerchief tucked into his breast pocket. The suit made a beautiful contrast with his black hair and dark skin, and he recognized him right away from the Metro commercials he saw every day on the way to and from work. This was Nabeen Singh, the smiling CEO of DaiSin, waving at his people and soaking in their adulation like a god. Tall as a skyscraper, he looked down upon them now, and Wen thought he should be terrified at having this man staring directly into him, but somehow he could only feel complete happiness, his rush of fear redirected as exhilaration and admiration.

"Good morning!" he said, and Wen felt as if he spoke only to him. The arena exploded in response with every person answering as one. Wen realized that the man he stared up to spoke directly into every person's mind, making speakers useless. Silence, the kind you could hear, it was so loud, fell upon the assembled crowd, which stood motionless and ramrod straight, waiting for instructions. Singh made the motion to sit, and all did so immediately, eager smiles plastered on their features.

"I want to begin today by telling you all how much of a great job you are doing for the company, and especially for me. It is an honor to have you as employees. Give yourselves a round of applause," he said, and the clamor that rose deafened Wen in its violent outburst of cheering. Singh once again raised his hand and the clapping ceased.

"I'd like to welcome all you employees who have just joined the family. You are a welcome addition, and we hope you feel safe in your new home," he said. Wen felt as if Singh had singled him out, talking for him and him alone. No matter how much he tried, he could not bring himself to hate this man, not even dislike him. It was hard to bear any kind of ill feeling in the presence of such overwhelmingly loving sentiments. They filled him to the bursting point, and he felt confused as to how to deal with what he suspected was emotional manipulation. There was no turning away from the towering figure's face, looming above him like some legendary statue come to flesh. He vaguely noticed his neighbors shaking his hands and patting him on the back, welcoming him to DaiSin, so entranced had he become.

"Work hard, and you can achieve anything; that is, after all, our motto. I want you to work as hard as you can because you deserve to achieve your full potential! Who here doesn't want the better things in life? Who here doesn't want to aspire to great heights? Who here only wants mediocrity?" Singh said, a look of disdain on his enormous features, and the assembled crowd replied: *"No one!"* in unison.

"Exactly. No one wants to be last. You must therefore work hard to be better than each other, to climb higher, to gain those heights, to win your rewards," he said, and in that moment, in Wen's torpor state, he realized why no one seemed to notice those who had fallen by the wayside: they simply did not matter. Those who did not make the grade were the chaff separated from the wheat. He wished it were not so, but he no longer cared either. Vigor and want were being infused into him, a hunger for perfection, and love for his fellow man and woman, like a living battery that had been empty, now gaining in strength. All was energy, spreading from his core outward, bursting from his extremities in waves, his senses overcome. For a moment, he felt connected to all present, that he very much was a part of an immense, caring family, fused through the nervous system, a node in a living machine.

"I wish you a great day and an even better week. Don't ever stop making me proud."

Wen felt a surge of horrible energy, some kind of polar negative zipping through his body like a precursor to what might happen should he forget those words, and then calm and stillness like a diaphanous envelope caressed his body.

Singh faded, becoming more and more transparent, losing resolution, until he was invisible, giving them the illusion that he was always there, yet unseen to the naked eye. The other employees around chatted excitedly about the day's sermon, disappearing in droves from the arena, making Wen come to the conclusion that he, too, could disconnect. Rising from the sensornet chair, he felt loss, and a bit of sadness, but hope as well. Next Monday was not so far away.

⏃ ⏃ ⏃

The following weeks were repetition: classes during the day and practice at night. Wen was allowed to see his brother on holographic display in his room once a week. He had settled into his new routine as best he could manage, his brother's absence weighing heavily on him. At least they seemed to be treating him well, and for that he could relax and concentrate on the task at hand. There was still no news about Andrei and Taz, and for them he worried still. Perhaps they were being tortured somewhere, their knowledge the only thing keeping them alive. There was no use inventing scenarios of doom without evidence, and he pushed the thoughts away. He could only do so much, and for now, he empowered himself.

In his spare moments before going to bed, he would enter his jungle clearing and forge weapons, penetrating the sweating jungle with his attempts, confronted by an ever-increasingly hostile fauna. His first gun grazed a large brown rat. The second finished it off. With proficiency came wilder and more dangerous game the deeper he ventured. His temerity augmented also, and he tried his hand at bladed weapons to take on some of the larger, mythological creatures that populated the virtual forest. The first katana he had forged and wielded had broken on the back of a Chimera, sending him running back to camp, pursued by the demented beast. It had taken him several more days and dozens of attempts to get the coding just right to defeat lesser beings. The lion, goat, and serpent heads of the Chimera now adorned his hut as trophies. None of his creations decorated the walls of the arsenal, but that wasn't surprising; there was nothing among them they could use successfully in any kind of battle that the seasoned soldiers couldn't make better.

His other discovery was one that troubled him far more than the increasing difficulties he encountered within the program. During his battles, he had tried to pause the program when he thought he had encountered real trouble, with no success. Whoever or whatever controlled the simulation refused to activate failsafes that could potentially save his life if it ever came down to it. He truly was on his own. No matter how curious he was to try to see what happened in case of his death, he was loath to actually attempt the experience for fear of permanence. Fighting on became his only option, and one he embraced with increased savagery and determination with every successful kill.

His sensornet chair became a second home, where he scrambled every time an alarm sounded. He observed the outgoing soldiers, taking note of their gear and preferences as they grabbed them from the walls of the arsenal. Most had forged their own and carried them with dignity. Of course, they were available to all, but the more hardened warriors took pride in handling the devastating power of the arms they had created themselves. Some of the younger novices chose those of the heroes they admired, following their leaders into battle with the assurance that both the weapons and their creators could not fail them. They, in time, would improve upon the design of their mentors if luck and skill let them live that long.

Older soldiers were always happy to enrich his theoretical knowledge with their experience, discussed over a cold beer in the common room at the end of long days. Wen listened, nodding gravely, making mental notes of strategies he could use in the slaying of his own practice partners in the shadowed darkness of the jungle. They offered tips about the kinds of weapons and armor that served best in various scenarios, and Wen never let an opportunity for him to put them into practice go to waste. They often mocked him for his inexperience, but even though he had not seen any actual firefights, he felt as if they grew to like him. There was a kind of mild rivalry between the trained soldiers and their tech counterparts, they of the computer warfare class. Wen felt more affinity with the people on the ground than those ordering from above, advancement be damned.

Many nights, he quietly strode from one section of the company to the other by Netmind, looking for the tiniest clue as to his brother's or his friends' locations, spying on unprotected minds on the upper levels. Either DaiSin had secret prisons, or they were kept offsite. In any event, he got no closer to finding them.

As the weeks passed, he felt the hum of the place grow stronger, more insistent, but never unpleasant. A live wire giving him a soft trickle of energy, subcutaneous and vague, like a thousand voices softly whispering their love for his very existence, accepting and nurturing him in ways he had not felt in a long time. Despite himself, he began to feel a kind of peace as the music of DaiSin fell like droplets on the armor he tried to keep intact began to thin.

ᛚ ᛚ ᛚ

The alarm rang, as it always did, toward the end of the afternoon, predictably, really. Mondays were dreadfully slow until the impending attack arrived. No longer surprised, Wen sauntered into the sensornet chair in his room and arrived in the Arsenal, ready to lend a hand for payload duty as all the other soldiers geared up for battle. Mood was febrile, a din of machine gun fire and mortar rounds resonated through the blast door, sending some of the veterans ducking in anticipation.

Ulrick approached from the side and yelled at him, "Gear up, Harkwell; you're going in!"

"What? Are you kidding me? I'm not ready!" he said, looking around for someone to back him up. Some of the other recent initiates reluctantly put on armor designated by the soldiers, as well as the weapons that suited them most.

"Get your ass in there, Harkwell; we're done babysitting," Ulrick said, spitting. Wen's heart galloped at a hundred kilometers an hour as he approached one of the sergeants he knew.

"Gotta gear up, Sarge. What do you recommend?" he said, holding his trembling hands behind his back as he perused the walls of gear.

"Well, it's a heavy assault. You're going to need ballistic armor like this one," he said, pointing to a massive piece of hardware, "and the tank-buster to go with it," he said, tapping a rocket launcher by its side. "Try it on."

Wen put his hand on the armor, and an exact replica wove itself around the contours of his body, becoming opaque. He picked up the rocket launcher, heaving it on his shoulder. Infantrymen rushed out the door at the far end in a half-crouch. Soon there were only the dozen or so recruits, himself, and Ulrick Werber left standing in the arsenal.

"What are you waiting for? Get the hell out there!" he bellowed, red-faced.

Wen's head swam. He clutched his rocket launcher in a death grip and led the charge, legs jelloing as he vaulted toward the egress. His stomach churned so bad he thought he couldn't contain himself. Two meters, he squared his shoulders, rock solid, and bared his fangs. One meter; he let out an animal scream and jumped through the aperture, the others close behind, ready to kill.

They tumbled into a silent white room. All the veterans stood at attention in formation, facing the door and dumbstruck recruits. Deguchi stood at the forefront and came forward to greet them.

"Congratulations, initiates, you've passed. You're now grunts," he said, and the room erupted with cheers, laughter, and applause. Veterans surrounded Wen to congratulate him, slapping him on the back and offering him a drink when they were out of the simulation. Wen glanced at Deguchi, trying to appraise his feelings toward him, but he wore a perfect mask of calm.

When the adulations were over with, Deguchi spoke again. "You've done well, and you're ready for action. Next time won't be a simulation but the real thing. Be prepared. Now get out of here and go party." The crowd dispersed, returning to the arsenal to discard their gear, most of them vanishing on their way out.

The Common Room was ablaze that night. War had been declared on sobriety, and heavy artillery lined the counter, fired back by those determined to kill it off, once and for all. The bar was overflowing with shot glasses and beer glasses, the soldiers-cum-bartenders struggling to keep up. Heavy metal music filled the packed room, smashing off the walls, overpowering the cacophony of voices and cheers. For one night only, the smoking ban was lifted, and the air hazed with strong cigar. Everyone on the floor was invited, and all were toasting the new grunts' graduation.

They toasted to DaiSin's freedom and war and victory; Wen toasted to his own. In the humid, fetid din, Deguchi came to him.

"You've been affected to your trainer's group. You know them, they know you; it'll help you get acclimated to the insanity," he said, pointing at Ulrick, Jenna, and Robert.

"Who's the leader?" Wen said, fearing the answer.

"Ulrick. He's the most capable. The other two are good, but…" Deguchi caught himself, looking at his beer and saying no more. He took a long quaff. "Oh, good news," he said, tapping his head, "with the promotion comes more liberty of movement. You don't need an escort to go around anymore. Feel free to go up to the 200th, or even to the other floors of the Department. You can't leave the building yet, though. Report to Ulrick tomorrow morning at the Command Center." Wen raised his glass, took a drink, and then saluted with the other hand.

Wen looked around, appreciating the hubbub. He turned to Deguchi and said, "I challenge you, sir, to an arm-wrestling match." He smiled.

Deguchi choked on his beer. "Are you serious?" the big man said.

"How else am I going to prove my chops around here?" Wen smirked, rolling up his sleeve. He yelled so that everyone could hear him. "I challenged the boss to an arm-wrestling match; do you think he'll take it up, or chicken out?" Cheers and beer mugs went up across the room as Deguchi's lip curled in an evil grin.

"You're on. You're going to get your ass handed to you, son." He removed his jacket and rolled up his sleeve over his enormous biceps. A table was cleared near the center of the room.

"I put 2000 yen on Harkwell!" he heard from behind him.

"Ha! 4000 on Deguchi!" a woman's voice declared. Soon, a bookie was found to take on the wagers of the crowd.

Gardner sidled up to Wen: "You're not seriously going to do it, are you?" he said, putting his hand on his shoulder.

"Do I look like I'm kidding?" Wen said, emotionless. He sat before the big man, the gathered men and women surrounding the two at a table still puddled with spilled beer, a single light shining above the two men like some cheap movie prop. A hush came down on the crowd. Wen put his elbow on the table, taking Deguchi's mitt in his diminutive hand. Both arms pressed hard against one another. Jenna placed her palm overtop both men's hands, and made the countdown. A ripple of excitement surged through the assembled crowd, shouts for the favorites gushing all around.

"Three, two, one…go!" she said, lifting her hand. For an instant, Wen's arm seemed to swing forward, but was thrown back onto the table with a crash, smacking him on his sore knuckles with a thud.

"The winner!" Jenna said, taking Deguchi's hand and raising it skyward at the jubilation of the crowd. Those few unlucky enough to have bet against him looked disappointed for a moment, but then new matchups were made to try to recoup their losses. Wen and Deguchi ceded their spots to the next contestants, Wen shaking the large man's hand.

"No hard feelings?" Deguchi said, squeezing his hand a bit too hard.

"None whatsoever," Wen answered, wincing. Deguchi walked away, triumphant, accompanied by a slew of admirers and others who wanted to take him on. Wen rubbed his sore knuckles, trying to shake out the prickling pain.

Gardner gave him a beer and said, "Told you that was a pointless idea."

"Bah, have to challenge the alpha dog sometimes, even if you know you're going to lose," Wen said, keeping an eye on Deguchi. "Cheers, Gardner. We're on the same team."

"I know," he said, raising his bottle, "and please, call me Robert."

"Will do, Robert," Wen said. He noticed that Jenna was looking at them, and Robert waved.

"She's gorgeous, isn't she?" he said.

"She's something," Wen said, nonplussed. "Listen, I have to jet. I don't like to drink too much anymore. If I stick around too long, I'll regret it in the morning. Thanks for the beer. See you tomorrow." He drank the rest of his beer in one straight chug and put the empty on a table.

"Gotta do what you gotta do, Wen," Robert said, heading off to see Jenna.

Wen left down the corridor and got lost. The right combination of beer and fatigue had erased what little he knew of his most recent surroundings. He knew he should have gone to the bathroom before leaving, but he needed to get out as quickly as possible. An array of black wall plates blanketed the walls, and he touched one. A screen formed before his eyes, a voice sounding from the wall. "How may I help you?"

"Wen Harkwell's private apartments, please," he said, hoping that would do the trick.

"One moment, please," the voice answered. "Follow me, please." Purple footsteps rose out of the black carpeting, ghost steps leading the way. Wen followed the tracks back to his apartment and entered, taking care of his business as fast as he could.

At his sensornet chair, he sat down, feeling a bit buzzed. No matter, he thought, he could do this blind drunk. Introspecting into his jungle clearing, he turned off the sun, the sky going from radiant and sweltering to star-filled and cool in an instant. The crucible waited for him. Yellow flames illuminated the glade from beneath it after he had lit it. He rolled up his virtual sleeve and dipped his arm into the cauldron. What popped up over the pot was an ID card; one with Douglas Deguchi's info.

Wen brought it into the hut and put it into a drawer. Then he opened his eyes and squeezed his arm to erase the evidence.

▲ ▲ ▲

The next day, his real training began, and he was handed a professional-looking automatic weapon and armor within the Arsenal. Jenna, Robert, and Ulrick were there, gearing up. Wen was among three other new recruits that had been imported from other levels of the pillar.

Ulrick lead the crew through the wide blast doors to the ramparts. A vast nanotide plain stretched before them, below the high defenses. Magnetic winds blew from a far-off server bank. Bits and bytes of dead program strewed the blasted grounds, spiraling into bit-devils before getting carried off on some stronger current. Less a clean-cut structural construct than an entropist's wet, flaking dream, the previous overseers of the systems having constantly battled and lost against the deleterious effects of data frittering and conversion loss, the visual Net proved once and for all that the universe cooled in the virtual as well as the actual, every loose byte swirling in the data currents as information-heavy as pellicles of dead skin.

Along the iron walls rose a purple haze of fractaled electroshielding, whirling metadata along every open node. The mesh hummed in low voltage tones, like the background radiation of the universe.

It was early, and the day's battles had yet to be fought.

"Alright boys and girls, take up positions along the wall," Ulrick ordered the new recruits. He lifted his hand, and bull's-eye targets appeared in the distance. "Take aim." They sighted their targets. "Fire!" A deluge of pulse-gun fire rained down on the distant targets, most going wide. "Pathetic," Ulrick said, scowling. "And they aren't even moving. The enemy won't be standing still for you to shoot them, you know. One more time! Sight carefully, butt stock comfortably against your shoulder. Squeeze the trigger gently; don't jerk it." This time, a few shots landed on the targets, nowhere near the centers. "Again, you maggots!" he bellowed.

"What good will virtual guns do against virtual people in a virtual world?" Wen asked, raising his head. Ulrick pinched his septum and closed his eyes.

"Harkwell, do you know what a computer virus is? I only ask because you seem to know nothing about anything," Ulrick said.

Wen's face reddened. "Of course I do!" he said.

"What you are blasting out aren't ion canon pulses or bullets; they are viruses of different types. They are designed to disable whatever part of the enemy projection they hit. Hit them often enough and the virus will disable a part of their actual brain. Any more moronic questions, Harkwell?" Ulrick said, fuming.

"No, sir," Wen said, his lips tightening to a white line.

The morning was spent target shooting under the orders of the bellicose Ulrick. During the afternoon, however, Wen continued his own practicing in the jungle, finding it much more soothing to be on his own than to have that howler monkey Ulrick on his shoulder denigrating his every shot. He began by target shooting objects he placed on the other side of the clearing. He built a stand where he could comfortably rest his elbows and steady his aim. By nighttime, he had progressed to the outer circles of the targets. Not enough to attempt "live hunting," but satisfying nonetheless. It was quite different to shoot long-range targets than the small animals he encountered a mere meter or so away in the jungle.

What he had been eager for, though, was the evening. He retrieved Deguchi's ID and reinstalled it on himself. Many options opened to him this way; he could enter people's minds through the back door, at least, most peoples', or he could simply impersonate Deguchi. At Fujii-Hashimoto Heavy, the managers possessed skeleton keys that could unlock any one of the employees' personal lockers, in case they suspected someone of drug dealing or carrying illegal goods. There was an almost certain chance that DaiSin would do the same, and that Deguchi's ID would have that power. It was a lie, he knew, that their choosing a password would protect them from intruders, at least, within the company. Access from the HYVE had to operate somehow, without direct control by the concerned party; therefore, a different, hidden port had to exist.

Wen wondered if the interference Zella had been talking about was what made it difficult for them to enter his mind without permission, through that theoretical opening. He still had no idea if the HYVE could sneak in, but he had to hope not. He introspected, leaving his body behind. Ulrick's mind was the one he was looking for. It was the most likely to have access to the Outer Nets, beyond the confines of DaiSin Corporation's physical structures. Wen wanted to muddy his tracks as best he could. He would have used more minds, if he had known exactly how the network operated. As it stood, he was going in blind, without a manual and his hands tied, it felt like. The old trick of creating multiple addresses to cover his tracks would surely work in this system as well, using multiple people instead, he hoped.

In the shimmering darkness, he zipped up the filament to Ulrick's mind. A sphere having no obvious up, down, left or right, he inspected the thing closely, hoping to find some sort of flaw that would indicate a back door or alternate port. A fine mist flowed from a certain area, like a tiny spigot that accepted as well as expelled water. The surface of the sphere was unbroken, yet when he approached his ex-corporeal self, a tiny green rectangle of light appeared on its surface, around the expulsion of what could only be data. This had to be it. Wen attempted to insert himself into the port, and Deguchi's VID fit the lock, shimmying through the bluish membrane and taking him with it. There was a real chance the man might be within his construct at the moment, but Wen had to take the chance anyhow. He had studied the man's habits, and if he stayed true to form, he would be drinking a beer alone in the mess hall. Wen floated down through to the chip and landed at the furthest entrance of his operating system, as a matter of precaution. Ulrick's "skin" was the castle theme that had been a part of the choices he had previously been offered but heavily modified over time. A thick-walled utilitarian medieval bunker, vaguely Teutonic, ramshackle, and looking as if a plague had decimated the countryside, dominated the plain on a stubble-covered hillock. Dark pennants floated listlessly over grim barbicans in the foreground of a perpetual burnt-amber half-dusk. Night insects threw an occasional chirrup as a murder of gorecrows threw him sideways glances and croaked at his approach from naked and twisted trees along the path. The whole set-up screamed "I'm trying way too hard!" in its attempts at scaring off intruders.

I should have guessed, thought Wen. If he was quick, Ulrick would never know he'd been there. Silence and stealth were of the essence. He pushed the front door of the castle open and sealed it again. Great bare stone halls echoed soundlessly with his soft steps. Dull metallic armor stood erect along the way, empty shells nonetheless sending shivers down his spine despite himself. Empty pedestals where other potential decorations could have been harbored diminutive brass plaques reading "Purchase Now? Click For Store," completely breaking the spell of the already ridiculous overall low-rent aura of the place and forcing a snort of disbelief out of him. There would have been no surprise on his part at seeing "spooky" vampires try to jump at him from the shadows, or some equally benign classic movie monster, and he half-expected, half-looked forward to such a corny event.

He climbed a wide crimson-carpeted staircase to the upper chambers and snuck into the master bedroom. The memory player was an enormous drop-down screen on the sable and brown stone wall, serviced by a projector over the massive four-poster bed. Wen turned it on and made a quick search. He needed Ulrick's Netrode address so he could spoof it and then exit the DaiSin firewall. A blank section of tape came up under the desired directory. Ulrick had deleted it from his memories. *Clever*, he thought. A "physical" copy had to exist somewhere. Wen searched in the lumbering wooden dressers, the gigantic closet, and even by the bed stand.

Footsteps resounded outside the chambers, climbing the staircase, getting closer. Wen panicked. If he was caught now, Ulrick could kill him, of that, there was no doubt. Scrambling around the room, he tried to find the thirteen-digit Netrode ID code. It was nowhere. The steps were close now. In desperation, he looked under the thick mattress, and found a rolled up parchment scroll. He snatched it, unfurling it as fast as he could, his fingers trembling. He glanced at the door, his throat dry, the footsteps just on the other side, and then a pause. He scanned the code with his arm, rolled the parchment, threw it back underneath the mattress as the door was opening, closed his eyes, and exited Ulrick's mindspace without a trace.

Swimming in the open blackness of Netspace, he circled Ulrick's orb until he found a less opaque section, staring through it like a frosted crystal ball. The man was in his chambers, lying on his bed, replaying a memory. Wen's tremulous hands settled, and he returned to his mind. The process of copying and IDing Ulrick's Netrode was done. He now had Deguchi's Virtual ID as well as Ulrick's Netrode address.

With Ulrick's Netrode identifier loaded as his own, he headed to the glasslike DaiSin firewall, was green-lighted, and slipped through without a hitch, crossing air. Now came the hard part; he had to find the old servers at Cape Canaveral. He rose as high as he could above the physical Netspace, hovering over the lights and dots that made up Tokyo; above him shone the red sun, illuminating the world and its Netlights. In the distance to the west floated clumps of dots, separated by their own firewalls, Netted countries with an Elite population. This one had to be China, the myriad lights indicating an enormous concentration of members of the upper echelons. He frowned and turned the other way, and a single string, nigh impossible to see with the naked eye, ran over a curved distance, a thin silk thread disappearing into infinity. Wen followed it, recognizing as he approached it the architecture of the late American Web. He had gotten so used to going in 'blind' that it was odd to navigate in three-space for the first time. His program identified the code for the server banks he had been searching for, and he went in to retrieve the files he had stashed what felt like eons ago. The clicking jaunts of the computer banks almost carried a musty odor with their ponderous plodding, and Wen wondered how people had survived with such infuriating sluggishness.

As he copied the files, he thought, *What makes* you *so special?* as he watched the lines of code in cryptographic form unfurl into his mind.

He sped back to Japan with the information. Once returned to his clearing, he attempted to make something, anything out of the file. The crucible only returned error messages. Deguchi had been right. He needed the key to decrypt the files if he wanted to find out what they were for and why they were so important.

The Code, he reminded himself. *I'm only alive as long as they don't get ahold of it.*

⋏ ⋏ ⋏

For the next several weeks, Wen practiced shooting moving targets in the distance of the Netplane and hunting the wild beasts of his forest. With proper authority, he borrowed an array of weapons from the Arsenal and improved upon his. He kept working on the Code until he managed to get a tiny fraction deciphered, a splinter he appended to a weapon in the crucible, to see what would come of it. The thing it birthed was a mean-looking, slick-black hand canon. Now he needed to try it out and see all the nasty it could do.

At the other end of the clearing rested an unsuspecting cardboard target, one he intended to put out of its nonexistent misery. For reasons unknown, he had named it Ulrick, and Ulrick, like all practice targets, needed to die. He leveled his arm, the thing in it whirring with power, beginning to glow red with anticipation. The trigger clicked, a tiny pellet like a spit wad flew to the target, and nothing much happened. Disappointed, Wen walked over to it to see if any damage had been caused at all. There was a hole big enough to admit a midget ant, a tiny little hole, near the center of the target. He peered through it and his forehead went cold. The miniature hole continued beyond the target, boring through the tree directly behind it. He followed its course to see where it had stopped. The deeper he went into the forest, the more his amazement grew. Tree after tree was penetrated through and through by his little invention's projectile.

As he was contemplating his gun, a rush of undergrowth parted before him, an enormous lizard careening out of the bushes. Its fanged mouth parted evilly and it let out a shrill cry as it pounced on him. Wen raised his gun and fired, sending the creature scattering in a fine red mist. Now he was truly impressed. He added The Pulverizer to his personal armory on his weapons roster.

⋏ ⋏ ⋏

He came on as observer with the other initiates during raids on the company, analyzing the movements of the enemy, their methods of attack and the way DaiSin soldiers reacted to them. It became obvious to him that it was a constant stalemate. The enemy assaulted and was repelled just as quickly. Dropped weapons were isolated and taken apart by a secure server in the HYVE, their structure added to that of the new weapons made at the Arsenal if seen fit to. A new enemy group would appear a day or so later, the soldiers would fend them off, their weapons picked up and analyzed, introduced into the Arsenal: wash, rinse, repeat. Wen was starting to doubt Deguchi's dire threats of death at the hands of the enemy. So far, he hadn't even seen one of theirs suffer so much as tousled hair, let alone a scratch.

One morning during practice, a small contingent of enemy dusted the pixels in the background of the null-space of the Net, nearing the outer limits of canon fire. No more than twenty mercenaries, lightly equipped, led by a single puny-looking hovertank with a loose tread and thin shielding, huffing asthmatically as it advanced. At first, they were mistaken for targets, but as the soldiers scrambled behind their energy shields, surprise turned to hilarity.

"What the hell are they doing?" said Robert.

Ulrick brought up a floating screen that showed their whole platoon. "Those idiots are just cowering behind their shields. Don't even bother sounding the alarm."

"That's a suicide attack if I've ever seen one," Jenna said, cringing.

Robert looked at the screens showing the cowering enemy. "I wonder what they did to their superiors to suffer this kind of punishment."

"All right, fire at will," Ulrick said, and they blasted at the invaders. The hovertank returned fire, as did the soldiers behind their cover. They soon began to retreat, the hovertank backing up by increments. "Let's go hunting," Ulrick said, eyes slitted.

"Are you serious?" Robert exclaimed.

Ulrick gave him a nasty look. "Are you disobeying orders, Gardner? Everyone, let's go." Jenna glanced at Robert and the other new recruits. Ulrick stepped through the force field and jumped down to the plain. The rest followed suit. Ulrick charged after what was left of the enemy platoon, firing as he ran. The others fanned out, doing the same. They passed by the practice targets and stopped. The attackers had gone away.

"That was easy," Ulrick said, smiling. A rumble sounded from above, followed by the appearance of five hovers, and a full contingent of soldiers from every direction.

Horrified, they stared for what seemed an eternity before Ulrick cried, "Retreat!" Jenna sounded the alarm, but the enemy was encircling them. "Log out!" Ulrick yelled. No matter how hard they tried, they were glued in place, no way of using the instantaneous route out. The defensive walls looked a million miles away. An army of Golems sped from the DaiSin Tower, shooting toward them at incredible speeds. The enemy fired at the six who ran for home. The Golems jumped over them, taking the rounds and shells aimed at the retreating humans, disintegrating as they did. They ran with the devil on their asses, glancing behind them to spy the Golems firing back at the invaders. The enemy outflanked them, and soon they were in the middle of a crescent, protected by the cubes, being shot at at point-blank range. Ulrick cowered in the middle of the circle.

"What do we do now?" Robert yelled over the din, shots flying overhead.

"Shoot! Shoot them!" Wen retorted angrily. The Golems were being consumed by live rounds, melting onto the ground at an incredible rate. They would be left defenseless in less than a minute if nothing was done.

A female recruit was shot and fell lifeless. The hovertanks drew nearer, the enemy soldiers spreading out to let them in.

The Pulverizer, Wen thought. *I have no choice.* He traded weapons on the spot and screamed, "Duck!" The others and the Golem cubes all flattened against the ground, Wen taking aim straight at the hovertank. He squeezed the trigger, aiming for the barrel of the massive canon. It bulged at the back and was engulfed with a huge fiery explosion rending it apart, shaking the ground beneath it and engulfing the surrounding soldier in its blast radius. The enemy soldiers looked around in surprise at the scorched black hole where one of their state-of-the-art hovers used to be, allowing Wen the time to fire off two more rounds into the other incoming vehicles. They blew apart like lava-filled water balloons, spraying molten fire in every direction, taking the crouching soldiers with them.

A cry came ringing from afar, and Wen turned to see DaiSin soldiers running to the rescue, their hovertanks leading. The remainder of the enemy fled in terror, and Wen sent off one last round and demolished another tank.

A commander came up to Ulrick, who was getting off the ground. "By the looks of things, you didn't need us all that much. You looked like you were in trouble there for a while," he said, patting pixel dust off of him.

"Yeah, ah, we were all right," Ulrick said, sheepishly, taking the man's hand and rising on wobbly knees.

"What do you mean, we were all right? You almost got us killed!"

Robert erupted. A soldier spoke up just then.

"Sir, this one is gone," he said, showing the fallen recruit, whose signal was transparent and blue.

"All right then," the commander said, shaking his head. "This action will go up for review. Download your memory of the event into my recorder."

Jenna, Robert, the surviving recruit, Wen, and finally Ulrick put their hands on the device, transmitting the memories as they saw them onto the commander's recorder.

"You can log out of the system now. There was some sort of interference field over you. We couldn't get you out even if when we tried. It dissipated with their retreat though."

"Thank you, Commander," Wen said, saluting him, grim-faced, and everyone else did the same.

"You're welcome, soldiers," the man said. "Go home. That's an order."

"Aye, sir," they responded, and one after the other, they vanished. Wen opened his eyes on his sensornet chair in his room. He sighed with relief and got to his feet to go see how the others were doing. When he arrived at the Command Center, the body of the recruit was being removed on a stretcher.

"What will happen to her?" he asked Jenna.

"She'll be cremated," she answered, eyes glistening. She brushed it away with her sleeve. "What was that thing you used on them? It was lethal!" she said.

"Yeah, I want to know too," Robert said, ascending the steps from the lower rung of the room. Others were beginning to leave as well, going for lunch.

"I made that," he said with the same tone he would have used to describe ordinary weather or the taste of a bland sandwich.

"*You* made that," Jenna said.

"That is some seriously hard-core shit you brewed up, Wen. That has to go in the Arsenal. How come it isn't already?" Robert said. Wen thought he detected greed in his voice, but no, Robert was a company man, and only wanted what was good for the collective.

"I thought my weapons weren't good enough; that's why they weren't added," Wen answered.

"Not good enough? Are you kidding me? You just pulled off four one-shot kills on hovertanks using something the size of a handgun. Which base program did you tweak to get something like that working?" Robert asked.

"Oh, you know, a little bit of this, a little bit of that; it's all in the Arsenal already. Plus I've been getting pretty good at forging," he lied.

"Pretty good is an understatement. Let me buy you lunch," Jenna said, taking him by the arm. Robert smirked and followed them to the Common Room.

Later that day, as Wen lay on his apartment's sofa, a summons came. The team had been awarded the rest of the day off, pending the results of the investigation, and Wen had used his time to attempt to get over the ordeal he had just experienced. How lucky was he to have survived, he wondered, and how long would this incredible luck last? Was Ulrick always this reckless with his men? It was one thing to have to fight for DaiSin, but to do so at the hands of a complete incompetent was another entirely. How could such a person have been given any kind of authority? It reminded him of what his father had once said, something about power not going to the most competent but those most desirous of it. Ulrick Werber was the purest embodiment of one who deserved none of the power he wielded but had tricked fate somehow and grabbed it for himself, to Wen's and everyone else's detriment. The sibilant ring interrupted his brooding, and he answered the holophone device wearily. A salt and pepper haired man he had never seen appeared in his living room. He wore long, thick red robes with theater-curtain velvet pomposity that would have been worth a snicker if not for his utter lack of humor and deadly serious demeanor.

"Wen Harkwell. I am Deliberator Kenji Miyazaki," he announced drily. "Your presence is required in room 347A, on the 245th level, in half an hour. Please do not be late." Then he extinguished.

That was quick, he thought, getting up. He met Jenna, the other two recruits, and Robert at the elevators. Ulrick fidgeted, biting his nails, looking like a trapped animal.

"If you get me in trouble, you're all going to pay for it," he said under his breath as the elevator doors closed.

"What was that?" Jenna said, turning and shooting daggers with her gaze at the man.

"You heard me. If I get blamed for this, I'm taking you down with me," he said, glaring at her.

"You're an *ass*, Ulrick," she said, holding his stare. Ulrick looked down and stared at the carpet. "If it wasn't for Wen, we'd all be dead or worse because of you," she added with the look of a woman who wanted an excuse to rub out some ugly bug with her heel.

Worse than death? What's worse than death? thought Wen.

"You lying bitch! I had the situation completely under control! Don't start spreading lies, or I swear you'll regret it," Ulrick said, his face distorted in a rictus of hatred, practically spitting in Jenna's face.

"We'll see about that," Jenna said, crossing her arms and lifting her chin in disdain, ignoring Ulrick's muttering for the rest of the trip to the 200th level. The lower level elevators were situated on the outside perimeter of the building, and they exited near the front entrance of the tower, in front of the guard station. Wen hadn't been back since his mother's abduction. The edifice remained grandiose; a marvelous sight to behold. The sun shone in from its myriad facets, inundating the dais with light. He was taken aback for a moment, his heart clenched. Robert strode forward and was saluted by one of the guards at the front desk.

"Here to go to the 245th, Disciplinary Verdicts room," he said.

"Right this way, sir," the guard said, getting up and designating the turnstiles. The group stepped through and were allowed to proceed to the elevators.

A long wooden bench lined the vertical wood-latticed walls on the 245th level. They all sat, save Ulrick, who paced back and forth, his steps smothered by the beige curlicue carpeting. A guard pushed open a wide wooden door, and a group of dispirited–looking, white-shirted workers walked out.

"You may enter," he said to the group. In the large, high-ceilinged room, the padded walls rendered the silence funereal. Rows of empty chairs filled the room. At the very back sat two men and three women dressed in the same red robes as the man who had summoned Wen. As a matter of fact, he was one of the two men presiding.

A bespectacled older lady rose, thin hands with blood-red nails palms-down on her pedestal. "Approach the bench," she said. The six walked down the aisle and stood before the ancient-looking Deliberators.

"We have reviewed the case," the lady said, adjusting her thin spectacles. "It would appear Mr. Werber conducted himself in a way unbefitting an officer. He will be removed from his duties as lieutenant."

"That's not fair!" he exclaimed. "How can I be punished for a simple mistake?"

The lady peered down to him over the rim of her glasses, visibly angered by the outburst. "Your 'simple mistake' cost the life of one your charges, with no discernible reason to do so. You should probably receive a harsher sentence. We have been lenient in light of your excellent service so far. Don't push us, Mr. Werber," she said. The accused demurred, peering at the others through slitted eyes. "Your new leader will be Mr. Robert Gardner," she added, hitting the table with a gavel.

Robert took a step forward. "Your Honors, I must decline the appointment," he said. The lady Deliberator's eyebrow lifted, her lined mouth opening in a small *o* of disbelief.

"Why is that, Mr. Gardner?" she said.

"I don't feel that I'm fit to lead. Besides, it was Wen Harkwell who saved us. You saw it yourself in our memories, I'm sure. Without him, we'd all be dead right now. I nominate Wen as our leader," Robert said. Wen looked at him in surprise.

She crossed her long fingers together under her chin. "This is highly unusual, Mr. Gardner. Mr. Harkwell is a new addition to the Company. He is not yet fit to lead."

You're telling me! he thought.

Robert clenched his fists. "I stand by my decision, ma'am."

"How does the rest of the group feel about this?" she said. "By a show of hands, who here thinks that young Mr. Harkwell would qualify as your leader?" All save Ulrick and Wen lifted their hands. "Very well. You may return to your duties. We will inform you of our decision within the next day. Dismissed." And she rapped her wooden gavel on the desk before her.

"What are you doing, Robert?" Wen whispered as they walked out of the room.

"The right thing. You saved our asses, Wen. I froze. I discussed this with Jenna earlier; you're the best choice," he whispered back. Wen shook his head.

They returned to the 200th floor, and as they were about to leave for the lower elevators, Wen recognized Mauritius Lewes behind the head desk.

"Go on without me," he said. Ulrick was already ahead, fuming. Wen approached the desk and saluted Lewes. "I need to talk to you."

Lewes returned the salute. "Looks like you're going up in the world," he said, sizing up Wen's uniform.

"Yeah, I went down to go up," Wen said. "Can we take a walk?"

"Isn't that always the way?" he said, grinning. "And sure." He gave Wen an inviting gesture, and they went toward the building's rotunda.

"Why did you thank me that night?" he asked Lewes, who walked with his hands behind his back. The sun shone through the myriad facets of the building's shell, warming Wen's skin in a way he hadn't fathomed how much he'd missed.

"Sometimes information takes too long to get processed, or gets lost. You gave me a piece of info that I needed. Without it, I might still be hoping to hear about it. Know what I'm saying?" he said, nodding nonchalantly to a woman passing by.

"Aren't you angry at me for my involvement?" Wen said.

Lewes shrugged. "Once again, did you do it?"

"Still no," Wen said.

"I believe you, and I can spot a liar. I have no reason to hold a grudge against you. Of course I'm upset at what happened. But the right person has to pay for what they did. I'm not in the business of wholesale retribution," he said, looking at Wen, who nodded. They rounded a corner, and a large indoor pond complete with carp and wading turtles revealed itself, lotus flowers unfurled around its edges. Further off was a café where employees sat at tables near a burbling waterfall, chatting and drinking, the far glass wall of the DaiSin Building looming in the background.

"One more thing. Don't take this the wrong way, but how did you get the police there so fast? Even calling them by Netrode would have taken longer," Wen said. This had been a particular sticking point he hadn't been able to resolve since that fateful night.

"I didn't. I thought it was a happy coincidence at the time, perhaps one of my neighbors having seen a strange man go into the apartment and calling them for me." They walked back toward the front desk. *Was it a coincidence then*, he thought, *or is there more to it?* On the one hand, it was entirely possible some neighbor had called the cops on him, but he had been careful enough that it seemed unlikely.

"Sorry about the arm," Wen said, as he remembered the slamming he had given Lewes during his escape.

"Apology accepted," Lewes said, smiling. He extended his hand, and Wen shook it.

"I have to get back. I don't have full access yet. Be well, Lewes." Wen walked through the turnstiles to return to the lower levels and his department. It just seemed too perfect timing to be a coincidence, he thought, as the elevator brought him back down. That evening, he received his weekly holophone call from his brother.

"I've got great news!" Sammy said, beaming.

"They're letting you out?" Wen asked, dubious.

"I wish. No. I'm getting implanted. I'm getting my Netrodes, Wen! Isn't that incredible! Everybody is getting them, apparently." Sammy practically vibrated with happiness, and he looked about at people that Wen couldn't see.

"Aren't you too young to be getting Netrode implants?" Wen said, a worried look creeping onto his features.

Sammy waved his worries away with his hand: "They said it was fine. New procedure, less danger of interference."

"But you're only thirteen! Why the hell do you need Netrodes?" Wen said, pacing back and forth in his room.

"Who cares? You're not jealous, are you?" Sammy said with a sly grin.

Wen paused. "No, of course not, Sam. I'm concerned, that's all. I had to wait until I was eighteen, when I was growing up, like everybody else."

"Ah-ha! You *are* jealous!" Sammy said, pointing an accusatory finger and letting out a giggle.

Wen mumbled to himself and then said, "I might become team leader. I can't talk about it yet, but this is an awesome opportunity."

"Well look at you, Mister 'I'm So Important.' You're not falling to the Dark Side, are you?" Sammy said, in mock concern.

"No, Sammy, I'm not. But they're giving me a chance. I shouldn't turn it down."

"How screwed up is this? I had to get kidnapped for you to get a real job," Sammy said, sticking his tongue out sideways. Right, because this was an incremental improvement over their previous life, he thought. No matter how bored he might have been at his previous job, he was fairly certain he would have picked it over this. As things stood, though, he was no longer entirely sure. There still loomed the overarching problem of Sammy's incarceration. Just because he, for now, successfully walked the tightrope did not mean he'd make it to the next safe point without getting pushed off into the yawning void. Seeing his brother before him was a constant reminder of the fact.

"That's not funny," Wen said, glaring at his brother.

"No, it's ironic, though." He smirked. "I have to go." And his signal faded out of the room, leaving empty space and silence where his body had been. Wen stared at the wall. Sammy was getting Netted. What kind of technology had they come up with to counteract the effects of pubescent hormonal release, he wondered. Now he had to trust that DaiSin would do right by his brother as well, another stress to add to the list.

Wen exited his body and took on the persona of Douglas Deguchi. He broke into Jenna's, Robert's, and Ulrick's minds and stored the Code in three parts, erasing some of their more unpleasant or boring memories to make room for it, leaving the original tags and short sequences at the beginning to hide the new info. His own version he deleted completely, wiping any trace it had ever been there. He could always go back and gather what he needed at some ulterior time. There was little chance the others would be scrutinized or scanned as thoroughly as they tried him.

CHAPTER 9

HE NEXT DAY, Jenna came ringing at his door as he was getting out of bed. "Morning, Chief," she said, rocking on her heels and toes, smiling.

"Morning, Jenna," he said, wiping sleep out of his face.

"Morning, *Chief*," she said again. Wen's eyes grew large.

"Are you serious? How come I wasn't noti—" he began, and his holophone rang.

"That would be your notification. Go answer your phone. Sir."

Wen said, "Answer," and the head of the older Deliberator appeared, disembodied, in the middle of the living room.

"Mr. Harkwell. You have been granted leadership of your group, effective immediately. Your original crew, plus any new recruits or transfers are now under your command. Any questions?" she said, tilting her floating head.

"Mm, what's the pay like?" Wen asked jokingly.

"Is that truly something you want to discuss in the present company?" she said, peering around his shoulder at Jenna waiting in the hallway.

"No, I guess not. Thanks for the good news." The elderly head evaporated. Wen stood in his pajamas in his living room, stunned.

"Your orders, sir?" Jenna said, hands behind her back, her face serious.

"Meeting in the Common Room in twenty minutes. Jenna, I nominate you as my second-in-command."

"Aye, sir," she said, straight-faced. She saluted and left. Wen dressed in a dream state. It was just so bizarre.

Get a grip, he thought. *I have to* lead *people now*. He thought of all the role models and bosses, heroes and idols he had ever had, and which would be the best one to emulate. Lately, the pickings had been slim among worthy gurus. He shook his head sadly for not having thought of it sooner: his father. The man was a myth among the rebels he had led. He had to be the responsible, patient, irreproachable man his father had been. Someone had just fitted him with a cement coat of responsibility. He clenched his jaw; he would make it fit.

In the Common Room, he waited for the others. Robert and the other two recruits congratulated him, and Wen took the time to learn their names. Whereas before he didn't care one bit about anything that transpired at the Barrier Department but his own travails, the game had changed, and he needed to know the players. Their names were Sonia Avilant and Abakar Essouf. Sonia was a French transfer, and Abakar was an Englishman of Chadian descent. Both were in their early twenties. Ulrick glowered a meter or so away from the group.

"You, come here," Wen said to Ulrick, pointing in front of him. Ulrick glared at the man who had taken his job and rank. *What a princess*, Wen thought. "Mr. Werber, you have five seconds to comply, or you will get the first reprimand under my command. What'll it be? One, two, three…" Ulrick shuffled toward the group and joined them, arms crossed, lips a tight white line. "As you all know, I'm in charge. Here is what I need from you: I want you to obey me to the best of your ability. I want you to share any concerns you have with me. I want you to relax when it's time to relax, and step up your game when we're neck-deep in shit. I do not expect you to do anything I can't or won't do. We are a team, and we will act that way. If anybody doesn't like it, too bad. Jenna will be my second-in-command. If I bite it, you bow to her, got it?" he said.

"Got it!" they all answered in unison.

Wen cupped his ear and said, "Got it?"

"Got it!" they answered louder.

"Good. Off to the Arsenal. We're going to do target practice this morning, but after that, we'll try other things. Dismissed." The group saluted and left.

A red-cheeked courier arrived after lunch with a brown paper box for Wen. Inside he found his thin bars, one for each shoulder. He removed the backing and applied the quick-dry adhesive in the appropriate spots, according to the folded instructions included with the decorations. Jenna looked happy for him, and Robert nodded approvingly. Ulrick refused to look at him, preferring to snarl once in disdain.

After the meal, Wen was summoned via holophone to the Command Center by a tall, smoke-skinned commander, her black hair tied back in a single braid. Wearily, he rehearsed on the way there what he wanted to say. Theoretically, nothing incriminating remained in his mind, and he just had to wipe the guilty look off his face to sail through unscathed. She would undoubtedly order a memory dump of his most recent experiences, which was why he had taken the precaution of transferring the Code onto the others. With any luck, the altered files would not be discovered and he could claim malfunction over any singularities that arose. He took a deep breath and closed his eyes for an instant before he entered the Command Center, the room empty save the Amazon that stood before him. Even under her uniform, Wen guessed a lithe yet powerful frame, a woman not to be trifled with, if the perceptive look in her eyes was to be trusted. Here stood a true warrior.

"Lieutenant Harkwell, have a seat," she said, and he nodded, reclining in the proferred sensornet chair, closing his eyes. They met in front of a gold-roofed, bell-shaped temple or palace in the middle of a large city in a tropical country. The out-side air smelled sweet, with tinges of strange yet somehow familiar spices. Hawkers in short-sleeved, buttoned shirts announced their wares under the hazing sun; fruits, vegetables, and flowers in the market, as well as T-shirts for the tourist crowd under rows of tall palms. Green, yellow, and blue three-wheeled vehicles sped about; tiny open taxis carrying couples about town. The air was hot and humid, the sun passing its zenith.

"Let's take a walk, Lieutenant," she said. They crossed the threshold of the im-posing structure before them, an enormous white arch that both looked pyramidal and step-like, walking among tall, thin statues of curled-toothed humanoid demons, bulging eyes staring at them from beneath their horrid gazes. By the architecture, Wen guessed they were somewhere in Southeast Asia, preflood. Among the religious-looking structures grew cultivated gardens of exotic flowers, watered and lovingly tended by men in orange robes.

"I'm Commander Surimat. The jerk-offs who had you pinned were Japonica Inc., a French-Japanese conglomerate. They've developed a new jamming technology, as you could plainly tell. We're not the first they've used it on, I've found out. Just the first they've used it successfully with," she said.

What is our weak point then? he thought. "Will we be able to replicate it?" Wen asked, as they walked among the jewel-encrusted golden colonnades.

"We don't have the device that creates the jamming waves, only the wave signa-tures. That's not enough to reverse-engineer anything. Congrats on your new com-mand, son," she said, noticing the shoulder bars.

"Thank you, Ma'am. I still think it's undeserved," Wen said.

"Ha, more deserved than that worm Werber. No real soldier would have fallen for such a stupid trap. Just because some people's grandfathers are on the Board of Directors doesn't make them eligible for command," she said.

So that was it, thought Wen. They took a right and entered a long, silent room with high, vaulted ceilings. At the end of the darkened chamber sat a Buddha in gold vestment, seemingly made of jade.

"I can only try to do my best, sir," Wen said, his voice echoing in the large, empty hall.

"That's all anyone can do, son. Now, as for this weapon of yours; that is some piece of work. You say you built that with Arsenal weapons?" the commander asked, staring Wen in the eyes, searching for lies inside his green pupils. It was hard to hold her gaze without flinching, but that was probably what she was waiting for, he mused.

"And my own trial and error, sir," Wen said. She nodded, pinching her chin. Wen's sweat dried on his face in the cool interior hall, his features remaining placid and unworried.

"That's some trial and error. May we have a copy of it, Mr. Harkwell? We can't seem to access your mind to retrieve it. Are you blocking us somehow?" Her gaze sharpened once again. Wen's face flushed, his pulse pounding.

"I assure you, I am not attempting to block anyone, sir. I seem to be having this problem with my Netrodes since they were implanted. I will upload the Pulverizer immediately," he said, holding his sweating hands behind his back.

"Good on you. These things happen sometimes; not to worry," the commander said, her intensity dimming as Wen retrieved a copy of his gun and handed it to her. It felt out of place in this peaceful setting, a desecration of something holy and unused to violence. Surimat caught his uncertainty but said nothing. "We'll have to analyze it, of course. You just kicked the R and D department in the butt. You may go."

"Glad to be of service," Wen said, and logged out, leaving the tropical palace behind. He released a long, unsteady breath once he had crossed the hallway door outside the Command Center, feeling as if he had held it ever since he had entered. Now began the waiting game to see if they would detect his meddling with their armory and the files they were after. The stress of knowing they were taking apart his new weapon was nerve-wracking to say the least. If anyone got a whiff that there was outside material, he would probably end up getting scanned and probed—and then mind-wiped. Nevertheless, he continued trying to crack the rest of the Code, without any success. It was odd how he had been able to unseal that one sliver but not the rest. Perhaps it hadn't been encrypted like the whole.

The Pulverizer was now public domain, and everyone borrowed it freely, improving on the design, which was already potent. With every new attack, the weapon made *definitive* casualties. Nothing could survive a direct hit, neither human nor hovers.

After a week, the attacks on DaiSin lessened. Wen believed the opposition was regrouping, perhaps attempting to create a shield that could deflect the terrifying power he had unleashed. Word from the spy networks was that the opposition was losing employees so quickly that any further attacks on DaiSin would permanently cripple their enterprises.

Meanwhile, he had begun a class of his own, unsatisfied with the basics of target practice out on the ramparts. The group gathered every day inside the jungle clearing of Wen's mind. He had moved the hut to the rear, placing large metallic shapes as cover in no particular order around the terrain. It was his team against a platoon of heavily armored androids he had forged, based on the Golems. These robots were a lot meaner looking than the little cubes but served the same functions and were activated by the HYVE Golem matrix. Their weapons set on stun, they would cause pain but no deaths. They would make his team into an unbeatable force. With much attention, he had neutered them so that they were unable to report the goings on inside his mind space; the clearing in which he now prepared these war games. It would not have done to throw the door wide open to spies.

Every day, they battled the androids, and every day, they got their asses handed to them. It wasn't supposed to be easy, and Wen had made sure that the robots were faster than their human opponents. If he wanted to make them improve, it was going to be by being tough on them. Period.

Once a week, he split the team in half and organized hunts in the jungle, where the prey was the other team members. Having had robotic enemies to contend with made grilling humans an easier and more satisfying sport, he thought.

The android-shaped Golems won less and less often, even though Wen turned up their abilities by increments, proof, perhaps, that his team was getting that edge.

⋏ ⋏ ⋏

Sitting against a steel wall after one of their successful battles, the group took a rest in the false sunset of the jungle.

"I think you're going to kill us," Robert said, breathing heavily, toweling his forehead off, crickets chanting in the thickets beyond.

"I'll make you *fit*, Robert," Wen said.

"You'll turn him into a weapon," Jenna said, punching Robert on the shoulder.

"If you don't mind my asking, sir, why do you push us so hard?" Abakar asked.

"Is that a complaint, Abakar?" Wen said, smiling.

The big man shook his head. "I wouldn't dream of it, sir," he said, frowning.

"Aba, you don't mind a little hard work, non?" Sonia chimed in, pinching him from where she sat, a strand of mussed blond hair covering one of her eyes under her helmet.

"It was just a question," he grumbled.

"I'm pushing you to be the best, that's all," Wen said to Abakar.

"But sir, we already have the best weapons; isn't that enough?" Sonia asked.

"The best weapons deserve the best soldiers, Sonia, n'est-ce pas?" Wen replied. She nodded in agreement. It was something that trained soldiers understood quite readily; that it wasn't just the equipment that had to be in top shape but the wielder as well. Harder to make techies follow the logic, since in this day and age, it was principally the equipment that did the work. In the setting of Net Defense, though, both were critical and had to be inculcated into his charges. It didn't matter that all this exercise was purely mental; in the end, it was their reflexes and intelligence that would gain from the experience, at least he hoped so.

"Hey, where's Ulrick?" said Robert, scanning the area. A cold chill went down Wen's spine, and he took off at a run toward the hut. Ulrick was inside, staring wide-eyed at the collection of pelts and skulls covering the walls, Wen's hard-won virtual trophies hanging from the ceiling as well.

"The hell are you doing in here, soldier?" Wen barked.

"You never said it was off-limits, chief," Ulrick said, still not looking in Wen's direction, transfixed by so many prizes. "That's quite the haul you have here. I know they're all virtual creatures, but still…" he said in awe. "Did you buy all these?"

"No. Out," Wen said, pointing at the door. "It's off-limits." He felt stupid for having let him out of his sight, even for a moment. If he'd been snooping long enough, everything might have been compromised. Wen had a sudden flash of being dragged to the first level by black-clad mercenaries, dropped to his knees in the filth, and capped unceremoniously in the back of the skull and repressed a shudder.

"Wouldn't want me finding things I shouldn't, would you?" Ulrick said, perceiving weakness, as he walked by his commanding officer. Wen could've easily reached out and broken his virtual neck, but what then?

"Out!" Wen hollered, following Ulrick out of the room and back to the others. "I didn't think I'd have to say it, but the hut is my space. It's no-go territory, comprende?" he told the assembled crew.

"Aye, sir!" they replied in unison, looking at each other in dismay. Only Ulrick seemed to be smiling a sick little rictus of hate.

Wen waited for them to leave, sealing all access ports, before rushing back into the hut and opening the drawer. His pulse ran at a thousand kilometers an hour as he searched among the myriad baubles he had collected over the months. How stupid of him to not have even placed the simplest of security on his own belongings; all he wanted to do was to punch himself in the face. There! There, under a picture he had wanted to frame; Deguchi's ID and Ulrick's Net address. Had he seen them? His stomach felt full of lead. He'd have to do something about that bastard at some point in time; too bad he still needed him; the information he had stashed inside his head was much too valuable to lop it off in anger.

CHAPTER 10

WEN STARTLED AWAKE with the raging woot of alarms. He jumped out of bed and ran to his sensornet chair, wiping crust out of his bleary eyes. The woman commander, Surimat, was gearing up when he arrived in the Arsenal.

"What's the situation, Ma'am?" Wen asked. Soldiers ran past, armed for war and a fear he hadn't yet seen in their eyes.

"Well, we've got several regiments heading our way. Administration Military Corps," she answered. Wen's head recoiled in disbelief.

"I thought we had a truce with Administration?" Administration wouldn't call in a full scale invasion unless they were assured of total victory, he knew. This was bad.

"We did. It's over. Man the tower guns," she said without emotion, grabbing a new-model long-range Pulverizer and leading her platoon out the blast doors.

Wen turned around and told his assembled crew, "You heard the commander. Gear up; roll out!"

Outside, the plain was thick with the enemy, far away in the distance and advancing carefully. Wen jumped on an ion pulse canon, swiveling the turret down and aiming at the advancing forces. He sighted through the target screen and fired; direct hit. Nothing happened but a powder of blue sparks sizzling off their shields. He fired another booming blast, the recoil and clack of thunder deafening. No better. All around him, the resonant blasts of canons barked and spewed blue flames at the enemy, with little effect. What he'd feared had become reality: Administration was aware of DaiSin's new advanced weaponry and had built defenses before coming to take it away from them. Shots began to rain upward from the field, shaking their own shields, pounding them like hailstones. The concussive effect of the enemies' weapons was identical to their own. Wen realized with horror that they already had Pulverizer technology! Worst yet, Administration had superior shield technology. How could they have made it themselves? How could they have developed it without the Code? Wen felt sick to his stomach at the realization: there was a traitor inside DaiSin, no two ways about it. It didn't take a genius to know how this battle would end if the strategy remained the same.

The recognition made Wen's brain want to explode. The DaiSin force shield was showing signs of stress. Cracks spidered along the lengths and widths of the voltaic wall, threatening to collapse it with every thumping detonation, each blast leaving a glowing orange pock-mark in the swirling program and shreds of code falling away like burnt shale.

Wen jumped off the canon, calling on his group to assemble. "The guns are ineffective. We have to get down there and fend them off hand-to-hand. I know; it's suicidal, but they have a blanket shield over them. We can shoot from up here until we're blue in the face, but we'll just get destroyed in the end. Grab a contingent of Golems and follow me."

The copper cubes began to appear around them, and Wen ordered them to lead the assault; they would use them as cover. He set them on glass mode, and the only thing that could be seen from the enemy's point of view was the other side of the cube, not the soldiers they hid. Even if they themselves had used optical camouflage, the enemy would certainly have detected them using thermal scanners; Golems emitted no heat.

Other soldiers had taken up position at the tower guns, and Wen ordered them to concentrate fire on the center front of the incoming army, like a moving blanket of black ants crawling toward them.

Wen jumped over the wall first, landing underneath a barrage of incoming fire. The cubes aligned in a half-circle wall between him and the invaders. The rest of the crew followed closely. Running in zig-zags, they assaulted the incoming soldiers, their camouflage leading, perfectly timed with their every move. Wen's blood felt cold, and he hoped they would not be discovered as they flew at top speeds toward the adversary on wings of fear, legs pumping like mad.

In the distance, Wen saw a black hover unlike the others in the center of the invaders; it had no canons but what looked like an antenna. Glancing around, he saw two more, on the right and left flank of the incoming army, releasing energy over the troops like liquid tesla coils: portable shield generators.

Wen gave the order and raced to the left flank, bullets whizzing above their heads toward the tower defenses. The sound of thundering canon rounds pounding into the enemy shields deafened them as they raced on and avoided the angle of descent of friendly fire. They crawled, penetrating the shields directly in front of the soldiers, protected only by Golem cover. The tower canons kept the bulk of the army busy by attempting to break through the front and center shields, bit by bit, firing relentlessly and avoiding his group by shooting around but not at them. The smell of ozone was thick and suffocating, and sweat dripped into Wen's stinging eyes. If any of them shot in their direction at this moment, they would be discovered and eradicated. While all enemy guns were upward and on the canons, he opened a tiny slit in his camouflage, big enough to fire off a Pulverizer round, right into the generator's flank.

It exploded in shards of shattering program, infecting and taking out the nearby soldiers. A third of the enemy were now without protection.

Wen got on the com with tower defense and whispered, "In ten seconds, canons 23 through 58 fire on the enemy's left flank!" The soldiers around the burning shield generator milled about, trying to figure how it could have been destroyed.

His crew ran as fast as they could back to the middle distance while the left flank was shredded by the tower canons. The enemy knew something was up now and began firing at ground level, trying to flush out whoever had taken out their generator.

"Right flank, now!" Wen cried, as they ran through the nanofields. Random shots were taking out their wall of Golems, tearing holes in their camouflage.

"I'm hit!" Ulrick yelped, falling flat. Wen ran back and picked him up, Ulrick's disintegrated lower leg pixelating. Their Golems formed a single, double-thick wall.

"Can you log out?" Wen yelled over the sound of snapping gunshots.

Ulrick's eyes unfocused and then returned. "I can't!"

"Then we have to fight it out," Wen said as they ran for the far right of the troops. Wen called the tower canons again. "Concentrate fire on the center of the enemy, all of you, now." The canons redirected and began to fire in the center of mass, damaging the enemy's shields. The advancing troops fired toward the center of the field, believing the canon fire was for cover, to attack them from the center. Abakar penetrated the right flank shield first and sent a volley of Pulverizer fire into the right shield generator, blowing it up in a massive explosion. The rest of the group swept in and fired on the confused soldiers, killing many.

"Right flank in ten seconds!" Wen ordered the tower canons, and they circled around the right, taking the enemy from behind, heading for the center. Now the soldiers fired toward the right and front, but Wen's group was already behind them, speeding toward the last generator. Wen lagged behind because of Ulrick, so Jenna led the charge with Sonia and Abakar, Robert covering the rear. Sonia cleared a path to the hover, and then Jenna fired a volley of destructive shots into the last generator, blowing it to fiery bits. The group kept running to the left to avoid the rush of retreating soldiers.

"Fire on the last of them!" Wen called to the tower, and a hail of blast-fire rained down on the fleeing soldiers, tearing them apart. "Ulrick, can you log out now?" he said. Ulrick's gaze waxed in the middle distance, and he was gone.

Wen turned to watch the fleeing soldiers and noticed a curious object flying toward him. It was a dark gem, glinting as it landed at his feet. He barely had time to realize it was a weapon before it flashed like the sun, turned vortex, and sucked him in.

CHAPTER 11

E WOKE UP naked, strapped to a table. Arms by his side, glued to cold metal by black rubber restraints. White soundproof tiles covered the walls and ceiling. He could only see in front of and above him, his helplessness reflected in an enormous one-way mirror five meters away. He was at an eighty-degree angle, his head cinched down like the rest of his body. He'd never been to an interrogation cell, but once in a while, he'd run across someone on the bottom levels who was still lucid enough after their lobotomies to tell him fragments. *Let the games begin*, he thought, and smiled inwardly. There existed in his mind the assurance that everything would be fine, that no matter what happened, he'd be safe. *Where does that come from?* he wondered. Fear, like a cleaver, threatened to slash this feeling in two, but when it loomed, the sly cockiness gripping him reasserted itself, independent of his natural reaction.

"Harkwell, Wen," came a tinny voice over the loudspeaker.

"Who?" he asked, feigning puzzlement.

There was some silence, and then the same voice said, "We will give you the chance to help us, Wen. You are in a unique position to tell us what is going on at DaiSin."

"Whatever happened to torture being beneath you?" he said, and grinned. A slight rumble came from the table, and it began to descend. He felt, more than saw, panels opening below him. His feet touched frigid water like stabbing blades, and his heart constricted in shock. Prickly needles had replaced his body hair. The table lowered by centimeters and he shook uncontrollably, banging his head against the headboard, feeling as if he were going to puke. It stopped once the water reached his knees.

"Your cooperation would be greatly appreciated," the voice said in an even tone.

"Suck it!" he yelled at the top of his lungs, shaking as if he was having a fit. The table hummed and began to lower again. Blood froze in his legs, and he couldn't feel his feet anymore. The water was getting to places he didn't want it to, creeping up his thighs. It burned, it was so cold. He no longer felt his bluish extremities.

Wen's neck muscles tensed to the snapping point: "I'll help you! Stop, you sick fucks!" The table stopped.

"What is DaiSin up to?" said the same monotonous voice.

How the hell should I know?, he thought, anger rising. "Get me out of here, and I might tell you. Not before," he yelled. It felt like minutes went by, and the table started to lower again. He screamed his lungs out, wiggling and shaking in his restraints, trying to loosen his bonds but lacking the energy to do so.

"I'll die in this thing, and you won't get shit!" he hurled at his unseen persecutors, his teeth chattering and lips turning blue. The one-way mirror reflected his anguish and pain. His neck was stiff with effort. Ping! The table stopped again and then rose slowly. His lower body was bluish white. He felt as if a heart attack was coming on, and his body rattled spastically.

"What are DaiSin's plans, Mr. Harkwell?" the voice reiterated. Wen knew he held the big end of the stick, for now.

"Get me out or you get jack!" he yelled.

"Bylaw 3856 dash B states that the control and dissemination of information is done so solely at the discretion of the State, and permission to publish or withhold has to be obtained, pending review of said information. You are in possession of something highly illegal, Mr. Harkwell. That in itself is a death sentence. We know about the files in your possession. If we do not obtain your full cooperation, we cannot stop your probable execution."

He felt a hard lump climb into his throat. They were bluffing. They couldn't get rid of him until he told them what he knew. He wanted to kill the traitor personally when he got out of there. If *I get out of here*, he thought.

"I don't talk while I'm strapped to this thing." His voice seethed between clenched teeth. A robotic arm popped out of the ceiling, on the end of which was attached a syringe. It went straight for the bulging blue vein in his forearm, and his senses faded.

Compared to the torture chamber, his cell was an oven. It was made of shiny, glowing nonslip red plastic material, the corners smoothed out. It was empty save a cavity in the right-hand corner, like a funnel. He was fairly certain it wasn't a watering hole. Sweat poured in buckets, pooling under his naked body.

Fine, so they wanted to make me sweat. I'm still in control. Until I give them what they think I have, I'll be OK, he thought. *Am I near a furnace?*

He had regained the feeling in his legs, and his groin was intact. There was still a chance he might have children someday.

Sex should probably be somewhere after taking a vacation on my list of priorities, he thought, reclining in a salty pool of his own bodily fluids, his breath hot, the air so thick he could taste it. He touched the back of his neck and was astonished to feel his Netrodes were no longer there. Had they removed them somehow? Avenues of escape closed to him with the realization he was back to being a flesh and blood man, no longer connected with the Net and its infinite possibilities—alone, truly and fatalistically. The red room pulsated hypnotically, and he felt as if he would melt into the plastic floor.

Three black-armored men barged through the door and picked him up, letting in a cool stream of air. They shackled his arms and legs together and marched him out of the cell. The corridor was screaming whiteness, and the shiny gray floors echoed with their steps. The sweat congealed on his skin and his black hair stuck to his scalp as the refreshing currents of air rejuvenated him. Not a word was spoken while he was lead to a different, much larger room. The faceless trio sat Wen down on a metal chair before a metal table, tied him to the floor, and left. There was a suspicious-looking drain under the table. The room was empty, another one-way mirror the only indication he was not alone.

"Wen Harkwell, you have been convicted of crimes against the State: treason, possession of illegal goods, intent to subvert the people, withholding information, belonging to a criminal organization, working for a known subversive corporation, war crimes—"

"Why am I here?" He interrupted the voice coming from the ceiling. There was a pause.

"You have been convicted of crimes against the State: treason—" the emotionless voice repeated.

Was there any person behind that window? Was he being interrogated by a machine? "Why am I *really* here?" he demanded. "I have been convicted. Why am I here? Let's get this over with quickly, all right? You want the files. I have the files. All I ask is to know the name of your mole within DaiSin. Then I'll tell you what you want to know. All of it. You won't scare me into giving you anything, and you won't be able to get anything through torture. Give me a name, and I'm all yours," he said, staring dead center into the mirror.

"You are in no position to make demands or strike deals, Mr. Harkwell," the voice said.

"Oh, I am, though. Think of the damage I could cause. You know as well as I do what I can unleash. That'd be terrible for you if I did, wouldn't it?" he made a mock sad face.

"You cannot implement anything from within your detention cell, Mr. Harkwell. Your threats are meaningless. Besides, what would you accomplish by this?"

"You seem pretty sure of yourself. Strangely enough, we're talking, and I'm not in my detention cell. Do you actually believe I can't do squat, like, say, oh, have someone else create a better, more powerful weapon to use against you? Accomplish? I hadn't really thought that far ahead, honestly," he said.

"Come now, Mr. Harkwell. We could strongly influence the outcome of your sentencing if you helped us in the comprehension of your present employer's actions, as well as handing over any and all copies of the files you have in your hands. Not so long ago, you were their worst enemy, and now look at you: a willing slave. Will you truly defend them with your life? Besides, you do not fit the psychological profile of a martyr. As of today, you are responsible for the death of 152 people. You *murdered* 152 employees of the Administration, Mr. Harkwell, not to mention any other corporation's personnel whose violent death you might be responsible for. That also hangs quite heavily in the balance."

Wen was nauseated. His eyes felt moist, and a lump was slowly rising and falling in his throat. "You *lie!*" he screamed, holding back the tears that were trying to escape his eyes.

"Now why would we do that, Mr. Harkwell? Perhaps you need some time to think about our counteroffer. We could, of course, take you back to the pool *right now*, but you seem like a bright sort of person for someone so young. We will grant you half a day, no more. Afterward, we will return to the methods you so deplore." There was an audible click, and the door behind him opened. The guards unlatched the floor pin with a flip and dragged him back to his cell. He could barely walk, or think. They took off his chains and tossed him into the crimson sauna that was his cell.

Alone again in the ultra-clean glowing cube, all possible thoughts worming their way into his brain discouraged him to no end. He had no idea how much time had elapsed since they had brought him back. His biological clock was broken; no help there. They were showing their "kindness" by lowering the temperature. It was now bearable, even though he still hadn't been provided any clothes. A meal was brought to him on a plastic tray, and it was gone in under a minute. The resulting stomach cramps were atrocious, and he hated himself for his stupidity. He rocked back and forth on his haunches against a wall, wishing the pain away. Was it true? Had he killed that many people? Should he assume everything was a fabrication?

With no concept of time, it was hard to figure out what to do. He eventually used the hole in the corner, and his stomach thanked him for it. He was still on the same square, nothing had moved. If he gave them what they wanted, he had no idea if they would honor their word, and DaiSin would execute his brother, Taz, and Andrei. If he didn't, they would torture him and then kill him.

Hard to get a shittier deal going, he thought. *I have no leverage and no reason to trust them. There is no way out of here. Where the hell am I? How did I get here?*

He lay on the floor and closed his eyes, sleep refusing to come. He was tired but too paranoid to let his guard down. Twelve hours came and went. The armored guards arrived with the shackles and slipped them on without a word. He was led back down the corridor to the interrogation room and sat down. The silent guards departed.

"Your answer, Mr. Harkwell." The voice was different this time. A bit more high pitched but masked nonetheless.

"No," he said. No use beating around the bush. "You'll just have to keep jerking off behind the glass." He bore holes in the mirror with his hard stare.

"You disappoint us, Wen. Very well." The door behind him opened, and three guards entered, carrying truncheons the length of his arm. They surrounded him and beat him, hitting him in different areas every time. Whack! He felt the cracking stings on his shoulders and back, the sides of his face, and his thighs. Crack! He yelled and tried to cover his head and groin. He had fallen off the chair and lay on the floor, and they kept hitting him and hitting him. Time disappeared, all thoughts having fled in a swarm of pain and humiliation. A minute could feel like an hour when you were enduring this much pain. His head swam, and a small pool of blood formed under his face on the cold cement floor. All he could see was the underside of the table, one of its legs, and the far wall. He hurt. He hurt like he had never hurt before in his life. There was a weird keening sound coming from somewhere far, far away, underwater. What was that sound, and why wouldn't it stop? It took him a while to realize it was him, crying uncontrollably.

"Perhaps you feel a bit more forthcoming now?" came the voice from somewhere above him.

"Fuck you," he croaked, sobbing, and a string of blood followed a broken tooth out of his mouth as he did. He cried and was ashamed of it; it only made him cry louder.

"Take him away," he heard from above. The guards picked him up and his body screamed. A low, guttural moan fell from his lips, unending: he felt broken. Was he? Dropped into his cell, he lay there clutching himself, weeping. A thin, white lab-coat-clad man entered a while later, followed by one of the guards. Tight-lipped and be-spectacled, he turned him over and palmed him all over, inspecting him as a livestock checker might have. *Bruises? This one's no good; throw him back, haha!* He must have been some sort of doctor, because he had a stethoscope around his neck. *I'm not a real doctor, but I play one on TV; buy Allevoril for all your torture aches and pains.* Wen felt it more than saw it being used on his back. He was soon alone again. Alone with strange, disjointed thoughts, seesawing between the physical wants of his body for attention and care and his mind misfiring in odd directions.

Is this what my life is going to be like from now on? Pain, from morning until night, whenever the urge takes them? Feedings to keep me healthy enough to torture? And checkups for same? he thought.

He wished he could bleed out and die. There was no way he could take this much abuse and go on, but he had to. There was no choice. *Never choose death over pain. Never let them win!* Rage would be his survival tool. Hatred would keep him going for as long as he had to. The need to rest stretched him thin, but he was torn between screaming in anger and melting in anguish. *A sign, anything to tell me I'm doing the right thing!* But there existed only himself to count on in this place: there *was* no one else. He lay there forever and waited.

The lights never went out. *Just another tool in the psychological warfare bag,* he thought. He would have to make do with the place where there was no darkness.

Days went by, flowing into each other like crushing waterfalls. Woken up just as he was going into deep sleep, dunked in the frigid waters of the water torture cham-ber, beaten with batons, scorched in his cell, and made to listen to the discordant and horrifying sounds of screaming children at all hours of the day and night. No matter the iron he thought his will was made of; it was bending. The pain rocked his shell, but his core remained solid, for the time being. The shell chipped bit by bit, though, and the time would come where it would collapse entirely. It was a time he dreaded almost as much as the daily torture sessions. The walls had begun to talk to him, and the things they said were atrocious. Insects buzzed inside his brain, and he had to en-dure them for lack of a tool to extract them. All day long, the voices grated like nails on the roof of his skull, shrieking his uselessness and coming final moment, distracting him from the physical realm of agony. The spark came dangerously close to blowing out of his being.

A light flashed in his eyes from the door of his cell one day after the doctor had left, shaking his head, and he believed he had lost his mind even further. He muttered and covered his purple-rimmed eyes, but the light somehow shone through his fingers, blinding him still. It carried a warm sensation, like holding hands over a spot heater after coming in from the cold; something he hadn't felt in eons. He creakily rose to his feet, holding the wall for balance, emaciated and grizzled form taking step after careful step toward the light. It literally came *through* the door in a single concentrated beam. An intense beacon of gleaming photons, aimed directly at his face. Wen winced, still trying to block it out. He put his hand on the cell door, and his fingers fell through the door. He retracted them. Cocking his head, he held himself up with the doorframe and put his hand against the door once more. It slipped through it as if it were a hologram. Wen pushed his whole arm through and then squeezed himself after it, shutting his eyes.

When he opened them, he fell to the ground. A cool, grassy earth received him, and he rolled a bit downhill before regaining his senses. It was nighttime. An enormously bright full moon shone close enough to touch, illuminating mountain peaks on either side of it. The upper part of a summer valley greeted his sight, surrounded by sleeping flowers and grasses: lemon balm and linden, sage and peppermint, wild thyme and horehound, blooms encased for the night yet still suffusing gentle scents from patchy thickets. Crickets chirped in the vicinity, and an owl hooted from a dark copse of trees, yellow eyes blinking slowly. The beam of light was in front of him, leading him in the calico darkness. A soft breeze caressed his face, bending the grasses in a gentle rush. The outline of conifers could be guessed at, higher up on the mountains' flanks. Patting himself, he realized he was no longer naked but back in his uniform. Touching his face and body, he noticed they had stopped hurting; the mental scars, though, would never go away.

A small log-house lay ahead, completely out of place for such an area. It belonged in nineteenth-century frontier America, not wherever he was at the moment. The two windows on either side of the door suffused a dim golden light from some inward source, a pale blue smoke ghosting from its stone chimney. He walked toward the door, swishing through the grasses, still following the beam, which now sat squarely on his chest. The wooden steps creaked as he climbed the porch and knocked on the solid door. It swung open, and a small hearth-fire crackled, haloing a hunched figure before it. The interior was simple, rustic, with a few pairs of deer antlers hung on the eaves, a pot and kettle hung by the fire, a cot with white linen blankets in one corner and a wooden table with chairs in the other. Wen cautiously entered the house and cleared his throat. The hunched figure turned around. It was Joe. He held the beam in his hand. It extinguished as soon as he closed it.

"It's not right, is it?" Joe said, getting up.

"What's not right?" Wen asked, coming closer, too shocked to react.

"Whole thing. For the life of me I can't remember what it's supposed to look like. I keep getting back bits and pieces, scattered all over the place. Have you ever seen mercury?" Joe asked.

"The planet?" Wen said.

"No, the substance." Joe opened his hand again, and the silver liquid within it joined and separated. "It coalesces. It's one of those weird properties it has. Split it all up, and eventually is comes back together. That's what my mind feels like right now," Joe said, fingers splayed over his head.

"Like mercury?" Wen asked.

"Yeah, but it's not coming back together very well. It seems right, but it isn't. Come back when it's right, will you?" said Joe, covering his eyes with one hand and waving Wen away with the other. Wen found himself outside the log cabin, but the mountain valley had vanished, and he stood on a stony outcropping on which slammed an angry sea directly below. Behind him, a white lighthouse extended from the cottage, sending its flaring, revolving light searching in the roiling obscurity. The waves crashed like walls into it and he woke up in the sensornet chair, panting.

Jenna, Robert, Abakar, Sonia, and Ulrick stood around him, their anguished faces turning to relief as his eyes fluttered open.

"How long was I out?" he said.

"Five minutes. Your sine waves flatlined. We couldn't get you out of there," Robert said.

"I was in some sort of prison. They tortured me for days," he said.

"Mindlock. They had complete control over your internal body clock. How did you get out?" Jenna said.

"Just lucky, I guess," he said. "How are we doing here?" Wen bounced out of his chair. "Give me a progress report, Jenna." The crew looked at each other.

"Administration officially denies everything. They destroyed sixty percent of our defenses. Another attack, and we'll be toast. Techs and soldiers are working inside and out, trying to find all burned-out ports and are fixing or replacing them. Deguchi is furious, and Surimat wants your hide. She wanted to see you as soon as we figured out a way to wake you," Jenna said.

"Where is she?" said Wen.

"Still on the ramparts, getting things under a semblance of control," Robert said.

"I'm going back in to face the music. Go and see if you can help out as well. Dismissed. And...thanks. Now get out of my apartment," he said, smiling, and then closed his eyes to go back to the Arsenal. He walked out the blast door and found Commander Surimat barking orders at some hapless soldiers who weren't moving fast enough for her taste. The tower was a mess. Black blast-marks fissured the nacre walls, the shield fizzling in places.

"Harkwell, what the hell do you think you were doing?" Surimat asked as she spotted him coming toward her.

"Destroying the enemy, ma'am," Wen said, saluting.

"Did you have my permission to go on a suicide mission, Harkwell?"

"No, ma'am, I did not."

Surimat glared at him and then smiled. "I'll let that one slide, soldier. You did a damn fine job." Commander Surimat beamed.

"I believe there's a traitor in our midst, ma'am. Administration Corps was using the same technology as we are," Wen said.

"We'll look in to it," the commander said. "You may take the afternoon off, Harkwell."

"I'd rather help out if I could, ma'am," he said, eyeing the surrounding damage.

"That's an order, soldier."

"Yes, ma'am!" Wen answered, and opened his eyes in his sensornet chair. His stomach grumbled, and he went in search of food. It was five in the morning. The attack and his incarceration had lasted a little over seven minutes. A knock came at his door, and he went to answer; it was Ulrick.

"I...wanted to thank you, sir. If you hadn't..." he said, biting his lower lip.

"It's OK. I did what I had to for my team. You're one of us, Ulrick," Wen said, extending his hand. Ulrick shook it fervently.

"Thank you, sir." he reiterated.

"You're a good soldier, Ulrick," he said, and Ulrick went off.

So who's responsible for this mess? he wondered.

CHAPTER 12

WEN PONDERED ALONE on his couch. What had happened? Who could possibly be in league with Administration from within DaiSin? He wanted to find the traitor and crush him, just wail on him (he had to assume it was a he) until all the life slipped out from the sticky, broken pulp he would leave behind. Whoever they were, they had given Admin the most powerful weapon DaiSin had, and the bastards had built on that to create an even better shield. He regretted having destroyed their portable shield generators; now there was no possibility of assimilating their tech. They would be sitting ducks unless they came up with something as or more powerful than this new foe's shields and weaponry.

The other question that burned his mind was about Joe, if that had really been him; how had he gotten him out of mindlock? He recognized the beam of light as the one that they had shared on the streets of Shinjuku1. How had it come to him in the deepest recesses of the prison? Technically, it wasn't a jail, he realized. It had been his own mind, fooled to think it was. Then, the bond between them was that strong. What had he said about mercury? It coalesced. Poor Joe's mind was lost, and he thought he could find it somehow. In any event, he owed him one. Wen was now even deeper in his debt. He sighed.

He needed to start working on a more powerful weapon; something that could not be re-created or stolen by the in-house spy. He could, of course, try to access everyone's mind and search their memories, but what a waste of time that would be. The traitor would reveal him or herself eventually. For now it was of paramount importance to prepare for the next onslaught. Damn but they were in poor shape, even with all the techies working day and night, it would take a solid week to reset the system to optimal capacity; and then what? Have it demolished again at Admin's whim?

Wen returned to his sensornet chair and went directly to his jungle clearing. He stood over the crucible, thinking about what he wanted to create, appending different code and seeing what came out. Nothing stronger than the Pulverizer ever did. He was baffled. If only he could...

He returned to Jenna, Ulrick, and Robert's minds and took the pieces of Code he had stashed for safekeeping there. He put them into the crucible and held a powerful weapon in his mind. He knew what they said about insanity, but he was determined to try anyway. He had to keep trying to crack this Code no matter what it took. The crucible stalled for a moment. Wen peered at it with his head cocked sideways. The pot had this word floating above it: Compiling. The word would appear and disappear, the closest thing to indecision a machine could express. Wen crossed his arms and waited. After ten minutes, he decided to let it run and go relax somewhere else. He returned to his apartment, turned on the Net set, and started thought-flipping channels.

A serious Japanese man in a black suit presented in front of a hologram of the Administration Building. Wen paused for a moment and leaned forward, turning up the volume.

"...cials say that the accident in the computer department of Administration Building resulted in the death of over one-hundred and sixty people, as well as multiple injuries. No news yet as to the origin of the blast that took out an entire room; an investigation is pending. In other news, Uehara Motoharu is expected to sing at..."

Wen stared at the screen. It was true. He had killed all those people. He was a murderer. It was war, dammit! It's not like he was given a choice! He hadn't been alone in their dispatching, either. They would have done him, given half a chance. They still could, if DaiSin didn't get the upper hand. He'd be looking out for those little trapping jewels from now on.

A tone rang, and he answered the holophone. Deguchi appeared before him, worry creasing his forehead.

"Wen, I heard about the mindlock, are you all right?" he said. Wen was taken aback by his solicitude. This was not an emotion he thought Deguchi had ever been imbued with or was even capable of.

"Apart from permanent psychological scarring, I'll be fine," he answered, twirling his finger around his ear.

"We could go take a look and erase those for you..." Deguchi began. This made more sense then; just another excuse to go trolling through the inner recesses of his mind, once again. Wen cut him short: "That'll be all right. I'll live with it as a reminder of my carelessness. Did you want anything?"

"Yes, as a matter of fact. We've fully analyzed the energy signature of those blasts in our shields. Whatever they were using was completely different from our Pulverizers," he said. Wen's mind went cold.

"Which means they've developed their own tech. We don't have a traitor in our midst," Wen said.

"Correct. Since we destroyed everything they had, we can't make an antidote or *borrow* their tech. We have to go back to our old blasters if we want to get anything off them next time," Deguchi said.

"But that's stupid though. We have to stay a step ahead of them, that's all!"

"And how do you propose we do that without knowing what they have?" He had him there. "What did you tell Administration while they had you?"

"Nothing. I couldn't tell them anything. I didn't know what they wanted to hear," Wen said, shrugging.

"What did they want to know, exactly?" Deguchi asked, his gaze narrowing.

"What we were up to. Since I have no idea, I told them as much, but they didn't believe me. I got the crap kicked out of me for that," Wen said, a shiver running down his spine at the awful memories.

"How did you escape?" Deguchi said.

On a beam of light, he thought.

"I forced my way out. I can't describe it. One minute I was in a cell, the other I was back on my sensornet chair," he said, lying back on his couch, arms over the cushions.

"You just forced your way out?"

You don't believe me for a second, do you? Too bad there's nothing you can do about it, he thought. "Yes."

"Of mindlock."

"Precisely." There was a pause, and Deguchi seemed to be trying to penetrate his thoughts again. The twitch on the corner of his lips told Wen he had once again failed, and he smiled inwardly.

"That's all I wanted to say. Your foolish actions are up for review by the Deliberators. I don't expect you'll be punished much for endangering your team's lives," he said, sounding disappointed.

"Why is that?"

"You seem to have made a fan out of Surimat." Deguchi said, and he winked out of existence.

He returned to his jungle clearing and found, hovering over the crucible, a black glove, striated with length-wise green, flat wiring, like an alien circuit board. It shone like volcanic glass and was slick to the touch. It warmed his hand when he slipped it on. As he gazed upon it, it evaporated. It felt like it was there when he touched his hand, but it was invisible. He removed it and put it in his drawer for safekeeping. He would try it out later.

What concerned him most was how, if there was no traitor in their midst, had Administration found out about his possession of the Code?

⊥ ⊥ ⊥

In the weeks after the incident, his notoriety grew, and so did the amount of recruits. Inevitably, many of them heard about Wen Harkwell and his crew, the daredevils who had saved DaiSin from annihilation. Abakar related to him the rumor that they had jokingly been named the Honey Badgers for their sheer fearlessness and odd tactics, but after having heard about the pseudonym, Wen had made it officially theirs; after all, the sobriquet fit. A new patch starring the tiny carnivore's ferocious face now adorned each member's shoulders, worn proudly in defiance of the haters. Hyperbole ran rampant, but so did sign-ups to be in his platoon. Within a month, Wen led a group of twenty recruits, all young and ignorant of the dangers that would come from the mouth of the enemies' canons. They were put through the same insane training program he had devised for his original unit, fending off the attack of hyper-activated Golem android fighters.

Deguchi came to see him one day. He appeared happier than his usual dour self, and Wen imagined he must have drowned a bath-full of kittens to achieve this state of nirvana.

"Come with me, Harkwell," he said and did not explain further. They took the elevator to the lobby, and Wen expected to go through the turnstiles, perhaps to go for another formal interview with the Deliberators, but Deguchi stopped him. "Wrong way." He pointed at the front door. Wen's heart began to beat faster. He could leave? Was that it? Sammy was still somewhere inside and so were Andrei and Taz. Where on earth were they going? He looked back once at the interior of The Needle before following Deguchi, apprehensive.

A black sedan idled in front of the building with the rear door open. Freedom had been taken away from him for so long, he felt elated at the outside air. It was a gorgeous February day. The air smelled crisp. Deguchi led him to the car, and Wen stepped into the back, relaxing on the beige leather seat. The car lifted without a sound, drifting into afternoon traffic with ease, the whisper of the engine barely audible. The uniformed guard nodded to Wen as their eyes locked in the rearview mirror and the glass separator rose between the driver and passengers.

"You've been quite an asset to DaiSin these last four months. Honestly, I didn't believe in you, but someone else did. You have a guardian angel, Harkwell, never forget it. As long as you protect the interests of the company, you will remain in his good graces," Deguchi said.

"Who? Surimat?" Wen asked.

Deguchi chuckled. "No, not Surimat. Someone even higher up. We're here." The car stopped in front of the old Shinseki Arms building. Wen looked at him with suspicion. "This complex is owned by DaiSin." They stepped out of the car and entered the front lobby. In the elevator, Deguchi pressed the button for the eleventh floor. He swiped his arm at number 1143 and entered. The basic décor was much the same as Oscar's apartment had been: gray walls and carpeting, slab of granite for a countertop, hard edges, and little imagination or fantasy.

"It's yours," Deguchi said.

Wen spun around. "Mine? What do you mean?"

"This is your place. Someone saw fit to give you an apartment of your own," Deguchi said, glancing around. "Your uniforms will be brought here for you tonight. Show up for work at seven every day. You have weekends off," Deguchi said, walking toward the far bedroom. "If there's an emergency, you'll have this." He opened the door and pointed to a sensornet chair surrounded by the black plates on the walls.

"Couldn't I work from home?" Wen asked.

"We'd miss the pleasure of your company. Besides, there's a half-second delay from here to the Operations Room. It's a bit annoying. That's why it's emergencies only. Oh, and you have full Net access, now." Deguchi stuck out his hand, holding a credit-card-sized plastic pass. "Your Metro card."

"What, no car to go with the apartment?"

"Don't push it. A banking app was added to your Operating System. The balance of your account is in there. You can go shopping, if you like," Deguchi said, giving him a piece of paper with a series of jumbled letters and numbers. "Your access code. Happy?"

"Freaking ecstatic. Will my brother be joining me?" Wen asked.

"What did I tell you about pushing it? We'll see. It depends on how things go from here on in." Deguchi pulled open the drapes, letting the afternoon sun play with the dust motes in the living room. "I'll be at the office if you need me. You already know one of your neighbors; you broke into his place several months ago. Surimat will be your direct overseer from now on. I've been assigned to, uh, other duties." He left Wen standing in the middle of the living room.

Wen walked to the balcony, unlocked the sliding doors, and stepped outside. It was a magnificent day. On his left, he could spy a part of Shibuya Station's glass cupola abutting its skyscraper. Down below, the sounds of passing traffic made its own kind of melody. Apartment blocks of various sizes filled the landscape among the enormous white towers. Virginal elephantine nimbus drifted carefree in the cool breeze, coming in from the ocean, the air filled with the angst of spring. Wen felt a prickle on his scalp. He was steps away from being truly free, he felt. Where before there were many, now only three strands pulled at him from unseen places, refusing him complete liberty of movement. He took the railing in his hands and admired everything he had once taken for granted. It was all his again. He had come here as a thief not so long ago, and now he belonged, like all the others. There was no more need to pretend. He took a deep breath, letting his heart expand to encompass it all, and returned inside. A question burned in his mind, though: who could it be that was watching over him, if not Surimat? With every answer, there was always one more question. Unanswerable, he put it aside and explored his new environment.

Barren rooms, save a bed in the first bedroom and a sofa in the living room, comprised the whole of his new lodgings. All the appliances were accounted for, but the fridge was dismally empty. Wen felt a pang of hunger, his stomach mirroring the interior of his icebox, and he decided to go out for supper. He remembered he was wearing his gray DaiSin uniform. It didn't matter; he was too famished.

Hard soles clicked on the spotless pavement as he walked down the street. *My street,* he thought. The looming station promised an assortment of restaurants for varying tastes and wallet sizes, and he mentally juggled the most promising foodstuffs he craved. The afternoon crowd was once again rushing out of the station, serious faces affixed to rigid, tired frames. A smirk crawled up his lip when he noticed the sideways glances from the passersby. He might have to rethink walking around in his uniform. A men's clothing store caught his eye, and he stepped inside. He was fortunate enough to find a non-net-based store. This one sold their wares on the spot instead of offering only samples, the actual product to be purchased and delivered. A dapper man in a blue pin-striped suit walked out of the store with his gray uniform tucked into a polymer bag, looking nothing like the officer he had walked in as. Any stares he would get now would be solely on the basis of his good taste and looks.

A well-known sushi restaurant called to him from the rows of popular dining spots, lines forming as the subways spilled their human contents. It had been years since he had enjoyed fresh fish, and he wouldn't let the occasion slip by so easily.

After his meal, he returned home and relaxed on his couch. With no Net set to watch, his entertainment options were limited. He climbed into the sensornet chair and turned inward, closing his eyes and rediscovering his clearing. Walking to the hut, he remembered about the glove. With a click, the desk unlocked, and he picked it up and slipped it on his hand. It became transparent and seemed no longer there.

Neat trick, he thought. It was very much like optical camouflage, but even more effective. A lot like the mirror glass effect that the Golems were equipped with, in fact. But what did it do, besides disappear? Walking out of the hut, he pointed a finger at a distant tree. The tree waved a bit in the simulated wind, but not much else happened.

Fire? he thought, and a bolt of raging flames slammed out of his finger, throwing him backward, almost breaking his arm with the recoil. A copse of trees lay charred and writhing where he had been pointing previously. He got up, dusting off his pants.

Laser, he thought, pointing to another part of the forest. An intense beam of blue energy burst out of his finger and sliced through a section of forest, trees crashing in a one kilometer radius in a straight line. He turned his hand left and right before his face. This thing was more powerful and versatile than the Pulverizer, no doubt about it. Sharing it with DaiSin would induce a full inquiry as to its nature and origins. He had been lucky enough that they had thought the Pulverizer was the result of his hard work and ingenuity. It would be impossible to do the same for this...What could it be? What were its limits? Whatever it was, it would remain his, and a secret. He put it away in his drawer, locking it behind him.

Three new applications had been uploaded while he was out: a piggy bank on his desk and a list, next to it. The third was a new remote control beside his television. He pressed the piggy bank and was asked for his access code. He logged out for a moment and retrieved it, went back in and punched it in. Wen's eyes went wide when he saw the amount in his possession. Without being a millionaire, he was far wealthier than he had ever been. There was enough there to seriously think about taking a few trips, or even buying a small vehicle, and it was all his.

Moving backward, he touched the shopping list, and a new window appeared, with the DaiSin logo in the upper-right corner. Pictures of a plethora of items, their prices and descriptions scrolled eternally upward. A shopping cart was soon filled with the bare minimum of necessities for his new home. He pressed "send," and within the day, he would be receiving his order. He hated to admit it, but being a DaiSin employee had its advantages; there was even a discount.

He clicked on the remote, and the TV lit up, showing him an incredible array of channels to choose from. The programs, though, could be viewed through the eyes and emotional responses of the audience members. He tried a reality show where he was a woman on some kind of date, and the first thing he saw was a man sitting across a table from him, smiling.

I really have to scratch my pussy, he thought, puzzled. The realization struck him that he was listening to the woman's intimate thoughts. He signed off, wondering how people would either want to watch or participate in such drivel. There were, however, a few porn channels he thought he might want to try at some other time.

The doorbell rang, and he went to answer. Robert and Jenna stood in the front lobby.

"What can I do for you guys?" he said in the intercom.

"May we come up to congratulate you?" Jenna asked, staring into the camera.

"Of course!" Wen said.

Jenna held a bottle of champagne in her hand, and Robert held a gift box, he saw, as he opened the door. Robert and Jenna both wore civilian clothes; Robert a dark suit and Jenna a knee-length blue dress with matching high-heeled shoes.

"What's the occasion?" he asked.

"Your promotion," Robert said.

"A new apartment isn't exactly a promotion," Wen said.

"No, your promotion is a promotion," Jenna said, smiling. The holophone rang, and Wen turned to answer. He threw Jenna a strange look and took the call. Deguchi was in the middle of his apartment.

"Harkwell, you're captain. I just got the word. Make us proud. Wolinsky, Gardner." He nodded and evaporated.

"Jenna, how the heck is it every time something happens, you're always the first to know?" Wen asked, an eyebrow cocked.

"Woman's intuition?" she said sheepishly.

"Come on, really," Wen said.

"I have very good connections in the hierarchy. That's about all I can tell you." She pinched her lips tight.

"Fair enough. Shall we pop that cork then?" Wen said, smiling. Robert removed the foil and twisted off the cage. He twisted the cork firmly and let it out with a slight pop.

"Glasses, please!" he said, and Jenna went to the cupboards to find some. All of them were bare, devoid of even a layer of dust.

"That's embarrassing," she said, turning back to the men. "Then, let's go out. Captain's paying." Wen shook his head, smiling.

Darkness rose like a slow wave over the clear, navy-blue sky. They walked in the opposite direction of the station, in search of a decent watering hole, the street on a soft decline. The three cast short shadows under the pale white halogen lamps. Semi-residential districts made way for businesses: restaurants, jewelry stores, clothing and accessories shops, as well as upscale bars and night clubs. The King's Head Pub was still relatively empty when they entered. A lone android bartender polished the long oak bar, the three reflected in the mirror behind it. A few customers drank at stools before him, ties loosened, faced with an array of tap handles from around the world. The bartender's smile stretched slightly under rubber skin in greeting. They ordered the first round and headed to the privacy of the worn leather booths at the back.

"You know what that means, right, this promotion?" Robert asked Wen, as they sat down at a window booth.

"That I'm faster, smarter, and better looking than you guys?" Wen said jokingly. In truth, he was curious as to the nature of his promotion. He didn't feel as if he had done anything remarkable in the past while to deserve the distinction. Of course, he would have to be a fool to refuse it, but its purpose still itched at his mind. It was all too convenient, in some way.

"That goes without saying, Captain," Jenna said, smirking. "It also means that we're now a part of the attack forces. We'll be carrying out stealth operations against our enemies." Wen had noticed the ramping up of hostilities in the past few months, as everyone had. So far, it had only seemed to be outside forces coming to DaiSin for a trouncing at their hands. It shouldn't have come as a surprise that DaiSin attacked others as well. He was now a part of those troops. Yet he was still curious to know why a so-called neutral party would come at them with everything they had. It just didn't make sense in his mind.

"Why is Administration so rabid against us now, do you think?" Wen asked, observing the last of the liminal light in the sky phase toward darkness.

"Who knows? They decided the truce was over and wanted a piece of the action," Jenna said, shrugging. Wen frowned, unsatisfied, and then scratched his head.

"I thought they were supposed to stay neutral in all this corporate warfare," he said, staring at her, his brow furrowed.

"Neutral? Who gave you that idea?" Robert snorted. "Administration is under the purview of eleven of the most powerful corporations in the world."

"After DaiSin," Wen said. He made a mental note to remember the meaning of *neutral* as meaning someone or something that refuses to get involved one way or the other until they had the upper hand, as cynical as that sounded. Still, this business with Administration portended poorly, especially since his attempted incarceration and torture.

"Naturally," Jenna said.

"The employees are given suppressants to ignore that particular fact, but the higher ups revolve between government positions and board positions for the eleven. It's all very private and incestuous. You can't expect any kind of 'neutrality' or 'objectivity' from those folks," Robert explained.

"That still doesn't explain why they would attack now," Wen said.

"Their CEOs are fairly smart. Like I said, they saw an opportunity and took it," Jenna said.

New weapons and a pressing need to use them, Wen thought, *but why?*

⋏ ⋏ ⋏

As the night went on, the pub filled to capacity. The three were surrounded by a clamor of joy and good times; the clinking of glasses and the laughs that accompanied hearty toasts. A few empties waited on the edge of their table to be picked up. DaiSin was cheered, the war was celebrated, the Administration was booed (quietly), and their heads grew lighter as the evening progressed toward the witching hour.

Wen looked at his lieutenants and said: "You guys are my friends, right?" they both nodded their heads gravely. "I just was wondering...was curious. How often do employees get, you know, promotions at DaiSin?" he asked, splaying his hands.

"As often as they like," Robert slurred, and Jenna burst out laughing.

"No, I'm seriously...I'm serious."

"Usually takes about a year for each promotion, sometimes more," Jenna said.

"So how come I get, like, two in a row in such a short 'mount of time?" Wen said, cupping his chin in his hands.

"Cause you're special," Jenna said, imitating his gesture and gazing into his eyes.

"Cut it out, you two," Robert said. "There'll be none of that."

"I'm sure I have no idea what you're talkin' about," Jenna said, giving him a cross-eyed look.

Wen gazed out the window at the pedestrians in spring coats, couples walking by with love in their smiles. They could go wherever they wanted, just like him. His heart pinched; only him.

"Can you keep a sssecret?" he asked, gulping.

"Aye-aye, sir," Jenna said, saluting somewhat less perfectly than she was used to.

"My younger brother...he's...somewhere inside the DaiSin building. So are two of my friends," Wen said, the words coming out with difficulty, as if he was coughing up gravel.

"That's OK; a lot of people have family working for the company. No shame in that, Cap'ain," Robert said, shaking his head.

"No, I mean...they're prisoners. I'm not supposed to talk about it, but..." he looked at them with haunted eyes. Jenna and Robert stared back at their captain with comical Os of surprise. Wen released a nervous titter, suppressed when his eyes began to water. He wiped his sleeve across his face and cleared his throat. *What have I done?* he thought, looking at the table intently.

Jenna leaned forward. "Captain, this is quite out of the ordinary. Are you certain?" She seemed to have sobered up completely in an instant. He rubbed both his eyes and gazed into her face.

"I'm not lying, if that's what you're implying," Wen said, his lips going taut.

"I shouldn't be listening to this," Robert said, looking around for potential spies. "I have to go. Please excuse me." He rose to his feet, gave a swift salute, and stormed out of the pub.

"I guess I am picking up the tab after all," Wen said, his gaze following his second lieutenant's exit.

"When did this happen?" Jenna said, searching his face for any trace of deceit.

"Before I arrived."

"I can't believe I'm contemplating treason," she muttered to herself. "What are your friends' names?"

"Scott 'Taz' Till and Andrei Yurushcenkov. I haven't seen or heard from them in months. I don't even know if they're still alive."

"Why wouldn't they be?" she said, puzzled.

"I said too much. I'm sorry. I'm going to get you in trouble, Jenna. That wasn't my intention. I just...wanted to get it off my chest." He guzzled the last of his beer and stood, walking over to the bar. Jenna followed him. He picked up the tab, and they left the rowdy pub behind, entering the cool outside air like sailing ships leaving the shore.

"I think I'm going to go home, Jenna. I need to think."

"As your second-in-command, sir, I recommend for you to take an escort," Jenna said, her brow furrowed in mock seriousness. Wen did not respond and began to walk toward home. Jenna caught up to him. Wen walked with his head bent and his hands deep in his pockets.

"Hey, I'm sorry I doubted you. Don't take it like that," she said, slipping her arm around his. Wen turned to her in surprise and felt a mild electric pulse course through his system. They walked in silence, and Jenna lay her blond head on the side of his shoulder. As they passed an all-night convenience store, she said, "Stop, I have to pick something up." She rushed inside and came out with a plastic bag. They continued their walk, and Jenna slipped her hand into his pocket and grasped his fingers with a tender touch. Wen slipped his fingers through hers.

When they arrived at his door, Wen said, "Thank you, Lieutenant; that'll be all."

She leaned in for a kiss. He felt his heart jump and run mad, his cheeks prickling. His mind went light, and she said, "I'm not done yet."

Wen opened the door, and she pushed him inside. She went to the refrigerator and retrieved the chilled bottle of champagne. There was a bag of plastic glasses inside her shopping bag, and she filled two with the drink.

"What are we drinking to?" he asked.

"To the future," she said, smiling. They went to the bedroom and sat on the bed, sipping the champagne. She deposited her glass on the floor and unbuttoned his shirt, caressing his chest with her soft hands. He slid one strap of her dress off her shoulder and leaned in to kiss her neck. A shiver ran through him as she unclasped his belt. He stroked her from her slender neck to the bottom of her spine with the tips of his fingers, and she arched her back taut. He kissed her neck at the juncture of her collarbone, lowering his head toward the slight bulge of her breast, hidden under the soft fabric of her dress. She removed the second strap of her dress, allowing it to fall to her midriff. She removed his clothes with a playful tug, and they were soon in heated embrace, she pushing him down on the bed and taking control, caressing his entire body with hers, his kisses hardening her resolve. Their moist interlocking rhythm became the music of their bodies, undulating in tempo, bucking in soft gasps. Fingers palpated soft, warm flesh, mouths and tongues danced, their passion mounting, moans of ecstasy escaped in rivers, arching in finality, both glistening with the pleasurable effort. She lay on his chest, still joined to him, breathing deeply.

They lay beside one another for a long time, holding each other, wordless. When he woke up the next morning, she was gone. The only proof against a dream the empty glass lying askance on the carpeted floor.

He walked through the apartment to find the gift box he had forgotten to open the night before: it was his captain's stripes.

CHAPTER 13

E WENT TO work that day anticipating trouble. The Metro ride to the DaiSin Building was punctuated with him mentally slamming his face into a wall for his indiscretions. He should never have slept with his officer and he never should have told them about his brother and friends. They worked for the enemy, they were bugged, and if anyone found out, the jig was up. The rules of engagement at DaiSin were simple as well. Use any leverage you can to advance yourself. He was guilty now of handing over the tools of his own destruction to two upwardly mobile people. Maybe Robert wouldn't use the information against him. After all, he had given up a promotion in favor of Wen. What about Jenna, could she be trusted anymore? Did he consider them friends? Over a beer and at arm's length, perhaps, but this was a screw-up of epic proportions. He worried especially about Robert, who had left in such a rush at the prospect of discovering illegal information. Was he the kind of man who would go off and turn him in for such a thing? He shivered at the conflicting thoughts. He needed to find him as soon as possible. Hell, he should have stopped him from leaving the pub entirely. Taken him aside and tried talking sense to him before he could run off and make up his own mind about the best course of action. His brain whirled with 'could haves' and 'should haves,' but the damage was done. Now was the time to go into spin control mode. He walked into the Command Center and was greeted by Jenna with a smile, and Robert with a smirk.

"Morning," he said, averting his eyes.

"Morning, Captain," Jenna said, smiling.

"Captain," Robert said, his voice chill.

Wen drew in a long breath and said, "Shall we begin?" The recruits were already in the sensornet chairs, twenty of them, getting ready for training in the Arsenal. Wen,

Jenna, and Robert took a seat, joining them. They entered the jungle clearing of Wen's mind, and the war drills against furiously fast android-type Golems began. On a covered platform overlooking the maneuvers, Wen observed with a hard stare. The long wooden overlook covered the length of the practice field, making it possible to follow the various team's efforts along the way. This had been one of Abakar's suggestions. The big man was presently leading a group of three around a treacherous opening between walls, fired upon by relentless androids.

Wen approached Jenna while Robert was further down the walkway.

"About last night…" he began.

"Yes, sir?" she said, turning to face him.

"I…I know this sounds weird, but I don't think we should continue," Wen said.

"Yes, sir," she said evenly.

"That's it?" he said, confused.

"I understand, sir. It was fun while it lasted, though wasn't it?" she asked.

"Yes, of course, but…"

"But it would be improper to continue down that path," she said, smiling.

"Something like that." He stared off into the distance. "I have a hard time believing you are taking it this well, I think."

She laughed. "Sorry. No offense, sir, but I'm not looking for a relationship."

"You're not?" he said, baffled.

"No. I wanted to have a good time with you, and I did. If you hadn't told me what you have, I would've."

"I see. I have to speak to Robert about last night," he said.

"I've already spoken to him, sir. That won't be necessary. I let him understand that you were going through a difficult time, and that you need our help. He is on your side, as I am. Sir." She smiled.

"Why does he seem so angry with me at the moment then?" Wen wondered aloud.

"Because Robert is in love with me, sir. I can't change his mind about that. He doesn't know what we did, but he is extremely overprotective of me. He won't turn you in because I told him not to," she said with a sigh.

"Oh, bother," Wen said, shaking his head.

"Not to worry, sir; everything is under control."

"What are you planning to do, if I might ask?"

"About what?" she said.

"That whole business about my friends and brother?" Even though she had a leash on Robert, it didn't mean she herself might not use his terrible secrets against him.

"I will help you, sir," she said, sounding serene and sincere, looking at the new recruits running the obstacles and those standing on the sidelines cheering them on as the sun belted down on them. Wen leaned with his arms crossed on the deck's wooden railing, looking at the young recruits getting pounded by the black androids' shock blasts, and wondered what the hell it was all about.

"Why, though?" he said.

"Because you're a good man. Because you need help. Because not everybody in the world is out to get you. Because...just because," she said, and walked over to where Robert was standing, and he shook his head emphatically. She put her hands on her hips, and Robert seemed to deflate. He walked over to Wen, and she remained at the far corner, staring into the distance at nothing in particular.

She looks just as lost as I feel, he thought as Robert drew near.

"I apologize for last night, sir. I am embarrassed by my behavior. If anything, I should be proud that my commanding officer would share something so personal with me. It won't happen again," Robert said.

"I need to apologize as well, Mr. Gardner. It was never my intention to burden you with my personal problems," Wen said as Robert stared at him, wide-eyed in surprise.

"I don't know what to say, sir," Robert said.

"How about 'apology accepted'?" Wen said, smiling.

"Aye, sir, that it is. Your secret is safe with me, sir. Anything...uh...happen after I left?" Robert asked.

"I was escorted home and went to bed, Mr. Gardner," Wen said.

"Ah, I see...thank you, sir," Robert said, sounding relieved.

"Dismissed," Wen said.

"Yes, sir," Robert said, and walked off happier than he had been a few moments before.

⋏ ⋏ ⋏

"Happy birthday, Sammy!" Wen said as his brother appeared in the middle of his living room for his weekly visit. It was the beginning of March, and their visits would not coincide with his anniversary, so Wen had taken the jump on it by getting a cake, some candles, and decorations for the apartment.

Sammy looked around, delighted.

"Holy smokes! That's awesome!" His voice cracked.

"Just wait!" Wen turned off the lights mentally and got the cake from the counter. He had prelit the candles in anticipation of his brother's visit, and in the dark, a beautiful Black Forest cake shone under fourteen colorful candles. He held the cake before the apparition: "Make a wish, Samuel."

Sammy's eyes closed, and when they opened, he smiled, but the corners of his mouth wavered. His took a deep breath and blew, Wen extinguishing the candles for him.

"Hey hey! Good job!" Wen said. "What was your wish?"

"If I tell you, it...it...it won't come true," Samuel said, his voice becoming a croak. He cleared it and turned away from the camera for a moment, only his lower body appearing before Wen. He heard the sound of someone blowing his nose, and Sammy leaned back in. "I'm all right. I'm OK." He chuckled. "They're bringing in a lot of people now. I've made a bunch of new friends in the last coupla months."

"That's great, that's great!" Wen said.

"I miss you, Wen."

"I know. Me too, Sammy. It won't be long, now. The way things are going, we'll probably be living together in the next few months. I can't promise anything, but word on the street is that if I behave, I get you back."

"Really? Are you serious?" Samuel said, his eyes round.

"Maybe. Don't get your hopes up, now, OK?"

"Are you kidding? How can I not? Wow!" Sammy said, looking as if he vibrated with excitement. An off-camera voice said something Wen didn't comprehend.

"It's my birthday, though; can I just have a little long..." and Sammy vanished.

Wen stood with the cake in the dark, empty apartment. This was a promise he had to keep, even though he had not promised anything. He only wanted to free his brother once and for all and live a normal life with him. His two friends, locked away in some other part of the behemoth building, or some unknown location, would have to wait, if they were still among the living, that was. He opened the drapes and let the sunshine destroy the gloom. He placed the cake on the cold granite slab of his kitchen counter, smoke still rising from the dead candles, and let himself slide down its side to the floor. He let his head drop between his knees and stared at the carpet. His carpet. In his apartment. In the Heights. For what it was worth.

A few days later, during training in the clearing, Jenna came to see him as he paced the ramparts.

"I have good news and bad news, sir," she said.

"What's the good news?" he said.

"Your acquaintances are not within DaiSin property, nor are they presently incarcerated by the company."

"What? Are you serious?" he said.

"There's no doubt about it," she said. Rage billowed inside him as he clutched the wooden railing.

He lied to me. He's been lying about everything; I'm sure of it, he thought. *Damn that Deguchi!* His voice trembling, he said, "So where could they be?" He pierced Jenna with his stare.

"That's...the bad news, sir. They're being held by Administration Military Services. If my information is correct, they will be executed within the week."

"What?" he howled. "How can you be so sure? What are your sources? Are they trustworthy?" Wen said, his body electric.

She hesitated. "I'm...certain, sir. My sources are placed fairly high up." Wen's mind reeled. He held on to one of the posts.

"You're absolutely positive," he said.

"Well, yes."

It made sense, though. How else had Administration gotten such similar tech as the one he had made if there were no traitors inside DaiSin? Administration got ahold of them, somehow, and tortured them, just as they had tortured him. They could have done it for months. His stomach churned. Deguchi had lied to him. Deguchi knew. He had to lie to him to get him to cooperate. Deguchi knew, and he let him believe DaiSin had them. Wen punched a post with all his strength.

"Are you OK, sir?" Jenna said, concerned, as she put her hand on his shoulder.

"Take over. Watch over my mind until I come back." He bolted.

"But where are you going?" she cried. Wen ran like a madman to the hut. He unlocked the drawer and picked up the glove and slipped it on. In the past weeks, he had found out just how much it could do. The truth was, there wasn't much it *couldn't* do. It was like having a portable all-powerful weapon that responded to his every thought. He had named it The Hand of God.

Running by the jousting labyrinth, he called over four of the Golems.

"You are coming with me right now." The slick-black bots saluted and tailed him in formation. Human recruits replaced them for the duration.

He ran into the forest down a slim, well-worn path, slashing at tall grasses and vines with the backs of his hands and summoned the manticore, jumping through its portal without slowing down, followed by the bots. Once in the null-space of the starry void, he redirected himself according to the vermilion sun, aiming for the heart of the Administration Building. The trailing bot's electron charges scintillated. He cored through the placental glow of the various firewalls between DaiSin and his target, never slowing down. Containment fields, bubbles within bubbles, none had any effect on him now. The spider silk of the link he careened on hummed in unison with his mind. In an instant, there it was; the tower projecting from a bottomless pit into the sky, its every level aglow with the sparks of the Netted, all unconscious of the danger that cometted toward them that instant, redolent with sanguine fury and tensile vengeance.

Wen mentally ordered the Golem to specific tasks and then masked his and their paths into the servers. He counted to ten and then plunged into the Administration Mainframe computer. With the help of one bot, he sifted through thousands of prisoner files and execution orders.

On the midlevel, chaos reigned. A hovertank had risen from the police garage and fired indiscriminately into the building and vehicles, destroying everything in its path with explosive-tipped photon blasts. Fire-repellent foam nozzles sprayed everywhere, and the screech of alarms blared like mad. Personnel ran in every direction trying to avoid the murderous rampage of the out-of-control tank. The living dragged the maimed out of its path, and the dead were strewn around like so many disarticulated mannequins, charred and burnt. The hover flew out of the building and began to fire at its flanks, blasting house-sized holes while flying sideways, aiming for the police levels of the Administration Building.

On the prison levels, all doors slid open at the same time. Curious, the prisoners stuck their heads out. Twenty levels of convicts were released in an instant, with no one to stop them save the handful of guards who had been left behind, the others busy trying to shoot down the maverick hovertank. Uproar overcame the stunned silence as a thousand orange-clad prisoners stampeded the exits, slaughtering what little resistance they encountered with homemade weapons and a newfound outlet for their pent-up bloodlust.

Wen and his aide combed the archives, every now and then appreciating the carnage he had sewn, through the eyes of the Golems that he had ordered to it, but no trace of his friends were to be found. Not even a mention. Even with all the commotion tearing apart the various levels, Administration was equipped with automatic systems to detect intruders. These had found them, now. The helper bot turned to fire on an incoming defense drone, and Wen gritted his teeth in frustration. He had been duped. If he survived this, he would have a word with Jenna's source, possibly two. Live guards followed the drones into the system, firing on Wen and his bot in the Server Archives. Wen and the team fled, leaving behind a small time bomb. The guards closed in on them from every corner, even as they ran down the virtual file racks. Shots rained down around them, and Wen fired sizzling death behind him, slicing the pursuers in half. An explosion rang out, filling the server with null-space. The contraction bomb had imploded everything within a 200 terabyte distance, leaving only the absence of a sphere in its wake. Wen turned around and jumped down into the cavity, resuming his run at the bottom of the server. He attempted a logout but was trapped.

A masked guard appeared before him and yelled, "Stop!"

Wen raised his fist to the guard's face.

"Wen! Stop!" the guard said, and raised his mask. Wen's blood stopped in his veins, his throat constricting; it was Taz. The Golem prepared to fire, but Wen raised his hand and stopped it.

"Wh...what are you doing here? I came to rescue you!" Wen yelled, his fist level with the man's face.

"You went to the enemy, Wen! I don't need rescuing, you idiot! I work for the Administration!" Taz said, his gun level with Wen's head.

"You what?" he said, his mind reeling in shock. Wen clutched his temples with his free hand. "You...you..."

"I...I...listen to yourself! I told you I could get you into the Heights, but you refused! I even tried to get you to help us, but you sent us packing! Now you're in league with the devil!" Taz screamed.

"You bastard! You're the one who killed Oscar, aren't you?" Wen said.

"Of course!" Taz said, rolling his eyes.

"You gave the Code to Administration!" he said.

"You catch on so quick, mate!" Taz said, sarcasm sliming from his words.

"You were my friend, Taz; I trusted you!" Wen said, his fist squeezing tighter. A slow maelstrom raged within his mind, lightning striking his synapses, pandemonium threatening to be unleashed through direct interpretation by the glove. Taz looked oblivious to the hellfire that could so easily be rained down on him, which Wen held back like a rabid dog on a leash.

"You have piss-poor choices in friends, my friend. I told you I look out for *myself*. Now be a good boy and turn yourself in. Whatever tech you leeched from the Code will be quite useful to us," Taz said, waving his gun to the right.

"You want me to go into mindlock, Taz; is that it?" Wen's face was red, and he exhaled acid. Wen raised his fist, a flush of blue light covering his body. He walked toward his former friend, the ground fizzling and crackling with every step. Taz fired shot after shot as Wen drew nearer. Wen's sneer as the bullets ricocheted off his virtual armor grew ever fiercer. He grabbed Taz by the throat and squeezed. The shocked man's slack mouth gagged, and his eyes exorbited. Somewhere, in a quiet, dark room, Taz was choking to death. Taz stood, mouth agape, like a fish gasping for water. Wen had him, and did not want to let go until he croaked.

"Where is Andrei? Is he one of you too?" he whispered savagely into the dying man's face, small darts of current running up his cheek, tesla-coil-like. Taz shook his head no, his eyes bulging, his face turning blue. He seemed to be trying to disconnect, but the hold Wen had on him prevented him from regaining his body. "Where is he?" he screamed. Taz shrugged, gurgling.

"I did what I did because of you, Taz. You forced me to do this. This is on *your* head. Remember that, always." Wen spat into the frightened man's face and then let him go, slamming a fist into the wall behind him, cracking code in the construct. He aimed at the closest server wall and cut a circle with the laser that reached the outer shell of the virtual building and then flew out, followed by the bot.

The hovertank was overtaken by the army's own weapons after fifteen minutes of intense combat. It plummeted to the depths, crashing into girders on the 50th, and then it burned all the way down into the Heap—the Golem that had taken possession of it pulverized in its demise.

Prisoners streamed out of the Administration Building at a gallop, the police force that could have contained them either busy tending to the wounded and dead or putting out fires in the crumbling halls of the station. The Golem controlling the computer systems for the prison doors was found and destroyed before it could escape.

⊼ ⊼ ⊼

"Captain, what happened?" Robert asked, worry lining his face as Wen reappeared in the jungle clearing. All the recruits stood in silence, facing him.

"I had to take care of something. All of you, leave!" Wen said, anger in his gaze. The recruits vanished one after the other.

"The Administration Building, it's...totaled!" Jenna said, listening to a live report from outside the simulation.

"I had no choice. They weren't held captive; who was your source, Jenna?" Wen said, walking menacingly toward her.

"They weren't? I...I can't..." she sputtered.

"You can, and you will. Who. Was. Your. Source?" Wen said.

"I was, sir," Robert said, his head bowed in shame.

"What? How could you have known?" Wen said in surprise, walking toward his second lieutenant.

"Ulrick told me," he said.

"Ulrick? What the hell does he have to do with any of this?" Wen yelled.

"I spoke to him; I needed his opinion. He promised to help me. He told me your friends were there. I believed him. He has access to info through his connections. It was the only way..." Robert said, red-faced and avoiding Wen's glare.

"I can't even..." Wen said. "Dismissed, the both of you. Get out of my sight!" They both vanished, their faces painted in shame. Wen wanted to incinerate something, regretting having let Taz live. He let off a blast of his arm-canon and sent the bot who had accompanied him back flying into nothingness, disintegrated. He brandished his malevolence at the forest and turned the flamethrower on, burning everything as tears of rage ran down his face. Betrayal upon betrayal sickened his shriveled heart, and he wanted the planet to burn, to explode, to extinguish, and he wanted to be the hand that did it. His soul blazed with fever in every molecule, and its fuel was infinite. Wen raised his arms above him and screamed like the damned, wave upon wave of plasmatic fire billowing out from him, setting his mind on fire.

⋏ ⋏ ⋏

He took the next day off. He needed the rest. Deguchi had congratulated him on his incredible success, without a trace of irony. To the brass, he was a hero. His methods had been wholly unorthodox, but the end result being what mattered, he had taken down the most powerful entity outside DaiSin. He was not allowed to leave the building. A wanted man, the army, or what was left of it, would have loved nothing more than to snipe his black head of hair from a kilometer distance. Wen didn't care about that or much of anything else, for that matter. He watched the news reports, helicopters circling the mangled Administration Tower on every channel. Criminals had invaded the Depths and were running rampant through the streets. As a precaution, DaiSin had "lent a hand" in offering their own security forces. Blue uniformed men and women patrolled the streets, restoring order now that the Administration had been mortally crippled. DaiSin was taking over. Thanks to Wen.

The number of dead ran in the hundreds: office workers, prison guards, police, men and women who had served the government. There was no shirking responsibility for it now; Wen was a killer. And he felt he was not done killing.

▲ ▲ ▲

Even a week later, when he stepped into the Command Center, his recruits regarded him with a new kind of awe and fear. Was this still the same man under whom they had trained?

"Today we go after Kanako Security Inc.," Wen said, glaring at each and every one of them. A rustle of murmurs ran through the room.

"Quiet. Yeah, they're tough, but they're not *that* tough. I've trained you well, and I want to see you go after something harder than a piggy bank. If you think you can't do it, you shouldn't be in this unit. You're not a Honey Badger after all." Set jaws nodded in agreement. "Gear up; we're going in. Full frontal assault. Ulrick will lead the charge." Eyes swung to him in surprise. Ulrick puffed up with pride, cocky as hell and ready to kick ass. They went in hard, riding four hovers and sending in the Golems as scouts, a platoon of thirty men and women, split under Jenna, Robert, and Ulrick, supervised by Wen. The meta-plain was strewn with bit-traps and data falls. On the walls of Kanako, all was silent, and the group took off on a full charge, blasting their way toward the fortress.

An electronic boom exploded all around them, and a shield device was thrown over them. They were within a gold dome, with no possibility of escape.

"Charge!" Wen cried, and they ran for the walls, shooting their way in, pock-marking the inner shields as they went. Guards popped up along the wall, firing at the onrush. Sections of the wall began to rise. Giant canons extended ponderously from the depths of their defenses, a whine filling the air. Wen threw out a protective wall with his hand along his entire offensive line, save one person.

Ulrick was ahead of all, screaming his head off in bloodthirsty glee. He did not look back when the defensive projection was erected behind him. He did not stop when the canons made their ponderous way out of the enemy walls. Wen watched him attack, a sick smile on his lips. He raised his fist and smashed the golden shield that prevented them from disconnecting. Canons fired, and Ulrick shattered like a mirror, his particles scattering in the virtual winds. The canon fire bounced off the shield he had erected and went straight back to the senders, bursting their shields and canons and demolishing a part of the wall. Soldiers fell from the ramparts onto the plain, dispatched by Wen's crew.

"Abort!" he sent out, and his personal army disconnected, returning to their sensornet seats. He feigned surprise when they discovered Ulrick's lifeless body lying on his chair. Jenna and Robert, though, traded uneasy glances.

"There'll be an inquiry, you know," Jenna said, concerned.

"It doesn't matter. He was a casualty of war," Wen said dismissively, receiving the adulation of the others as they left the room, brimming with pride over their win.

"You shouldn't have done that, Captain. They'll see you set him up; it's obvious," Robert whispered.

Wen didn't care. He had what he wanted: revenge. Why should he stop now? More needed to die. The liars and the traitors and those who had made his life a living hell. They had to pay. In time, they would all pay, all of those who deserved it, and all of those who got in his way.

⋏ ⋏ ⋏

The call came for him the next day. He was sent to the Deliberators, in whose grim faces he recognized that he might have taken matters too far. At a chair alone before them, he felt the weight of their judgment press down on his shoulders. As much as they could elevate, they could destroy, and woe unto those who forgot it. Wen had done just that. He was not immune to penalty, no matter how powerful he felt he had become. Should he care, he wondered, what these decrepit old beasts thought? Whatever their logic, could it touch him in any meaningful way? He certainly thought not. No one would touch a hero of the company. Would they dare to take away the privileges of someone who had done so much for DaiSin?

"Mr. Harkwell. Captain now, is it?" the woman in the center asked.

"That's right, ma'am," he answered, the tip of his finger running along the cold frame of the chair on which he sat.

"You have done this company proud in the past few months. We must commend you on your efforts." She leaned toward him.

Ha! He was right: adulation and respect, as he was owed. "Thank you, ma'am," Wen said, his ego inflaming.

"You've made a terrible mistake, however," she said, lifting a tablet and adjusting her anachronistic glasses as she analyzed it. His finger stopped.

"Ma'am?"

"Your loyalty is to the company. You have broken your oath to protect its assets. For reasons unknown, you sent a man to his death for no reason whatsoever. Does this situation sound familiar? We saw what you did for the others. You singled him out; why?" she said, peering down on him, brow furrowed.

"I cannot say, your honor."

"Cannot, or will not? It is quite a shame to have to punish such a rising young star for such a stupid mistake. Believe me, Harkwell; from our position, it looks rather idiotic, unless you have an explanation that could supersede our judgment."

"He was a traitor!" he blurted out.

"And for that he had to pay," she said flatly.

"Yes!"

"You disappoint us, Captain Harkwell. You were doing so well. You will keep your command but will receive a warning," she said. "Dismissed."

That's it? A warning? This is a joke! he thought. They were obviously powerless before his might.

"Yes, ma'am," he said, holding back a smile.

"Captain, report to level subsection 49 in the East Pillar for your warning. Find Lewes if you don't know the way. You will be given instructions there," she added.

Whatever, he thought, cackling inwardly. He nodded and saluted and then left the room, attempting to keep the bounce out of his step as he did. As he walked down the carpeted hall adjoining the rail that peered down onto the first floor of the building, he wondered, *Subsection 49? East Pillar? Where is that?*

He looked around him at the ground floor as he rode the elevator down. Then he walked to the front desk and found Mauritius Lewes, who saluted him at his arrival.

"At ease, Mr. Lewes. You're still the Head Guard in this place," he said.

"You outrank me, sir; I have to salute," he responded.

"Mr. Lewes, I've been sent to subsection 49 in the East Pillar. I'm a little embarrassed; I have no idea how to get there."

"That's not surprising. Follow me." Lewes said, and headed toward the elevator banks that Wen had just left. He kept on going though, entering the café and striding past the counter, into the back. There he opened the door to a walk-in refrigerator and went to its furthest wall. He lifted a plastified health poster and placed his hand against a detector. The back wall slid open and an elevator door revealed itself.

"Let me come with you. I haven't been to the medical ward in a while," Lewes said.

"The medical ward?" Wen said, raising an eyebrow.

"Yeah, where DaiSin does most of its biological experiments. I love how they can get away with hiding so much from the authorities. There are four more pillars holding up the Tower, and all of them are filled to the brim with DaiSin's 'off the books' activities. Well, you'd know that; you work for the Barrier Section," Lewes said, and chuckled. "What floor?"

"Uh, forty-nine," Wen said, becoming uncomfortable. Why was he being sent to the illegal medical department at DaiSin for a warning? As the elevator descended, his apprehension grew. What could he possibly find there? No matter; it was a warning, after all.

The door opened with a ding onto an immaculate white hallway with shining white tiled floors. Gurneys lined the hallways, equipped with beige leather restraining straps. From somewhere down the hall, he could hear an awful moan. A pinched-looking woman in a white lab coat tromped up to them out of nowhere and snapped up a board with a form. Her long, frizzy red hair partially covered her face.

"Captain Harkwell?" she said, like a whip-crack.

"Yes."

"Follow me, sir," she said, turning around without waiting to see if he was following and walking off. "You've been sent to sign off, so I'll ask you to please sign at the bottom of this page." She handed the board to him without turning around, walking at a brisk pace, her hair bouncing like a giant puffball.

"What is this release form, exactly?" Wen said, growing more and more worried after having read the header on the page.

"Oh, it just says you will take care of costs and incidentals, that's all."

"I see." He signed the paper while trying to keep up with her. Mauritius Lewes was close behind, a grim look on his face. She extended her hand, and Wen gave her the board back. They came to a room with rows of metallic refrigerator doors, small, square and mirror-like, from one end of the room to the other, and from the floor to the high ceiling.

She looked at the form and scanned the numbers on the doors. At 212, she paused and pulled the handle. A sliding panel came out, and the cold, blue-lipped body of Samuel Harkwell came with it.

A strangled cry escaped Wen's throat as he struggled for air. This couldn't be happening! This was impossible! They couldn't have done this to him. They killed Sammy! Wen's head swam, and he fell to his knees, wheezing in pain. A distant cry rose from the pit of his soul, and he felt a prick in his shoulder. He turned around to see the white-clad woman holding an expended needle, and he fell to the ground, unconscious.

CHAPTER 14

T WAS OVER. There was no longer any reason to live. He lay in the bed of his old DaiSin apartment, where once he had been an initiate, staring blankly at the wall, under heavy sedation. A guard had been placed at his door on suicide watch. In his muddled mind, Wen thought that he had been put there to tell the others as soon as he was dead. They could rejoice at his passing. The room spun, no matter how he looked at it, and it was only worse when he closed his eyes. It was no longer a spin but a drowning. No more revenge; what was the purpose? His brother was dead. His mother was dead. His father was dead. His best friend had betrayed him. Gods only knew where Andrei was. He should have expected it from Ulrick and Deguchi, but it only added to the agony. He existed in a void, with a fine filament of drool puddling on his uniform underneath his chin.

Wen closed his eyes. It hurt. It hurt so damn much! All of it, crushing him. What was the point of going on? He opened them again and rolled from his bed, falling to the ground on his stomach with a thud. Heavy body and unresponsive limbs made any movement excruciatingly difficult. Dragging his arm forward, his neck rubbery, his muscles refused to move. He slid his leg and sobbed, groaning under the effort. Anger refused to come to help this time. Helplessness filled him, and he stopped in the middle of the carpet, panting. There was no stopping, even now. With all the effort he could muster, he propelled himself onward. Drool and tears pooled under him as he crawled to the sensornet chair in the other room. The rooms spun like mad, the sedatives making his progress sluglike.

After an eternity, he reached the chair. The effort had made some of the drugs wear off, and he lifted a trembling arm to the edge of the seat, taking it in a death grip and pushing himself higher with his shaky legs. An arm lifted and plopped down. The drain of effort and the spike of meds made him feel as if he was having an out of body experience, nothing as pleasant as projecting onto the Net. All was sheer agony and nauseating exertion. Finally, he lay on his back and looked inward.

He sat in the middle of the midday clearing, the sun blinding him. With a blurred thought, the lights went out. Complete darkness covered the world. No sounds came from the forest. No light penetrated his mind. It was as cold as a crypt, and he lay down in the sand. Why had he thought he could take on DaiSin in the first place? What mistakes had he committed to make him end up here?

Plenty.

More than he could count. There would be no more mistakes. It had to end. There was no one to blame but himself. He would be the one to end it.

Even now, they analyzed his new weapon, his Hand of God. If he hadn't used it so foolishly, it would still be a secret. They would know he had the Code. They would get it from him. If they didn't, they would tear it out of those around him, those he had *used* to hide it. He mentally smacked himself. What a man he had become. What would his mother have said? Would she be proud of the boy she had raised? Surely not. It was too late for Jenna and Robert. Why should he care about them, anyhow? The only way to avoid torture now would be to erase himself. He had the power to destroy his own mind. He had the Hand of God. Surely it could take away all his memories. It would be like death. He'd become a different person, if he wasn't in a coma for the rest of his life. All he had to do was...

A light. A long white beam, parallel to the ground, shone onto him. *Ignore it this time.* It became warmer. Backing away only made the light burn, "physically," into his clammy flesh. It only cooled down as he got nearer. If he waited too long, the light became warm again and then hot, and at that point it scorched through his skin. No choice but to crawl toward it. His mind cleared as he advanced, and he rose to his feet, his energy returning. The manticore waited, a few meters away, its long scorpion's tail swaying gently. The glow suffused from the portal in his chest, illuminating him. Wen exited and found himself in...

The room where everything had been set in motion, restored to new. This was the apartment that stood at the bottom of the still inexistent towers, millennia ago, windows unbarred, night and an ancient city beyond its panes. The light was eclipsed by Joe's closing hand. On one of the leather sofas by the lit fireplace, he sat and observed Wen's astonished face with a gentle smile.

"I found many of my old memories, Wen," he said. "This was my home. It's a reproduction, of course, but I found it in the old architectural archives of a décor magazine that was popular long ago." He admired the bookshelves and tapestries. "I had good taste, don't you think?"

"This...this is your home?" Wen asked.

"Yes, or more precisely, one of them. I'm pretty sure I had several. I don't know why I know this, but there's an incredible familiarity to it," Joe said. "Come, have a seat." He waved him over.

"I have something of yours," Wen said, recalling the Code from his mind. It suppurated from his palms like quicksilver and began to pool in his upturned hands.

"You? You have them?" Joe said, getting out of his seat and extending his hands. Wen placed the swirling metal liquid in his old friend's cupped hands, and it began to sink into his body. Joe's eyes closed and his eyelids fluttered briefly.

"Joe, are you OK?" Wen asked as his friend shuddered.

Joe's eyes opened. "Yes, but please, call me Yusuke."

"Yusuke?" Wen said, wrinkling his nose.

"Yusuke Daiko. That's my name. Thank you, for giving me my memories back."

"Yusuke Daiko? Any relation to the Daikos of DaiSin?" Wen asked.

"He is me," Yusuke said.

"What do you mean?" Wen said.

"There was always only one Daiko, and that is me," Yusuke said, straight-faced.

Wen laughed. "But that would make you..."

"A tad over three hundred years old, yes."

"How is that even possible?" Wen blurted out.

"Cell regeneration therapy. Nabeen and I participated in some of the first clinical trials. Of course, I stopped getting my treatments when he double-crossed me," Yusuke said, frowning. He walked over to the bookshelves and picked up a tome. "Man, I missed these."

"You mean to say that the present CEO of DaiSin is over three hundred years old?"

"Now you're catching on. We started DaiSin together. I created products, and he sold them. He was a master at marketing, you know. A real genius. About a hundred and fifty years ago, he decided he no longer needed me. He erased my mind and dumped me on the lower levels. Fortunately, I always made backups of my memories. Sure took me a while to get them back though. Still, I do appreciate it."

"It's me. I owe you. I've owed you for so long. Ever since we landed on the streets of Shinjuku1, Sammy and I. If it hadn't been for you, we would have *died*. You found us shelter and food, and protected us. I've never known how to repay you in full, I think I might have resented you a bit." Wen said, with sadness.

"You poor boy. I never expected you to 'repay me', as you say. Everything I did, I did it out of love. You never had a debt toward me to begin with," Yusuke said, with a half-smile. "I appreciate your giving my memories back, however. If it can alleviate your conscience, consider this 'debt' of yours paid in full." Wen nodded. A pressure he hadn't realized was there, was lifted from his body, making him crane his neck sideways and smile back at his friend and savior.

"This place looked like a museum..." Wen said, admiring the décor once again.

"Just a little trick to distract would-be thieves," Yusuke said, and winked.

"What happened? Why did you two fall out?" Wen asked.

"Ideological differences, as is always the case. I thought people should be free to choose their own paths, and he thought otherwise, probably still does. Dropping me penniless on the streets was his way of showing me that people were inherently evil, I think. He was wrong though; I survived. He brought our mutual venture down a very dark road. Aw, look at that; they redacted the whole thing," he said, holding up the book whose pages were all blank in one hand and then placed it back on the shelf.

"But DaiSin is a great company! Anyone who works there knows that. Besides, I was getting my freedom back, before I screwed up."

The older man stared at Wen: "Getting your freedom *back*? Who told you it was his to take in the first place?"

"I...I...should respect authority!" Wen blurted out, and a curious look crossed his face.

"Does authority respect you? Let me answer that for you: no it does not. If it did, you wouldn't be in this mess. Therefore, you owe it nothing, this *authority* of yours. Less than nothing, actually. It's the chip talking."

"The chip?"

"Yeah, that crystalline chip inside your head. I invented that, you know. Nabeen decided it would be a good idea to add a bit of extra programming. Make the faithful more...faithful. It's another reason for our disagreement." Yusuke slapped his hand on Wen's forehead, and he fell down on one of the couches as if touched by a faith healer.

"What did you do that...for...hey, DaiSin is a douche factory!" he said, his mind clearing.

"Yup. The longer you have that in your head, the more you become enthralled to the company. Nobody as loyal as a DaiSin employee, he used to say. I got sick of it. You're truly free now. Free from poisonous doctrine, anyhow."

"Your ex-business partner killed my brother. Probably my mother as well," Wen said, standing up.

"That surprises me. He's greedy. That means he doesn't usually eliminate his assets," Yusuke said, void of irony, going into the kitchen.

"I saw my brother's body," Wen said. "That's convincing evidence enough."

"Still. It could have been a ruse. He's cunning. That body could have been a fake. I don't know how much he's changed over the past hundred and fifty years, but as far as I know, he still hoards as much information as he can. That's what keeps him on top." Yusuke reached into a cupboard and removed a small box. Water boiled on the stovetop in a silver teakettle.

"How does a person get to be like that?" Wen wondered.

"You ever play chess?" Yusuke asked, getting a teapot out of a cupboard.

"A little," Wen said, sitting back down and watching the blue flames of the fire dance.

"Imagine you have a pyramid. At the bottom, you have your pawns. They're practically worthless. You can throw them away for all you like. Higher up the pyramid, you have your better pieces, rooks, knights, castles. At the top, you have the king and queen. Thing is, when you're the king, everyone under you is expendable, to a degree. To Nabeen, people are pawns to be used in a game of power. It's the same all over when humans are given it, unbridled. The kings of various factions send out their pawns, and knights and rooks and castles to do their bidding. They're alone at the top of their respective pyramids, and their game is to topple other kings, simple as that," he said, coming into the living room with a tray holding a Japanese teapot and cups. He set it down on the glass table.

"But people aren't pawns!" Wen said.

"Go tell that to the kings," Yusuke said, smiling. "When people have power, they believe they are allowed to manipulate. Or to kill." Yusuke's eyes narrowed as he gazed into Wen's soul.

"I...I guess you're right," he said, feeling ashamed. "I had no choice though!"

"Someone put a gun to your head and told you to attack the Administration Building, killing hundreds, wounding thousands, and smashing any semblance of order to this city, effectively handing all power to Nabeen Singh? Is that what happened?" Yusuke said, growing cross.

"I just wanted to save my friends," he said in a whisper as his gaze unfocused.

"Are their lives worth those of hundreds?" Yusuke said, pouring the tea.

"I thought they were," Wen said, looking up.

"Then you might want to go play with the kings, if you're going to act like one of them. Your brother is alive. He is somewhere inside DaiSin; I'm sure of it. Stopping Nabeen Singh should be our priority though. There is now no more dangerous man alive. If you thought he was a cruel tyrant within his own domain, just wait and see how he will be with an entire city or country under his belt. I can see him growing already, every time I close my eyes," Yusuke said, frantic.

"What can I do?" Wen said.

"It's not about *you*, Wen. It's about everybody. There is no magic bullet; there is no magical hero. This isn't a fantasy world you are living in. We have to gather everyone we can to oppose him. I'm with you now. Who else can help us?" Yusuke said, lifting his cup.

"Maybe my lieutenants. I don't know how to get them to oppose the company, though...they helped me once, or tried to anyway," Wen said, chewing on a fingernail, eyeing the amber liquid in the cup.

"That's a start. Now that I have my memories back, I have all my old ideas and power back. I'll also attract Nabeen's attention, unfortunately. I have to lay low until the right moment. Go and find as many people to help as possible. You still have a copy of my memories; here's the cipher to unlock the rest." He gave Wen a small gold lighter.

"How was I able to unlock your Code...memories...in the first place?" Wen asked.

"You were in contact with me; that was enough, I think. Everybody rubs off on everybody else, in some ways," Yusuke said.

"And the Administration?"

"Sheer dumb luck and a force cracker. If you put enough computers on a problem long enough, they'll come up with the solution in time. Not as efficiently as a human, mind you. Go back, and act normally. They can't know you're no longer under their influence."

"But my lieutenants are!"

"And you can do to them what I did to you, if you believe you can trust them."

"I don't know who to trust!"

"You have to trust someone. Sometimes you get a bum deal. Sometimes you get a truly horrible, life shattering stroke of rotten luck. If you don't get back up and brush yourself off, you might as well be dead. There will always be bastards in this life. But there are some truly wonderful people as well. For all your faults, Wen Harkwell, you are one of those," Yusuke said. Wen nodded, finding the pill hard to swallow.

"They have the last weapon I made from your memories."

"Doesn't matter. You don't need weapons anymore. You need something better."

"But I only know how to make weapons!"

"Every invention can become a weapon. Every thought can be used to hurt some-one, but it does not need to. A hammer is just as good to build a house as it is to whack someone over the head; it's the intent and motive that matter. You will find a way, Wen. Now go!" Yusuke said, and Wen felt repulsed out the door.

The impenetrable darkness surrounded him once again. He wished for dawn, and a stream of orange-yellow light appeared over the treetops. Was his brother alive? He fervently hoped so. Decoy, subterfuge, illusion, all would be better to believe than finality. The real question remained: what was the truth? Without it, he could only trust his eyes; that the frail figure they had shown him was the lifeless husk of his sibling. What could he be capable of if he had Yusuke's intuition? On that point, he had been right though, it was pointless to end his life with Nabeen Singh growing stronger and subjugating everyone. It took courage to end it all, but it was also needed to keep on fighting, whether there was anyone waiting for him at the end of the line or not. Eyes creaking open, he felt a massive headache pounding at his skull. Whether it was the drugs wearing off or the effects of Yusuke's destroying the chip's programming, he neither knew nor cared. Wen staggered from the sensornet chair and stumbled into the bathroom. The cold water he poured on his face in handfuls wiped away the last of the cobwebs hanging inside his thumping skull. Long draughts of liquid cooled his aching throat. He knew he could go on if he had purpose, if he could find meaning in his actions. Only he could imbue every act he perpetrated with sense and therefore have a reason to continue. Were these his thoughts? They sounded like his, but he had a feeling Yusuke's memories were becoming a part of his own. Now he had to trust. For that he had to be truthful. How much would that cost him?

Jenna and Robert came when he contacted them and met him in the clearing. They looked him over as they would a terminally ill yet contagious patient, half-piteously and half fearfully.

"How are you doing, Captain?" Jenna said as she sat on one of the logs in the glade.

"I've been better," Wen said, his mouth smiling below his purplish, tired eyes, taking a seat on a large tree trunk in the sand. He felt he looked like he was suffering from a life hangover, one that might never entirely go away. "Where are your bodies at the moment?"

"In my room," Robert said.

"Same? Why?" Jenna added.

"I want to be sure you won't be bothered or interrupted. I need to talk to you both," Wen said.

"We heard you got a warning. For Ulrick," Robert said.

"I did. I'll never do that again," he said. "I wanted to tell you both how sorry I was. I acted unlike I should have. You have every right to be afraid of me, or hate me. If you want, you can transfer platoons."

His lieutenants regarded each other, and Wen heard the background chatter of a private mental conversation.

"You've been punished enough, sir. We made mistakes as well. You are the best we've ever had, and we trust you implicitly," Robert said. "Would you want to be under someone else's command?" he asked Jenna.

"Never. Robert is right. You're a great leader," Jenna said.

"Come closer, you two," Wen said, rising and putting his palms on both their heads. A surge went through them, and they both staggered backward in surprise. Jenna grabbed her head in pain, falling to her knees. Robert writhed in the sand, clutching his hair. Wen watched, sitting back down on the trunk and crossing his legs while they bucked and squirmed in the sand.

The tremors relented, and they stopped moving. Both were covered in sweat, breathing heavily, the veins on their foreheads pulsing with the strain. They held themselves up on shaky arms, staring in shock at their captain.

"How do you feel now?" Wen asked them.

"Like a bird that's found the door to her cage open," Jenna whispered.

"Like I've just seen a false god murdered," Robert said grimly.

"You're free now, just like me. I have to admit something to you, and I'm sorry I didn't tell you sooner. I've been using your minds to hide pieces of a very dangerous set of data. It's still there. I will show you where it is, and you can delete it, if you want."

"Is that how you created the Pulverizer and that...thing you used to destroy the Administration?" Jenna said.

"Yes."

"You used us? We trusted you, and you used us?" Robert said.

"I did. I am sorry; from the bottom of my heart, I am sorry. I didn't think there was any other way. I know better now. If you still want to leave me, I understand," Wen said, holding his hands on his knee.

"I might have to think about this," Jenna said, hands on her hips and staring up at the sky.

"I don't. Wen Harkwell has freed my mind from something I didn't even know was there. Thank you, Captain. I am grateful. I forgive you, sir," Robert said, saluting.

"That was quick," Jenna said.

"Lieutenant, this man just liberated you. He told you the truth of his actions. He has been straightforward in everything he's done," Robert said.

"Not everything," Jenna said.

"I slept with Jenna," Wen said flatly.

"Excuse me?" Robert said, cocking his head sideways.

"It's the truth. I slept with her that night we went to celebrate my captaincy. I hid it from you. I didn't think it was any of your business. I regret that. I also regret doing it." Robert and Jenna both turned beet red. "You are free to go. I will let you ponder my actions for as long as you need. I need your help. I won't lie to you anymore. If you truly feel that what I have done is a betrayal beyond forgiveness, you may do as you choose. But I need you. I desperately do. You are two of the only people in the world I feel I can trust at the moment. I'm sorry for what I've done; I can't say it enough. You are dismissed."

They looked at each other, saluted Wen, and vanished. Wen stared at his hut in the distance. The noon heat baked his shoulders. He stepped to the crucible and wondered what he could possibly make that wasn't a weapon; something strong enough to defeat the most powerful man in the world.

CHAPTER 15

OR THE NEXT few weeks, relations were awkward, to the say the least. Wen had returned from the brink, much to everyone's surprise. Like most of the others, he believed that what had been done to him in retaliation for Ulrick would make him finish himself. Wen strode in confidently and without guile. He told them all that he had made a mistake, and that he had paid for that mistake in blood. Missions resumed with regularity, even after he handed over the weapon he had created.

The Hand of God was a misnomer; he recognized it as quite the opposite. Anything as dangerous could not have emanated from a benevolent and all-powerful being. It was renamed Asteroth's Claw before anyone could think any good could come of it.

Strangely, the Deliberators did not ask him for the source of his power. Wen decided not to elucidate the mystery. Their motives were unclear, apart from their undying loyalty to DaiSin. Delving deeper would have meant asking questions for which he would have been asked some of his own. It was better to let this topic lie idle until he faced them again, as he inevitably must.

DaiSin mercenaries scoured the streets for the missing criminals. Those who defied the new order were vaporized. Many inmates were hired on to work in the various departments in need of interesting subjects. The Administration, diminished and ailing, could only look on as the tendrils of DaiSin's might spread like a poisoned vine throughout all the levels of the city. Curfews were instituted; death was the penalty for breaking them.

Even the strongest alliances of syndicates were no match against the might of DaiSin's newly equipped military. A thousand men armed with Asteroth's Claws were like the invading Spanish troops of Christopher Columbus armed with guns against the spears or bows and arrows of the natives. There was no contest. Every day, Wen saw another company fall to DaiSin. Every day, he felt the impotence grow inside him, twisting him. Every day, he led the charge against those defenseless people and returned home with their scalps. Killing became a necessity of the job, not something he enjoyed even remotely.

During training one day, he noticed one of the Golems jolting about in a peculiar manner, attracting undue attention to itself.

"Something wrong with that thing?" he asked Abakar, who shrugged. It stood in place, bouncing. Then it stopped, and after that it bounced more quickly but then stopped again.

"You want I should get it checked out, Captain?" Abakar said.

"Nah, concentrate on the drills. These new ones are flabby. We need to get them in shape," Wen said. He had picked Abakar and Sonia as his new lieutenants, since the Board had given him even more recruits to contend with. "You, go stand in the corner," he ordered the Golem. The robot kept jolting about, as if having a fit of hiccups.

That night, as Wen lay in bed, he couldn't help but think that there had been some sort of regularity to the bot's movements. It almost seemed like it was trying to communicate with him. Was there a sequence to his movements? The more he thought about it, the more ludicrous it seemed. It was a defective Golem, and he would have it dismantled and reassembled the next day.

It was still doing it when he came into the jungle clearing the next day.

"Abakar, can you get the IP address of this bot and send it over to the IT department? They'll have to check the HYVE to see which personality is off. Might have to erase it and start over," Wen said. As Abakar stepped toward it, the android-like Golem raised its arms defensively. Abakar stared at it in wonderment.

"Did that bot just fend you off?" Wen said, bemused.

"It did. First time I ever see that, Captain," Abakar said, taking a step back.

"Think it's dangerous?" Wen said, raising his loaded fist. The Golem swung its head from side to side.

"Never seen a bot do that either," Abakar mused. The Golem began its frantic up and down jumping, sometimes in quick succession, and then a short wait, always in the same order. It was communicating the only way it knew how.

"Abakar, you and the others take over training for a while; I'll be back," Wen said.

"Not going to go destroy a city on your own again, are you, sir?" Abakar asked, apprehensive.

"No, not this time. That's an order, Lieutenant," Wen said. Abakar gone, he asked the Golem to follow him. The forest foliage hid their direction. Wen wanted to be absolutely certain no one noticed their departure. "Do you know where Sammy is? Jump once for yes, twice for no," he said, and the Golem jumped once. "Can you take me to him?" The bot jumped once more. Wen felt incommensurable joy filling him. He summoned the manticore, and they both fell into the void of Netspace. As they were in the Barrier Department's pillar, the Golem's orb projection trail sped upward, veered at ninety degrees, went a short distance, veered once more at ninety degrees downward, and vanished. Wen paused. The filament just ended, no trace of continuity. Another light popped from the ether and headed in a different direction. Wen was unsure as to what he should follow. He hovered over the nonspace, and noticed that unlike most other areas of DaiSin, there were no Net orbs glowing below him. Some sort of blind spot was situated directly beneath. He approached it and was pushed away. There was no way to go in through the Net. A tiny electric charge appeared from nothingness and hovered before him. This had to be the bot he had followed. It seemed to want to tug him, but Wen had no way of advancing. The spark returned to the nothingness it had come from and did not return. Wen backtracked all the way to his mind and pondered what he had seen.

"Everything OK, sir?" Sonia said, when she saw him reappear.

"Sure, fine," he said, his gaze far away.

"Did you want to regain command, sir?" Sonia asked.

"Hm? Oh, yes. That I will. Thank you," he said, coming back to reality. Another dirty secret at DaiSin. The bot had stopped somewhere on the 150th floor; he was sure of it. During the entire afternoon's exercises, his mind kept wandering back to that place where the Golem had vanished. He mentally triangulated the location, and realized it was in the vicinity of the central pillar. Lewes had mentioned there were five hidden departments in the recesses of the supports. Were all towers in the city built like DaiSin headquarters? Were they all of them hiding some monstrous and illegal activities that they could not admit openly?

That night he went the Net way, knocking at Lewes's mind, finding his glowing orb in his office of the 150th. Lewes allowed him to enter, and Wen found himself on top of a skyscraper in a large city. It was nowhere as big as Tokyo, but the view was impressive nonetheless. It was even possible to see all the way down to the ground. A river snaked its way further east, and two stark black towers stood in the distance. Yellow cars like tiny pebbles drove down the surrounding streets. It was a cloudless day, and a thin breeze blew through his hair.

"How can I help you, Captain?" Lewes said, smiling.

"I need your opinion on something," Wen said.

"What would that be?" Lewes said, walking to the edge of the fence.

"How do you like this place?" He tapped the DaiSin insignia on his lapel without looking away from Lewes.

"The Empire State Building? I find it frustrating at times, but a challenge as well." Lewes said, cocking an eyebrow.

"Would you say you have trouble with this construct? Are there other sceneries you would rather visit?" Wen said.

"I have been growing unsatisfied with this view for the past little while, but it is the only one that is afforded me. Do you have any leads on how to change my perspective?" Lewes said as he walked toward Wen.

"I might. I just wanted to sound your feelings on it before I could introduce you to an alternate vision. Would you say you feel trapped in this particular panorama?" Wen asked.

"What penalties might I incur if I were to agree with you?" Lewes asked, fidgeting.

"You know the rules. I will let you decide if you want to look elsewhere or not. This is New York, isn't it? Before the Americans went insane? Must have been nice. Have a wonderful evening, Mr. Lewes. Come and knock on my head with your answer," Wen said.

"And to you, Captain," Lewes said, giving him a sly grin that meant *What are you up to, Harkwell?*

CHAPTER 16

ONE NIGHT, WHILE Wen slept at DaiSin, he was awoken to his Net set beeping softly. He turned on the screen before him, a newscast in progress. A black man in a green suit was announcing the day's weather in Kinchasa, describing the sweltering heat the New Zairian capital would suffer that day. Wen was about to turn off the set when he noticed the scrolling ticker at the bottom of the screen:

Andrei Yurushcenkov released from Administration prison during attack and in stable condition. —Joe

The ticker went on to announce major events around the world. Yusuke was a genius. How else could he get the message into DaiSin without attracting attention? Wen turned off the Net set and went back to bed. Finally a bit of good news.

⋏ ⋏ ⋏

Jenna and Robert came around a few days later. At first, their attitudes toward each other had been one of animosity, but Wen saw that things had returned to a semblance of normalcy. The cold, hard stares of the first days were now the complicit smiles he had grown used to.

During a heavy firefight with the East Russian Federation, where the two armies disputed a previously neutral territory, Jenna approached Wen.

"We've made peace, Captain," she yelled over the shelling that rained on their heads.

"That's great, Lieutenant; glad to hear it," Wen said as he signaled for Abakar to surround the right flank of the enemy. A data mound lay between the two armies, the destroyed remnants of a server tower blasted to bits. Neither army was ready to rush the mound, fearing exposure at the top. Two other brigades had joined Wen's, Surimat leading them.

"We're ready to follow you into hell, sir," she said.

"I am honored to lead the way," Wen said, as he pointed to the top of the hill and motioned for the troops to charge. He was first in line to go, and his screaming battalion followed. Wen felt a surge of hope.

Seeing the enemy rush over the mound struck fear into the Russians' hearts, and they fired even more heavily. Their tech was just as powerful as DaiSin's. The contest was no longer weighing heavily on their side. Wen had a mind that Yusuke had been helping their opponents, evening the odds. He smiled. It would no longer be a complete roust for Nabeen Singh.

⅄ ⅄ ⅄

Wen had not been entirely certain about Mauritius Lewes. He seemed to be a company man, but appearances were deceiving, he knew. There was a reluctance in his actions, more as if he was forced to perform abhorrent duties than taking pleasure in them. He risked much in being so open with Lewes, even in his covert way, but choice was a factor that had little sway in his decision. Intuition, though, had nudged him on. Something about him was right, despite what he had witnessed that night in the blood-spattered room where Sayeed had died. Like himself, Lewes was in thrall to something bigger, and he could only use a small voice to express it. The weight of responsibility was on Wen's mind now for having offered the man freedom with a strong chance of death. What other choice was there though? If he wanted to be free, did he not have to risk his very being? For a chance at a better life, didn't they both have to stand up, no matter how fearsome the consequences, even if it meant putting their own heads at risk of being sliced off? Wen now thought so. How curious the way his thoughts had evolved in such a short span of time. Once again, he wondered if these were his own or Yusuke's. He came to the conclusion that very seldom his own thoughts, unless they were driven by his base emotions, were his own. In acquiring alternate means of interpreting events, decisions, and reactions, his foundation changed to the thoughts of those who posited them and were no longer emanating from his core. Yet in having taken them in and accepting them, they had transformed his mind and therefore had become his thoughts. An open mind had saved him from self-destruction, which he would always remember. Having a rigid ideology strapped to his body like a time bomb would never happen again. There was room enough in his mind for all the ideas in the world now, and he no longer would be forced to adhere to a single one. The pressure-testing machines from Fujii-Hashimoto Heavy came to mind. Ideas were the parts that comprised his mind, and for them to be efficient, he had to rigorously test each one using proof as the one constant that made the thought worthwhile. Without it, it might as well blow up and be gone for all he cared. There was no longer room in his working mind for lies. There was much refinement he would add to this new development, but for now he would go with proof as his basis in truth and the rallying point for his most concrete thoughts.

Lewes knocked at his mind as he was deep in contemplation. He let the man into the jungle clearing at night, and invited him to take a seat around a campfire he had going. The crickets chirped in the forest, and a blanket of fireflies could be seen hovering over the forest thicket, an unconscious and comforting projection he had plucked from his childhood memories.

"I'd offer you a drink, but all I have is green tea," Wen said.

"Virtual tea, huh? You sure know how to live the high life, Captain." Lewes smirked.

"Call me Wen. I've given up on alcohol. It doesn't like me very much. Might as well stick to it in the Net as well," Wen said, smiling. "You've considered my offer then?"

Lewes's gaze seemed lost in the fire's embers. "I have. I'm a soldier, Wen, or at least I used to be. Fighting is what I'm made for, but not like this. I was campaigning in Southern Europe until I was recruited by DaiSin. Urban warfare. Everybody was the enemy. UN World Police had some sway back then. We quelled riots, brought *peace*. That's where I met Oscar, incidentally, during the Greek Wars. We weren't even on the same side back then. He made me see that what I was doing was being the tool of oppression, pure and simple. I couldn't keep going after that. We both ran away, got jobs on a ship, and did mercenary work for a while. Then we snuck into Tokyo. DaiSin hired us pretty quickly. I thought I was lucky; we both did."

Wen rose to his feet and paced before the fire. "What happened?"

"After a while, choice was taken from us. The implant does something to you. It makes you blind to anything but one opinion or direction. I've been fighting it, mentally, for the past ten years. It's like being stuck in a cage with a tiger circling around you, attacking when you are weak, attempting to devour you. It's...draining," Lewes said, wringing his hands.

Ten years, my goodness, thought Wen. "I'm surprised you can talk about it." "It takes quite the effort, but yes." Lewes looked up at Wen.

Wen walked over to Lewes and placed his palm on the man's forehead. A jolt took hold of him, and his head snapped back. He let out a small cry and leaned forward, putting his fists to his temples. He removed them and stared at Wen in astonishment.

"How? How did you do that?" Lewes said.

"I have gifted friends." Wen smiled, stepping back.

"Thank you."

"I need your help, Lewes," Wen said.

"Maury, please. Anything," Lewes said.

"What lies in the Central Pillar, and can you get me in there?" Wen said, gazing intently at him.

Lewes shook his head slowly. "That's the HYVE Supercomputer Array down there. Only machines can access it."

"How do they fix it if anything goes wrong?" Wen asked, surprised.

"It's all automated. The techies put the spare parts in elevators along the top of the column, and they're taken over by bots when they get to the computer. Keeps the area free of contaminants, I suppose. What do you want with the HYVE?" Lewes asked.

"I've been told my brother was alive. That he may be hidden there," Wen said.

"Impossible; nothing living goes into the HYVE. I'm sorry to say this, but we both saw your brother..." Lewes said.

"I have to. I have no choice," Wen said, his determined face set in a way that said there was no changing his mind. Lewes nodded gravely.

"Is there any way I can do that little trick you did on me?" Lewes asked, pointing at his forehead.

Wen smiled and shook his hand.

⅄ ⅄ ⅄

A day later, during war games, the Golem that had dragged Wen to the HYVE entrance tried to communicate but could not make itself understood. For most of the morning, it went along with the activities but was not as concentrated as the other machines. Wen took it off the field. It had to be used, of course, so that no one would think twice about it, but it acted so awkwardly that it attracted attention to itself nonetheless. Wen hid it in the forest. It would have to return to the HYVE at some point, of course, or its absence would be noticed by the Central Computer banks.

It had to return.

Wen had an idea.

"Bot, give me your Serial ID and address. I want you to stay here tonight. You will only go back to the HYVE when I come and get you, is that understood?" he said, and the Golem jumped once.

Wen extended his arm. "I want you to download the information onto my forearm. Do it; I'm adapted for it." The Golem leaned forward and touched Wen's arm with his square hand. Wen projected into the nonspace of the Net and retraced his steps to the area where the bot had led him before. He slipped through the firewall and found himself in a gargantuan cylinder, looking top-down into it. Orbs, like diamonds, scintillated like ice-fire all along the walls of the cylinder, as well as smaller rods arranged in the center. An occasional flare saw one extinguish, and certain lights flew past him and into the building, off to assist the humans they were programmed to. Wen followed the filament he was on to the address he instinctively knew would be the computer home of his Golem. He slipped inside it and opened his mind's eye, attempting to communicate with the machine. It balked and repulsed him, and Wen felt fright emanating from it. It was not frightened of him, he felt, but of the repercussions of his being discovered in the forbidden area. Wen hesitated and then flew out of the machine, returning to his own mind, where he allowed the Golem to go back to his home, in the secretive hollows of the HYVE.

Wen was even more curious than before. If he wanted to interact with the Golem, he would have to somehow get its memory chip out of the socket where it was kept. It obviously had its own address, as they all did. They worked together but as individuals. It was an interesting arrangement. He wondered if that had been another of Yusuke Daiko's inventions. The question would be asked the next time they came in contact.

"May I have a word with you, sir?" Robert asked as he walked back to the training ground.

"Of course. What's on your mind?" Wen said as they both went back to the top of the gangway overlooking the exercise yard.

"Jenna and I...we were wondering if you could share that power you used on us... the one that freed us."

"It's not a power, Robert, just information," Wen said, smiling at his lieutenant.

"It sure feels like that, sir."

"What do you intend to do with it?" Wen asked.

"We know of others who would like to have more leeway. We would like to free them, sir," Robert said, turning red. Wen looked out over the obstacle course, his mercenary group outflanking and taking on rapid androids like it was nothing. They were under his command, but ultimately their allegiance went directly to DaiSin.

"Granted, Lieutenant. Do be discreet," Wen said, staring at the man hard.

"Of course, sir," Robert said proudly. Wen stuck out his hand, and Robert took it. A current went through them, and Robert observed his hand. "All I have to do is...?"

"Touch their minds. It destroys the program in the chip."

"Thank you, sir," Robert said, saluting. He left to find Jenna.

᛫ ᛫ ᛫

That night, Wen sat on the sensornet chair in his DaiSin apartment. He closed his eyes and opened them in the darkening glade. From his hand, he shone forth a beam of light, which he directed to the open portal of the manticore. Within a few moments, another beam, identical to his, touched his chest. He flew out the portal, following the beam. It led him away from the capital and through another portal somewhere over Europe.

He was in a small town square, surrounded by three-story stone buildings. A café with painted green wooden chairs stood off to his right. At one of the red-checkered tables sat Yusuke, sipping a green liqueur from a tall, thin glass under the tarnished striped awning. He closed his hand and the beam vanished, already almost invisible in the hot midday sun.

Wen strode over and sat by him.

"I thought you were a tea man," Wen said, leaning on the table and admiring the scenery. "Where are we?"

"I am a man of many tastes; why limit yourself? We are in a small French town, before the First World War. Beautiful, isn't it? Did you come to discuss tastes?" Yusuke said. He looked younger, his previously matted beard shaven. The lines in his face remained, but poise had come into his previously haggard demeanor.

"No, of course not. What can you tell me about the HYVE?" Wen said, shaking his head in negation when the *garçon* offered him a menu.

"I don't know what you're talking about. What hive?" Yusuke said, cocking his head toward Wen.

"Not hive, but H-Y-V-E. It stands for 'High Yield Virtual Entities.' It's part of a supercomputer at DaiSin. You really don't know anything about it? I thought you might have designed it," Wen said, saddened.

"*Garçon, l'addition, s'il vous plaît,*" he said in perfect French. The waiter, in spotless white chemise and black vest brought a black leather billfold and stood at attention while Yusuke signed his name at the bottom.

"We are in a simulation, aren't we?" Wen asked.

"Yes, but why break the magic by doing something out of the ordinary like not paying?" he said, handing the billfold back to the waiter, who bowed slightly. "Shall we?" he said. They walked down the quiet street of the town, watching washerwomen carrying laundry back from the lines behind the houses. A chimneysweep stepped precariously atop a slanted roof while his assistant held a long wooden ladder below.

"I've never heard of this HYVE. When I was still there, it didn't exist," Yusuke said, nodding to a gentleman in a black suit with tails and a top hat.

"What was in the central pillar of the DaiSin Building then?" Wen said, admiring the workmanship that had gone into the details of the town's construction.

"Why...nothing, as far as I know. Unless he had something installed in secret during construction," Yusuke said. "Nabeen's been busy. What do you want to find out about this HYVE?" Yusuke said as they walked toward an impressive and stately church. A star-fire pattern of stained-glass adorned the front, between two arrow spires to its sides.

"What it has to do with my brother. I can't get in physically, but I have to. I was able to get in by projecting, but whatever address belonged to the bot that led me there was, it kicked me out before I could question it," Wen said, scratching his chin.

"What stops you from getting in?" Yusuke said.

"Nothing biological can enter," Wen sighed.

"So go in as something nonbiological."

"I'm an idiot," Wen said, lifting his head and staring into the sky.

"No, not at all. I'm honored you would ask me for my help. Sorry I didn't know more about this HYVE," Yusuke said as they walked up the steps of the church and entered. Inside, a cool and peaceful serenity reigned. A choir of young boys practiced canticles in soft, echoing voices, and behind the hostel, at the front of the fifty rows of wooden pews, stood intricate ormolu statuary. The smell of incense mixed with age permeated the air in a soothing admixture, something that reminded Wen of his hometown in an indescribable way. A flash of red temples and the memory was gone.

"This is a gorgeous reproduction. What's the name of this town?" Wen asked, enthralled.

"St-Lô. It was almost completely destroyed during the war. The second one. Part of this church is the only thing that survived. They left the actual ruins intact to remind people about the destructiveness of war. This place was 'built' by the descendants of the inhabitants to show what is annihilated when we forget." Wen observed in silence and then wished him farewell.

Once back at DaiSin, he called for the Golem and made it wait in the clearing. He went straight for the 150th floor, physically. There would be few guards and no lab technicians at this hour. The small, square doors were situated at regular intervals on the inside walls of the building. Wen found a closet and hid within. He projected his mind, hiding among the scents of ammonia and disinfectant, using the bot's address, and went back inside the HYVE. This time, he was right next to its location and jacked directly into one of the robots that handled repairs. A camera turned on, and he was able to see in the dark using infrared. He was only able to see the scintillating lights when he was in free flow down the HYVE's cylindrical structure. Being inside the robot and seeing only in tones of black and green made it difficult to make his way forward. He wished he could see both views at the same time, and the darkness of the camera filled with the lights of the HYVE Golem's energy signatures.

The technician bot he had invaded was an arm attached to the wall of the pillar. It could go in any direction, as long as it followed the magnetic "streets" arranged along the way. In this way it was similar to the robotic arms he had so admired back at Fujii-Hashimoto Heavy. No dancing here, though. The activity prevalent was more akin to the tapping of a keyboard. An arm would reach into one of the server doors, removing or adding a part, and then go on its way. This motion went on constantly, all along the walls of the pillar. Wen dove down the length of the pillar, aware of the buzzing lights behind every server door. He arrived at the address given by the bot and opened the door.

There was no computer. A Plasteel jar sat nestled among various cables. Inside it, in a reddish liquid, was suspended a brain, its connection to the outside a link between its Netrodes and the jar. Instantly Wen knew: it was Sammy. With the robot arm, he reached into the alcove and picked up the casing. As he was removing it, another arm lowered itself above his and tried to take the braincase away from him. Wen sped down the length of the pillar toward the bottom, where he could see other arms taking identical casings. They were opening the tops of the jars and spilling the contents straight down into a rotating blade. Dead minds, devoid of light, vaporized on contact. Wen changed direction, pursued by the intruding arm. He felt a pressure inside his mind. Someone was coming for him; he had to escape back to his body. There was no way he would leave his brother's mind to be destroyed. Escape was the only option. He leapt off toward the right, heading around the ring of the pillar, and then turned again to head upward. He accelerated, turning the camera to the brain to see if it was all right. A few bubbles formed, but the pulsing light coming from inside the mind glimmered steadily. An elevator appeared. He took its contents and replaced them with the case he held and then sent it back up. The chasing arm caught up to his and snatched whatever he held in his pincers. It returned to the lower levels in what Wen could only describe as a snit. Wen logged out of the arm.

He walked out of the closet and checked for newly arrived elevators from the lower levels. He discovered his a few minutes later, two hundred paces down the corridor. A pair of guards walked by, and he took the braincase back to the closet where he had hidden. If he could have, he would have kicked himself. There was no way he could take his brother's mind out of there without being caught.

He called Lewes. "I need a hand with something."

"What can I do for you?"

"Bring a body bag to the 150th, near the computer elevator entries. I'll tell you afterward," Wen said.

Lewes showed up fifteen minutes later with a black rubber bag. Wen motioned for him to get inside the closet.

"What's going on?" Lewes said, handing over the sack.

"Were you aware that the HYVE was *this*?" Wen said, holding up the braincase.

"What the hell is that?" Lewes asked, recoiling.

"This is most probably Sammy's brain. That's all there is down there: human minds, connected to the computer. I saw them throwing dead ones into a giant blade. I'm sure that's where everybody goes eventually."

"That is insane! How can they even do that?"

"I don't know, but I want to put a stop to it," Wen said. "Please take my brother's mind and bring it to these coordinates." He handed Lewes a piece of paper. "I couldn't leave with him without getting caught. You, however, have the dubious honor of getting rid of the bodies. That talent'll come in handy for once." Wen smiled wryly.

"Yes, sir," Lewes said, and walked off with the black satchel in hand.

Wen returned to his apartment and took the sensornet chair. He sent a simple message to the fourth Golem, correction, person, he had left hidden as a spy in the communications array at the Administration Building before his attack.

There had to be a way to stop the use of the so-called bots. He was just as guilty of using and discarding them as everyone else, but that was before he knew the truth. How many Golem had he taken onto the field and allowed to be blown to smithereens so he could have cover for a few moments? Wen shivered in disgust, another notch on the long belt of his mistakes. If only he had known sooner. How many lives could he have saved? Then again, there was little help for all those poor souls running as ragged slaves for all the supposed humans above ground. Where could they go? It didn't matter as long as it was no longer toward the slicing blades at the bottom of the pit. The time for action was coming soon.

⋏ ⋏ ⋏

CHAPTER 17

"SIR, HAVE YOU seen your Net presence, lately?" Robert asked him a few days later as they walked down the halls of the Barrier Department. As a matter of fact, he had not turned around to see his own sphere in quite some time. Not since he had come in as an initiate, fresh from surgery. He exited his mind and observed what he had become. Behind him hovered an energy field the size of a small house, pale yellow and pulsing, getting larger. Filaments sprang in all directions to other, smaller orbs near and far. He could stay awake and see inward now, since the incident in the HYVE a few days previous. It was an odd feeling, a kind of double sense. It was possible for him to superimpose both reality and the Net, a bit like when he used to wear his father's Zipper glasses but completely different at the same time. He could see Robert's sphere, shining bright, right inside his head. It was a strange feeling to see people send out their consciousnesses around him. Wen could coordinate with them with his mind, sending vocal commands to all of them, if he chose. In only a few short days, Jenna and Robert had converted over a hundred people. The totality of his unit now obeyed his orders out of their own sense of right instead of being imposed upon from the crystal within them.

"What does it mean?" he wondered aloud.

"You grow more influential by the day, sir," Robert said.

"For what it's worth," Wen said as he wondered what would be needed to defeat the most powerful man on Earth. "If you'll excuse me, Lieutenant," he said, sensing a familiar presence approaching him on the Net. He took a deep breath and returned to the jungle clearing. Taz stood there, disguised as the energy signature of the missing Golem, still waiting orders in the Administration systems.

"I got your message," said the Golem.

"Sorry for the disguise. It's the best I could do to get you in," Wen said evenly.

"What do you want, traitor?" Taz said through gritted teeth.

"A chance to redeem myself," Wen said. "Did you receive the package?"

"Yes. Whose brain did I smuggle?" Taz asked, disgusted.

"Sammy's. DaiSin is powered by the minds of its employees. There must be thousands of people's brains in this building, all as expendable as the next. That's just one of the things DaiSin is up to. Did you contact Andrei?" Wen said.

Taz nodded. "I did. Your brother's...brain is in his custody now. You will be executed for what you've done, you know," Taz said. So he had done as Wen had asked, for that much he could be thankful. He could see an inkling of the old Taz in him yet. Not enough to call a friend, of course, and probably never again, but at least there stood a man in whom he might learn to trust to do simple tasks, if only under duress. The coming days would be crucial to test those poisoned waters.

"That's what I wanted to discuss. You and your superiors might get the chance to take back the power I so blindly destroyed, but I want immunity. Call it services rendered," Wen said, holding his fingers crossed behind him.

"How dare you? How dare you even try to play politics after what you've done? Do you really think we'll just let you walk away?" Taz said, turning red.

Wen smiled sadly. "I do have to protect myself, and frankly, you're in no position to threaten, yourself. Only I can help the Administration get back on its feet. How long do you think you can hold out against that line of tanks parked outside your door? We've also begun to attack other sovereign countries over the Net, not just corporations anymore. The situation is getting dire. I can help, but I need immunity. Take it or leave it," Wen said, crossing his arms.

"I'll have to discuss this with my superiors, of course," Taz said, clenching and unclenching his fists, giving the Golem a comical look of anger. Wen felt different from the little boy he had let be bullied by the man who stood before him. How many lifetimes ago was that, six months? There was even footing now, and the ball was in his court; at least Taz seemed smart enough to recognize it.

"Don't take too long. Things are accelerating around here. Have been for months. I don't know how large my window of opportunity is, so please, chop-chop," Wen said, clapping his hands twice.

Taz pinched his lips and then said, "You've grown cocky, old friend. Don't let it go to your head." He used *friend* almost as a mild epithet, something akin to *reptile* or *bastard*. Wen felt in no way insulted, affected, or disconcerted. It barely registered as a blip on the radar. Curiously, it was as if the roles had been inverted, and he was now the adult dictating terms to his childlike friend, and he took no pride in this either.

"Use the Golem's signature to come back in undetected. Don't do anything foolish with it, or people will die. I don't mean to sound like a hypocrite saying that. I don't know whose mind that Golem belongs to, but I don't want to see any more people bite it unnecessarily. I *am* sorry for what I've done. Good-bye, Taz," Wen said, and the humanoid bot form eclipsed.

⋏ ⋏ ⋏

Four hundred people were freed within a few days. It seemed his lieutenants as well as Mauritius Lewes had taken the liberty of spreading the method to their adherents, and the action had become exponential. Wen physically saw people's Net presences tending to stick to his, whether the person was physically there or not. Seen from outside, his orb looked like it was surrounded by a glowing throng of frogs' eggs, stuck to him in a clump, and more joined by the hour. It would soon be impossible to hide this from the higher ups, and Wen worried about what would happen when the chainsaw would come down on all their heads. Immediacy was in the air, impending momentum, the falling over a tall vertical into nothingness, with no ropes or nets to hold them up once they did. He felt neither ready, nor willing to face this eventuality, yet he knew it had to happen, and sooner than they all expected. Every moment was a rush, a heartbeat too long, every scrap of news coming from the Net a potential doom from the ether. As he wandered the corridors of the Barrier Department, he could instantly tell those who would follow him by their alert looks, the same as mice who expect the cat to pounce from behind when they wouldn't be ready for it. The vibration coming from the walls was a steady, heavy thrum now, alien to the ears and mind of those who had successfully blocked out the pernicious fingers it planted in the still thralled millions. Wen was of the silent opinion that the enemy already knew that he waited. He was of the sickening realization that they'd all soon be slaughtered, every one of them, once their true nature was revealed and their fates sealed. None of the others had to know yet, but the odds were that the smarter among them had come to the same conclusions as he had. The worst part, it turns out, was the wait.

Mauritius Lewes came running into the mess hall unannounced as most of Wen's adepts were sitting down to lunch, yelling, "He knows! Someone told him! You have to go after him now!" he screamed, before falling to the ground in the middle of the assembled soldiers.

"Lewes, what's wrong?" Wen said, getting to his knees to help him. Blood flowed from his nose, gushing out. The vein on his forehead bulged, gaining size and finally exploding. Lewes clutched his head, which grew swollen before their eyes. His eyes exorbitant, his screech inhuman, his head pulsed, and the assembled group backed away, but not fast enough to avoid being splattered by his detonating head. Mauritius Lewes lay before them, cut off at the neck, the remains steaming where they had landed.

"What the hell happened to him?" somebody yelled from the crowd. A young woman clutched her head, screaming. The crowd backed away from her, knocking over plastic chairs. There was a loud crack of bone snapping, and her head split like a melon, spraying brain matter and blood everywhere.

"It's Singh. He's been tipped off. Mauritius was one of us. We have no choice. We have to go after him now!" Wen yelled to the assembled soldiers. Most people stared at the ground and stayed silent, terrified.

"We're not ready for that!" said someone else.

"Do we wait until all our heads get blown off? Do we stay here, cowering, until every single one of us has been decapitated? What will you do? Fight for your life, or hide until you're dead?" Wen yelled. He sent out the mobilization order to all who were now free men and women connected to him through the Net. He pasted the memories of the HYVE as well as that of Mauritius Lewes and his now deceased recruit, and sent it as a mass e-mail to all employees, so they could see who they were truly working for.

"Let's go, people! I'm not waiting around!" Jenna hollered.

"Come on!" Robert said. Wen sent the images to Yusuke, hoping there was something he could do to help. The groups assembled and began riding the elevators to the 200th floor. In the lobby, half the guards were dead, their heads vaporized. The others looked around in horror at their fallen comrades. A voice came thundering in their minds:

"This is what will happen to all those who oppose me. You pledged loyalty to me, remember? Stop those who are stupid enough to fight us." The blood-covered guards saw the soldiers coming from the elevators and raised their nightsticks, running toward them. The weaponless soldiers rushed out and surged toward them. Every so often, a sickening detonation spread blood and brain matter all around, covering the combatants in gore.

Yusuke's voice came to Wen: "He's using the crystalline chips to concentrate microwaves: he's frying everyone's minds!"

"Is there any way you can stop him?" Wen thought back as he fought off a guard while trying not to slip on the blood-soaked floors.

"I'm trying, but as long as he's got control of the servers, there's nothing much I can do. I was able to slow him down in the pillar where you just were, but he's in full control up here. You have to go stop him!" Yusuke said.

"Where is he?" Wen yelled, ducking a blow and punching a man in the jaw.

"Top of the tower. Get in the elevators; I'll hack the controls. Nabeen is too busy killing everyone to stop outside signals at the moment," Yusuke said.

"Small consolation, that," Wen said. He raised his arm and called everyone to him.

"We have to get to the top! Everyone with me!" he hollered. The survivors got rid of the remaining guards and ran after Wen.

Yusuke's voice came to him again: "Sammy says hi. We set him up to communicate with us. Andrei found me, and we're in his lab. Listen, your brother's chip is inactive. For whatever reason, he retained all his memories. I'm guessing because he's so young, they weren't able to erase them."

Wen felt a wave of relief, even as people died all around him. Nabeen Singh would have a lot to answer for. He looked up, and noticed for the first time that the top of DaiSin Tower pointed directly at the enormous red sun he had grown used to when entering Net space. What he had mistaken for rays of light were millions of filaments connected to the fantastically large orb. The closer they got, the more he realized that this "sun" was in fact comprised of an exponential amount of individual spheres, packed so tightly into one another that they appeared as one. The elevator passed the last official level and before it penetrated the darkness, Wen looked down one last time to see the river of blood that had been spilled down below. The other ten people who rode with him were blood soaked and grim faced. None knew what awaited them. The few weapons they carried were the batons they had stolen from the guards. More would be coming from the depths to stop them at any time now. They could be killed by their own implants, or so Wen had communicated to them. They felt naked and afraid, but that alone would not stop them.

The spy bot showed up inside his mind: "What did you do, Wen? The hovers outside Administration suddenly redeployed and are in a ring formation, their turrets pointing at each other like some sort of Mexican Standoff!" Taz said.

"I didn't do that, Taz; it's going down *now*. I don't care what you've decided, just get the army down here and stop the DaiSin mercenaries, will you? If you could find a way to shut off the wireless servers, that would be great too. Singh is exploding our heads like grapes," Wen said, pushing him out of his mind before he could get an answer. The elevators stopped in a huge glass dome. The white floors shimmered like plastic. On one side of the dome was a smaller one, opaque with no apparent opening. It was the size of a house, though smooth and glowing, like a half-sunken egg. Wen could see through the Net that it contained the source of all power within The Needle, that filaments by the thousands shot straight up from that cupola into the crimson sun above. Fifty people from various departments at DaiSin had made it to the top, all of them loyal to Wen. Pulsating lights only Wen could see shot down from above and attacked them, turning the stunning white floors into a bloody mess. A circular portal opened in the side of the mound. Nabeen Singh walked with slow, deliberate steps toward them, and the portal closed again. He raised his hand, and most of Wen's followers fell to the ground, unconscious. Jenna and Robert kept coming forward, behind Wen.

"Stop," Singh commanded, and all three froze. "I just want this one." He pointed to Wen, and he became unstuck. "You can't harm me, so do me the courtesy of not trying. I could make you suffer the same fate as all your traitor friends," he said. Nabeen Singh turned around and scanned his arm before the portal. It ellipsed, and he stepped inside, Wen following. Within, the walls glowed like diamond ice. Hundreds of thousands of crystalline chips were encrusted into them, reflecting a brilliant light that came from the center of the room, a Plasteel throne. Nabeen Singh sat upon it and smiled at Wen.

"I have to admit; you surprise me, Wen. I did not expect you to live for so long. You have outdone yourself. Bravo," he said, crossing his legs and resting his palms on his knee. "You can't stop me, you know. I can think of several good reasons why you might want to just give up."

"Such as?" Wen said evenly, staring down the man on his throne.

"You're an accessory to everything that has happened in the past few months, for starters. If I turn you loose, Administration will devour you. Thank you, by the way, for enabling me to go through with my plans. I was right to give you some latitude in your actions; you came out for us in the end. I'd like to give you one last chance, though, to join the right side in this little fight. You've been so good to me; I'd be remiss to dispatch you without even trying to change your mind."

Wen looked at him, wide-eyed, and said, "You want *me*, to join you? Are you serious? Those are some powerful drugs you must be on, Singh. What could possibly make you think I'd want to do *that*?"

"You and I are very similar. We both know how human nature works," he said, and the lights went out inside the dome, leaving perfect darkness and the two men alone. Wen looked around himself in surprise, trying to spy the exit, or some sort of reference point, but the only thing to be seen was his enemy, sitting a few meters away, contemplating him. Reaching behind him, he tried to feel a wall, the door, something to ground him, but there was nothing there. He could feel his pulse rising in his breast. An ice pick plunged into the back of his mind, and he gasped for air.

"The operative word in *human nature* is, of course, *nature*," Singh said, and as quickly as they had plunged into darkness, they found themselves on the shady floor of a boreal forest, populated with tall elms and maples, chestnuts and firs. Wen's first reaction was to grab a tree, which he resisted, his brain reeling and trying to bolt for the nearest exit. *I'm in mindlock again; calm down. The bastard has me in a construct,* he thought. A white rabbit bolted past his legs, chased by a fox, who caught up to it and snapped its neck, dragging it away. On the dry leaves at his feet, ants carried off various twigs and other insects to feed the colony. A mother sparrow fed its chicks higher up in a nest on the upper branches of an elder elm tree, regurgitating live worms to the chirruping birdlings.

"We are of nature, and survive from it. We use the same techniques for our survival. This is evolution," Singh explained, spreading his arms.

"Right, survival of the fittest. Here's the problem, Singh; that's not how humanity does it. We help each other. That's how we made it to the top of the so-called food chain. Yeah, we make mistakes and we attack each other, but it's through collaboration that we've come this far. Even *you* should be able to see this," Wen said.

Singh smirked, and the scenery changed to that of a small wooden village, smoke rising from some dozen stone chimneys. "Indeed. Collaboration has been a *great* thing. Let's fast-forward a bit, shall we?" The village began to grow and grow until it was a town and then a city. Industrial zones appeared, and garbage dumps on the outskirts. Soon, other towns became large enough that they bordered the original village that had mushroomed into this monstrous thing. The camera pulled skyward, and Wen felt the familiar nausea of too-rapid acceleration. From a satellite view, he could see the cities of the world lighting up the night skies, and factories by the millions belching smoke into the air, nature chewed up by constant human expansion. Polar ice caps shrank, melting, and the millions of gallons of water they held in check flowed into the oceans, raising them exponentially, until all those lights went out like birthday candles.

"That's human collaboration for you. Are you still convinced it's the best way forward? My method keeps the human population in check, at least the part under my purview. If I could control the rest of it, we might actually get somewhere. If not, we'll keep going through the same thing over and over again; humanity be damned. You think you're helping people by attacking me? You're not. Not by a long shot," Singh said, shaking his head sadly at the sight of a once again dark earth. Wen sat down on the invisible floor, looking at the dead planet from orbit, shocked into silence.

"It got better, didn't it?" he whispered from his crouching position. Singh laughed out loud.

"Of course it got *better*! For the ten percent of the population that *survived*! How many times do you think we can go through this and pull through? How much, apart from *us*, has been lost, do you think? Wake up! It's time for us to rejoin the natural order of things!" he said, and they were once again in the boreal forest, whizzing through it at dizzying speeds, like hawks flying through a maze of branches. Wen held his head and grunted, feeling sick to his stomach. He got up on his feet, legs cottony and shaking, but new energy flowing into him from some distant place. He stared at the self-satisfied man before him with loathing such as he had never even imagined before.

"You're no savior. You're no god. You have no say in the future evolution of Homo sapiens. You're lying about what ruined us. It wasn't cooperation. It was because of little snakes like you who refused to change the way we lived on this planet out of simple greed. And now, out of greed, you want to enslave us. You only know lies and pretty light shows. You're a charlatan, Nabeen Singh. What else you got?" Wen said. The louder he spoke, the more the scenery wobbled and fell, spinning finally into oblivion until the lights returned and they were once again inside the glittering diamond-encrusted room. Singh looked around him, his gaze darting around the room. He snapped his fingers a few times, looked again, and when he realized nothing would happen, he once again concentrated on Wen.

"So much for convincing you to join; perhaps it's time for you to just quit in the face of impossible odds? What would your girlfriend think of what you've done? Your life is *over*, Wen." He smiled lasciviously.

"Jenna's not my girlfriend," Wen said, nonplussed.

"I'm not talking about Jenna. Shawna, the girl you left rotting in jail without even a second thought. The girl who swore she would wait for you. What would she think about Jenna?" Singh said, leaning forward.

Wen's stomach turned. No one knew about Shawna...how?

"How do you even—?" he asked, trying to hold the anger out of his voice.

"You're mine, Wen." Nabeen cut him short. "You belong to me. Your life and the lives of all within this company belong to me. I know absolutely everything about you: every call, every transaction, every covert meeting. How could I not, in this day and age? I know every thought ever recorded on your chip. Every. Single. One."

"Ever heard of privacy, Singh?" Wen said, his lip curling in disgust, his stomach churning with cold anger.

"Since when does property deserve privacy?" he sneered.

"And I thought you would be impressive. You disappoint me, Singh. Sorry, those aren't very good reasons to give up, quite the opposite. I think you've gotten too used to your puppets over the years. You're still a sad excuse for a human being, and you need to be dispatched like the garbage you are," Wen said, shaking his head. Nabeen Singh's smile faded.

"Is that the mouth you kiss your pimp with?" he said; all niceties evaporated.

"Why did you kill them all, Singh?" Wen said, extending his arm to where he had come from.

"What else do you do with unsightly pimples, boy? You *pop* them. I can't have my people turn against me. Think of what it would do to morale!" Singh answered.

"What is all this?" Wen asked, raising his hands to the diamond-encrusted dome.

"Memories. Personalities. Souls. They belong to me. Just like you," Singh said, pointing at Wen, an evil grin plastered across his features.

"I see. You steal people's memories and call them your own. You need to go out and get a girlfriend of your own, Singh. You have some morbid hobbies," Wen said, looking bored.

"For a *maggot*, you have a pretty big *mouth*," Nabeen said, leaning forward. "I have a feeling I'm going to get bored with you very soon."

"Good, it's about time. That means you'll be able to catch up to me, finally." Nabeen rose to his feet and hollered, clenching his fist. The room shook, a few crystals falling from the ceiling with a tintinnabulation of glass. Wen felt a crushing blow to his head out of nowhere and fell to one knee, holding his aching head. A drop of blood fell from his nose onto the floor.

"That's where you belong, on your *knees*," Nabeen said, sitting back down. "Tell me, Wen, how were you able to go against me? You might be the first, you know."

"I had a little help from my friends. I don't kill everyone I disagree with; it makes for longer relationships," Wen said, wiping his nose.

Yusuke's voice came on in his mind, crackling with interference: "I can...bare... hear you...distract...im...a lit...long..."

"What were you hoping to do, Wen? Did you really think you could come here to kill me? Or did you want to make peace?" Nabeen said, mocking him. "Who was that, just now, I only caught a part of it. Distract me? Why? What could you possibly accomplish by that? Poor Wen, no one told you life wasn't fair, did they?"

"Oh, I think we're beyond that now. That was an old friend of *yours*. I believe he was the first to go against you." Wen stood up on shaky legs, blowing a spray of blood out of his nose.

"Did you find Yusuke? No, really? I should have killed him when I had the chance instead of letting him go on in a living hell. My bad." Nabeen smiled giddily, rising as well. "It doesn't matter. I'll just have to kill him after I'm done with you," he said, clenching his fist and smiling, a curious look on his face.

"Now, Wen!" came Yusuke's voice. Wen bolted toward Nabeen Singh, grabbing his arms and pushing him down on the throne. Singh raised his legs and ejected Wen onto the wall, his back slamming into a million points of pain. He slumped over on the ground, his back on fire. His gray uniform shredded, crimson began to flow from the wounds punctured by razor-sharp crystals.

"You little bastard. I'm practically immortal!" Singh said, laughing. "You need to learn your place, little one. Only I have the power over life and death in this place!"

"I'm counting on it," Wen said, giving the order for all the crystal's personalities to eliminate the loyalty commands and to return to their minds in the HYVE, with the help of Nabeen Singh's stolen ID, which he had just now taken from him. A shockwave surged through the orbs, high up above them. They obeyed as if they had received the order from Nabeen himself.

Few events of this magnitude have ever been witnessed by so many in the course of human history. The Net, and all of its residents, became aware of DaiSin's troubles when all external firewalls suddenly dropped out of existence. From the point where they saw so many rise to the top of The Needle, all eyes were riveted on the unfolding drama, collective breaths choked back in anticipation of the outcome. Anyone on the Net that day can attest to this: the sun that had shone so brightly above the DaiSin Building shattered in a silent supernova, sparks raining down like apocalyptic fireworks, straight into the recesses of the base of the building as if sucked in by a black hole through a straw, vanishing. One last point of light remained at The Needle's apex: a very small, barely visible flameche next to Wen's large, amber sphere. There was a pause, when all thought it was over.

A surge of fire came from the depths of The Needle, a magmatic eruption of crimson light, lightning fast and indomitable. It rose to the light at the top of the tower like a plague of nightmarish locusts, devouring it with insatiable fury.

Wen pressed his wrist before the throng could mistake him for Singh. At first, Singh scratched the back of his head. Then he began to peel himself, grunting in agony. He fell in a heap on the ground, tearing off the skin from the back of his neck, screaming like the damned, trying to remove his own Netrodes. They set alight, and a fire like roman candles fizzed and popped from his trodes. Blue flames lit from his head and he crawled toward Wen, the skin of his face melting in a horrid mask of pain. Wires and tubules exposed, Wen saw that the man was more machine than human. The air reeked of burned polymers, and Wen coughed, turning around to open the portal but could not do so without Singh's ID, which would make him a target for the wrath of the people. Black smoke filled the airtight space, choking Wen and turning his eyes red. He heard a detonation from outside the confined space, and the building shook.

Wen slammed his fists on the sealed portal. He hit it as hard as he could, the life draining out of him like the snot and tears running down his face. Something brushed his mind, a soft stroke, unlike the disagreeable feeling of an intruder; it warmed him against the pain. Then, the unimaginable happened: the door reticulated. Wen dropped outside, gasping for air. Greeted by the sight of his friends and comrades waking slowly from their induced comas, he staggered. A hovertank, over by the shattered glass wall, rested, turret pointing toward him. An enormous, smoking black hole had been blasted into the dome. A panel opened on top of the tank, and Andrei's disheveled head popped out.

"What are you waiting for, an invitation?" he said, waving Wen over. Wen shook his head in disbelief and stumbled over to the awaiting tank, Yusuke coming out of another port.

"I can't leave them behind!" Wen said, helping his dizzy lieutenants get up off the ground.

"We don't have much time!" Andrei said, peering at a monitor before him. "One minute before they show up!"

"Then help me get everyone aboard, dammit!" Wen yelled as he lifted Jenna and Robert under his arms, helping them hobble to the tank. Andrei and Yusuke scrambled out, finding anyone whose head was still intact and taking them in through the back of the hover. All told, a dozen people had survived the CEOs wrath.

They boarded the hover as the elevators arrived at the top floor. Administration guards fired indiscriminately at the hovertank as it slid backward out of the hole in the dome.

"Where's Sammy?" Wen croaked, his face caked in blood and soot.

"I'm back at Andrei's lab." A voice came over the hovertank's intercom.

Wen looked at the speaker in surprise.

"I had to hook him up to the Net to get him 'working' again," Andrei said, taking the hover as far away from DaiSin Tower as he could. Wen saw on the screen that Administration tanks surrounded the base of the building, DaiSin guards coming out with their hands over their heads. An explosion resounded. More hovers appeared from the depths like black flies. They attacked the military, attempting to escape, but stopped in midair, frozen. The military hovers surrounded the DaiSin mercenary's tanks and dragged them onto solid ground.

"That'll teach 'em," Sammy said with a note of pride.

"Did you do that, Sam?" Wen exclaimed, observing the motionless tanks.

"Yeah, I also hacked into the ones that were threatening Administration," Sammy said. Wen nodded, impressed.

"Where are we going?" Wen asked as they flew between towers, their optical camouflage protecting them from pursuit.

"Back to my place until things cool down," said Andrei, looking back from the controls.

"Taz knows where your hideout is, Andrei. They'll be there waiting for us," Wen said.

"I don't think so. He promised us to keep quiet until everything was resolved. Something about a deal with you?" Yusuke said.

"I didn't think that would pan out," he said. "How are you feeling, guys?" He addressed his surviving unit. Their silent nods told him volumes: they were all happy to be alive, of course, but now there would be an inquiry and the scapegoating that went with it. It was a pyrrhic victory, and none of them could foretell the future and what was in store for them. Wen felt dizzy at the loss of blood and fell sideways between hover seats, unconscious.

The tank descended as the last rays of sunlight disappeared behind the monoliths, back into the stygian darkness from whence it had come.

Epilogue

A THIN, GELATINOUS PINK pad covered his naked back, still, as he wandered the corridors of Andrei's hideout. The hover slept under its tarp in the corner of the garage once again. He would forever carry tiny points of scar tissue where so many crystals had pierced his skin.

These past few weeks, he had pondered the irony of the weird arc his life had taken: from watching over artificial workers to slaving for a man who had lost all his humanity. Whatever decisions would be taken from now on would have the people under his protection squarely in mind. There would be no more running away from responsibility. He ran spread fingers slowly along the plywood wall of the hallway, feeling the rough cut after every smooth section, thinking, *Something is there. Everything has depth and meaning. You just have to look for it.*

A delicious odor drew him to the kitchen, where half a dozen of his "soldiers" were busy making breakfast. Rations that Andrei had calculated for a single person for years were rapidly depleting.

Gozen Samurai's *Rock Child Demagogue* came whispering from some unseen speaker in a back room, no doubt enjoyed by Sammy for the millionth time.

Wen's attempts at finding Shawna had revealed fruitless, yet he would not give up the search until he could face the woman he loved and explain to her all that had happened, inevitable consequences notwithstanding. He wanted to be a man of honor from now on. His odds would greatly improve once they could escape the confines of Andrei's bunker.

Jenna jumped into the kitchen from the lab hallway: "I've got news!" she said. They had been waiting for two weeks in cramped quarters. Morale was dismal. The news from topside was that all DaiSin employees had either been arrested or killed, making their little group the last free men and women.

"Administration wants to negotiate," she said. "With you." She pointed at Wen. He calmly walked to the lab and picked up the receiver, followed by the rest of his unit and friends.

"Hey, Wen," Taz said, smiling on the screen. "They thought you might want to discuss things with a friend." Wen looked at his old nemesis disconcertedly for a moment and then took it in stride.

"What are your terms?" Wen asked.

"Slow down, slow down, cowboy. First come congratulations on stopping a world war; for that alone, the Administration is willing to give you *all* immunity," Taz said. They all looked at each other, stunned.

"What brings on this overly generous gesture?" Wen said.

"Well, we caught Douglas Deguchi at the spaceport as he was trying to make himself scarce. He's been extremely cooperative in implicating just about everyone from the top down. The Administration is aware of the coercive methods that were employed against you and has weighed them in the balance," Taz said, smiling broadly. "He's trying for a plea bargain to reduce his sentence. You were set up, Wen, pretty much from the beginning."

Just like you set me up, he thought, chuckling inwardly, without animosity.

"What will happen to him?" Wen asked.

"Life in prison, minimum, I would warrant," Taz said. "We have a favor to ask of you."

"What's that?" Wen said, cocking his head.

"There is a swarm of millions of orbs around the Administration building, has been for days. It's big, it's angry, and it collectively demands you be put in charge of the company you took down. Apparently you had the crazy idea of releasing them from bondage, or so they say. Now they're wreaking havoc on the Net systems and promise to be a pain in the ass until their demands are met. No doubt that if we don't, there'll be hell to pay."

Wen stared at him, dumbfounded. "Is...is that all?" Wen stammered.

"Isn't that enough?" Taz smiled. "Please do hurry; they're holding our communications array hostage."

Wen nodded.

"And, Wen, I'm glad you survived." The screen went blank.

Pandemonium ensued as everyone present jubilated and hugged one another. It was a tearful release to so many days of tension and doubt. Wen patted the glass case in which Sammy's brain was encapsulated.

"Don't worry, Sam; I'll take care of you," he said.

"I hope so. I don't want to be just a brain for the rest of my life, no matter how much smarter than you I am," came the reply from a nearby speaker. "Besides, I think I can take care of myself, if I could save you!"

"Ha! You won't be, I promise. You're right; you did good, Sam," Wen said, and he meant it.

After a pause, Sammy said, "I've been thinking, Wen. You said the porthole opened on its own after you detected something familiar. Do you think Mom could have been among those memory chips?"

"Only one way to find out," Wen said and smiled.

Andrei erupted from down the hall, out of breath: "What's this I hear about everybody getting off scot-free? It's a trap, isn't it?"

"I don't think so, Andrei. Admin has a whole lot of people watching their next move. I'm fairly certain their generosity has a lot to do with the pressure they're under right now," Wen said, his lip curling in a wry grin.

"Crap, are you telling me you're taking the job?" he said, eyes wide.

"Definitely. I'd be hard pressed to do a worse job than the previous owner. Besides, if I don't, it'll fall directly into one of the Elevens' hands, which isn't much better if you ask me. I've been told that life is all about misery, mortal struggle, and stepping all over people to get somewhere. I have a bit of a different take on things now. I would love nothing better than to prove that bastard wrong," he said, and gritted his teeth. His fist in the air, he yelled, "Who's with me?" As one, all assembled detonated in a resounding "Aye!"

If you enjoyed this book, please consider heading over to Goodreads. com or Amazon and leaving a review. That way others will know about it, and I get to bring you more of this. Thanks.

Made in the USA
San Bernardino, CA
16 August 2017